For Betsy:
with much love.

Florence Mae Brentano

# The Recycling of
# Joan

# The Recycling of Joan

Florence Mae Brentano

Copyright © 2015 by Florence Mae Brentano.

Library of Congress Control Number:   2015907088
ISBN:        Hardcover         978-1-5035-6725-2
             Softcover         978-1-5035-6726-9
             eBook             978-1-5035-6727-6

All rights reserved. No part of this book may be reproduced or transmitted in any form or by any means, electronic or mechanical, including photocopying, recording, or by any information storage and retrieval system, without permission in writing from the copyright owner.

This is a work of fiction. Names, characters, places and incidents either are the product of the author's imagination or are used fictitiously, and any resemblance to any actual persons, living or dead, events, or locales is entirely coincidental.

Any people depicted in stock imagery provided by Thinkstock are models, and such images are being used for illustrative purposes only.
Certain stock imagery © Thinkstock.

Print information available on the last page.

Rev. date: 05/05/2015

**To order additional copies of this book, contact:**
Xlibris
1-888-795-4274
www.Xlibris.com
Orders@Xlibris.com
702667

For

dj

# Chapter 1

There's a place where Highway 203 curves to the right just thirty miles from the coast. A road, nearly hidden from view, branches off and continues six miles along the river to the logging camp. Natural beauty changes to small farmers' fields that blend into hills with deep canyons. Here and there along the way, a solitary tree grows in the middle of a field . . . mute testimony to a long-ago pioneer's bright dream. Further on, an old orchard filled with wild berries clings to life.

Joan remembered how the hair on the back of her neck stood up when she was deep in the vines picking berries when she was a child. She *knew* a great big black bear would be standing, waiting for her when she turned around. She'd stand paralyzed with fear. She enjoyed the feeling—later.

The Newabram River Valley was lovely all year with each season displaying its own special kind of beauty. The new soft green of spring gave way to the dark shady green of summer. This turned to yellow and gold in autumn; then fine stalks faced winter with stark nudity that made one wonder if spring and life would ever follow or if the long days of winter might ever end. They did. Spring again. A welling. A victory. Survival. Then the cycle began. Again.

A dirt road wound twisting, steep and flat, built on a path of least resistance. It rose and fell as it afforded passage to the hardy few who needed access. At a place where the river met with a roaring clear stream in a wide valley filled with tall white-barked alders mingling with cedar, fir, and spruce, the camp was built.

The camp deep in the forest attracted people from all parts of the country: south, east, west, and north. Some were drifters who stayed a short time. Some were drifters who would never leave. Some were *so* good. Some were *so* bad. Fighters and pacifists, preachers and sinners, families and single men. Young and old. Each found the camp for different reasons. Some loved it. Some didn't.

Rough-built unpainted houses testified to the impermanence of the camp. Here and there in the row of houses, a fence appeared, sometimes lined with bright flowers, snapdragons, geraniums, and a rosebush or two. Other houses reflected the disenchanted people who lived within. Not a blade of grass grew. Boardwalks. Hard-packed soil. A big chunk of wood with an ax stuck deep was usually near the back door. A pile of kindling and firewood sometimes blocked the entrance—depending on the time, season, and disposition of the man of the house.

It didn't take long for the camp to establish a personality of its own. The mix blended. A society formed quickly. Gossips surfaced. So did brave men and cowards. It didn't take long in such a confined area where people might be together for weeks on end without leaving the camp for them to come to know each other very well—and their weaknesses.

Everyone knew the worth, or lack of worth, of each man, woman, and child. Families loyally protected each other, and a camp fight brought out fierce passions before abating from the torrent and settling back and forgiving but not ever forgetting. Once a man did something base, no one ever forgot it. It was better (and wiser) for him to leave camp.

By 1940, with the proper antenna, radio reception was a reality. Long winter months were spent listening to the radio. Adults played pinochle in the light of electricity generated by a large generator in the center of camp. Water heated in the reservoir on the side of the handsome cookstove, a shiny block of beige porcelain with chrome trim. Saturday night—weekly family bath night. Water dipped from the reservoir and poured into a large galvanized tub in the center of the kitchen floor felt warm and soft. In addition to Saturday night baths, Monday was wash day; Tuesday, ironing; Wednesday, cleaning; Thursday, mending; and Friday, baking. Most of the mothers died on Sunday.

By summer children roamed the hills, swam all day in the sun (no one ever came to see if they had drowned), walked to the store (six miles away), picked berries, and peeled chittam (cascara bark) to sell (it was used as a laxative). They clambered over the rocks in the river, which ran low and slow in the summer sun. To the eyes of a child, the river was very wide. One of the most exciting memories of that time was when the men in camp came down after work to challenge the older kids to a race across the river. Everyone was surprised—by who could and who couldn't swim across.

There were late-night bonfires with potatoes thrown in and roasted among red-hot coals. Flames flickered on surrounding trees. A few feet from the fire it was cold. No-man's-land between hot and cold. Back to the fire. So warm. Then it faded. Embers glowing in a hypnotic swirl. The youngest children were first inside—then the older ones.

Joan had fun remembering the camp—the freedom.

They played the same games children still play: hopscotch, marbles; King of the Mountain; tag; hide-and-seek; and Run, Robin, Run.

The only time Joan had known fear in the camp (besides the forest fire) was in winter when the swollen, swift river left its banks, and huge logs and other debris went crashing by. There was always a feeling of impending disaster, but, except for the excitement and rush of adrenaline, nothing serious happened.

It seemed the rains started in early fall—and didn't stop until late spring. One family had a tin roof, and the sound of rain on it was especially pleasant. Joan liked to go with the lady who cleaned the bunkhouses where the single men lived. She loved the smell of wool blankets, Copenhagen, hand-rolled cigarettes, tobacco, and wood burning. She could see the little potbellied stove nearly dance in the corner. Big cracks in the iron revealed orange-yellow flames spiraling skyward.

The camp always smelled good. The trees and the river produced a scent that permeated camp during the warm days and caused the bees to buzz a melodious tune. After a hard rain, the air held a wonderful clean fragrance and the promise of a new beginning.

Wild iris, trilliums, jonquils, and wild mint grew among the lush green fern. Where there were no flowers, the different colors of the forest were still very beautiful especially with the sun sifting through branches. The enchanted forest.

Joan smiled in memory. All that was long ago. Now she had children of her own. Since then, they'd bulldozed the old schoolhouse, machine shop, office, cookhouse, bunkhouses, and even the houses. A county park now stood where the old camp was. They put in a footbridge over the wide swift creek. Except for a tree or two and the shape of the valley and the way the river meets the creek and the big rock in the middle of the river, no one who lived there would recognize the place. Alder trees now grow where houses used to be.

Joan's first year of school was the first year of the Second World War. The schoolhouse was a half mile from camp—a one-room school for eight grades. It was a good building painted white, and there were little outhouses for the girls and boys. They were to the side of the building because they were built into the side of a hill, and that was the only place there was room. There was little space to play. An iron ring hung in a huge maple tree near the road that ran by the schoolhouse. Big trucks loaded with chained logs rumbled by, which caused the little building to shake. Red clouds of dust spewed forth when the road was dry. When it rained, the trucks cut deep ruts in the road, and the ruts filled with mud. The children loved to slosh through the mire on their way home.

Later a school bus transported the students six miles to a roadside berg where two buildings took care of grades one through four and five through eight. The older and larger building sat majestically on a hill. Below, the newer building also housed the gym. Inside the newer building, a black cast-iron woodstove sat cold and silent in a far corner of the room. In cold winter months, the metal glowed red with heat, and the large room was cozy and warm.

Ms. Ferschel had just graduated from college, and this was her first teaching job. She was petite, pretty, and prim. She smiled a lot and was patient and kind. She wore soft plaids in pastel colors. All the young men (old ones too) in the area fell under her spell. When she left to marry her college sweetheart, everyone was disappointed.

The year after she left, Mrs. Parker came to teach. She was an old pro. She knew her business. She reminded Joan of Abraham Lincoln. She was tall and rangy and wore severe navy-blue crepe dresses with white collar and cuffs, well-laced orthopedic shoes, and an unbecoming bun hairdo that accentuated her long thin nose and caused people to ignore her rather attractive face. Her forbidding manner precluded any insurrection, and only the bravest and/or stupidest child caused any kind of trouble in her room.

On special occasions, the lower classes visited the upper classes. The entry to the big building was lined with coatracks, lunch pails, rubber boots, and, in a corner, bats and balls. A rope attached to the school bell dangled in the north corner. It was dim in the entry. A door opened into the schoolroom filled with big desks. Ink wells and a depression for pencils and pens were on the top surface of the desks. Some desks had hinges and could be opened from the top.

The Christmas party was the most fun of all. The scent of fir trees, school paste, oranges, candy, wood burning, and excitement filled the room. Joan trudged down the aisle. She knew her older sister, Grace, wouldn't move over to let her sit with her. Not that she wanted to. She quickly found a seat with one of the *neatest* girls in school then smugly turned back to look at Grace. Grace smugly returned her smug look. Sometimes Joan hated her sister—and with good reason. When they both got a candy bar (which was a rare occasion during the war—all they had was something called horehound, which tasted like it sounded), Joan gobbled her chocolate, while Grace nibbled daintily. Then Joan followed Grace around, hoping for a bite. No. Grace just ate hers slower. Joan hated her for that . . . and other things.

Buelah's across the highway from the school served sandwiches, ice cream, pop, and beer—kegs and kegs. There were pinball machines and slot machines in Buelah's. Buelah's was the social center of that end of the county. Loggers and farmers and their wives congregated there from early morning until late at night (depending on the weather, the lack of excess funds, and the inclination). Many loggers went to work the day after an evening at Buelah's with monumental hangovers and were a menace to the men who worked with them and depended on them for their safety. They were tough men doing tough work at a time when their brothers, buddies, and neighbors were being killed overseas. Maybe they felt guilty. There was a lot of talk about 4-Fs. Nobody could stomach a 4-F.

Most of the loggers were 2-As. That classification was given them because of the importance of the logging industry to the war effort. They were home, safe (except for an occasional falling tree), drinking away their frustrations at Buelah's and fighting with each other. They found any little excuse to fight. A simple statement like "I don't like your looks" could touch off a wild encounter . . . and an evening's entertainment at Buelah's.

In the early '40s, a law was passed that made it illegal for children to be in taverns. Consequently, many children spent long hours in cold cars with frosted windows waiting for their parents to tell one more story and have one more beer. It was too cold to sleep.

They heard the raucous sounds of drunken men and women leaving the tavern. Loud laughter, shouts of parting, then the menace of drunk men caused the children to wait in apprehension as they passed the car. They crouched low in the backseat so no one would see them. The sound of gravel grating under heels subsided. They relaxed. The door opened again. Was it them? No. Another lone person staggered out the door lit with a bare bulb high overhead. Then he too moved out of sight.

Tired eyes in miserable bodies root around the car searching for comfort and warmth that are not to be found this night. Soft beds with warm blankets are not here. Minutes turn to hours, misery multiplied. Finally. They're here! Then home through the night, the heater of the shiny black Packard sending waves of heat through grateful little cold bones. Home. The cold house waits. Moonlight bright as stardust lights the house through frosted windows. Silent shivers and chattering teeth find their place in chilled beds. Blessed sleep. Then only the memory.

The woods was a dangerous place to work. Snags fell. Highlines broke. Chokers snapped. Logs were upended and went sliding and crashing down mountainsides. Shorthanded and manned with inexperienced workers, it was difficult to maintain production. Many of these men were lured from taverns in Watertown when they were just drunk enough, just willing enough, and just stupid enough. Not many good men were left at home to carry on the vital work of the war effort. Joan's father, Paul Powers, the superintendent of the company, took any man he could find wherever he found one. Some of them lasted a day. Others became an important part of the crew. Valuable. As good men always are.

Fatalities soared as the combination of inexperience, lack of men, hangovers, and negligence took their toll. One camp became so well known that wandering loggers avoided it like the plague. It was a highball outfit. Every machine ran at full throttle. Men died. Trees split on high climbers. Logs rolled over fallers.

Mulligans (large vehicles for transporting men) became ambulances. Grim-faced men with hands in their pockets and anxiety in their eyes waited for word by the office. In time, the call would come. The men lived or died, and those waiting were stricken to silence or threw up their hats and shouted for joy. Good or bad, the camp was affected for days.

When the man died, the camp mourned, took care of the widow and children, arranged for the funeral, brought food, and did the necessary things. In time, the widow moved or stayed or remarried. She was (from that time forward) known as *poor so-and-so's widow*. The camp settled into an uneasy restlessness . . . waiting for the next accident and wondering who would *get it*.

The women in the camp were a composite of all women. They were clean and dirty, small and large, smart and stupid, pretty and ugly. They varied in increments along the scales of measure. Some were pious (not many). Others wicked as sin. One wore a red fox fur jacket with jodhpurs (then in poor taste) and high heels with thick wool socks. Another was the epitome of the well-dressed woman. She was black velvet, satin, and lace.

Most of the homes were surprisingly clean. The smell of laundry soap Purex, floor wax, and Lysol permeated them. Except one. There a large mound of dirty, smelly diapers in the middle of the floor dominated the decor of the kitchen. The pretty mother of two small daughters seemed perfectly happy to live in that manner.

When the women weren't cleaning, they were playing pinochle and gossiping. The camp divided almost equally between the smart women who knew the score (and had a hell of a good time) and the older, uglier, fatter, more frustrated faction. Neither group liked the other. The smart ones didn't care what the others said about them. They went on their merry way cooking up all the deliciously naughty things women can cook up given time, money, and a restlessness caused by hardworking and inattentive husbands. They whispered or spelled, hoping the children wouldn't get wise to their latest escapade.

They danced and drank through the forties. Gas rationing made travel difficult, except for those with an *in* or a priority. They had it made. They could go anyplace and as often as they pleased—and they did. Camp shut down most weekends during summer because of humidity. Then it was deserted, except for wives whose husbands had better things to do elsewhere and men who had no cars or places to go.

Dogs barked here and there. The sun shone. Birds sang. No one stirred. The camp died.

Joan amused herself in various ways when she was alone. One of her favorite places was Carrie's cookhouse. Carrie was a Southern woman reared in the tradition of Southern hospitality. Her husband, Jake, was an older, dark, scowling man who looked at children as though he didn't see them or want to. He never seemed to be on the premises even when he was. Carrie had four children, two girls and two boys—and a phonograph. "When the Red, Red Robin Goes Bob-Bob-Bobbing Along" and "If I Had the Wings of an Angel" and "Back in the Saddle Again" emanated from the Victrola, and anyone listening sprang to wind it when the music slowed. The house was always filled with good house sounds—crackling fire, music, laughter, whistling, and humming. It smelled like heaven might smell. The fragrance of good food simmering, good bread baking, and good coffee perking permeated it.

Carrie often let Joan help in the kitchen. She watched in fascination as Carrie's girls buttered loaves of fresh bread, placed buttered slices together, and stacked them into tall stacks. Then they spread them with fillings, wrapped them in waxed paper, and placed them in freshly washed lunch pails that would return that evening caked with mud. The girls worked in an assembly line operation, laughing and joking as they worked.

Carrie belonged to neither of the two groups of women. She had a warm voice, a warm heart, and a warm kitchen. She had no time for groups. Busy women seldom do.

The camp kids ran in packs. Usually they played well together. Sometimes they fought. Their lives were so intertwined, and they shared so many of the same experiences that in many ways they became like brothers and sisters. The main division was sexual. The boys didn't want to play with the girls . . . until they wanted to *play* with the girls. The other division paralleled the two women's groups. The children of one group usually didn't play with the children of the other.

Joan's young life was one of immense frustration. There were few children her age in camp. There were some much younger and many much older, but no one her exact age—and very few girls. This lack of female companionship did not distress her. She found from a very early age that she preferred the company of boys to the company of girls. Boys did things. They went hiking up the creek with fishing poles, they caught polliwogs and salamanders, they whittled with pocketknives, and they played Cowboys and Indians and *war*. They were fun.

It wasn't long before Joan found the boys didn't enjoy her company all that much. She always started out with them on one of their sojourns, but as soon as they were out of sight of camp, they hurried up the bank of the creek in order to get away from her. They shouted, "Go home, Joan!" or "Your mother's calling."

"Why can't I go with you?"

"We don't want you to go with us."

"I'll be quiet."

"You're never quiet." "You scare away the fish." "Run. Run, guys."

"No. Wait!"

"Go *home*, Joan."

With that, they left her fighting her way through dense brush that lined the creek. Then she was alone. They had done this to her before, but she never learned. She kept following them, hoping they'd let her stay. They seldom did. They were ordinary mean boys.

Joan was very lonely until someone in camp discovered the game of *doctor*. Then Joan had plenty of playmates.

"How do you play it?"

"It's easy. You lie on your back, and I'll examine you like a doctor. See?"

"Then after that, can I be the doctor and examine you?"

"No. Girls aren't doctors."

"Well, if we're just playing a game, why can't we pretend that girls are doctors?"

"Look, do you want to play or not?"

"I don't know. Maybe I do and maybe I don't."

"I'm getting tired of this. Yes or no?"

"OK. What do I do?"

"Just lie on your back."

Joan started to giggle. This was silly—and fun. Her little boy playmate looked so serious that she said, "You're not going to hurt me, are you?"

"Naw. I'm just going to see if you're sick."

"How come you're doing that?"

"I'm just examining you."

"There?"

"Yeah, that's where you have to check."

"Oh."

"Does it hurt?"

"Kinda."

"It's supposed to feel good . . . doesn't it?"

"I don't know."

"Whattdaya mean you don't know?"

"It feels kinda funny."

"Do you like it or not?"

"I do like it."

They giggled, and he continued *examining* her for some time.

"Do you ever touch yourself there?"

"I'm not supposed to."

"Yeah, but do you?"

"My mother told me not to."

"Joan!"

"Yes, I've touched myself there, but I'm not *supposed* to. I'm getting sore."

"All right . . . but you have to come back to me in one week for a checkup. That will be two dollars."

"OK. Here's your money." She handed him two bark chips, then got up, pulled up her panties, and brushed off her dress. "Now it's my turn to be *doctor*."

"Aw. No, you don't . . . I ain't having no girl be the doctor for me."

"That's not fair . . . Besides . . . maybe you'll like it."

"No. I won't do it."

"Then I won't be back for my checkup."

"Aw."

"I promise I won't hurt you. Just lie down and I'll *examine* you." She moved toward him. He started to turn and leave, then reluctantly fell to his knees.

"Just lie down. Oh. I think you've been hurt. Let me see how bad it is."

Joan had never seen a penis before, and her eyes widened with anticipation and excitement as he unbuttoned the fly of his pants. She was disappointed with what she saw. It was such a strange-looking thing, pink and wrinkled and little.

"It looks like a snake."

"It does?"

"Yeah. I've never seen one before. Aren't you afraid it'll fall off?"

"No."

"If I had one of those things, I'd be afraid it would fall off. Gee, you've really got to be careful of it, don't you?"

"No."

"I'm glad I don't have one of those things."

"I'm glad I do."

"Now let me see. Does it hurt if I touch it . . . just a little?"

"No. Go ahead."

"OK . . ." Joan looked at the strange thing, then carefully touched it. She moved her hand up and down on it. "Hey, it's growing . . . wow!"

"Can't you shut up?"

"Is it supposed to do that?"

"Yes."

"Are you sure it's all right? I've never seen anything like that before."

"Yeah, it's OK."

"It's fun to play *doctor*, isn't it?"

"Yeah, Joan." He smiled. Then the sound of voices made Joan's hand freeze. "It's our mothers calling us. They're looking for us."

"They can't see us in here. They'll go right by."

"I'm scared."

He jumped to his feet and hurriedly buttoned his pants. Then he peeked out through the underbrush.

"They're down by the creek. As soon as they go around the bend, I'll run out. Then you follow me in a few minutes." He started to leave.

"Hey, wait."

"What?"

"You owe me two dollars!"

# Chapter 2

"Good morning, Mrs. Kent."

"Good morning, Joan."

Joan smiled at the older woman as she boarded the bus. At five o'clock in the morning, heavy dew covered the shrubs, the road, and the big dirty berry bus filled with half-awake scroungy berry pickers wearing old clothes caked with dried mud. Joan plopped into the seat next to Mrs. Kent, who always reminded her of the Lincolnesque Mrs. Parker. She closed her eyes and saw strawberries. They'd been picking for over a week, and whenever she closed her eyes, the strawberries were there. Mrs. Kent sighed and looked out the window.

"Is anything the matter, Mrs. Kent?"

"No. I just didn't get to bed early enough. I'm tired."

"So am I. Donna is so lucky to have her job and not have to work in the fields . . . and be *sixteen*." Joan ran her fingers through her short cropped red hair and made a face.

Mrs. Kent smiled a sympathetic little smile. Donna, her youngest daughter, and Joan, their neighbor, had been inseparable until Donna became an usherette at the local theater. Now their schedules conflicted, and Joan obviously missed her friend.

"Don't you like to pick strawberries, Joan?"

The bus hit a bump. Trees and houses zipped by. They were a few miles from town . . . and a few years from when all the fields they passed, the earth that grew some of the best produce in the world and the trees themselves, would be given over to subdivisions. The best farmland in America—under subdivisions.

Joan's answer was immediate and predictable. Mrs. Kent had heard it daily and on the trip back and forth to the field, when everyone was happy and tired. While others sang, Joan grumbled. Mrs. Kent threw back her big head and snickered when Joan started her litany.

"I hate picking strawberries. My back is broken. My knees are sore. Every muscle in my body aches. I hate to get up early, and I hate going to bed at nine o'clock. I can't sleep. I just hate it."

"Then why do you do it?" chided Mrs. Kent.

"I need the money for school clothes," moaned Joan.

They laughed and stood as the bus stopped. They got off, grabbed flat-bottomed carriers that held six hallocks of berries from the huge pile, and went to their row. They had finished about half of it the day before. They picked on opposite sides of the row. Both hoped they could finish early today, but they wanted to earn as much money as possible. They picked through the morning, past lunch, and into the middle of the afternoon. The hot sun cooked them as they silently worked. After the first few days of chatter, they'd settled down to concentrated picking. The voice became an intruder.

At about three o'clock, Joan was startled out of a fantasy . . . by Mrs. Kent's voice.

"What did you say?" Joan asked.

"I said Mrs. Schultz called last night. She needs help with her babies. She's got some kind of bone problem and isn't able to lift heavy things. She wanted Donna to spend the rest of the summer with them. They live in St. Eames. It's a pleasant little community."

"Donna told me about it. She had a lot of fun there."

"Every summer, when we lived in the cabins and picked hops, she never told me she was having fun."

"She had fun *after* work. I would like to have a job like Mrs. Schultz's. How much does it pay?"

"She said they'd pay fifty dollars a month. Are you really interested?"

Joan knew the berries would be over soon and there would be no crops to pick until the middle of July—and she did hate picking anything.

"Yes, I am interested." *Yippee.*

"Mrs. Schultz is going to call again tonight to get Donna's answer. I told her Donna wouldn't give up her good job to go and take care of children, but Mrs. Schultz was desperate and said she'd call again. I'll tell her about you when she calls."

"Great."

Joan brushed the dried mud of morning from her pants. Sweat ran into her eyes, and her back ached in unison to her heartbeat. Oh.

"I hope she hires me," she muttered. "I'm probably not old enough for that either."

It was hell to be fifteen. You couldn't do anything. You couldn't drive or work (except at jobs like picking berries, which were *so* easy). *Big joke,* thought Joan.

She waited expectantly for the bus the next morning. Her whole future depended on the job. She rushed into the bus, tripped on the top step, and flew forward into a metal column. She wasn't hurt, but almost immediately a bump appeared on her forehead. Cheering rose from the pickers. She gave them a contemptuous glare, then sat down with Mrs. Kent.

"Are you hurt, Joan?"

"Just a little."

"Let me see." She turned Joan's sleepy face toward the light and looked at the bump. "We'll put some cold water on it when we get to the field."

"Cold water?"

"It takes down the swelling."

"Tell me! Tell me! What did Mrs. Schultz say?"

"You got the job."

"I did?"

"Yes. Her husband will pick you up this Sunday at about four o'clock. I gave her your address."

"That was nice of you, Mrs. Kent. I appreciate it." She frowned a little and tightened her jaw. She hadn't said anything to her parents . . . but that was no problem . . . She was sure they'd love to have her go away for the rest of the summer.

They would.

At four o'clock the next Sunday, a Ford sedan pulled up in front of Joan's house. There were five men in the car. One got out and came toward the house. He looked around at the flower-filled yard, then rang the bell.

"I'm John Schultz," he said as he shook Paul Power's hand.

When both men and Joan's mother, Rose, were satisfied, John Schultz carried Joan's suitcase to the car, stowed it in the trunk, and then motioned for her to get into the backseat. They rode in silence for a while. Then the men started talking. At first, the talk was general. Then they fell into familiar ways of speaking. Joan listened closely. Patterns began to emerge. She approved when John Schultz quietly reminded them of her presence after one of them told a dirty story. They'd all laughed. Except John. He'd been clearly embarrassed; when his eyes caught hers in the rearview mirror, she could see his anger. She blushed. She'd never been in a situation like this before. She didn't mind a dirty story or two, but this made her very uncomfortable. A silence fell. Then one of the men noticed a sign along the road.

"It's only three more miles to Martha's."

"What's Martha's?" asked Joan.

"It's just a place we stop on our way home from the ball games. We usually have a beer or two before we go home."

They pulled into the dusty parking area. Country Western music filled the air. Hee-haw.

"Come in with us, Joan . . . You can have a soft drink."

"No. I'll wait here." *I hate that kind of music, and the place looks like a dump.*

"OK, suit yourself."

They trooped into Martha's. At first, Joan amused herself by counting out-of-state car licenses on cars that flew by. Soon, that bored her, and she began to think. The longer the men kept her waiting, the more she wondered with apprehension if she had made the right decision in coming. Finally, they tromped out of Martha's. They seemed happier and louder than when they'd gone in. Joan was glad to be on the way once more. It was still daylight, and as they crossed the Williams River and drove toward St. Eames, she was impressed with the beauty of the lush green rolling fields, the dark-green fence rows, and the clusters of tall green trees dotting the landscape. Every scene reminded her of a picture postcard.

"Have you ever heard of St. Eames?" a voice asked from the front.

"I never did . . . until this week."

The men laughed. Joan didn't understand the humor, but she assumed they had a private joke, since they laughed so hard.

St. Eames—population 204—was a gem of a little town. It consisted of a few stores, a bank, a post office, two taverns, a city hall, nice little houses, and a barn or two. The streets, wide and silent, served the people who came from around the countryside to get groceries, parts, and mail, to borrow, to pay back, and to buy and sell seed and produce. The largest structure inside the city limits was the old brick church with its magnificent classic spire set back on a huge perfectly manicured lawn. The parish house, newer but with matching brick, lay nearer the street and on the southwest corner of the immense lot. South of the parsonage, across the road and running east and west, stood a row of tall birch trees, which could be seen from a great distance on the flat prairie.

When each man had been deposited at his door and they were at last on their way home, Joan was relieved. They'd curved and driven around St. Eames and the countryside for quite a while, finding, first, one home and then another on the dirt roads that crisscrossed like string on a ball.

John Schultz finally stopped in front of a two-story bright white colonial home that stood welcoming them in the gathering twilight. John's wife, Christina, a beautiful woman of twenty or so, met them at the door.

"How do you do, Joan?"

"Fine, thank you . . . and you, Mrs. Schultz?"

"Oh, no. You must call me Christina, and Mr. Schultz is John." Her light lime-green eyes laughed, and when she bent to her, Joan was amazed at the color of her hair. It glistened deep dark brown with highlights of copper—breathtaking.

Joan liked the idea of calling them Christina and John. It seemed so friendly to her. She looked around the kitchen. "Did you decorate the kitchen yourself?"

"We did." Christina was obviously pleased and glanced quickly around the cheery room. Her eyes passed the blue-checked walls, the frilly sheer white curtains, the flash of copper tools and pans, the couch she'd designed in the corner, and the almost-always spotlessly clean dark-blue tile floor.

"You did a wonderful job. It looks like something out of *Better Homes and Gardens*."

"Thank you. I'll show you the rest of the house in the morning when the children are awake."

They chatted for a while. Then John helped her to her room. She hadn't brought many clothes. She wondered if she'd have enough to wear. She looked around. The floor shone; the curtains, crisp and white, hugged gleaming windows; moss roses without vines covered the papered walls; and the fluffy white bedspread promised nights of regal rest.

"Excuse me, John, I forgot to ask where the bathroom is?"

"It's right off the kitchen. When you want to use it, just turn on the light at the head of the stairs." He looked around the room. "I hope you'll be happy here, and I'm glad you could come." He winked a friendly little wink. Joan noticed his eyes were almost black—strange.

"Thank you." *No one's ever said things like that to me before. That's really nice. I wonder if he likes me? Or if he just needs help. I'll find out tomorrow. This is a great adventure. No more berries. No more dirt. Yeah!*

She got ready for bed, then climbed into the sweet-smelling sheets. In just a few minutes, she was dreaming she was getting on the berry bus . . . again.

"Joan . . . time," Christina's soft voice called.

Joan looked out the window near her bed. *Still dark.* She glanced at her watch. *Six o'clock.* She hurriedly dressed, then went downstairs. The big bright light in the kitchen ceiling glared in her eyes.

Christina smiled sweetly. "I wanted you to get up early so you will have time to catch on to our routine. Since I've been almost incapacitated, I need help to take care of the children and the house. While you're waiting for them to wake up, you can set the table."

Within a few minutes, the three children appeared—Blair, three; Johnine, two; and Carter, baby (in Christina's arms). They were hungry and hurried to the table where they waited expectantly for food. They banged on the table, hit each other, and yelled. Christina called, "John . . . breakfast." She set dishes of food on the table, then dished up for the eager children. When breakfast was over, Christina showed Joan how to wash the dishes to suit her, and throughout the day, she explained and taught Joan how to use the various appliances in the house. All during the day, Christina kept one hand on her back. Toward evening, her manner reflected her pain. She wore a veiled look. Joan looked at her with admiration. She had obviously been in much pain all the day, yet she hadn't complained.

A few days later, at one o'clock, Joan became quite warm and went upstairs to change into shorts. She'd put the children down for their naps and finished the lunch dishes. Now, in a few minutes, the last batch of clothes would be ready to hang in the backyard. While she waited, she heard a commotion and looked out the back door. A big load of hay lumbered down the back lane aimed at the big old barn a few hundred yards from the house. Four tanned, hay-covered, handsome young men rode on top, laughing and shouting.

*They're feeling their oats,* Joan thought, then congratulated herself on her cleverness and drew back into the room to hide from them.

"Joan."

"Coming."

Christina had been lying down most of the day but now held a chilled pitcher of lemonade and indicated a tray of glasses. "I want you to take this out to the men. Daddy loves lemonade."

Joan balanced everything and went out the door. She walked carefully so as not to spill any of the frosty yellow liquid. She noticed with pleasure an extra glass for her. She walked over to the man she assumed was *Daddy*. When he saw her, he stopped the operation (the men were putting hay into the barn) and called for the others to come. Three heads appeared in the upper opening of the barn. When they saw Joan, they whistled and called out to her. Joan blushed. *Daddy* looked amused and pursed his lips to whistle. She self-consciously poured each man some lemonade and was careful not to stare at them. When she peeked, she saw glistening bodies with rippling muscles. She smiled to herself. This wasn't going to be such a bad summer after all.

The next day they all came to dinner at lunch. Joan never could get used to calling the huge meal in the middle of the day dinner. Dinner should be at night. But this was their dinner.

It was hard for her to do her work with all that male attention. They eyed her curvy body and stared at her pretty face. At times, it seemed they quit eating just to watch her. She gleamed. She loved all the interest. It continued for a few days. Then Joe Schultz, John's younger brother, pulled her aside after dinner one day. "Want to take a ride tonight?"

"What time?"

"What time for you?"

"After dinner . . . I mean after supper. About seven. OK?"

"Fine. Bring your bathing suit—we might want to go swimming."

All day, as Joan did the household chores and took care of the children, she thought of Joe Schultz. He was good looking with his sun-bleached hair. He had his brother's almost-black eyes with enormously long, black, thick eyelashes and a surprising sprinkling of freckles on his fine straight nose. His face was angular and fine planed. Sometimes when she looked into his eyes, it seemed she saw into *him*. She'd been watching him from the first, and she was pleased he had asked her for a date. Restlessness was part of her. She could sit so long, be quiet so long, then she had to have a change. Anything.

She was ready at seven. She should have been tired, but she wasn't. She felt great. She heard Joe's footsteps on the front porch and hurried to open the door before the buzzer disturbed the baby. The other children were ready for bed in their light summer pajamas. They squealed with delight when they saw their favorite uncle. He wore a plaid shirt, Levi's, and a Stetson cowboy hat. Yum. Yum. Yummy.

Joe came into the house, kissed the children and threw them into the air amid cries of delight, paid his respects to John and Christina, then took her hand and led her to his waiting pickup.

He shot her a big wicked smile that revealed straight white teeth and a hint of naughtiness. The engine roared. "How about a beer?"

"Sounds good," she said as he handed her the bottle. Her eyes rested on the full case in the backseat. Wow.

They drove down by the river where a sandy beach ran for nearly a half mile. About halfway across the river, a gravel bar protruded and cut off most of the main flow of the river. What was left on this side of the river was an ideal place to swim.

They swam for some time, paddling back and forth in the eddy. Then Joe built a small bonfire for warmth and to keep away insects. They lay on the blanket, watching the fire burn and listening to the sounds of night, sounds that carried on the stillness and came from miles away. A train tooted; a cow mooed. They looked at each other and laughed. They talked about a lot of things that night. Joe said he wanted to be a millionaire.

"Why?" Joan asked. "All the rich people I've ever known have spent all their time thinking about money. They don't have time or energy to do anything else. They live for money and don't enjoy anything that isn't connected to dollars in some way. They don't relax. Ever. They are always preoccupied with the next *deal*."

"I hope I'm not like that. I want to be a millionaire because I want to be able to afford to do what I want to. My goal in life is to be a millionaire," he declared and shook his fist at the sky.

She laughed. "Good luck, J. Paul Getty!"

He reached over and tousled her hair. "What about you? I know what you want to be. You want to be an English teacher."

"What makes you say that?"

"Your vocabulary. You always use big words."

"I don't. Not always. Christina and John and their friend Barney, the short man with the beard, were teasing me about my vocabulary the other night. What can I say? I love words. I love books. The first novel I ever read was *Forever Amber* by Kathleen Winsor. I can still see Amber in her beautiful dresses riding in a carriage. It was wonderful. Do you like to read?"

"No."

"No?"

"I'll tell you the truth. Whenever we were supposed to do a book report in school, I skimmed the book and wrote it from that."

"Joe, if you ever found the right book, you'd enjoy reading."

"I don't know."

They talked on into the night. What Joe had said bothered her. She was always an A student, and she'd been teased too much about her interest in words. She guessed she was defensive about it. It was like being called an egghead—by dummies. There was really no defense. Except maybe to learn more words.

They talked about a lot of other things that night. They necked. They drank beer. When they got home, Joan didn't feel very well.

She had a hint that something was the matter the next morning when Christina called her to get up; her voice sounded strained and unfriendly.

Joan went downstairs and began her chores. Christina coolly watched her as she worked. Finally, when the kitchen fairly burst with aroma, and just before the men came in for lunch, Joan couldn't stand it any longer.

"Will you please tell me what is the matter?"

"Nothing is the matter."

"But you've been so unfriendly all day . . . Something must be the matter."

"Well, there isn't anything the matter."

"If there is, I wish you'd tell me. Is it because I went swimming with Joe?"

"No, it's not because you went swimming with Joe. It's because you were drinking with Joe and you didn't get home until one o'clock."

"What's the matter with that?"

"We don't do that in St. Eames."

"And how did you know we were drinking?"

"I happened to look and saw Joe take a drink."

Christina's mood dampened the usually good-natured lunch hour . . . for a while. Soon, everyone competed to be heard, as usual. The crowded kitchen strained at its seams. Then when everyone had eaten, one by one, they left until only Joan remained. She sighed as she surveyed the disaster. "Maybe I should have picked strawberries," she muttered as she started to clear the table.

"Joan, I'll be in my room lying down," Christina said as she shuffled into the bedroom.

She seemed her old self, and Joan was happy the problem had been aired. She'd be more careful in the future. She wondered what else they didn't do in St. Eames. The days passed quickly. She and Joe were together almost every evening. They were careful to get in earlier, and they kept the beer out of sight. Christina was watchful but didn't say any more to Joan.

A few days before the Fourth of July banners appeared across the main street of St. Eames. Written on them was "20th Annual St. Eames Rodeo—July 3, 4, and 5th."

"You mean you've never been to a rodeo, Joan?"

"I don't even know what a rodeo is."

"We'll ride over there tonight on the horses. Then you can see how it is before it starts."

When evening came, they rode over to the rodeo grounds. Huge pens held milling Brahma bulls, wild horses, and cattle. They tied their horses, then found an open door and went inside the grandstand. The freshly worked dirt smelled good and would provide a soft landing for the cowboys. They walked through to the other side of the arena. On that side were colorful rows of stands: cotton candy, hamburgers, barbecued chicken, ring toss, milk bottle pitch, fortunes, and others. Several big rides struggled for life.

Joe's eyes glinted with excitement. He walked with an air of expectation. Joan looked puzzled.

"It's a carnival," she said.

"It's a carnival, but it is a rodeo. I'll take you."

"Would you really? I'd love to go."

"If Christina will let you."

"She's having a lot of company."

"I know, and John is a director. You'll be lucky to get away."

"Joe, I'll ask as soon as I get home. Will you want to go on the Fourth?"

"There's no point going any other time. That's when *everyone* is there."

"Let's ride down to the bottom before we go home. It's such a nice night."

"It's getting too dark for the horses. We'd better be getting home."

Joan tried to get Christina in a mellow mood so she could ask her about the Fourth. They'd be chatting—something they had started doing—and Joan would be sure the moment was right. Then it would pass, and she would have missed her chance. She walked by the rodeo grounds almost daily on her way to pick up the mail. There was an urgency about the work being completed. Men shouted and waved to other men holding pipes or pieces of boards or cans of whitewash. Joan stayed away from the animals. They frightened her, and while she liked the horses, the bulls seemed too threatening.

She delayed asking about the rodeo as long as she dared. It was the first of the month, and Joe had to get tickets.

"Christina, could I please have the afternoon of the Fourth off? Joe has asked me to go to the rodeo."

"You have Sundays off."

"Yes, I know," she said. She'd enjoyed going to church with John, while Christina stayed home with the children. "But I would like to go to the rodeo."

"I'm having company."

"If I did all my work early and had everything done, couldn't you take care of the children for the afternoon?"

"I'll talk it over with John."

*Gee,* thought Joan, *we've been getting along so well. We've had such good visits. Christina tells me all about the people in the community—whom they're related to and how and why. I really have enjoyed the stories. You'd think it wouldn't kill her to take care of her own children. What did she do before I came when there wasn't anyone to help her?*

A deal was made. Joan would take off Saturday the Fourth instead of Sunday the fifth. She looked forward to meeting more of the local kids. She'd met some down by the river when they'd been swimming. She liked the boys just fine. She had never seen so many handsome faces in her life. The girls seemed edgy, but Joan found that she liked two or three.

An air of supercharged electricity crackled around St. Eames as the rodeo drew near, and as if to participate in it, the heavens crashed through with a spectacular display of lightning and thunder the night before the rodeo started. Lightning zapped across the sky from one direction, then another. Big bolts split the black sky. Loud thunderclaps sounded as though they were directly over the house. They watched the spectacle from the window of the blue-and-gold dining room. Christina and the children in their pajamas edged together for a good view of the show. It started to rain. Big drops fell in ploppy plops and quickly turned the dust to mud. It didn't rain long, and when it stopped, Joan noticed little rivulets of water running near the sidewalk.

Now it was the day of the rodeo. The sun broke through the morning mist early. Cowboys practiced near the corrals. People in the stands gave their businesses a final check, then opened so they wouldn't miss a single customer. New sawdust, carefully raked, blanketed the area. Outdoor toilets stood white and glowing in the sun, the final coat of whitewash still not quite dry. Men on horses with saddles of silver rode through the rodeo grounds on the road that ran around the outside of the arena, hurrying with an air of importance to deliver unimportant messages.

As the day wore on and it became noon, people started jamming into the rodeo grounds. Indians, farmers, cowboys, housewives, businessmen (with cowboy hats), and just about every other kind of person came to the rodeo. Drunks and teetotalers (in short supply) attended. Fourth of July celebrations around the state brought drunks out of the woodwork. Drunk Indians from reservations put on a special show. They fought. They cursed. They made love under the big tree at the edge of the grounds. Wild Indians.

Young people, old people, and even babes in arms went to the rodeo. They bought balloons, Kewpie dolls, and gaily colored banners. They dunked firemen, tested their strength, and had their weight guessed. They ate hamburgers, hot dogs, fresh corn, barbecued chicken, cotton candy, candied apples, ice cream with chocolate and nuts, and a sampling of Mexican food. Gypsies told fortunes (no one from St. Eames—against their religion),

At one o'clock the show would begin. Joan and Joe found their seats. Soon, a fine male voice announced the beginning of the rodeo. A rocket whooshed into the atmosphere. A small American flag on a parachute descended into the arena. Everyone stood as the national anthem echoed through the stands. The grand march began. Posse after posse rode into the arena. Each group wore distinctive clothes of jewel-like colors. Green, blue, ruby, white, and pink satin shone in the early afternoon sun. When all the different riding groups, performers, and clowns were inside the arena, fire trucks, ambulances, and other sundry maintenance vehicles crowded in. Then around and around in a swirl they rode, drove, or ran. Chaotic excitement blurred before the spectators. Suddenly the parade began to leave the arena. In a flash they were gone. The rodeo began.

That was the best part of the show for Joan. The rest was dull and boring (except when the bulls chased the clowns), and she watched with disgust when the cowboys roped the terrified little calves and then twisted their necks until they fell to the ground. She couldn't wait until it was over. Joe watched with great interest, obviously enjoying the activity. Joan decided not to hurt his feelings; she would remain silent. He was not fooled.

"You didn't like it, did you?"

"I liked some of it."

"Uh-huh." He nodded his head and averted his eyes. They climbed down the stairs and went into the rodeo grounds.

"I really did like it, Joe. I liked the grand entry and the people who did the tricks on the horses—and I loved the clowns . . ." She could see he was disappointed, so she stopped trying to convince him. It was hopeless. She knew that the summer would soon be over and her time in St. Eames would end. She'd probably never see any of these people again anyway.

Everyone in the community worked hard during the summer. The men who planted in the springtime spent long hot days irrigating their fields. Almost all of the crops raised in St. Eames needed large amounts of water. Corn, wheat, sugar beets, red clover, strawberries, hops, beans, and other crops grew well in the area. The main crop was hops. They were irrigated from wells and the swift flowing river that formed an ever-changing boundary around the farms. All through the summer, farmers irrigated and kept the fields free of weeds. In late August the main harvest began.

While the men worked in the fields, the women worked at home. They picked fruit and vegetables, and canned and preserved jellies, jams, pickles, and anything they could stick in a jar. It was said of one miserly housewife that she probably canned grass.

By August Joan looked better than she'd looked in a long time. Christina was a gourmet cook, and she served small portions. Every serving dish was quickly emptied, and there were no leftovers for Joan to nibble. She slimmed down in a hurry and felt wonderful.

"Let's go to town shopping, Joan."

"Who will take care of the children, Christina?"

"We'll find someone and then you can shop for your school clothes."

Joan thought of her money. When she was paid at the end of August, she'd have one hundred and fifty dollars minus what little she'd spent that summer (mostly for candy bars). "I'll have about a hundred and thirty dollars to spend."

Joan wondered why Christina acted like she hadn't heard, but she wasn't too concerned. She should have been. She'd heard Christina and John quarrel about money often. Christina loved beautiful expensive things. John ranted and wanted to know how much this or that had cost. Christina smiled. Then he demanded. She smiled again and never, never told him.

Joan's money disappeared as if by magic. Christina guided her. Two cashmere sweaters from Scotland, Bally shoes from France, a few other fine items, and Joan owed Christina fifty dollars. She wasn't worried about it, though. She knew she could earn that much during the winter months.

Joe came to dinner the Sunday John drove her home. Joan knew she would miss him, and when it was time for her to go, she was surprised when he pulled her to him and kissed her in front of everyone.

Christina sat at the littered table. "Joe!"

"Well, I want Joan to know I'm going to miss her."

"She knows it. She knows it." John shrugged his shoulders and shook his head. "It's time to go. Let's get in the car."

"Good-bye, Blair, Johnine, Carter, Christina, Joe . . . Good-bye. Good-bye."

They were halfway to her house when it occurred to her that the summer was over and that the people she'd met meant a great deal to her. "Good-bye, John. Thank you. It was nice knowing you."

John reached for her hand. He held it tenderly. "It was nice knowing you too, Joan. We'll be in touch. Take care."

Baby tears formed in her eyes as she went toward the house. She felt dumb. She didn't cry. She was tough. She was a logger's daughter. Should have been a boy.

Joe and Joan wrote to each other a few times that winter. *Hi! How are you? I am fine.* Joan also wrote to Christina. She was unable to earn any money that winter because her family moved to the coast where there were virtually no jobs for teenagers in the winter. When summer came, Joan wrote to Christina and made arrangements to return to St. Eames.

# Chapter 3

This year would be different. Joan would get her board and room in exchange for babysitting, and she would be free to work on the farms around St. Eames. She could earn ten dollars a day irrigating hops for John. This was very hard work. Hops grow on vines trained around vertical wires about twenty feet high. These wires are attached to horizontal wires that are anchored to large posts at intervals around the hop yard. In order to manipulate the long irrigation pipes through the vines, it is necessary to go forward, then back, turning the pipe into the proper row. If the ground were dry, it would be easy; but as soon as the water goes off, the pipe has to be moved. This means that with every step, the workers sank almost to their knees in wet, oozing mud. Joan's legs ached as she pulled first one and then the other from the leaden mud. It was nearly quitting time, and she couldn't wait. She saw John's pickup in the distance.

She'd just settled in amid all the tools, ropes, and wires when John said, "How'd you like to stop in at Irisher's for a Coke on the way home?"

Joan knew about Irisher's. It was where the men in the community hung out. It was the place where hard liquor was served. There was another place called the Steer Inn that only served beer and soft drinks. The young people went to the Steer Inn to listen to music and to dance. "Yeah, John, I'd like a Coke, and I'd really like to see inside Irisher's. But we don't want to be late for dinner."

John rolled his eyes and nodded his head. "No, we mustn't be late for dinner."

They bumped out of the bottom (where the hops grew) in the old blue pickup. Its window was broken, and rope tied the door shut on Joan's side. Big clouds of dust rolled behind them until they reached the main road, which was blacktopped and smooth. They shouted at each other over the sound of the motor and sighed with relief when they pulled up in front of Irisher's.

Joan's pants were dirty and wet. So was she. Dark coolness enveloped them as they entered the establishment. Red lights illuminated the long back bar mirror. Incandescent lights glowed behind a display of liquor bottles that seemed quite lovely to Joan. Booths lined the wall, and when Joan's eyes became accustomed to the interior, she was surprised to see twelve different trophies (deer, elk, and other unfortunate animals) hanging above the booths.

John had a couple of drinks, and Joan watched everything that happened with fascination. Men drifted into Irisher's after their long day's work. Each one looked Joan over on his way to the bar. They were surprised to see Joan with John. It occurred to her that there'd be hell to pay if Christina found out—but who would say anything?

By the time they got home, Christina knew about it. She was furious. John got just as angry, so Joan took the children out to the yard, while John and Christina had a fine battle. She snickered when she heard Christina shout, "We don't do that in St. Eames!"

No one enjoyed dinner that night, except the children.

Summer came to an end; crops were harvested and preparations were made for fall. It was nearly time for Joan to return home to the coast. Christina had invited her to live with the family and go to school in St. Eames, but Joan thought that might not work out too well. That night she had her last date with Joe Schultz.

Bright stars hung in the late summer sky. They seemed closer and brighter than usual. The air held scents of harvest. Sweet-smelling chaff from the combines swirled around their feet as they made their way to their favorite place on the edge of the field and down the trail lined with berry vines, mint, and brush. The dirt path held enough moisture to keep it wet, and Joan felt mud between her toes as Joe pulled her along behind him. She carried the blanket under her left arm, her swimsuit under her right elbow, and a portable radio in her right hand. Joe hoisted a case of beer high over his head. They navigated the short path in record time, then began gathering wood for a fire. In no time it burned brightly on the sandy beach and cast dark shadows onto the bam trees lining the river. The water made rippling, trickling, lapping sounds at the edge of the sand. Joan washed her feet in the warm water, then dipped her sandals and rinsed them off. She looked back at Joe on the blanket and saw him opening a bottle of beer. She raced back to him, knelt down, took the bottle, and drank a long drink.

"Oh, that tastes good."

"Nice and cold . . . like you."

"Joe Schultz, who said I was cold?"

"I did."

"Well, I'm not!"

"Prove it!"

"I don't have to *prove it*. Let's go swimming." She jumped up and disappeared into the shadows to change into her suit. Joe waited on the blanket. He smiled when he saw her and took her hand when she came close. The fire crackled and snapped as they ran into the water. They swam for a time. The water felt warm, and the current flowed swiftly. They swam into the dark center of the fast-flowing river.

"I'll race you back," Joan called to Joe. He nodded, shouted "go," and easily outdistanced her. He pulled her from the water, and they both collapsed, exhausted, on the blanket. Their wet bathing suits made big spots. Joe opened more beer, put more wood on the fire, then lay down beside Joan. They talked and drank and talked and drank until nearly midnight. Then Joe, who had been playful, suddenly changed. He held her tight against him. At first, she tried to pull away, but he wouldn't let her go. Her head was woozy from the beer, and she knew her reflexes were slow. He kissed her. And kissed her. And kissed her. After the first tide of resistance, she kissed him back. A strange feeling enveloped her. She'd never felt like this before. It seemed her body temperature soared. She was hot.

Frantically and with shaking hands, he pulled off her bathing suit. Again, she started to protest, then was taken away by the urgency of his feelings and her own inability to stop what had been started. Then it was over. Joe lay spent and breathing hard next to her. She looked at him in amazement. She had never experienced anything like that.

Two weeks later, she knew she was pregnant.

She hadn't wanted to believe it when her period was late, but now waiting for the bell to ring, signaling the end of this day's school, she knew it was true. She thought about ignoring it; maybe it would go away. But she knew it wouldn't, and she knew she'd have to do *something*. She just didn't know what. Joe would be there the next weekend. They'd talk it over then. In the meantime, she decided to say nothing to anyone. It would be a tasty morsel for the school gossips, and Joan didn't want that.

Joe came in late Friday afternoon.

"Hi."

"Hi."

"Aren't you going to ask me in?"

"Of course. Come in."

"No kiss?"

"Of course." She kissed him, and the warmth of his skin and the scent of his body made her want to stay near him. He gently pushed her away.

"Is anything wrong?"

She wished she were more clever at hiding her transparent feelings. "I'll tell you later. Let's take a drive. My parents will be coming home soon, and I'd like to talk to you before they meet you."

"Fine."

They stopped on the way to the car and looked at the scene below. Fishing boats chugged back and forth across the bay. Blue water mirrored green mountains in the background. Little clouds, puffy white and propelled by jets, streaked across the sky. A stiff breeze came up, and Joan rushed back into the house for a sweater.

"Let's go someplace where we can see the bay," Joe said.

They drove to the top of the mountain where a football field had been dozed. They parked near the edge. The view from there gave a sweeping panorama of the bay. They watched the boats for a while. Then Joan shifted in her seat.

Joe pulled her over to him and kissed her. "Now what do you have to tell me?"

"I'm pregnant."

"You are?"

"Yes."

His expression didn't change, but his high pink color became a pale green as Joan watched with fascination.

"What are we going to do?" His shoulders sagged.

"I was hoping you'd have the answer to that."

"There's only one thing to do—we'll just have to get married."

"I don't want you to *have to get married*."

"I didn't mean it like that—I mean we'll get married."

As soon as she was sure she was pregnant, she'd begun thinking about what she would do. She knew what she wouldn't do. She wouldn't have an abortion, and she wouldn't force Joe to marry her. She knew she didn't really love him, but watching him now as he tried to *do the right thing* made him seem very dear to her. She also knew that if she couldn't learn to love him because of his goodness, she'd never be able to love anyone.

"Joe, if we get married, you'll have to quit school and get a job."

"Yeah, but only until Uncle Lester retires from the farm. Then I'll take over his interest."

"I'd love to live on a farm."

"A job would just be temporary until he retires."

"When will he?"

"I don't know. Before too long, I hope."

"Why can't you farm with him?"

"The farm only produces enough for one family. When I take it over, I'll have to make payments to Uncle Lester. I'll be buying it from him."

"Oh."

They sat. They didn't see the boats, the mountains, or the flag that snapped in the breeze at the high school far below. Engrossed in conversation, they were unaware of the dramatic speed with which their lives were changing.

"Let's take a walk. It's getting stuffy in here." He didn't wait for her to answer. Quickly he opened the door and swung his long legs to the ground.

"Wait for me." She scurried out of the car. She followed him up an old dirt road to the right of the playing field. He slowed, reached for her hand, then continued walking.

"We'll have to get married right away."

"Won't we have to wait for the banns? What are banns anyway?"

"The banns do have to be published. They're just announcements in church. They announce three Sundays in a row before a wedding is, that a wedding will be."

Joan laughed. "If all goes well, we could be married on the tenth of November."

"Yeah. Then we'd have to figure out when, where, and how?"

"I want a simple wedding. I'd like to wear a pink dress and have just a few close friends. I'd like to have champagne to drink. Pink champagne."

"No, we can't do that. In St. Eames they have big weddings."

"This isn't St. Eames, and we don't know anything about Catholic weddings. My parents have never been inside the church. I'll just have finished my instructions to become a Catholic. Couldn't we go away and have a quiet wedding someplace in another state and then someday get married in the church?"

"No, we just can't do that. We have to have a big wedding whether we like it or not. Have you told anyone?"

"No."

"Good. Don't say a word to anyone . . . not your folks or your girlfriends or anyone."

She didn't say a word. All the next week she hardly spoke to anyone. All she could think of was that she was pregnant and the secret was about to bloom on the world.

She would miss school and all her friends. It was a small school. One day she stayed after the last bell and wandered through the rooms. The school had become a part of her life. It would be sad to leave it.

She remembered her first day there.

\* \* \*

The bell rang. Joan waited in the office, while the principal completed his duties. The office was old, cluttered, drab, and small. She'd surveyed the building from the outside before entering. It looked dangerous. Inside the aging boards and the ramp that served as a stairway would cause an inferno in case of fire. She hoped they didn't allow smoking in the building.

A new school; a new beginning. She hated the idea of being "new" again. In some ways she was happy to have left the old school. New faces, new thoughts, and new experiences held a certain fascination for her.

Mr. Taylor, the principal, turned and handed her a slip of paper. "You are to give this to your teacher, and when your records are transferred, we'll give him your grades. His room is the first one on the left." Mr. Taylor smiled at her with crinkly blue eyes, tan cheeks, white teeth, a kind of long nose, and intriguing soft full lips. Joan found out later that he was a veteran, the kids liked him, he was fair, he had a family of towheads, he had a nice wife, he was a disciplinarian, and he had an open mind.

As she left the office and headed toward the room already filled with students, she was struck by a wave of self-consciousness. She checked her dark-maroon wool skirt, her light-maroon cashmere, the silk scarf at her neck, her Armishaw saddles with their companion white rolled anklets, which were about five inches from her skirt, and she sighed. She hoped her breasts weren't sticking out too much, then wondered if she should thrust them out more. Moderation. That was the thing. Moderation. Neither out too far nor in too much.

She took two deep breaths, told herself to relax, and entered the noisy room. As she walked to the teacher's desk, a silence descended. All eyes followed her movement. She felt her face redden. Her chin came up, her back straightened. Just as she thought she had command of herself, a loud, low, insinuating whistle reverberated through the room. Then another. And another.

The wish to cry filled her throat. Mr. Taylor's voice brought her back to the present. He stuck his head in the library door.

"Joan, I'm locking the school."

"Oh, OK. I'm leaving."

"Did you want to get a book?"

"No, I don't. Thank you."

"Is something wrong?"

"I think I'm outgrowing this school."

"What does that mean?"

Joan laughed at her cleverness. "Time will tell."

He shook his head as Joan slipped away. She hurried down the cement steps and along the highway that led to the Heights. Big trucks whooshed by as she rushed home. She'd forgotten she'd told her mother she'd babysit her little sister, Ann.

"Sorry I'm late, Mother."

"That's all right, Joan, but you'll have to start dinner."

"What do you want?"

"Round steak. Do you remember how to fix it? Pound the meat and flour it?"

"I remember."

"You'll have to put it on soon."

"OK. Where's Ann?"

"Over at Mrs. Mallorie's. She can stay there for another hour. Then you'd better bring her home."

"OK, don't worry . . . Everything is under control."

With her mother gone, Joan started fixing the round steak. As she worked, her mind raced. She found herself thinking, *I don't want to get married. I don't want to leave school. I don't love Joe, and I don't want to marry him. I don't want a big wedding. Oh, I wish I hadn't let him do it!* She was surprised at the big tears that fell down her cheeks. She wasn't the kind to cry.

It was a lovely diamond ring. Joe gave it to her the next weekend. They talked to Father Vittorio. Joan had admired him since he agreed to give her instructions. His devotion to his faith served as a model for other Catholics, laity and clergy. He had traveled extensively throughout Europe visiting monasteries and learning the Gregorian chant. For a time he lived with an order of monks who ate animal entrails, wore hair shirts, and never bathed or spoke. For a time he entertained the notion of joining them. A sensible man and having a distinct dislike for animal entrails, he became a Benedictine. Until his magnificent voice gave out, he served his church by teaching the Gregorian chant to the seminarians at the abbey.

When he was sixty, a time when other men contemplate retirement, Father Vittorio found himself a parish priest. His round stomach, round face, and round body encased in flowing robes with hood attached became a welcome sight in northern coastal towns.

Everyone loved him, including Joan. She'd been interested in the Catholic Church since she'd been a child and found a rosary hanging from the brass head post of her grandmother's bed. It was a romantic religion with power to *forgive* Joan for her sins. She felt the need for forgiveness. Her conscience bothered her. She thought she was bad.

She went to the house near the church where Father Vittorio lived. It was sparse, cold, dismal, and colorless. He lived frugally and did his own cooking, cleaning . . . everything. He was dedicated to the people and refused to spend any comfort on himself—or money. At times, he would go to Joan's house. Then he enjoyed himself immensely. The family welcomed the kind, gentle, serious, warm man. Grace, Joan's sister, didn't like him and stayed her distance; but Ann, who was three, adored him and insisted on being swung into the air whenever he came to give Joan instructions.

"Now see here, Joan," he'd say whenever he knew she didn't quite believe what he was saying. He could read her face like a book. No one had ever been so able to tell what she thought—or cared. But he did.

Now as Joan sat facing him, she found it difficult to look him in the eye. She knew she was foolish to feel so guilty and ashamed, but she couldn't help how she felt.

She inhabited a room called shame. One door down, humiliation waited with anticipation. She had never been so ashamed or so humiliated. In her brief time on earth, it hadn't occurred to her that *anyone* could be so ashamed or so humiliated. She had no perception of such feelings. Disgrace rode with her like a cloud—for years and years and years. That incident, that beginning, was the soil from which a wart grew and grew—an ugly wart that caught on things when least expected. To have to get married. Ick. To have everyone know that you weren't *quite perfect*, especially on the sexual side, the side where *good people* never strayed. Bah. The red wart turned pink with the years, then, finally, white. One day Joan said, "Bullshit . . . no more!" Off it went. Gradually she began to be whole again.

Father Vittorio told them to discuss their problem with her parents and his guardians. They were surprised. His weren't as surprised as hers. They ranted, raved, and screamed. They decided for the sake of the child—the children should be married as soon as possible.

# Chapter 4

The only day open to them on the church calendar turned out to be the nicest, warmest, sunniest day of the month. The ocean storms howled and poured down torrents of rain every day but this one.

Joan was excited that on this day when she married Joe, she would receive Holy Communion for the first time. The wedding party dressed in the parish house. The house's interior was one-by-two-___ tongue-and-groove fir stained gray, and the floors were of linoleum. Noises of the wedding party echoed and reechoed, banging and clattering from walls to floors.

The bridesmaids wore blue ballerina dresses with big blue hats, white gloves, and white pumps, and each carried a pretty fragrant bouquet. Ann was the flower girl. Her long blond hair done in ringlets bounced up and down as she walked, and her patent leather shoes peeked from under her long dress. They had put lipstick on her—and rouge. She looked very grown-up-little. Precious.

The church filled with loggers, relatives, farmers, schoolgirls, college boys, and others. Joan had met a few of Joe's relatives, but when she walked down the aisle and saw all the strange people staring at her, she felt like running away. Her legs shook as she walked on her father's arm. Her mother, dressed in a green damask maternity smock, watched from the front pew on the bride's side of church.

Father Vittorio waited for them to come to the altar. At last everyone found his place, and the ceremony began. Joan looked at the flowers in high baskets on the side of the altars. She and her family had never had anything to do with a church or a wedding as long as she could remember. Her parents eloped one October night many years ago, and Joan planned to do the same thing. Joe had other ideas. No Schultz had been married by a judge. Ever. It just wasn't done.

The ceremony ended. Joan sighed. It had been long and boring. They rushed up the aisle. Then people were shaking their hands. Old friends and new acquaintances. The only thing Joan could remember later was that several said, "May all your troubles be little ones." Then they laughed, like it was a joke. She didn't understand the humor. Joan's classmates formed a circle around her. One of the girls began to cry. Then another. And another.

*Dear God . . . make them stop,* she silently prayed. Then someone took her hand, while her mother's friend Marjorie took movies in the sudden late fall sun. The girls dried their tears and began to smile. Then they went to the reception at the city hall. It had quickly filled with ill-at-ease-people who, an hour later, were babbling, first, in a din, then in a roar. Small children hid behind their mother's skirts, ladies bustled in the kitchen in last-minute preparation, and Joan's mother wore a look of dismay. So did her father. Her mother was pregnant. Her father had just spent a fortune for a wedding.

Some of Joe's college friends decided not to eat. Drinking was too much fun. They got *drunk*. When Joan came back from changing her clothes at the parish house, they kidnapped her. She broke away and ran down the street, clutching her black velvet hat while trying to keep her white coat from flapping in the breeze. Everyone from the reception laughed—and hooted. Joan hadn't gone far when they grabbed her. They threw her in a car and drove around town for quite a while before finally turning her loose in front of the hall. Joe waited with a pained expression. Everyone else thought it was fun.

They left town shortly after. Driving down the coast in a car smeared with JUST MARRIED seemed the final indignity. Years later and with a lot of bad days between, Joan still remembered her wedding day as the worst day of her life.

"I'll never get to know all your relatives, Joe."

"Yes, you will."

"I won't. There are too many of them. How many children were in your mother's family?"

"There were nine children in her family."

"And your dad's?"

"There were ten in his family."

"That makes nineteen people I'm supposed to know. Then most of them are married . . . I'll have to know their husband's and/or wives. Then they have children, and I'll have to know them. No thanks. I'll just pick the ones I like and get to know them."

"Don't worry about it. We don't see them that much anyway."

"Joe, did you think Mother looked good in the smock she wore to the wedding?"

"Yeah, she looked fine. When is she going to have her baby?"

"In February."

"And you're in June?"

"Uh-huh."

"Wasn't that a neat reception, Joan?"

"It was fine as far as receptions go . . . but I'm never comfortable around a lot of people. I much prefer them in ones and twos rather than a big bunch. I did think it was funny when your friend Murray started drinking out of the punch bowl. Mother looked like she was going to kill him. It wasn't funny when Daddy had to go get another case of whiskey."

"That didn't bother him."

"I think it did. See, he didn't expect any expense two months ago. Now he's had to pay for a big dinner, drinks, flowers, and photographer. It all adds up."

"I guess it does."

They rode in silence through the gathering haze of dusk. The winding coast road brought them into the next county—a distance of about fifty miles. Lights twinkled in the distance as they approached the town.

"Joan, the first thing I'm going to do is to get this car washed."

She knew how embarrassed he'd been driving the decorated car. People smirked as they drove by . . . and pointed. Oh.

"That's good because I have to go to the bathroom."

"I see a station over there."

He pulled in and then went around to rouse the lone attendant. Joan hurried to the restroom. When she came back, Joe was pacing back and forth in short paces.

"He can't wash the car until morning."

"Oh. Well, that's all right. Why don't we find a place to stay and leave the car here?"

The attendant smirked and wiped his hands on the dirty oilcloth he held. "The nicest place in town is only three blocks from here. You could walk that far."

"What's its name?"

"The Rochester House." He went toward the street and pointed down the highway. "You can see the sign from here."

"Thanks. Joan, let's walk down and see if we can get a room. If we can, we'll come back for our things."

They could get a room. They were relaxing in a lovely room overlooking an exquisitely kept garden within the hour.

When they were all settled and about to retire for the night, Joan said, "I'm thirsty."

"For what?"

"I want a Coke."

"Now?"

"Yes. Now."

"Oh . . . OK. I'll go get you one."

He put on his pants, shirt, and shoes. He wore no socks as he headed for the lobby. He was back soon, and Joan swore later that that was the last nice thing he ever did for her.

They saw San Francisco. They didn't know the streets, the neighborhoods, and the places to go (they were both too young to go into places that served liquor). So they really didn't *see* San Francisco. But they were there. For nine days.

They arrived in San Francisco at midnight. A big convention of veterans filled all downtown hotels. There was not one room to be had. They searched the backstreets for hours. Finally, when they'd decided they'd have to sleep in the car, they came across a hotel named the Rochester House.

"Let's try. I think it's too much of a coincidence. The first hotel we stayed in on our way down was the Rochester House. And you know how much we liked that. It was really a nice place."

"I liked it too. I did get tired of going after Cokes for you. Gee."

"I couldn't help it. I was thirsty. Let's go see if we can get a room."

They could. The lobby overflowed with graceful plants. A rich carpet and comfortable furniture lent an air of warmth. The price seemed reasonable, and Joe happily paid for what was left of the night. The desk clerk ushered them to a room. He opened the door, mumbled something, and left.

"What did he say, Joe?"

"I didn't hear him."

"Where is the bathroom?" She saw an ornate old sink in one corner of the room.

Joe surveyed the small room. "Down the hall."

"Oh."

He moved near the bed. "I guess it won't hurt us to sleep here one night."

Joan looked around the room. The 60 watt bulb in the chandelier bathed the room in a soft glow. On close examination, it also disguised dirty walls, a threadbare rug, and a lumpy bed.

"I think we'd better look at the sheets before we decide." She pulled them back. They were clean.

"I don't think I could look for another place tonight. We've been driving for hours, and I'm exhausted." Joe collapsed on the bed.

"So am I. I don't think we could get our money back either. But we'll have to find another room tomorrow. I don't want to stay here another night."

"We'll find something . . . I hope."

"We will. I'll go to the bathroom first, then put on my nightgown in the room."

"Fine."

"If I'm not back in ten minutes . . . come looking for me?"

"Nobody will bother you."

"You're right. There probably isn't anyone alive in this whole *so-called* hotel."

He was right. No one bothered her. She heard noises from the other rooms as she walked by in the hall. She wondered what kind of people would stay in such a crummy hotel. *Probably people like us,* she thought.

Joe had a job waiting for him when he got home. In a mill. He would work the night shift. Before the wedding, they'd found a little cottage that was attached to three others in a row near the state highway that ran close to the ocean. A huge barricade of boulders separated the ocean from the highway. The cottages were on high ground and in no danger.

They had twenty dollars when they returned from their trip. It had to last two weeks until Joe was paid.

"I'll borrow some from Mother."

"No."

"No what?"

"No, I don't want you to borrow any money from your mother."

"We only have twenty dollars."

"That's enough."

"To live two weeks?"

"Yes."

Three days later, they borrowed a hundred dollars from Joan's mother and prepared to move into the cottage they'd rented. It seemed smaller than Joan remembered—and dirtier. The furniture was old and saggy. The cushions were faded and matched the washed-out colors of the old frayed rug. The bed looked lumpy and uncomfortable. The ornate metal bed was dented and tarnished. Dusty curtains hid spiderwebs. Little dirty window panes looked out on a parking area, and the other cottages were so close, voices could be heard through the thin walls.

"Let's stay a few more days with my parents until we get this house clean," Joan begged.

"No," Joe said.

"No what?"

"I don't want to stay with your parents."

"Why not?"

"Because I just don't."

"We can't stay here. This place is filthy. It needs to be cleaned."

"I'll help you clean it. How much work could it be?"

He found out. Through a maze of detergents, polishes, cleansers, mops, brooms, brushes, and other heroic measures, they cleaned the little cottage. When at last everything was dried, polished, scrubbed, scoured, hung, unhung, and rehung, the cottage looked wonderful.

They flopped on the couch and drank a Coke.

"I'm exhausted."

"So am I, Joe. I worked hard for Christina cleaning that big old barn . . . which she loves so much . . . but I don't think I've ever been this tired."

"I had no idea housework could be so hard. It does look good, though." He stood up, stretched, looked around the room in smug self-appreciation, then reached for Joan. He pulled her to her feet and whispered in her ear, "Let's go to bed."

"Let's. Will you want a lunch in the morning, or will you come home?"

"I'll come home. It isn't too far from work, and I'll want to see you."

The alarm didn't go off (because Joan forgot to set it), and by the time Joe rushed out the door, it was clear he did *not* want to see her at lunchtime.

She dressed, tidied the kitchen, swept the floor, made the bed, noticed it was eight o'clock, sat down on the couch, and then looked around and shuddered when she realized her work was finished. She wondered what she would do with all her time. By the time she sorted through old letters, took a walk, took a nap, and took a shower, it was time for Joe to come home. She waited by the door for him. She heard sounds outside of his shoes in the gravel. She moved behind the door, and when he opened it, she flung her arms around him.

"Hey, let me go!"

"No, I'll never let you go. You belong to me."

"Later. Later. I need a shower."

"Was the work hard?"

"Yeah. It was hard, but I think I'll like it. They put me on the green chain." He thought about the day—about going to work, meeting the men. Wow. They were tough. He didn't stop to think that just as he judged them, they judged him. They saw a six-foot-three, light-blond-headed, well-muscled, almost-black-eyed, slightly uncomfortable, very young man. The men of the mill had once been the little boys of the town. They grew up. There were no jobs other than the mill, and so they took them. The bully, the coward, the hero, all were there. Each man did his best within his own limitations. They led hard lives. Hard work. Hard times. Joe smiled when he thought of the men. Wow. They were tough.

While Joe showered in the little bathroom down the hall from the kitchen, Joan finished making the salad for dinner. She surveyed her handiwork. The salad looked good. She'd spent the afternoon poring through the cookbook they'd received as a wedding present. She'd taken home economics in grammar school and had learned to make a couple of sauces. Other than that, her cooking experiences had been limited. Christina had taught her how to clean but not how to cook.

She checked the oven to see how the meatloaf looked. It looked good. Joe came out of the bathroom with a towel around his waist, dripping water on the floor.

"Dinner smells good."

"Hurry and dress so we can eat."

They ate in silence. Joe was too tired to talk. By the time he finished eating, he began to feel better.

"Would you feel like taking a little walk after I finish the dishes?"

"OK. You do the dishes, while I go over to the cafe and get a newspaper."

"I got one this morning . . . It's on the table."

Joan saw him look across the small room. From where he sat, he could see everything in the cottage, except the bathroom and the hall. Everything about the cottage seemed in miniature to him. The kitchen and living room were divided by the dining set that stood in front of the south end of the drainboard. In the bedroom there was hardly room for them to walk around the double bed.

"You know, Joan, it's hard to get used to living in such a small space."

"I know what you mean, but we were lucky to find a vacancy . . . Remember, we didn't have any choice. Everything was rented . . . or we didn't have enough money to pay more rent. We'll have enough next month . . . Maybe we should look for something else."

"Naw. We can stay here for a while . . . until we get some more money saved . . . Who knows . . . someday we might even buy our own house."

"I certainly hope we can, J. Paul. It'll have to be a two-story white colonial, like Christina's, only solid and elegant with cranberry glass in the windows and crystal in the cabinets at the right angle so the sun shines through." She finished washing the dishes, dried her hands on the towel, then went over to where Joe read. "I'm ready to go."

They walked on the railroad tracks that lay in front of the boulders on the ocean side of the bay. The night was clear and crisp, and lights blinking across the bay looked like candles flickering. Waves crashed against massive rocks, and now and then water sprayed high above them. As they made their way along the tracks, the rail bed rose higher and higher above the bay until they could hardly hear the waves crashing below. They could see the iridescence of the phosphorous that illuminated the shoreline. The moon reflected on the water, and overhead glowed pale yellow in the blue-black sky.

Joe felt the blister on his right foot. The boots he wore were too new, too tightly laced, and too warm. He felt a chill from the cold salt air that smelled like the coast—fresh, fishy, and wet.

"Let's go home, Joan, and go to bed. I'm tired, and I have to get up early tomorrow morning."

"OK. Thank you for coming with me. I wanted to get out of the house."

"What did you do all day?"

"I really didn't have much to do. I had the house cleaned and everything done by eight o'clock. I spent time writing thank-you notes and then in the afternoon I read and then I took a nap."

"There's not much to do in that small cottage."

"There really isn't. Tomorrow I want to go up to Mother's and get some of our wedding presents. I'll bring back whatever we can use. The rest of the stuff we can leave in the attic. We really got a lot of junk . . . didn't we?"

"Junk? How can you call it junk? Most of the wedding gifts are really nice."

"It's a bunch of junk, and you know it. Nothing matches, and we have ten sets of cheap glasses. The colors of the linens are garish, and frankly I hate the lamps."

"You seem to hate everything."

"No, I don't. I just don't like the wedding gifts."

"You know people spent good money to buy presents for us. I don't think you're being very nice about them."

"I certainly wouldn't discuss it with anyone but you. If I can't say what I please to my husband, whom can I say it to?"

They made their way back to the cottage. Now and then, Joe looked over at Joan, who walked beside him not saying a word. He reached for her hand as she quickly moved away from him.

The cottage was nice and warm when they entered. Their faces glowed, and their cheeks looked like rosy red apples. They hung up their coats. Then Joe went into the bedroom to get ready for bed. Joan sat in the big chair in the living room and started to read.

"Hey, aren't you coming to bed?"

"Not yet."

"Come to bed."

"No."

"Why not? Was it something I said?"

"I don't know if it was something you said or something you didn't say. I don't know what it is."

"Maybe you're just tired."

"Maybe I'm not."

"Maybe you are."

"Maybe I'm just pregnant."

"Oh, so that's it. Do you want to fight?"

"Yes, I want to fight."

"Well, I don't. I have to get up early in the morning, and I'm tired . . . so good night."

She sat in the chair and said nothing for some time. Then with resignation, she rose, went around the cottage, straightening things, then turned out the lights. She got ready for bed, and when she finally climbed in, Joe snored softly next to her. He roused a little, pulled her close, and then started snoring again. His body, big, warm, and soft, closed in around her. Her earlier petulance forgotten, she happily settled in for a cozy night.

The months rolled by. February came and brought with it another little sister for Joan. She was a beautiful baby, and her name was Neeley. Her eyes were big and brown, and her skin and hair were lustrous. Her fat little cheeks were dimpled. Seeing her made Joan even more anxious to have her own baby. She hoped hers would be as pretty as Neeley.

He wasn't. He had a pointed head, pointed ears and chin, a squiggly shaft of pale yellow hair, and a jaundiced complexion. His yellowed skin was dry and flaky. Even the whites of his eyes were yellow. His face looked gnarled like a little old man's. His arrival had been a surprise.

Joan had been to the doctor for her regular checkup that afternoon. She told him she'd had a bloody discharge. He didn't seem too interested. Her back ached, like it was slowly grinding in a circular motion.

"Mrs. Schultz, you are just fine. The baby will be born on time."

"Dr. Carr, I don't think I'll live that long." The idea of feeling like this for two *more* weeks wasn't pleasant to her.

"Go," he commanded.

That was about two in the afternoon. Now it was seven in the evening. Joan sat visiting with her neighbor at the cottages. Joe was on night shift, and she liked Mary Blair's company. Mary and her daughter, Kay, lived alone, while Lee Blair captained tugs off the coast.

That night, Kay, who was ten, kept watching Joan for any sign of the impending birth. It made Joan nervous.

"Mary, I think I'll go home and read. My back is hurting, and I keep having Braxton-Hicks contractions. Only they're harder."

"What are Braxton-Hicks contractions?" Kay asked.

"Braxton-Hicks contractions are the first stage of labor. They often start in the last month of pregnancy, I think," Joan answered.

"Joan, you go home, and I'll come check on you before I go to bed," Mary said.

"That is so nice of you. I appreciate your concern, but the doctor said the baby would be on time, so I'm not worried, but the pains do seem harder. I don't know what the real pains are supposed to feel like."

Mary smiled knowingly. "When they happen, *you'll know.*"

Joan laughed. "All in all, Mary, I'd rather be in Philadelphia."

"Look, Joan, we know how the baby got in there. Now we have to figure out a way to get it out."

Joan patted her big stomach. "Mary, I think God made a mistake. He should have fixed it so the baby could have been carried on the back of the shoulders. This (she patted her stomach) is always in the way. You can't bend over, you bump things, and you can't get near the drainboard to work. It's very inconvenient."

Mary shook her head. "When you get to heaven, protest."

"If there is a heaven, I doubt if I'll make it."

"You'll be queen of the angels."

"I'd be foolish to say any more. Good-bye. Good-bye. I gotta go!"

"See you later," Mary called. She watched Joan waddle to her cottage.

Joan dressed for bed with as much speed as her ungainly whalelike hulk could muster. At last she was snug between the crisp percale sheets. She picked up her book from the night side table and began to read. Pains that hadn't stopped since this afternoon enveloped her—one after the other. She read on. Pain. Pain. Read. Read. The pains seemed unending and intense. They ground on. At ten o'clock, just when the words on the page doubled and tripled, Mary knocked on the door.

"Come in, Mary. The door is open," she called.

Mary took one look at her and signaled for her to get to the car waiting near the gate, and without a word, they drove to the hospital. Joan could hardly talk. Time had been wasted. She hadn't recognized her need. Now birth was imminent.

They made it to the hospital with little time to spare. The doctor was late, and they held her legs together until he came. She used language she didn't know she knew. At last the doctor came smiling into the room—and the baby was born. Thank God. Thank God. Thank God.

Mary was waiting when they wheeled her out of the delivery room. She rushed over to the gurney and clutched Joan's hand.

"I was so worried." She seemed ready to cry.

"How good of you . . . I'm fine. Did you see the baby?" It made Joan feel warm to know she had a friend who would be so concerned about her. It also made her uncomfortable. This was harder on Mary than it was on her. "Could you get in touch with Joe?"

"I called him as soon as we came in. He'll be here soon."

They settled Joan into her room. Mary fussed with the curtains. "I'll bet you can't wait until Joe gets here."

"I am excited. He'll be so happy to have a son." Joan thought about all the long days of the pregnancy. The morning sickness, the gradual great growth . . . all of it. Now, as she waited expectantly for Joe to see their son, she knew it had all been worthwhile.

"Here he comes," whispered Mary.

Joe stood in the doorway. Joan wondered what his first words would be on this important occasion in their lives.

As he came toward her, she heard them. "Phew," he said, "you smell like ether."

\* \* \*

"Is that *my* baby?"

"Yes, Mrs. Schultz."

"Are you sure?"

"Yes, Mrs. Schultz."

When the nurse left, Joan carefully surveyed the infant. The only appealing thing about him was that he had two big dimples in his cheeks. She wondered if she'd ever love this ugly little bundle. *Maybe later,* she thought, *maybe after I get used to him, though that doesn't seem likely.*

He, Stan, was born in June, soon after the strike at the mill was settled. Joe had been off work, and they'd lived on unemployment for three months. One day when he was off work, they'd taken a walk around the Heights near where her parents lived and found a small house with a For Sale sign. When they inquired, they discovered the owner wanted two hundred and fifty dollars down and the balance in small monthly payments. Sixteen hundred dollars was the asking price. The house was very, very, dirty and unfinished and awful.

"We can't buy that house."

"Why not, Joe?"

"We don't have two hundred and fifty dollars, the house needs too much work . . . there isn't even a kitchen . . . the yard is overrun with blackberry vines, and I don't want to buy it."

"Maybe you don't right now, but think about it. Where can you get a house for sixteen hundred dollars? We can clean it up, paint it, put in a kitchen, and clear the yard. All the money we pay for rent could be saved . . . at least most of it."

"We don't have two hundred and fifty dollars for the down payment."

"We can borrow that from my parents."

"Oh, no. Oh, no. We'll not borrow more money from your parents."

"Why not? They don't mind. They like to lend money to us. And we always pay them back. Let's do it."

"No. No. No."

# Chapter 5

They lived in the little house for over a year. Joe built a charming kitchen of knotty pine. They cleared the yard of the blackberry vines and planted a lawn and dahlias around the edges. They enjoyed the view of the bay and the sound of fishing boats chugging through the water.

They were within walking distance of Joan's parents and often went to visit. Joan spent more time with them than Joe because Joe still worked nights at the mill and slept nearly all day. Joan enjoyed visiting with her mother, and she found it entertaining to watch the two babies play together.

The summer after they moved to the house, they got a call from Joe's uncle. A friend of his was retiring and wanted Joe to take over his job reading blueprints at a lumberyard. He would teach him all he needed to know, and he thought it would be a wonderful opportunity for him. After he learned the business, his salary would be twice what he was making working more than forty hours a week. Joe and Joan went to see the man.

"What did you think of him, Joan?"

"Mr. Hall?"

"Yeah, did you like him?"

"I don't know. I wonder if he has a drinking problem."

"Just because he had two drinks while we were there?"

"No, because he had a complexion like someone who drinks too much. Didn't you notice his red nose? Also, he's in that group of friends of your uncle's who drink too much. They use every excuse they can to get loaded."

"What difference would that make? I'd still have the job. I think we should take it. Working in a mill is not what I want to do the rest of my life."

They moved into an apartment over a tavern in the Albinate District in Watertown. They lived on a busy street, and the first few nights in the apartment, the combination of traffic and the reverberating sound of music from the tavern caused Joan and Joe to have insomnia. Even Stan couldn't sleep. His crib was in a large closet, and he hated being in the small area. He screamed and screamed.

The apartment cost $50 a month. It had a large kitchen with an old gas stove and a funny old refrigerator on legs, and a living room with a hide-a-bed for them and the closet for Stan. The floors were linoleum, the windows had wavy glass, and the high ceilings needed paint.

Joe worked in the lumberyard. He was to receive three hundred and fifty dollars a month until he learned to read blueprints and could take over Mr. Hall's job of ordering supplies for new building construction. When he learned this, his wage would double.

In the fall, after several months in the little apartment, Joan found an ad in the newspaper for a house on Seventy-Third. It sounded just like what she was hoping to find. She hadn't discussed it with Joe because he was a little upset about his job (Mr. Hall wasn't teaching him as he said he would), but she had been looking through the papers for a house for weeks. The house described in the ad suited her just fine.

"Joe, I've found a house that sounds great for us."

"A house?"

"Yes, we can't go on living in this little apartment much longer. We have to sleep on a couch that converts to a bed, it's noisy, there's no place for Stan to play, we can never have company because there is no place for them . . . We just have to move."

"How can you think of moving? We haven't any money. We are still paying payments on the house at the coast. We hardly have enough to get by on as it is."

"OK. Don't think about buying it. Let's just go look . . . I like to look at houses."

"No."

"Why not?"

"I don't want to."

"That's not a good reason. I stay home all day, every day, and on the only day we could go someplace . . . you don't want to. I'll tell you what I'll do . . . you can babysit Stan, while I drive over and look at the house."

"No."

"Why not?"

"The car isn't running right."

"What's the matter with it?"

"It's out of adjustment."

"Either you drive me or I drive myself. I'm going to see that house this afternoon."

They found it without difficulty. The ad said it was of colonial design. It wasn't. It was nondescript: two stories, gray, large lot, oil furnace, fireplace, four bedrooms, dining room, basement, and outdoors with a huge wisteria vine hanging over the driveway. The yard was fenced, and shrubs lined the walk.

The real estate lady, Mrs. Keenan, was very nice to them. Her gray hair pinned in a bun escaped here and there and gave her a homey appearance. She looked like a lady one could trust. Her clear blue eyes sparkled whenever Joan found something of interest about the house. She patiently showed them every detail of the house even when they assured her they were *just looking*. She treated them deferentially as she would any other prospective customer. When they were leaving, Joe and Joan thanked her for the tour.

"It's quite all right. I've enjoyed meeting you both. I want you to remember the house is on the market for $7,500. If you should be interested, you could buy it for a thousand dollars down and $75 a month."

Joe turned red. He looked at Joan, then turned to Mrs. Keenan. "We have no intention of buying, Mrs. Keenan. I thought we made that clear to you."

Mrs. Keenan laughed. "Don't misunderstand me. I know that you are not in the market to buy . . . still . . . one never knows. If you have the figures, it can give you something to work on if you should change your mind."

On the drive home, they talked about the house.

"It's too old, and there is too much maintenance on it," Joe said.

"It didn't look so bad to me. The foundation is sound, and the roof is good. Joe, I think if you'd look at it from another point of view, you'd find it is a good buy. If we bought it, we could save all our rent."

"We only pay fifty a month, and until the job situation is more certain, I don't think we should consider buying a house."

"Look, even if you don't get the raise . . . you still have the job. That house might get sold in a little while. While you stall around and try to make up your mind, that house could get sold."

"I thought we were just looking."

"We need a house!"

"Why?"

"You know why. We can't live in that terrible apartment much longer."

"Damn. I don't like the way you engineer these things."

"What things?"

"You know what I mean."

"Joe, you don't have time to do everything. You have to work all week. I just do the things you don't have time to do. Let me go talk to Grandpa and see if he'll lend us the money."

"Absolutely not. I will not borrow a dollar from your grandfather to buy a house."

They moved in the middle of November. It was cold outside, but the oil furnace and the fireplace kept the house nice and warm. They kept the upstairs shut off during the day and opened the door at night. Joan loved the cheery kitchen and spent most of her time in it. The only thing she missed about the apartment was the bakery across the street. Now that she was pregnant again, she had wild cravings for certain foods. She craved pumpkin pies. Before they moved, she'd often go across the street to get one for dinner, take it home, eat it piece by piece, and then have to hurry back and get another for Joe's dinner. (Of course, she never said a word.)

Here in the real house Joan spent a lot of time baking—and a lot of time eating what she had baked. Stan toddled around and spent most of his time with his arms curled around her legs. She couldn't move without upsetting him. She was like a horse with fetters. The only time she had to herself was when he napped . . . and he napped less and less.

Joan began to worry about Mr. Hall. He had become strangely evasive to Joe. Joe spent several weeks with him. Then he was *busy* whenever he called. Finally, Joe had given up.

"At least you have your job."

"I was looking forward to making more money."

"I know, millionaire. I was looking forward to it too. I wonder what happened to Mr. Hall?"

"I think I know what happened, Joan. I think he had too much to drink one night and told Uncle Lester there was a great future for me in sales. Then he found out I'm *not* a salesman.

"Let's not think about it anymore. Everything will work out for the best. It will soon be Christmas, and we'll have a good new year living in this house. We'll have a garden, and I'll plant some flowers . . . I'll find out which ones later . . . We'll have a happy life living here."

"I don't know, Joan. I don't know if I'll ever get used to living in the city. I miss the farm. I miss the quiet evenings, the sound of birds in the early mornings. I miss the smell of hay being cut. I miss the clean, crisp air that makes you chill in the early morning because you wore light clothes because you know the rest of the day will be hot. I miss it all."

"You'll get used to it. We have nice neighbors . . ."

"Who live five feet from us."

"And there isn't much traffic on our street . . ."

"But it goes by all night, and the horns honk and keep me awake."

"And this is where we live, and we were lucky to get it!"

On December 23, the company Joe worked for sent him home with a turkey. They also gave him notice that he had been laid off. He came home that night with shoulders sagging. Joan knew at once that something was very wrong. He told her about the layoff and that no work would be available at the yard for at least three months.

"Oh, Joe, we can't live three months without work. We owe money on this house, the house at the coast, the car, and the sewing machine, and in March we'll have another doctor and hospital bill for the new baby. We just can't live without you working."

Joe looked at her with irritation. "If you could just have listened to me before we bought those things."

"We needed the houses, the car, and everything else we've bought. You can't live without certain things."

"*I* can live without certain things."

"We'll sell the house at the coast in no time . . . Then we won't have a payment on it . . . you'll see. In the meantime, you'll have to look for work."

"Yeah, but I don't know where to begin."

"Start with the newspaper."

He pored over the ads. Finally, he had a list of twenty places that had advertised for help. He went to bed that night nervous and apprehensive. When he woke in the morning, he felt better. Armed with the list, he set out bright and early.

Joan watched the time pass that day. Every few minutes, she looked at the clock, and what work needed doing was done automatically. She was completely immersed in her thoughts. Even Stan failed to get her full attention.

At six thirty, Joe drove in the driveway. She could tell by looking that he had been unsuccessful. Her heart dropped. He came into the house and sat down in the chair at the kitchen table.

"Can I get you something to drink?"

"No."

"It didn't go so well, huh?"

"There's a recession on."

"How about the job for a laundry truck driver?"

"They wanted a college degree for that one. There were twenty guys with a BA or a BS waiting in line."

"Oh, no."

"Oh, yes."

"What are we going to do?" she asked.

"The first thing we are going to do is sell this house."

"We've only lived here a month and a half. We can't sell it. And where would we go if we did?"

"We'll move back to the coast," Joe answered quietly.

"We can't do that. There's no work there. All the mills are down."

"There must be something . . ."

"Let's just think about it and not get too upset, Joe. Maybe your uncle or my dad know of something."

"Let's drive out tomorrow and see them."

"We don't have to . . . They are coming in for dinner tomorrow. It's Christmas, and we invited them weeks ago to celebrate our new house, remember?"

"We are having them for dinner?"

"Yes. You knew that."

"I guess I did. I forgot. We don't have enough money to buy food for a dinner."

"We have the turkey and twenty dollars."

"Our last twenty dollars."

"And we're going to have a nice dinner. We can go shopping after Stan wakes up and we eat."

"Isn't he sleeping late?"

"He went down for his nap at four thirty. He should be awake any minute."

Several months earlier, Joan's parents had purchased a small hardware store in a little valley town. They had also found a lovely old two-story house with four bedrooms. Joan knew that if they had to, they could move in with them. Her father had intended to devote his time to the store, but when it became evident that business was slow, he decided to return to the woods. Logging was something he knew and understood, and he was much too restless to be confined. The running of the store fell to her mother, who was finding it difficult to take care of her two younger children and manage the business.

Joan was up early the next morning. She carefully followed her cookbook's instructions. The turkey looked good. She made cinnamon rolls, candied yams, and fruit salad, and peeled potatoes for mashed potatoes. Later she'd make the gravy, open the peas, and do other last-minute things. She was learning how to cook and enjoyed it.

"What time are they coming?"

"Dinner is at one."

They came early, before she had a chance to finish her work, change her apron, and comb her hair. Her face, reddened from the exertion of the dinner's preparation, broke into a big smile when she saw her parents. Her smile was not quite so big for his uncle and aunt, who followed them through the wide front door. None of them knew that Joe was unemployed. Joan hoped the news wouldn't spoil their dinner. She tried to catch Joe's eye to warn him not to discuss it until after the meal.

Her mother came into the kitchen. "How is the turkey?" She took a fork, opened the hot oven door, and prodded for a few seconds. "It's not nearly done."

Joan stepped back from behind her mother. "It isn't?"

"No. It won't be done for at least another hour."

"Oh, damn. Everything else is ready. I did just what the cookbook said."

"You can never depend on a cookbook for cooking meat."

"Mother, how do you know how long to cook different foods?"

"Mostly by experience. Don't be upset . . . We can visit until dinner is ready."

Joan put newspapers on the dining room floor under Stan's high chair. He was a sloppy eater. After each meal, the floor, the high chair, and Stan had to be extensively washed. Joan wondered how long the spattery stage lasted.

Finally, the turkey was done. The dinner turned out well. Everyone had seconds and thirds, and even Joe seemed happy—for a while. After dinner, they sat around the dining table visiting.

Joe took a deep breath. "We have some bad news. I have been laid off. There won't be any work for at least three months . . . Maybe they'll never need me again. In the meantime, I'm going to have to find another job. I was hoping that one of you would know of something. I can do nearly anything . . . except in the mechanical line. Do you know of a job, Uncle Lester?"

Mr. Schultz cleared his throat and adjusted his glasses. "No, Joe, I don't know of a thing. I did hear they were employing a lot of men at the nuclear site in Idaho. There is a lot of construction going on around there."

Joan's father shook his head. "More people are out of work in this state than at any time since the Depression. All the mills along the coast are down . . . There is no market for lumber, and the price has gone so low that it doesn't pay the mills to run. I think this is going to be a very hard winter."

Joe looked at the two men. He knew what they were talking about. His recent attempt to find work had left him frustrated and enlightened. There simply was not a job to be had in all of Watertown. And from what Joan's father had said, there might not be one in the whole state.

"Uncle Lester, it looks like I'll have to take your advice and go to Idaho. If I could just get a job to tide us through the winter, I'm sure I can find something next spring." He looked down at the table. "There is a problem, though... I will have to borrow some money to get over there."

Mr. Schultz frowned. "Borrow money?" His face turned red.

"Just enough to pay for the trip and to tide us over until I get my first unemployment check."

"Oh, yeah... yeah," Mr. Schultz stammered.

Joan watched him try to compose himself. *Joe should have asked him in private,* she thought. She knew that if Mr. Schultz refused to loan them the money, her dad would loan it to them. What mattered to her was that the money would have to be paid back.

Her mother sat upright in her chair. "Joan, you're not thinking of staying here in this big house while Joe is in Idaho, are you?"

"We've already decided to sell the house, but we don't know where to go. We can't live at the coast. We can't live here, but we have to be close to the doctor and the hospital for when the baby comes."

Her mother leaned forward. "Joan, why don't you move in with us? We have such a big house—there's lots of room. You could store your things in the shed at the back of the house. I think you would be quite comfortable. If Joe is gone all winter, you'll be lonely living alone."

"Thank you, Mother, but I'm not so worried about being alone, as I am about being able to afford being alone... or anything else."

Joe left for Idaho on the twenty-seventh. He found a friend to go with him and share expenses. The car was loaded down with clothes and blankets. They didn't know how long they would have to stay in Idaho, and they were prepared.

When Joe had driven out the driveway, Joan walked through the house. She made mental notes about packing. Her father would be there the next morning with a rented truck to move their belongings. Joan would be busy all that day getting ready for the move. Stan's bed would be about the last thing to be taken down. She hoped he would stay out of her way as she worked during the day.

Her father arrived at eight o'clock. Joan had been up since six. All of the things in the cupboards had been wrapped and packed in cardboard boxes. Her father started loading the truck. After two hours of hard work, he sat down at the kitchen table. "Whew. I'm getting warm."

"Would you like a beer, Daddy? There are two in the refrigerator."

"Sounds good." He relaxed, while Joan opened the bottle.

"Here you are."

He took a long drink. "Ahhh. That tastes good." Then he leaned back in his chair. "Joan, we haven't had a chance to talk since you got married. Are you happy? Do you like being married? Are you looking forward to having another baby?"

Joan looked at him and laughed. "I'm not deliriously happy. I'm not crazy about being married. I'm not especially looking forward to having another baby."

"Oh."

"Oh, don't look like that, Daddy. Everything is really all right. I just get so bored not having anything to do. After I do my housework in the morning, fix a light lunch, and do a few chores in the afternoon, it seems that it is such a long time until I have to fix dinner. I just have nothing to occupy my time most of the day."

Her father smiled. "I know one thing you could do to occupy your time."

"Really? What, Daddy?"

"You could clean your oven."

At last, the truck was loaded and ready to roll. They climbed into the cab. Stan sat in the middle, fascinated by the gear shift and all the gauges and dials. Joan's father wearily hauled himself behind the wheel.

"Are you ready to go?"

"We have to drop the key by the real estate office. It's just a few blocks from here."

"OK. Show me the way. Here we go!"

## Chapter 6

Four days later, Joe pulled up in front of the two-story residence on Elm Street, which his wife and child were in the process of getting used to. Joan happened to see him stop. She rushed to meet him. He had stubble on his cheeks, his clothes were rumpled, and he looked very tired.

"Joe, I'm so surprised to see you. Are you all right?"

"I'm fine, Joan. I just looked for work all over the state of Idaho, and the only place they needed men was in the potato cellars. The job paid eight dollars a day. I get five-dollars-a-day unemployment. By the time I paid for a place to stay, I'd have been in the hole. You know I'd rather work than sit around, but it just wouldn't pay. So I came home."

"I'm glad you did, but what are we going to do now?"

"I'm going to go to the coast tomorrow . . . Maybe I can get on at one of the little mills . . . especially since I have experience."

"Can I ride out with you?"

"No. I might have to stop too many places. Stan would never like that."

"You're right. I hadn't thought about him—or the girls. I'm babysitting while Mother is at the store."

"How is that going?"

"There's hardly a customer, but the store has to be kept open."

"Maybe it will do better later."

"I hope so. It's so tiring for Mother to be there."

"Doesn't your dad stay at the store at all?"

"He was, but now he's decided he'd better find something until the store starts to pay off or they sell it, whichever comes first. Besides, he is too restless to spend a lot of time there."

The next morning, after Joe left for the coast and she had finished the dishes and the other everyday chores, Joan bundled the children up and walked to the post office with them. There was a letter. She knew from the way the envelope looked that it was about the house. She ripped it open. She couldn't believe her eyes. The house at the coast had sold for twenty-five hundred dollars. She mentally computed: they'd paid sixteen hundred. They'd made a profit of nine hundred dollars. And just when they needed it so much.

It wasn't until they returned home that Joan had time to read the letter carefully. The buyers wanted to put down three hundred dollars. The rest they would pay on time. It would take forever for them to get their money out of the house. *Still,* Joan thought, *at least we won't have to make any more payments on it.*

Joe was smiling two days later when he pulled his car in front of the house. Joan knew without asking that he had found a job.

"It's at the plywood mill at Baldwin. I just happened to be there when another man didn't show up. The foreman asked if I wanted a job. I said *sure.* I worked that shift and then the one this morning. It's not too hard. Better than the green chain. And I have until Monday off."

Joan told him about selling the house. He relaxed visibly. "Maybe things are going our way for a change." He smiled at the idea. His almost-black eyes twinkled. He reached for Joan with his big strong hands. She moved away. She wasn't ready to play.

"What will we do about moving to the coast?"

"We've done enough moving for a while, Joan."

"What will you do? You can't drive back and forth every day?"

"I rented a room. Over a tavern . . . wouldn't you know? And I can fix food for myself. When things open up here in the valley, I should be able to find a job. In the meantime, let's stay here with your parents. It's not working out too bad, is it?"

"No. Everything is fine here. And to tell you the truth, I'd just as soon have my doctor deliver the baby. Living here will be hard on you, though."

"Why?"

"Mother will make you wipe your feet."

Joe drove home from the coast on weekends. He arrived tired from the long drive. He hated the work, and every weekend he toured the country looking for a different job. He searched for weeks without luck. When he had just about given up, he happened to be driving by the lumberyard in Plainsville when he noticed a new Help Wanted sign in the window. Joe applied immediately.

"I won't need anyone for four weeks," Otto Kent said. "I just wanted to be sure to have someone who could step into my son-in-law's shoes when he leaves for the air force next month. Think you can do the job?"

"Well, sir, I worked in a lumberyard for several months, and I know a lot about lumber. When I left the sawmill, I was being trained as a West Coast grader, so I know the different grades of lumber. I think I will learn whatever else I need to know in a reasonable time."

Otto Kent looked him over. Joe was nice looking, strong, and pleasant, and seemed bright. At last, and after what seemed an eternity to Joe, Otto stuck out his hand and said, "I'll go take the sign out of the window. You're hired. You'll start the first of April. I'll see you then."

"Thank you, Mr. Kent. I'll be here."

"Call me Otto."

Joe couldn't believe his good fortune. On the way home, he decided he wouldn't tell Joan about the job for a while, but he couldn't restrain himself, and the first thing he did was blurt it out.

"Oh, Joe, I'm so happy. Now we can move out of here."

"Don't you like living with your parents?"

"We're lucky to have a place to live, and it is pleasant living with them, but I want a place of our own."

"We'll have to stay here for now. It will be some time before we have enough money so we can move."

"I know we have to be careful of money, but it seems we can't afford anything," she said irksomely.

"We can't afford another baby. We don't have any insurance or money saved."

"I know, but what can we do? The Catholic Church says we can't use contraceptives, and so far the rhythm system doesn't work for us." Joan felt her huge stomach. She felt the baby move inside her. It kicked hard and made the fabric of her smock flutter. "Just think, in one short week, you'll be a father again."

It happened sooner than she expected.

Three days later, when she pulled the tea down from the cupboard, she had her first labor pain. She knew with certainty the minute it started. It radiated through her whole body, took her breath away, and caused her skin to turn a rosy red. She made no sound that would catch the attention of her mother or Joe's uncle Lester and aunt Emma, who were chatting in the living room while they waited for tea.

"Is everything all right?" her mother called.

"Fine. We'll have tea in a minute."

When the tea was ready, she carried it into the living room. She took a small cup for herself, served the others, then sat down to visit. She hoped the Schultzes would leave soon. She knew that she'd have to go to the hospital before too long. It was an hour away.

Mr. Schultz raised his voice as he condemned Republicans, Baptists, Jews, and the weather all in the same breath. Whenever he found a willing or unwilling ear, he couldn't resist.

Joan smiled. She wondered if anyone could see she was having labor pains. She hoped not. She would not have agreed if someone said she was shy. But she was. She would rather have died than have the

Schultzes know she was in labor. It was such a personal thing, and she was uncomfortable with them.

They made no move to leave, and then Joan realized that they were probably going to stay so long that her mother would have to ask them to dinner. She began to panic. A breathtaking, bottom-of-the-foot-pulling, stomach-stopping, throat-tightening, vein-constricting pain enveloped her. Her eyes widened. Jesus Christ. She knew she'd have to do *something* soon.

Then as if by some miracle, the Schultzes were standing. They moved toward the door.

"Are you sure you can't stay for dinner?" her mother asked.

Joan held her breath.

"No. Thank you. We promised our friends, the Tates, we'd stop by on our way home."

"Well, you know you're always welcome here. We'll look forward to seeing you again soon."

*Go. Go. Please go*, thought Joan as she smiled and waved them away.

Finally, her mother shut the door. She turned red from the force of another hard pain. "Mother, we've got to get to the hospital."

It seemed like hours before they were actually on their way. A babysitter had to be found—and picked up. And they had to get a few groceries. And. And. And. Actually not too much time passed. Joan wanted to be careful not to alarm her mother, who tended to panic. The pains were closer together and had increased in intensity. Lights began to flicker on as they drove northward. They traveled through uninhabited grazing lands, small towns, and small forests, and passed several lovely streams. Joan realized her mother was nervously pressing her foot on the accelerator, and the speedometer looked like ninety from where she sat.

"Don't be alarmed, Mother. I'm fine."

With that, her mother relaxed the pressure on the gas. She settled back in her seat and began visiting with Joan. She became so engrossed in the conversation that she slowed down to forty.

Another hard pain gripped Joan's body. She was afraid what the next one might be. That one had been so intense. "I guess we'd better go a little faster, Mother."

She was sure they'd never make it to the hospital, but they drove into the emergency entrance with time to spare. By the time she was admitted, examined, and put into a bed, the pains had almost stopped. They were far apart but much harder. It was a puzzle to her.

Her mother came into the room. "Joan, I'm going to have to leave. I have to get back home. You'll be all right here. I'll come see you tomorrow. Good luck."

Ten minutes after her mother left, the baby dropped; and she dilated to ten, on a scale from zero to ten, and was on her way to the delivery room. The nurse who greeted her inside the room looked as though she had survived many things. Huge, ugly, and mean, she lifted Joan onto the delivery table with strong hairy arms. She glared at Joan.

"My leg is getting a cramp," Joan said seconds after her legs had been strapped into the stirrups. It seemed as if the cramp would never leave ... Then she began to have another labor pain—out of the frying pan, into the fire. Oww. The pains became constant. Anesthetic administered through tubes in her arm made her woozy. "Oh. Son of a bitch," she moaned. "Let me out of this terrible place."

"Here, now, you stop that or I'll slap your face," Big Bad Nurse snarled.

Shackled arms and legs, Joan raised her head and glared at the woman. "You slap my face and I'll slap yours!"

The schoolroom clock on the delivery room wall said nine o'clock. The large round convex mirror was directly in Joan's line of vision. Every time she looked up, she saw her orange-painted vagina staring at her. Her legs, spread at 180-degree angles, were encased in long heavy stockings. Her orange vagina contrasted sharply with the white stockings.

"Oh. Oh. Oh."

"Are you having a contraction?"

"Yes."

"Good."
"Here's Dr. McCready."
"Good morning, Dr. McCready."
"Good morning, Joan."
Oh. Oh. Oh.
"How are you, ladies?"
"Fine, Doctor. Did you have time for dinner?"
"Yes. I had Swiss steak in the cafeteria. Very good."
"We missed you this weekend."
"Marge and I went skiing."
Oh. Oh. Oh.
"That sounds like fun."
"It was. Dr. Koch was there."
"He's a good skier, isn't he?"
"Yes, he is. He had an accident this time, though."
"Really? What happened?"
"He jumped off the ski tow and broke his ankle."
Oh. Oh. Oh.
"That's a shame."
"Yes. He won't be able to work for a while. When did she come in?"
"About twenty minutes ago."
"I'm going to examine you, Joan. It won't hurt."
"Fine." *That's what he always says.* "Yeow. What are you putting in me?"
"Just my little finger."
*It feels like a cannon.* Oh. Oh. Oh.
"When was her last contraction?"
"About one minute ago."
"They're a little erratic. Give her a little more gas. She's having another one. Push!"

Oh. Oh. Oh. Gas always made her dream the same dream. It was so real yet unreal. It took a full week for her to determine that then really wasn't real and now really is real. It was a terrible dream and yet so *real*.

There was a black spiral on a background of blazing light. The spiral spiraled. It moved endlessly—down.

*I know what hell is. This is hell. Everyone thinks hell is fires and burning, but it isn't. I am the only one who really knows. The stupid bastards. I wish I could tell them, but I can't . . . I've died and gone to hell. I am the only one who knows what it's like, and I can't tell them. But I know. I know. I've died and gone to hell, and the spiral of light is hell. Ha-ha. I know.*

"She's coming out of it."

"Did I have the baby?"

"Not yet, Joan."

Oh. Oh. Oh. Oh. Oh.

Back to hell. Spiral. Light. Down. Down. Hell.

"Did I have the baby?"

"Not yet, Joan."

"Push! Push!"

"Did I have the baby?"

"Yes, you did!"

"Thank God. Is it all right?"

"Yes. You have a healthy baby girl. Look."

*That makes me sick. The gas was bad enough, but do they have to stick a newborn baby with that creamy junk all over it in my face? That makes me sick.*

"Isn't she beautiful?"

"No . . . I don't want to look at her . . . She's all slimy."

"Well!"

"Give her a little gas. I'm going to take a few stitches."

"Stitches? I don't want any stitches."

"Now, now, Joan. I'm just going to take a few stitches."

Oh. Oh. Oh.

The recovery room nurse was waiting for her when they wheeled her in nauseous and groggy.

"What are you doing now? Please don't knead my sore stomach like that."

"I'm just making sure your uterus is in place."

"Please stop."

"I have to do it . . . I saw your baby. She's adorable."

"Thank you."

"You don't sound very happy. It wasn't that bad, now was it?"

"It was worse than bad. Delivery rooms are torture chambers."

"My daughter just had a baby. She said as soon as she went into the delivery room, she didn't feel a thing."

Joan didn't answer. It made the woman nervous. She tried to smile, then edged out the door.

"Well, at least you have a nice healthy baby girl."

"I'd rather have had a new refrigerator."

# Chapter 7

Hospital sounds broke the silence of early morning. Joan had not slept. She was too keyed up. Too tense. Too hyped. Her body ached. She felt like she'd been in a fight—or had a baby. A nurse came in to check her. *Go away. Leave me alone. I don't want to talk. Good morning. How are you? Fine? No. Leave me alone.*

"Good morning. Did you sleep well?"

"No, I didn't. I didn't sleep at all."

"Hmmmm. Well, you can sleep today."

"Could I see my baby?"

"Haven't you seen her?"

"They stuck her in my face before she was cleaned up, so I'd like to see her now."

"They'll be bringing in the babies before too long."

Joan looked at the little baby and saw with relief that she wasn't as ugly as Stan had been. This baby was darker and had finer features, though she was wrinkled and purplish in color. Joan checked out the fingers and toes, and noticed the ugly remains of the umbilical cord as she ran her fingertips over the baby's incredibly soft skin. The infant stuck her fist in her mouth, twisted it, made sucking, rooting noises, then started to cry. Joan cooed and gooed at her, then, after a short time, called the nurse. She'd nursed Stan for three long, long weeks. It was one of the worst experiences of her life, and she vowed she'd never repeat the mistake. The nurse could feed this one in the nursery.

That evening, after dinner, Joan saw her mother coming down the hall. Rose Powers walked erect, with her head held high. She wore her dark-red hair in a pageboy, and it bounced as she walked. Her new spectator pumps looked good with her navy coat. She smiled as she came into the room.

"Are you ready to go home?"

"No, I'm not ready to go home."

"Is something the matter with you?"

"Didn't they tell you I had the baby?"

"No. Oh. Oh. I . . . I called the hospital this morning, and they said you had false labor."

"I didn't. I had a baby girl. She was born at 10:03 last night. She's fine. Would you like to see her?"

"Of course!"

"I'll walk down the hall with you?"

"Are you well enough?"

"Yeah. You know how soon they get women up now."

Joan's mother liked the new baby. She tried to look at her from all angles, and the only thing she saw was the top of her head and the soft flannel blanket she was swaddled in. Joan wished that Joe were here. She knew he'd be delighted with the baby.

"Does Joe know about the baby?"

"I called the tavern. They said they'd give him the message."

"Are you sure they'll give it to him?"

"They said they would."

They didn't.

At nine o'clock in the morning of the day she was to leave the hospital, Joe suddenly appeared in the doorway of her room. He had a huge bouquet of flowers. He hurried over to kiss her and finally caught his breath long enough to tell her how he had found out about the baby.

"I went in for a beer last night. While I sat at the bar, I noticed a message for me. That's how I found out about the baby . . . and I had to work last night. I thought I'd never get here."

"I thought you'd never get here either."

"Well, I'm here now. Where is the baby? I want to see her."

"I'll walk down to the nursery with you."

The wide hall was nearly deserted. From far down the span, clanking noises could be heard. The window to the nursery was covered. Joan knocked on the door. Finally, a petite dark-eyed nurse opened the door.

"Could my husband see our baby? He's been out of town and hasn't seen her yet."

"Of course. Wait by the window."

Soon, the curtains parted, and the nurse positioned the little baby so Joe could see her. He rapped on the window. "Hey, she's all right. Is she all right?"

"Joe, she's just fine."

"How come her eyes are so puffy?"

"They put something in them to keep the babies from going blind."

"What is it?"

"I don't know . . . I'll ask the nurse."

"She's really a pretty baby, isn't she?"

"Yes. Will you be able to take me home today?"

"When can you leave?"

"I have to wait until the doctor comes in. He wants to check me and the baby once more before we leave."

"Oh." Joe seemed disappointed.

"Is something the matter?"

"It's just that I have to work tonight."

"You have to drive all the way back to the coast so you can work tonight? And you haven't slept?"

"Yeah."

"Can't you miss one day of work?"

"No. I have to be there. I get paid extra tonight."

"You'll be so tired."

"Maybe I can sleep for a while before I leave for the coast . . . after we get home."

"I hope so, Joe."

The doctor was late. He didn't come in until one o'clock. Joe slept in a chair near Joan's bed. The warm room and the comfortable soft chair caused him to fall asleep soon after he sat down. He didn't stir when the woman in the bed by the window started crying. She could be heard down the hall at first. Later, her crying subsided into loud sobs. Joan wondered why she always had to be near women who cried. It was disconcerting.

When the doctor finally finished probing and prodding, he smiled. "Everything seems to be in order. I've given the nurse a prescription for the baby's skin. She seems to be allergic to something. The salve should clear it up in a hurry. I'll sign your discharge . . . and expect to see you in six weeks unless something comes up. In that case, don't hesitate to call me. I'm always on call."

"Thank you, Doctor, and thank you for taking such good care of me and the baby. We appreciate it."

"My pleasure . . . I'll be going now. Good-bye."

After he left, the nurse came in and helped Joe and Joan dress the new infant. Each person tried to harness one flailing arm or leg. The baby cried all the time. Finally, she was dressed in her own lacy pink clothes. The nurse went to the nursery to get a bottle for her. Joan sat in the big leather chair, rocking and cooing to the screaming infant. "*Sssshhhh. Ssssssshhhh.* Now, now, Sarah, don't cry." When the bottle came at last, she rooted and then sucked as if her life depended on it—and it did.

At two they left the hospital. Sarah slept soundly in Joan's arms. Joan felt hot and weak but otherwise fine, and she was *so* happy to have the ordeal over. When they drove in front of the house, Stan peeked out the window. Then he rushed for the door and ran to greet them. He glanced at the baby, said she looked funny, then hopped on his tricycle and rode off down the street.

Joan carefully laid the baby in the bassinet. "Can I fix something for you to eat before you have to leave, Joe?"

"Yes, I'm hungry."

"I'll make you a sandwich."

He didn't say anything.

"Is something the matter, Joe?"

"Uh . . . no. I was just thinking that now I'm responsible for four people. That's a lot of responsibility."

"I guess it is. I have a lot of responsibility too."

"I mean financial responsibility. I am responsible for everything we eat and wear and . . ."

"Did you just think of that?"

"I guess I did. No, I've thought of it before. It kind of hit me today . . . bringing the baby home and all."

"Joe, I know you'll do your best, and that's all anyone can do. Whatever we need, we'll find. Don't worry about things."

"How can I help worrying? We've got a family to take care of, and that's a lot of responsibility."

"Yes, it is, but you have a good job coming up soon. We have a nice place to live, and when Mother and Daddy sell the store, they'll leave, and we'll have the house to ourselves."

"Why are they having such a bad time at the store?"

"There just aren't any customers. The man who sold the store to them told them the business was very, very good. He showed them invoices to prove it. The invoices only proved what the former owner had bought, not what he had sold. The store is well stocked with new merchandise that is not selling."

"Can't they sue the real estate man?"

"There's no way to prove he misrepresented the business to them. It would just be their word against his."

Three months later they had an auction. Everything in the store was sold. It was the only way Joan's parents could get their money out of the business. The night of the auction, many strange faces appeared. The townspeople who had carefully avoided the store were now out in force, hoping to find bargains.

A carnival air filled the building as the auctioneer put item after item before the bidders. The crowd moved from aisle to aisle and grouped into close-packed quarters in the back of the store where heavy hardware lined the walls. The store and the crowd started thinning out about ten, and by midnight, almost everything had been sold. By two the last buyer had left, the money had been counted, and the items that would be picked up the next day were placed carefully against one wall.

Joe and Joan and her parents walked home through the backstreets of the sleeping town.

"Daddy, how did you come out?"

"By the time we pay the auctioneer and sell off the fixtures and the building, it shouldn't be too bad. The auction brought more than we'd hoped it would."

Joe moved toward the curb. "That's great. I was surprised by the turnout. Did you expect so many people?"

"I didn't know so many people lived in this town. They sure weren't around when we had the store open six days a week!"

\* \* \*

When her parents moved to Hillsberg early the next month, Joan and Joe moved their furniture into the big house from the storage area. They had enough furniture to fill the big rooms; although it seemed a bit roomy in the living room. They had never bought new furniture, and the combination of used pieces added up to a dismal sight. Joan decided to refinish everything she could.

Joe drove to work in Plainsville. He started work early and finished by four thirty. He was home by five, and they had dinner by five thirty. He liked the work at the lumberyard much better than the work at the mill. He thought he was lucky to have found the job.

"What don't you like about the job, Joe?"

"Joan, when I've finished my work and there is nothing to do, I have to look busy. Usually we are busy, but it is really hard to look busy when you have nothing to do. I think that's the hardest part of the job."

"Are there many times when you aren't too busy?"

"No, most of the time we have too much to do. I think the hardest work is unloading railroad cars filled with cement sacks. Boy, that is really hard work. Anytime you have to unload a railroad car . . . you know you've worked."

"Do you have to wait on customers very often?"

"No, I don't do much of that, except when Mr. Kent is too busy, then I wait on people. I don't like to do that. They always want to know things I don't know, and they are hard to satisfy. I'd rather deliver lumber and windows and other materials for new houses. When I do that, I don't have to have much to do with customers. Some of them are really nice, though. One man had a beer waiting for me the other day."

"Did you drink it?"

"Yeah. It was hot, and I was thirsty."

"Daddy would never drink on the job."

"One beer is hardly *drinking on the job*. It couldn't hurt anything. Besides, the man would have had his feelings hurt if I hadn't . . . It was open when I got there."

"I guess it was OK then."

"Grrrrr. I don't want to hear another word about it."

Months passed. Joan and Joe settled into a routine. The children stayed healthy and grew from one size to the next with surprising swiftness. Joan's parents wrote that they were doing well. They lived on a small acreage near Hillsberg, and her father was once again involved in logging.

It was a lovely day in late summer. Nothing distinguished the day from any other in the season. Joan stifled a yawn then looked out the window and saw her cousin Greg getting out of his car. She thought, *He probably wants to arrange a fishing trip with Joe, or maybe he's just passing by*. He looked sharp. His well-creased tan wool slacks blended with his light-brown silk shirt. When he came closer, she noticed with surprise that he seemed upset. He was still cocky and strong, but he seemed to sag as he sat in the big chair in the bright yellow kitchen.

"Did you want to see Joe?"

"Not especially. I just came from my doctor in Plainsville. I thought I'd drop in and see you on the way home."

"Good. What did the doctor have to say?"

"He said I had to quit working on my garbage route."

"Oh my. Can you get someone to work for you?"

"I could, but there is no sense to that. The route doesn't take in enough for me to hire another man."

"What will you do with it then?"

"I'll have to sell it and find something else to do."

"How much do you want for the route?"

"I'm going to sell it for seven thousand . . . that includes the truck. It's not in perfect condition, but it still runs. Why do you ask?"

"We'll buy the route from you, Greg. I know how well you've done—we'll buy it."

"No, you can't. The fellow who lives near the dump has first chance. He really wants it bad."

"Damn."

"Where would you get seven thousand dollars?"

"I don't know. If something happens and the route isn't sold, let us know. We can work out something."

"Did it ever occur to you that Joe might not want to be a garbageman?"

"Joe wants to be a millionaire. You have to start somewhere."

"Do you think he would do that kind of work?"

"He'd do any kind of work that paid more than he's making. He brings home three hundred and five dollars a month. How much does the route bring in?"

"I make about four hundred on the route, and then three days a week I collect scrap iron, tin, and other metals. I make several hundred dollars a month doing that."

"That sounds wonderful . . ."

"Yes. Yes. *If* the other fellow can't raise the money, there is a chance you and Joe can buy the route . . . *if you* can raise the money."

"Don't worry about that. Can you stay and have dinner with us?"

"Yeah, I'd like that, and I don't have to be home for a while."

"Does your back hurt bad?"

"It aches most of the time. Sometimes not as bad as others, but I always know it is there."

"Did you hurt it on the route?"

"Originally I hurt it in the woods. Working on the garbage route just aggravates the injury. Now it's gotten so bad, any pressure hurts. I don't know who's going to buy the route, but I know I have to get off it. Until I sell, I'm going to have someone help me with the pickups."

Joan stood up and motioned to Greg to move his chair closer to the kitchen table so he could visit with her while she fixed dinner. She often became so engrossed in conversation, she forgot what she was doing when she had company. She found it difficult to cook and visit at the same time.

Dinner magically turned out well. Usually when she had guests, something or other was icky, but this time everything was delicious. The children ate with a minimum of fuss and then soaked in the tub while she did dishes. She could hear them giggling and splashing. She checked on them often, and every time she went into the bathroom, they had dumped more water and bubbles on the floor. Joe and Greg visited in the living room.

Later, when they went upstairs to bed, Joan was so excited about maybe buying the garbage route that she didn't think she'd be able to sleep.

"Maybe you're getting too excited." Joe rolled over on his back and looked at her. A T-shirt covered his chest and upper arms. The light from the bedside lamp caught the fine light-red hair on his arms and turned it into a golden shimmer.

"Why do you say that?"

"Greg isn't sure he can sell the route to us . . . and, frankly, Joan, I'm not sure I want to buy it if he wants to sell."

Joan couldn't believe her ears. "What do you mean?"

"I mean I'm not sure I want to buy a garbage route. You know I want to farm . . . I've wanted to all my life."

"I know. We've talked about it night after night. I want you to farm too. But there is no way you can now. We don't have any money, and your uncle isn't ready to retire."

"I'm not sure I would like the work."

"You aren't crazy about working at the lumberyard."

"No, but it's better than being a garbageman."

"Anything is better than being a garbageman, but Greg is making a lot of money."

"I don't know."

"You're the one who wants to be a millionaire. If you're going to work, you might as well earn as much as you can. Joe, any work, no matter how disagreeable, has a certain dignity."

"I want to be a farmer."

"There is no way you can be one now."

"But that's what I want."

"Can't you understand—it doesn't matter what you want? We may have an opportunity to buy a business that is doing very well. I say we don't have any choice."

"I've *wanted* to farm since I was a little boy."

"I know that, but maybe someday you can sell the route and buy a farm."

They talked on into the night. They couldn't sleep. They heard the horses in the barn across the street and the dogs barking three houses down. Light poured into the room from a streetlight. The bed was soft and comfortable, freshly made with sheets, sweet smelling from having been hung outdoors. Still they couldn't sleep.

The next morning, when the alarm rang, neither of them reached to shut it off. Finally, Joan couldn't stand it any longer. Sleepily she pushed in the button and lay back on the bed.

"God, I could sleep forever. I'm so tired."

Joe rummaged in his drawer for underclothes. Delighted, he found his favorite T-shirt. His drawers always looked as though a Mixmaster had been turned loose. He was not neat. No. He was not neat.

"Get up. I don't want to be late."

"Yes, sir. Yes, sir."

She moaned as she put her feet on the floor. Slowly she began her descent to the kitchen. Tying her robe around her, she hurried to fix Joe's breakfast and pack his lunch. She hoped the children would sleep long enough for her to read the morning paper after Joe left. Her luck held. She heard no sounds from their room, as she, more fully awake now, set to work.

She heard Joe's electric razor purring. As she cooked breakfast, she thought of new ideas to discuss with him. He came into the bright kitchen and squinted.

"What's for breakfast?" he asked.

"Pancakes, eggs, and bacon."

"Good. Where's the paper?"

"Don't read the paper this morning."

"Why not?"

"I want to talk to you."

He folded his arms. "You always want to talk *to* me."

"Yes, but not in the morning. You know I can't bear to talk to anyone in the morning. I never do. You know I don't."

"OK. OK. So you don't. What do you not want to talk about? We talked last night all night, and I don't think we reached any conclusions. I'm tired of talking."

"Well, let's just say that things worked out so we had an opportunity to buy the route..."

"Look, even if we had the opportunity, we could *never* raise the money."

"Don't say that."

"It's true. Where would we raise the money?"

"We could borrow it."

"Ha. Who's going to lend us money?"

"Somebody will... you'll see."

He made some funny, strangle-type noises as he went to get the paper. From the look on his face when he returned, she knew she'd better not talk about the route.

When he'd gone to work, the house seemed very quiet. She read her newspaper in the big comfortable chair in the living room. When she finished the last page, she heard a small sound from Stan's room. She hummed as she opened his door.

# Chapter 8

If it hadn't been for the Bible, they would not have had any savings. One day when Joe was at work, a salesman knocked on the door. He was selling the nicest Bible Joan had seen. It was red leather with gold trim, about eleven by fourteen inches in size and bore the imprimatur of an ecclesiastical office. Joan didn't have the twenty-eight dollars to pay for it, so the salesman wrote it up on a short-term contract.

Joan waited until after dinner to tell Joe about the Bible. She wasn't sure exactly how he would receive the news. Not exactly.

"How could you spend twenty-eight dollars for a Bible?"

"We can pay for it three dollars a month."

"Joan, I hate time payments."

"I don't like them either, but how else can you get the things you need if you don't pay for them a little at a time?"

"You don't *buy*, that's how."

"Don't you think we need a Bible?"

"We don't need a *twenty-eight-dollar* Bible."

"It's really nice. It's made of red leather with gold letters, and they're delivering it next week . . . and I wanted it."

"You want everything."

"I don't like your attitude."

"I don't like your wasting money on a Bible."

"*You're* supposed to be so religious."

"That's not the point, and you know it. We can't afford it."

"How would you know? I take care of the checkbook. As far as you're concerned, we can't afford *anything*. We haven't been to a movie in years or eaten in a restaurant or done anything that is the least bit fun since I can remember."

"You can tell the salesman you are *not* taking the Bible."

"I'll pay for it myself."

"Yeah. Yeah. How are you going to pay for anything? All you do is waste money."

"I'll get a job."

"Ha. That's a joke."

"I'll do it, you son of a bitch. I'll do it!"

\* \* \*

Finding a job was more difficult than she anticipated. She had no skills, and, except for berry picking and similar tasks, she had never held a job. Also, her educational background, or lack of it, limited her choices. She vowed she would never give up, but as she searched and searched and followed every lead, no matter how insignificant, she became increasingly depressed. Then when she least expected it, a sign magically appeared in the window of the local turkey processing plant.

She got the job. The fall season was about to start. They worked for a few weeks and paid more than the local cannery. Joan was delighted to have the work. The foreman, Harry, told her what to wear and to report for work the following Monday.

Joan arrived early Monday morning to find fifteen other women dressed like she was dressed, in white nylon dresses, long clear plastic aprons, hairnets with visors, rubber gloves, and rubber boots. The few men were dressed in similar fashion.

Harry ushered them into a large room that reminded Joan of the inside of a galvanized tub—white, windowless, concrete floor, and a metal line with hooks dropped from the ceiling. It carried featherless turkeys around the large room. As turkeys moved in front of them, each person performed his or her task. Few of the people were familiar with the operation, so Harry patiently explained the procedure to each individual.

Joan wanted the reamer's job. She didn't know what it was, but she heard someone say it paid ten cents an hour more than the other jobs, and she believed if you were going to work, you might as well make as much money as possible.

When Harry asked, "Who wants to ream?" Joan's hand shot up.

"Have you ever done this before?"

"No. But I can learn."

"Well, all right, I'll try you here."

Then he showed her what to do. Taking a very sharp knife in the right hand and holding the turkey's anus with the left, he cut, making a half circle in a clockwise direction. Then he inserted the knife directly under his left thumb and made another cut counterclockwise. This resulted in a perfect circle slightly larger than the turkey's anus. Then Harry pulled the large intestine free. Fecal matter ran out and plopped on the floor.

Joan gulped. Her nose vibrated. Her eyes widened. She felt nauseous. She had a very weak stomach. Whenever one of the children was sick, Joe had to clean up after them—if he was at home. When she had to clean up after them, she got sick herself—wretchedly so.

"Think you can handle it?" Harry asked.

The sight and smell of fecal matter mingled with the image of Joe's mocking face. "Of course," she answered.

Like an expert, she learned to make the necessary cuts. The line fairly flew at times. It hardly gave the women a chance to keep their knives razor sharp. They stood in water, fecal matter, and blood. After the first day, no one seemed to mind.

Thousands of turkeys passed in front of Joan during the day. At night she dreamed of them. When Thanksgiving was near and every turkey the plant processed had been killed, plucked, cleaned, reamed, washed, graded, cooled, placed in a plastic bag, and quick frozen, the season was over.

The second day she was home, one of the nut-packing houses called her. She had forgotten that she had even put in an application. The woman asked if she could report for work the following evening. Joan mentally counted the money she would earn and add to their savings account.

"OK, I'll be there. Thank you."

She arrived at the plant a half hour before the shift began. Lights above the loading ramps shone down on men unloading boxes filled to the brim with walnuts and filberts. Tires bit into the dust of the roadway, and the air filled with clouds every time another young truck driver hotdogged in.

Joan walked inside. She had no idea what she was to do or where she would be working. On her left she saw the lunchroom. Inside were several women. All of them looked older than she—and heavy. She could see by the way they looked at her that they didn't like her. And she could tell at a glance that she wouldn't like them. Suspicious old bitches.

At five minutes to seven, the women got up from the tables and headed down a long hall to the work area. Joan saw the foreman and went over to him and introduced herself. He hardly listened. He led her over to the belt and indicated a place for her to stand. Then he walked away.

"Will you tell me what we are supposed to do?" Joan asked the woman nearest her on the belt. The woman didn't look at her.

"You'll see," she said and stared straight ahead.

The warehouse was unheated with lofts for the belts. An odor of chlorine bleach hung in the air. Suddenly the belt started. A loud rumbling sounded behind the partition at the end of the belt. Soon, freshly bleached wet walnuts came onto the belt. It moved at a moderate speed. The women began picking out dirt, leaves, and other foreign material.

Joan shivered as she worked. Her feet began to feel numb. She hated to be cold. It was hell.

"Use both hands!"

Joan turned to find the crabby foreman glaring at her.

"What?"

"Use both hands." He indicated the woman by her side. She stood like the other women with both hands moving constantly, sorting, rolling, turning, and simultaneously removing culls and other material. Joan, slow and unsure at first, watched her left hand and surprised herself that it moved easily in a short time. She was able to keep up with the older experienced ladies.

She spent three cold months there. Finally, all the walnuts, filberts, and special mixed nuts were sent to the dryer. Joan was delighted. She thought she'd have time to clean the house and to rest.

Financially, things were worse than they'd been before. Instead of having more money because she was working, they now had less. All that she earned was put into a savings account. Her working expenses, clothes, babysitter, gas, and other costs were paid out of Joe's already inadequate wage.

Joan enjoyed working, until she got home and had to do the washing, ironing, cleaning, and cooking. It was enough to make her twenty-two-year-old heart cry.

She had only been home two days when they called from the cookie factory.

"Your job is to remove the cookies with this long spatula like this . . ." Mrs. Jones deftly removed several cookies from the cookie sheet with one twist of her wrist. She carefully piled the cookies together. "Then scrape the pans, being careful to remove all the crumbs, then stack the trays over here." She pointed to a large pile of trays behind the table.

It smelled good inside the factory—vanilla, chocolate, walnuts. There were other scents Joan couldn't identify. She'd been like Ferdinand the Bull, smelling cookies. The building was new and huge. It was a warehouse filled with ovens, tables, trays, machines to package, boxes, and other necessary items. Everything was immaculately clean.

"Hi, kid. What's your name?" The woman next to her on the platform leaned forward.

"Joan Schultz... What's yours?"

"Jenny Cummings. I'm pleased to know you. I been working here for the last three years. I'll show you what you need to know."

Mrs. Jones nodded at the two women, then walked away.

"Look at that old bag. She's so fat, she can hardly waddle." Jenny made a face.

"Why do you call her an old bag? She seems nice enough to me."

"Wait until you've worked for her awhile—you'll call her an old bag too."

They worked in silence for a while. Jenny was quick and sure in her working habits. Joan watched her, trying to get the hang of taking hot cookies off hot sheets and not breaking any. If they weren't handled in a certain way, they would break or pleat. Mrs. Jones hovered. Whenever Joan made a mistake, she was right there to watch, comment, or simply look disapproving. After a few hours, Joan thought, *I'd never call Mrs. Jones an old bag. She is a first-class bitch.* Joan had a certain respect for first-class bitches. Somehow they were able to infringe their behavior on others and still maintain their position in society. She knew she'd never be able to be one. No one would put up with such behavior from her. Not Joe. Not anyone. She wondered how the first-class bitches got away with being first-class bitches.

When the day was nearly over, the sights and sounds and smells of the cookie factory were not nearly as appealing as they had been that morning. Joan felt a little nauseous.

Jenny leaned toward her. "Joan, the best part of this job is you get to eat all the cookies you want."

## Chapter 9

Joe's uncle Lester called that weekend. He had found a small acreage near St. Eames that sounded wonderful to Joe and Joan. When they saw the property the next weekend, they had certain misgivings. The house looked like a giant jack-o'-lantern. Two windows on the second floor were the eyes. The mouth slit was a narrow window on the first floor. The house looked woeful and neglected up close. From the road, the house, barn, and outbuildings on the twenty-acre farm looked very good. The buildings were about a quarter of a mile from the blacktopped county road. A charming lane led into the house. The garden spot was in the center of a large loop that served as a turnaround.

Eagerly they inspected the grounds. The earth sank beneath their feet. The grass, still wet from an early morning frost that had melted, lay flat wherever they stepped. The garage, thirty feet from the house, tilted to one side. Except for a concrete floor, it was worthless. There were no doors on it, and Joan noticed old tools and license plates hanging on the walls.

The barn seemed huge. They couldn't understand how the floor could be dry (which it was) when big patches of daylight showed through the high-pitched roof of the building. Outside, and in, aged wood had turned to silver. A few stanchions still stood, mute testimony to the industrious efforts of a now-forgotten man. A field of strawberries lay dormant near the barn and near a small creek that ran through the draw.

Behind that, five acres of winter wheat had been planted. An old moss-covered fence sagged around an orchard of worn-out fruit trees.

"Near the south side of the orchard would be a perfect place for pigs."

"Joe, who wants pigs?"

"I do."

"Oh . . . let's go see the house."

The old house, vacant for years, smelled musty on that cold February afternoon. Old wallpaper hung from the walls along with gossamer spiderwebs that fluttered in the drafty rooms. The main house consisted of a kitchen and dining room on the first floor with two bedrooms directly above. In later years, the long living room had been added on the north. Above were two smaller bedrooms. The back porch, directly off the kitchen, served as a hallway to the bathroom and as a laundry room.

"How much did you say this place was?"

Lester Schultz's face turned red. He half turned away from Joan as he mumbled, "Seventy-five hundred."

"How much down?"

His face got redder. "He wants twelve hundred down and fifty dollars a month," he said evenly.

"Joe, we could handle that. We can use our savings for the down payment. The monthly payment would be just like paying rent."

Joe looked uncomfortable. "Let's talk about it later, Joan."

"All right, if that's what you want." She went to inspect the bedrooms. Mentally she made notes. This bedroom would be blue, that one beige. The living room would be papered; the dining room painted to coordinate with it. The first thing that would have to be done would be the floors. They had several layers of paint, and Joan felt sure the wood was good underneath.

Later, when they were taking the back roads home, Joan's excitement was evident. "You know, Joe, that house could be fixed up to look pretty good. It needs to be painted and papered, and the floors need refinishing . . . Then in the summer we could paint the outside."

"Hey, you've already got us moved in."

"Well?"

"Well, just take it easy. We have to think about it."

"Why?"

"You just don't buy a farm without thinking about it."

"If it's what you want, you do. We could make a lot of money from the strawberries, and the wheat looked good."

"And I'd have to commute to work every morning."

"How far is it?"

"About sixty miles, round trip."

"That's not so far . . . By the way . . . what made your uncle act like that when we were talking about buying the farm? I thought he wanted you to buy it so we could live in St. Eames. He sure acted strange."

"You know how he is. He doesn't think women should know anything about business."

"Even about their own houses and things like that?"

"Even about their own houses and things like that."

"I can hardly believe it. Do you mean to tell me that your aunt doesn't know anything about the family business?"

"That's right. She's given money for groceries and the things she needs to buy. Uncle pays the other bills."

"I don't mean the monthly things. I mean the important things, like how much did the farm cost? What percent interest is charged? How long is the contract? Does your aunt know anything about all that?"

"No."

"Joe, do you know that *I* have to know. *I* couldn't not know. It is important that *I* know."

"I know. I know."

"So?"

"So keep quiet around Uncle Lester. He doesn't need to know you know."

"OK. Keep quiet around your uncle and don't smoke in front of him or your aunt."

"That's right."

"Is there anything else, sir!"

He gave her a dirty look, sat up straighter, squared his shoulders, became intent upon his driving, and shut her out completely. They rode for miles in silence. Then when they were nearly home, he suddenly reached for her hand. "Do you think you could be happy in that house?"

She had already moved in, arranged the furniture, visualized the curtains, and wondered about the size of the upstairs closet, and was trying to figure out how to make the bathroom larger.

Joan sighed. "I think with a lot of hard work, the house could be quite comfortable. It really isn't a very good house, but then again, it won't cost much. We might make quite a bit of money from the strawberries and the wheat. We have enough in our savings account to pay the down payment."

"I was kind of thinking that if the garbage route is available, we could use that money for a down payment," Joe answered.

"We haven't heard from Greg for weeks. That means the other fellow will probably buy the route. And if it was for sale to us, we'd need more money than twelve hundred. I imagine Greg would want cash."

"Where would we get cash?"

"We could get it."

They drove on in silence. Joe seethed angrily. Joan was always so positive. So right. So irritating.

"Joe, aren't you glad *I* worked and earned all that money? We wouldn't have any money in savings if *I* hadn't worked."

"That money belongs to both of us. We spent the money I earned."

"I didn't mean that the money was mine. I only meant that if I hadn't worked, we wouldn't have anything in savings."

"And if I hadn't worked, we wouldn't have had any food in our stomachs."

"Oh, Joe!"

They decided to buy the farm. All the papers were ready within a few days. Since there was no one living in the house, they could move right in.

"I don't think we should move in until the floors have been sanded. We can paint and paper after we're in, but we can't finish the floors with furniture all over the place."

"All right, Joan, we'll sand the floors."

As soon as the floors were thoroughly dry, they moved in. They rounded up boxes from stores, several willing helpers (mostly male and mostly related), and a rented truck. It rained the day they moved.

It didn't take long for all their belongings to be loaded in the truck. They'd acquired a curious mixture of things from various sources. They had everything they needed, though they'd still purchased nothing new. All their furniture was used and collected piece by piece. It had been nailed, stripped, painted, varnished, and prayed over. It looked pretty good.

The men laughed, slipped, cussed, strained, and pushed as they loaded the last heavy things into the truck. It was late afternoon when it pulled away from the curb. Joan hurried to finish washing the mud from the floor. She'd been cleaning the house as she packed, so there really wasn't much to do. Her car waited filled with their clothes, some breakable things, and Sarah. Joan looked out the window just as the truck pulled out. Stan waved to her. He was overjoyed to be riding in the big truck next to Joe.

The rain moved with the entourage to St. Eames. Everyone got soaked. It didn't take long for the truck to be unloaded, the furniture arranged, the refrigerator and stove plugged in, and a fire started in the living room. The house had been open most of the day as the men carried boxes, furniture, appliances, and clothing through the kitchen door. Now the warmth of the fire chased the chill from the room.

Joan finished making beds then joined the men and the children near the fire. "Brrrrr."

"Are you cold, Joan?"

"Yes, Daddy. I wasn't while I was working, but now I feel chilled."

Paul Powers moved over to make room for his daughter beside him. "Do you think you're going to like living here?"

"Oh, yes, Daddy. I'm going to love it. As soon as the house is papered and painted and fixed up, and we get curtains and things, I'm going to love it. I always wanted a place just like this . . . down a lane, with a big garden and animals. I've always wanted to be able to raise our food—to be self-sufficient. Actually, Joe is the gardener. I wish the house were nicer, but we're really lucky we were able to buy it."

"If you say so."

"Don't you like it, Daddy?"

"I never was one to visualize anything. Some people look at something and see what might be. I look at things, and all I see is what is." He glanced at Joan and Joe. Their faces reflected their disappointment that he didn't share their enthusiasm. "Now don't get me wrong," he said. "I think you kids have gotten a *really good buy* . . . and I know that you'll have this place looking homey and comfortable in no time. I'll like it when you've done what you're going to do . . . I just can't visualize what it will be."

"Oh, Daddy."

"One thing you're going to need is a woodshed, Joe. I'll help you build it as soon as the weather changes. I can't imagine why you didn't get an oilstove."

"Paul, we didn't get an oilstove because we couldn't afford to burn oil. There's lots of wood around here. I'll either borrow one of your saws and cut some, or we can get Mr. Clark to bring some for us. Either way, it's a lot cheaper than oil."

Joan saw her father stiffen, so she cut in quickly. "Joe, I think we should get some plastic to cover the outside of the windows. It would cut a lot of the heat loss."

"I'll pick some up at the lumberyard."

"Daddy, do you think Mother would keep Stan and Sarah for a couple of days?"

"I don't know, Joan. You know how she hates to babysit."

"I know. I also know how Joe's aunt hates it. I thought grandmothers were supposed to dote on their grandchildren."

The last thing she promised herself before she went to sleep in their cold bed was that she would call her mother the first thing in the morning and try to get two days. She would need that much time to find all her pans and linens and to put everything away and clean the mud . . . and . . . God, she was tired.

"Good night, Joe."

"Good night, Joan."

"Are you happy?"

He didn't answer. He was asleep.

Joe's dream had come true. He had a farm of his own, even though it wasn't quite what he'd hoped. He would commute (the farm wasn't able to support the family—yet, but they could have a cow). The eight acres of strawberries might bring in several *thousand* dollars.

Spring came and brought with it blossoms. The cherry tree, the apple trees, the snowball bush, the flowers in the yard, and the strawberry plants blossomed. The air smelled good and fresh and old-fashioned. The garden gave off the peculiar scent of freshly turned earth. This year they'd have an even larger garden. Joe wanted to plant several miniature apple trees. The old apple trees would die soon.

It was a busy time for them. Joan worked at redecorating the house, while Joe commuted six days a week.

Their finances were strained. Joan was unable to work and the three hundred and five dollars that had seemed so meager in the old house now stretched to cover the expense of commuting sixty miles a day. More and more they pinned their hopes on the strawberry crop, which they faithfully hoed, irrigated, fertilized, and sprayed.

As spring turned to summer, the bumper crop started to ripen. By the fifth of June, big, red, juicy, luscious-tasting berries hung on deep-green vines. Joe had contacted Big George, the migrant labor boss in the area. Big George had promised to have a crew at the farm on the seventh of June.

Joe watered the berries for the last time the evening of the sixth. Warm weather would dry the cultivated ground by the time the pickers arrived.

On the morning of the seventh, Joe and Joan anxiously waited for Big George and his crew. At seven, Joe had to leave for work. He watched the clock.

"You'd better go, Joe." Joan fussed.

"I kind of wanted to wait until they came."

"I know, but you'd better go. I wonder what's keeping them."

"I don't know."

Joe left. Joan waited. And waited. And waited. They didn't come. All day. The hot sun beat down on the ripe berries. Finally, Joe drove in from work.

"Joan, what happened to Big George?"

"He didn't come. Are you sure he said today?"

"Positive."

"We'd better go see him . . . after dinner."

Brown eyes stared at the intruders as they made their way to Big George's. Joan waited in the car with the children, while Joe talked to the fat unkempt man. Big George lounged indolently against the door frame; his shirt was unbuttoned, and his half-tucked-in pants precariously clung to his mountainous belly. They looked tentative, like they might fall with every next breath. He wore no socks, and his shoes were untied.

Joan couldn't hear the conversation, though she strained to catch a word now and then. She idly watched the children playing in the dusty roadway. They seemed happy. Honeysuckle climbed the wall of the cabin nearest the car, sending a heavy pungent scent into the air. The sun shone through the dust in the dark-orange twilight. Insects hummed and buzzed. Joe didn't return. *Strange,* she thought. She shifted her back to get a better view of the two men.

Joe's wonderfully long legs stood rigidly flexed; his jaw seemed made of iron. *Trouble,* she thought. She wondered what was wrong. She wasn't worried. She never worried. Everything would work out *fine.* Abruptly,

Joe finished talking. He spun on his heels and marched to the car. He slammed the door.

"What did he say?"

"He said he can't come tomorrow."

"*Why not?*"

"He's got to pick Hal Jones's berries. Hal has over a hundred acres. Big George planned on having another crew for ours. They didn't show up for work this morning and probably won't tomorrow. He said he was sorry . . . He'll be there Wednesday for sure."

"We'd better hope it stays cool." Joan looked helpless.

"I can't see where two days will hurt that much . . . unless it does get hot."

"Couldn't we get some of the kids in town to pick for us?"

"Every kid in the county is signed up with a platoon before school is out. They go to the same farms year after year."

Joan shuddered. She remembered how it had been. He was right. "Well then, what are we going to do?"

"We'll have to hope the weather cools and that Big George keeps his word."

He didn't. They repeated the trip to the camp—several times. Big George promised. Each day the berries rotted a little more. Each day he promised to come the next day. The first picking didn't get picked, and by the time the second picking ripened, the first was completely rotten.

With the loss of the berries, Joe's and Joan's spirits sank. They'd counted on the crop with anxious anticipation. They had made grand plans. They would roof the barn and buy a cow—and some *new* furniture and maybe a dress for Joan and a new suit for Joe. Most importantly, they'd pay their bill at the feed mill.

The rotten berries dried in the warm summer sun. A moldy odor pervaded the farm as they sat under the light high in the black walnut tree. Lacy leaves were beautifully illuminated by the light cast, moving shadows on the sidewalk near where Joan and Joe sat.

"Who's coming down the lane, Joan?"

"I can't tell."

Greg pulled into the drive. He got out of the car and came toward them. "Golly . . . what is that smell?"

Joe shrugged his shoulders. "It's our entire strawberry crop rotting."

"Owee . . . it smells like horseshit."

Joe leaned back in his chair, smiling slightly. "Horseshit is just another name for *garbage*."

"Touché. Touché. Hey, come and look at my new *used* car."

They went over to look at the car.

"When did you get it?"

"Last Tuesday. How do you like it?"

"It's great!"

They sat under the tree visiting for over an hour before Greg cleared his throat and told them what had happened. The buyer of his route couldn't raise the money to buy it. Greg had thought everything was in order. He had to sell because his back was giving him such agony. Otherwise, he wouldn't. He just wouldn't. Who would give up such a deal? He had most of the small towns around the area. Of course, his route wasn't big, but Wayne Sharp (his wife's cousin) had told him he'd sell him his route when he retired. There was even a remote possibility Wayne's brother, Edgar, who had the largest route in the state, would sell him his. Then he'd really have something! If it wasn't for his back, Greg would never think of selling.

As soon as he made the deal to sell, he'd gone out and bought the Buick, shiny and blue with leather seats—used. But what a buy! Then the buyer of his route backed out, and Greg was stuck.

"So if you are still interested, you can have it—$7,000, cash."

"We want it."

"Not so fast, Joan."

"Why not?"

"I don't know if I want to be a garbageman."

"Why not? When we talked about it, you seemed very interested."

"I still have hopes of being a farmer." The conversation was taking a personal turn. Joe became uncomfortable and shifted his weight from one side to the other. He hated discussing personal or business matters in front of others. He vaguely wished Greg weren't there, then thought, *Maybe he should hear what I have to say. He may understand how I feel and why.*

Joan's hand caught his sleeve.

"I think this is a fantastic opportunity. Say, yes, Joe. After we pay back the money, you'll be able to hire someone to run the route. Then you can think about farming. Who knows, you might even like the garbage business."

"Who could like being a garbageman?"

"Joe, someone has to do it. If a man does an honest day's work, it shouldn't matter how he earns his living. Is it really so bad, Greg?"

"It's just like any other job. If you don't do it, you don't know what it is like. Frankly, the work is terribly hard at times. There are state laws concerning the weight of the can, but a lot of people don't know what it is. They fill their cans with concrete or dirt or bricks. In the winter, when the rain runs down your neck and rats jump down your shirt and maggots line the bottoms of some cans, it's not pleasant at all. Someone told me garbagemen were the real heroes in our society. Maybe we are. It's a dirty job. It has to be done. Somebody has to do it. It pays good. That's all I have to say."

"I never minded being a garbageman—it's an honest living. Some of Marlys's friends make remarks once in a while, and they tease Tess at school . . . no real problems."

"Who cares what people say?"

Joe glanced at her. "I do, Joan."

She looked at him and gave a weary sigh. "Let's talk more about this and let Greg know for sure in two days. That will give us time to explore the matter thoroughly. I don't want you to do anything you don't want to do, but we do have a lot of bills we can't pay from the strawberry crop. I think we should think it over. Is that all right with you, Greg?"

"Sure, that will be fine. You can let me know in two days."

They thought it over. Night and day. They talked and argued and plotted and planned and schemed. Joan's enthusiasm began to affect Joe.

"Let's call your uncle."

Mr. Schultz said he'd lend them four thousand dollars, interest-free. He was very nice about it. Joan wondered how she felt about the rather attractive uncle of her husband. She wondered why she didn't like him. He'd been good to them in so many ways. Then she realized what it was. Something was missing. A part of the man never existed. He lacked the capacity to love. Everything in life is muted without it. Everything is diminished. The joy of living never known. So who could blame the man for his smallness? Existing without the capacity to love would make anyone small.

"It would be nice if he could have lent us the whole amount. Then we would only have to make one payment."

"Joan, we're lucky he lent us anything."

"You're right. I wish you could go with me to borrow the money from Uncle Joseph and Grandpa."

"I have to work. Do you really think they will loan us the money?"

"They love me—how can they refuse?"

"Unless they don't have that much money to lend?"

"Then I'll have to think of something else." She wasn't as confident as she sounded. They'd never borrowed that much money before. What if those who *loved her so much* said *no?*

"How much interest does the bank pay, Grandpa?"

"Four percent."

"We'll give you five."

"Sounds like a fair deal."

"It is. We'll pay you back seventy-five dollars a month, plus interest..."

"You say you unclea gonna get you some money?"

"Yes, Grandpa, but he only has a thousand that he can lend, so we still need two thousand from you."

"You takea me to the bank. I get it for you."

"Oh, thank you, Grandpa."

Joan decided to stop in at Hillsberg and visit her parents on her way home. When she told her mother about the loans, her mother's anger flared.

"But, Mother, what is wrong with borrowing money from Grandpa? We certainly intend to pay it back, and we'll be paying him bank interest plus 1 percent. Besides, he seemed happy to loan it to us."

"He's an old man."

"Do you think I took advantage of him?"

She didn't answer. Her back was to Joan, who was sitting on the chair near the table in the clean all-white kitchen. Her mother's shoulders, rigid under her starched apron, fell. She turned quickly and shook her paring knife at Joan.

"Yes, I do. I think that anyone who takes money from an old man is taking advantage of him. Your grandfather has been saving his money all his life, and now he'll just worry and worry until it is paid back."

"You're a lot more upset about it than he was, believe me."

"Mark my words . . . you'll be sorry you did this."

"Yes, Mother. See you, Mother." *God, I'm sorry already.*

## Chapter 10

Greg applied in each community for a transfer of the franchises he held. They were granted without any delay. On July 1, 1957, the garbage business legally belonged to Joan and Joe. Marlys explained the details of bookkeeping to Joan. It was simple. Joan was sure she could do it easily. There were reports to file with the state, which looked complicated, but Marlys assured her they were simply routine.

Joe left early the first day on the route. He had to meet Greg at the service station where the truck was parked. It had been there ever since Greg's neighbors complained about the smell and the flies that buzzed around the truck.

Greg waited for him. He looked fresh and happy. "Morning, Joe. You ready to learn the route?"

"I guess."

"You should know it in two weeks. You can draw a map this week, and then after you've gone over it once more, it should be easy for you to follow the third time."

The day passed with surprising speed. Joe, completely lost after the first three turns of the truck, couldn't believe he would ever learn the route. Besides making the map, he picked up all the cans on his side of the truck.

By the time they stopped for lunch, Joe's map had become a labyrinth of main roads, side streets, alleys, private lanes, and some unintelligible scribblings. He wondered if he would ever be able to read it.

Greg kept up a running monologue about each customer, their habits, and their personal life. He seemed to know everything about the people on his route. He knew which ones were divorcing, marrying, and dying; how many children they had; where they were; and who they were. He named names. *What a memory*, thought Joe. He was amazed at his knowledge. Greg also knew who drank, who didn't, and why. He knew about how much money each family earned and how they spent it.

"You'll get to know all about these people same as I do. You can't help it when you see them every week—or at least what they throw away. I usually enjoy visiting with them, but when I'm in a hurry, it is harder than hell to break away—especially when they wait for me."

"They wait for you?"

"Yeah, and they'll be waiting for you the same way. A couple of old ladies on the Thursday route always have cookies for me when I come around. No matter what happens or what kind of weather . . . I get my cookies. The other things you've got to watch out for are the honeys."

"What's a honey?"

"That's what the men call them. They're frustrated housewives. Probably unhappy too. Anyway, there are a couple of them in the new subdivision that are especially dangerous."

"How are they dangerous?"

"They're good looking, and they parade around half dressed or completely undressed. They stand in front of windows where they can be seen only by the garbageman."

With each passing customer, Joe grew more and more silent. His muscles began to ache. His left shoulder developed red marks where the bottom of the carrying can scraped it. His legs hurt. It was only two thirty. Greg said they should be done by five. Joe hoped that were true. He hoped he'd make it until then. The sun came out about three. It was warmer than he remembered July should be. Sweat dripped into his eyes. He wiped it away with his shirtsleeve.

They stopped for a cold drink soon after they picked up the big restaurant on the edge of town. The cold lemonade felt good on Joe's parched throat. He hadn't worked so hard since he was in high school and had to hoe fifty acres of corn—by himself.

He remembered the day his uncle told him he was the only one to do it. After the first few hours, the sunbaked earth emanated heat. The cool mist of morning was replaced by the sun burning through his light shirt, and the six-inch corn gave no shade. He thought a lot while he worked. He thought he'd never finish. By the time the corn was all hoed, he vowed that someday he'd be rich—rich enough to hire someone to hoe *his* corn.

Joe had trouble in school. The other kids teased him. They thought his uncle was rich and that he was given money. (No one gave him a cent.) The truth was that he was forced to work on the family farm (with no pay) until all the crops were in and the season was over. Then he had to find ways to earn enough money for his school clothes and for spending the entire year. Everyone in the community knew how tight his relatives were (especially his uncle). Still his classmates teased him.

The sound of the truck's gears meshing brought him back to the present. The truck was a fourteen-foot garbage truck bed with sideboards. As the truck filled, another board was placed in a slot to close off more of the box and to gain greater capacity. The steel bed was mounted on a hoist, and there were two large doors that swung open at the back. When Greg didn't use it for hauling garbage, it was loaded with scrap iron or tin. It was old and worn but, except for minor imperfections, in very good condition.

Joan watched the main road for a sign of Joe's car. He should have been home two hours ago. Dinner dried in the oven while she stood near the front windows, searching the darkness for a sign of his headlights. At last, she saw lights cutting through the night. The children called to each other from upstairs. They hated to go to bed early—or at all. Their day started so early that Joan felt, for their sakes (and for hers), an early bedtime was necessary.

"God, you look awful!"

"I'm OK."

"Are you sure? You're pale and you look sick."

"I think I drank too much water. I couldn't stop drinking," he moaned.

"Tsk. Tsk. You know how that makes you sick."

"Yes, I know."

"And it was so *hot*. Did you have an awful day?"

"No, I guess not. It was kind of interesting, but the work is really hard. I'll get used to it in a day or two." *I hope.*

"Oh, Joe, I hope you do. You look awful."

"I'm just going to take my bath and then go right to bed."

"Can't you eat something? Your dinner is in the oven."

"I don't feel like eating anything."

"Well, look . . . wait until you're through with your bath. Then maybe you'll feel better."

"We'll see. *Ohhhh,* I ache."

Joan knew what a hard worker Joe was. When they'd lived at the coast when Stan was a baby and Joe had worked on the green chair, she'd been amazed at his stamina. Sometimes one of the other men wouldn't show up for a shift, and they'd ask Joe to stay and work a second shift. Then he'd only have eight hours before it was time to go to work again—doubles, they called them. He'd done it many times. But he'd never looked sick before. He'd been really tired, and he'd ached from the hard job of pulling heavy boards off the green chain. But he'd never looked sick before. *It must be the heat,* Joan thought. *Oh, God, I hope we haven't made a mistake!*

She hovered over the stove while she waited for Joe to bathe and wistfully thought that the stove was the first thing they'd bought on time. She smiled when she thought how hard she'd had to talk to persuade Joe to buy it. They'd spent the six hundred dollars he'd had in savings when they were married on a .30.06 rifle for him and an expensive refrigerator for her. They needed a stove for the little house on the hill they'd bought with the borrowed down payment from her parents.

As soon as Joan laid eyes on the stove, she knew she had to have it. It had a window on the door of the oven, and it was beautiful—shiny white porcelain with red numbers and black letters.

Joe didn't want to buy the stove—or anything else on time. He held firm. They left the store. Joan pleaded. She begged. She had to have that stove. Finally, as her last argument, she promised to bake him pies—coconut cream, chocolate, banana, lemon, berry, all kinds of pies.

"Yes," he said, "yes. We'll go buy the *son of a bitch.*"

"Stoves can't be sons of bitches."

"Grrrrr," he said, as he lunged for her.

It was funny . . . After they bought the stove, Joan never did bake many pies. She baked cakes and delicious cinnamon rolls and custards and bread puddings and other goodies, but she seldom ever baked a pie. Joe teased her, and it got to be a kind of a joke between them. Whenever she wanted something (often) and started to nag (often), he'd make fun of her and say in a voice mimicking hers, "Honey, you just buy me that stove and I'll make you so many pies." Then they'd laugh. Sometimes they wouldn't laugh, and she'd say, "You son of a bitch, if it weren't for me, you'd be working on the farm with your uncle for fifty cents an hour and living in a tent. You wouldn't own anything . . . and you'd be happy as a loon."

They both knew it was true. He liked the simple life. Though his old dream of becoming a millionaire persisted. Millionaire! Jesus. Joan shook her head when she thought how increasingly difficult it was to get him to spend a dime. He was beginning to want more and more money saved, and he looked on even the smallest expenditure with scorn—just like his uncle. More and more, Joan found herself buying things without discussing them with him. If she asked if she could or should buy something, he invariably said . . . *no.* If she went ahead and bought things he seldom noticed, and since he didn't look at the checkbook, it was painless to him—and her. He was a puzzle to her. She never knew when some innocent remark would send him into a rage.

Now she realized she hadn't heard a sound from the bathroom in some time. She went in to find Joe asleep in the tub.

"Joe."

"Yeah?"

"Wake up, Joe. It's time to wake up . . ."

He smiled. He always smiled when he woke up. It was one of his nicest qualities.

"Can you eat something now?"

"Yeah. I'll eat a little."

"Good. I'll go finish warming it. I hope it hasn't dried out too much."

When Joe came into the kitchen, he looked much better . . . and smelled better too. Joan watched him try to eat.

"You're going to have to have some new clothes. You won't be able to wear your work clothes more than one day."

"I know. They really smell bad."

"Yes, they do."

"Greg looked neat when we finished . . . and his clothes didn't have a spot on them."

"He's never gotten dirty. He looks good no matter how dirty the job. I don't mind washing your clothes."

"I know. It makes me mad that every time I wear a clean shirt, I get it dirty."

"It's no big deal . . . We may have to get a dryer, though."

"Oh, Jesus. Not now, Joan."

She was sorry she'd mentioned it. He had enough to think about tonight. And she could get by until it started to rain. She was glad she hadn't mentioned her other bit of news. That she was pregnant. Again. She wondered how he'd survive that.

He went off to bed so tired, he could hardly pull himself up the stairs. They had chosen the middle bedroom upstairs. Several of the young couples in the area with small children slept downstairs and put their children upstairs. Joan worried too much about fire to be satisfied with an arrangement like that. Two of her cousins had burned to death in the '30s when their mother left them alone to go next door for a cup of coffee. Their frame house caught fire, and within fifteen minutes, the house and the children were lost.

She finished the dishes, pulled the string in the middle of the room, plunging it into darkness, then groped her way to the stairway aided by the soft moonlight that came through the small-paned kitchen windows. She tiptoed up the stairs. She heard Sarah cough in her sleep. She stopped. When she was sure the child slept soundly, she again made her way carefully. Every board creaked. She silently covered the sleeping children, then went into her room.

As soon as she pulled the sheets around her, she reached for her rosary. It was the ivory one that Joe had given her when she'd received Communion for the first time on their wedding day.

People in the Catholic Church laugh and say that converts are often the strictest Catholics. In many ways, Joan was. She relished the religion and loved the pomp, ceremony, ritual, and society of it all. The interior of the churches she attended were filled with beauty—creamy white altars. Sky blue, ruby red, silver, gold, purple, all colors, rich and vibrant, were found in the paintings, stained glass, and accouterments of the churches.

Joan said one decade of the rosary and then became drowsy. She slipped it over the headboard. She began her examination of conscience. It was very difficult for her to feel guilty or contrite even though she knew she should be. Shouldn't she?

*Dear God, I'm sorry that I have offended thee. I have used bad language ... how many times? Twenty times? Or more? I can't remember. But I know I did it many times. Sometimes, though, God ... some people just can't be called anything but a son of a bitch—or a bastard—because no other word suits them. I just don't know any other word besides son of a bitch or* bastard to describe some people. I know. I've just got to do better. I've just got to. I can't go on using bad language all my life. The trouble is I was reared in a logging camp. As my sister, Grace, used to say, "We weren't reared in a logging camp for nothing." I guess I was probably a bad girl. What the hell, I know I was. Anyway, God, I'm sorry about the bad language. What else did I do wrong? Oh, yeah, I gossiped. I said Jean Lapport was a dumb bitch. It isn't very nice to say someone is a dumb bitch, and I don't think it shows much charity. But I did. I lost my temper several times. I wish I wouldn't do that. I know it is a sin to lose my temper, but sometimes I just get so angry. I guess you know that. I try not to, but like today when Sarah dumped ten pounds of flour on the floor and Stan spread it around with the broom, I was angry. I probably should have spanked them both, but really, God, I think the only time a child should be spanked is when they deliberately disobey. If they don't obey you, they might get hurt really bad sometimes because they didn't. Gee, God, I'm really getting sleepy. I know that you know that. I hope you will forgive me for these and all my other sins, and I also hope you'll remember—even a king falls seven times a day."

Being a Catholic was serious business to Joan. She was way behind the people in the community, and Joe who had been at the business of being a Catholic since birth, but she was making progress . . . and she really *tried*.

Before she had become a Catholic, she had been all mixed up about religion. Occasionally, she had gone to other churches. Because her friends had gone. And because certain cute boys went. When Joan was introduced to the Catholic religion, she embraced it wholeheartedly. The Catholic Church had a very clear set of rules to live by. There were church laws and canon laws, and every good Catholic knew which was which and why, and no one had to think about what was a sin and what wasn't. It was really easy to be a Catholic. You didn't even have to *think*. It suited Joan just fine—especially now that she was getting so busy and had so much to do.

Joe threw the blankets over her in his sleep. He always did that. He was too warm when he slept with even very light blankets. He jabbed her right breast with his elbow just as she was sound asleep.

"Damnit, Joe, move over."

The days passed quickly. Joe learned the route with surprising speed, and after the first few painful days, his muscles became used to the constant exertion, and his stamina increased. Greg left. He'd found a business at the coast. In the last days on the route, he'd been rather quiet. When he did speak, his voice was all choked up. Joe was surprised that Greg was so sentimental. He always knew how a person felt by listening to their voice. The pitch changes when they're sad or happy or lying or telling the truth or very, very tense. It takes practice to tell the difference. Joe's awareness of the sounds the voice makes had been of use to him many times.

Joe was happy to see Greg go. He didn't like to visit much, and Greg's usual cheerful chatter could easily have driven him insane if he had let it. Now all was quiet in the truck, except for the buzzing of the flies. He sprayed his cab often, but still they buzzed. He decided to try some of that new insecticide he'd heard advertised so often. Probably wasn't much better than what he had; still, he'd give it a try.

Joe usually didn't try new things. He liked things the way they were. He hated gadgets. Whenever he bought anything, he always chose the simplest model—the most efficient design.

Two months later, Joe sent out the bills. Joan helped him stamp them. That was all he would let her do. It didn't take him long to get them ready for mailing. Joan offered to help, but Joe wanted to make sure everything was done right.

"And I don't want you to open the letters when they come in."

"Couldn't I just open them? I would put them back in the envelopes. I want to see how much money comes in."

"Joan, just leave everything alone—I mean it. I'll take care of the business."

"And I get to answer the phone, right?"
"That's right."
"Lucky me."
"Jooooan!"
"All right, I'll shut up, but I don't think it's fair."

Four days later, there were three letters addressed to Ace Garbage Service in their mailbox at the end of the lane. Joan held them to the light from the window over the desk. She could make out the figures in one of the envelopes, but the other two were folded and hid the contents. She considered steaming the letters then decided against it. The steam might leave a trace, and also Stan and Sarah had overhead the conversation with Joe, and she knew they'd tell on her if they saw her steam the letters. She couldn't get away with anything when they were around. They were like bloodhounds. Worse, there was no way she could get them to take a nap.

Just then she heard the familiar sound of the truck bouncing and rattling down the lane. She was surprised and pleased that Joe would be home for dinner on time for a change, even though she'd planned on fixing the children a sandwich and then cooking a steak for him later. She was glad he was home. She hadn't had a chance to have a good talk with him since he started working on the route. He'd been so tired and busy. She went out to the truck.

"Are you home for dinner?"
"I'm home and I'll have dinner, but I've got to go back to the dump. Some pigs are loose."
"Pigs?"
"Yeah, they got in under the fence from the farm next to the dump."
"Daddy."
"What, Stan?"
"Could I have my ride in the truck when you go to get the pigs out?"
"No, son, not this time. Next time, OK?"
"Why did you come home so early, Joe, if you just have to go right back?"

"I split the seat out of my pants again."

"Oh, dear, how did you do that?"

"I took a big step out of the truck, and they ripped. Will you get me a pair of pants, Joan?"

"Sure."

Dinner was strained. Every time she opened her mouth, it seemed he got angry. She supposed it was because he was so tired. By the time dinner was over, he seemed to relax. The children ran out to play. When he felt comfortably full, he leaned back in his chair and sighed.

"Did you get enough to eat?"

"Yeah."

"Do you have to leave right away?"

"No, I can wait a few minutes . . . Did I tell you I met Wayne Sharp today?"

"No, you didn't. What is he like?"

"Really nice. You'd never think he had the second-largest route around. (Only his brother's, Edgar's, is larger than his.) He likes to joke, and he smiles a lot. When he talks, though, people pay attention. He's a strong-willed man. We had a good talk."

"Did he say anything about selling his route?"

"No. And we're not interested in his business."

"Why aren't we?"

"We just bought this one."

"I know. But Greg said Wayne Sharp was going to sell his business to him."

"So what?"

"So you should let him know we *might* be interested if and when he decides to sell."

"You might be interested—I'm not."

"Oh, shit."

"Will you please not use that kind of language *please, please, please?*"

"Will you please not shout and lose your temper?"

"I can't stand that kind of talk. I never talk like that. Do you ever hear me use that kind of language?"

"Yes. Sometimes I hear you."

"Well, not often."

Joan looked him directly in the eye. "Shit. Shit. Shit."

"One of these days, I'm going to belt you."

"That should be fun for you."

"You make me so mad, I can't see straight."

"It matches the way you think."

"Jesus, I'm getting out of here."

"Good-bye, asshole."

After he'd stomped out, she wished she hadn't been so mean. She also wished she'd remembered to tell him that one reason he never swore (hardly ever) was because he didn't have anything to swear about. Everything was done for him. His clothes were laundered—some were ironed—his meals prepared, and his house put in order. She'd probably never say *shit* if someone did that for her. She would remember to tell him that the next time they had a fight.

She hurried through her chores. She went to bed when the children did that night. It was unusual for her to go to bed early, but she was beginning to feel something was wrong with the pregnancy. She was especially tired, and after a brief examination of conscience, she fell right to sleep.

Joe woke her when he came into the room—on purpose. He was still angry. Her head hurt, and she squinted in the light of the bare bulb in the ceiling.

"Joan, will you do me a favor?"

"What?"

"Will you please stay in bed in the morning and let me get my own breakfast?"

"Sure."

"I can't stand to see you so grouchy in the mornings."

"You mean I can't get up at four thirty and get your breakfast anymore?"

"That's right."

"That suits me just fine . . . and, Joe . . ."

"Yeah?"

"You're a mean son of a bitch."

# Chapter 11

The months passed quickly. Joan had her third miscarriage. It wasn't as bad as the other two, but her doctor and another doctor, called in for consultation, recommended she have a hysterectomy. She consulted a specialist, who was mystified by the other two doctors' diagnosis. He told Joan there was no reason she couldn't have another child.

Joe relented about the bookwork—gradually. As the months passed and the work became harder and the route grew, it seemed more and more a good idea to let Joan handle the billing and banking. Joan enjoyed doing the work, and Joe hated it.

He tried to keep the route to three days a week, even though more people were moving into the area. The other three days, he cut, hauled, and salvaged scrap metal from the surrounding countryside. Nearly every farm had some old salvageable metal. Old cars were burned, their motors removed and saved for a load of iron. Radiators were cut out and thrown in the copper pile. Old copper tubing from refrigerators and copper wire that had the insulation burned off also went into the pile.

At first, Joe had a problem loading car bodies on top of a load of tin. Then he rigged up an ingenious A-frame loading device with the aid of Joan's father, who had vast experience in rigging trees during the years he spent in the woods. Joan watched with fascination as the first car was loaded. Joe raised the car high in the air. Then he backed under the swinging car, and miraculously, when the cables were lowered, the car was in place on top of the load. Unless Joe could cap off a load of tin with a car body, it didn't pay to salvage tin. It was too light.

Soon after he started salvaging metal, he met and became friendly with Gene Greenman from the junkyard. Gene found a winch for Joe to load heavy metal onto his truck. It came from one of the ships that was being scrapped. It was a godsend to Joe. He could load things he never could have loaded alone without it. Gene also sold Joe surplus battleship gray paint in five-gallon cans. Joe sprayed it on the two-story house and painted the window trim white, and the old place looked great.

Joe wished he could junk six days a week. He didn't mind working on the route, but junking was very profitable. A glass jar in the cupboard was nearly full of hundred-dollar bills. The money would pay for the loan to his uncle. The other loans were nearly paid. For the first time in their married life, they were almost out of debt.

"I think we should get a new car."

"Listen, Joan, if we buy anything new, it is going to be a new truck."

"We need a new car. There is nothing wrong with the truck. We're almost out of debt, and now we can afford a *new* car."

"I wouldn't mind trading and getting a used car—if we could find a good one."

"Even if we found one, you wouldn't know whether it was a good one."

"So I'm no mechanic."

"Or carpenter. Or plumber. Or . . . Or . . ."

"OK, so I'm just a farmer."

"Doesn't it make sense to buy a new car and not get something someone else got rid of because it was about to break down? And, Joe, it's no big deal that you're not good at mechanics. A lot of men couldn't do what you do. And you do have the nicest garden in the country."

"You're right, and don't forget that I built a fine kitchen in that house at the coast when we were first married."

"And you haven't built or fixed anything since."

"I built the woodshed."

"I forgot . . . but Dad helped with that."

"I'm going to have to get some wood."

"Where are you going to get it?"

"Out by the dump. I'll borrow one of your dad's power saws and cut some up."

"When?"

"Soon."

They'd nearly frozen the first winter in the funny old house. The woodstove in the living room was totally inadequate to heat the old house with the drafty windows. The wood, wet and in large blocks, simply wouldn't burn. Joe hadn't had time to get the wood when the weather was right. All he'd been able to find was some wood that wasn't dried and wouldn't burn well. Joan spent the days trying to light the fire. By some miracle, by the time Joe came in at night, the chill would have left the living room, and he found it difficult to believe it was as cold as Joan said. The upstairs door was kept shut, and since it was the only thing in the house that worked well, not a single unit of heat made it upstairs. Several times that winter, they awoke to find their noses iced with frost.

Joan took the children to her parents for two weeks that winter. Not only was the house cold, but also the water froze. They were without water, except for what they hauled. Joe was too busy working to take time to thaw the pipes, and the cold spell lasted longer than usual.

This winter would be different. There was a new woodshed. A trash burner in the kitchen would heat it, and with luck, they could leave the stairway door open, and some heat might go up to the bedrooms. And Joe would get the wood in time so that it would be nice and dry. He promised.

"Let's just go look at the new cars."

"OK, but I'm not buying one. We can just look."

"Sunday after church, we can take our Sunday drive and look at cars."
"OK, but I'm *not* buying one."

They could get an awfully good buy on a new Ford. They couldn't believe it. It gleamed in the Sunday sun. The man was so nice. He said "Yes, sir" and "No, ma'am" when he thought he should. He hardly said a word other than that. When he did speak, Joan was in complete agreement. She thought that black-and-white Ford was the most beautiful car she'd ever seen. Finally, Joe pulled her aside. "Don't agree with everything he says."

"Why not?"

"You're supposed to find fault with everything. That way you can get a better deal."

"Oh."

Joan didn't know how to bargain. To her, it seemed rude. She saw the salesman approaching. "Shhhh. Here he comes."

The salesman puffed up to them. Little beads of perspiration betrayed his anxiety. His unbuttoned plaid coat revealed an unironed shirt and a solid paunch. He put his foot on the front bumper. "The boss wouldn't ordinarily do this, but I convinced him that if he didn't, you might not buy the car." He gave them a conspiratorial look. "He said he'll knock off a hundred dollars if you decide to buy today. I've given you our best price already, so you can see it's a real bargain."

They drove it home that evening.

The sound of the truck bouncing in louder than usual should have alerted Joan, but it wasn't until she saw Joe striding tensely toward the house that she knew something was bothering him.

"What's the matter?"

He told her while he undressed and bathed. She sat in the bathroom, watching him and listening. "Well, there's nothing really to it. Wayne Sharp stopped me when I was on Main Street. He wanted to talk to me... so I said *sure*. We went in and had a cup of coffee, and he told me what he wanted me to do. He's been in the garbage business for years. He was one of the first to recognize a need for garbage service. He was unemployed one winter and started hauling small loads for people. Hardly anyone needed service then. They either burned their garbage or dumped it in their backyards. Or they hauled their own trash to the dump once a month. All that was years ago. The war came, and everyone got busy, and they had money to pay someone else to do the job . . . Now all but a small percentage just aren't interested in fooling with their garbage."

Joan still couldn't figure out why Joe seemed so tense. "People live differently now than they used to. A lot of people who lived through the Great Depression aren't about to spend a penny extra . . . even for something as necessary as garbage service. But what does all that have to do with Wayne Sharp?"

"To make a long story short—he did a fine job for years and never had any problems. Now he has a big one. He chose a disastrous time to ask for a raise. He applied to the city council six months before his franchise was to be renewed. He should have waited until he had the franchise taken care of. As soon as he asked for the raise, they put the franchise out for bid. Wayne has built the route into one of the largest in the state. Now that it's valuable, they want to steal it from him."

"That doesn't seem right."

"It isn't. And to make matters worse, the mayor's son would like the business."

"Do you think he'll bid against Wayne Sharp?"

"He'll be first in line. He's the main reason they're putting the route out for bid. He tried to buy the route from Wayne a year or two ago. Wayne wouldn't sell even when he offered a premium—much more than it was worth at the time. Now it's worth nothing—to Wayne—unless he gets the franchise back."

"What are you going to do?"

"I'm going to bid against Wayne Sharp."

"That doesn't sound right."

Joe had been surprised when Wayne first suggested the scheme, but the more he thought of it, the less distasteful it seemed. On the way home, he decided he'd discuss it with Joan and call Wayne that evening. He'd told him he'd call tomorrow, but there was no reason to make Wayne wait for an answer. He was upset enough.

"That doesn't sound right. I can't believe he'd ask you to do a thing like that."

"What's wrong with it, Joan?"

"I don't know. It just doesn't sound right."

"How do you know when it does sound right?"

"My body tells me. When something sounds right to me, I get a good feeling throughout my body. It moves around and then seems to come in pleasurable waves to the heart. When something 'sounds wrong,' I feel as though I am being silently and completely bound, with the finest elastic that, if applied in just the right way, can completely immobilize the strongest of men. It affects me that way—insidiously. After the feelings come, I give them names. Sometimes I'm wrong. I may mistake fear for anger, and then because there is no precise word to describe my particular feeling, I stumble along thinking I'm angry when I'm really only afraid. I think I'm becoming more in tune with my body, and I am amazed at how much better I am when I take time to listen to myself."

"This time you can listen to me." He told her about it then. Every detail of the proposal Wayne Sharp had made that day. Joe could see a few details that could be worked out. When he mentioned them to Wayne, he'd thought he'd noticed a little smile of appreciation on the older man's hard mouth.

"I can't believe he'd ask you to do a terrible thing like that. It seems dishonorable."

"I fight dishonor with dishonor." He did too. He thought of the *only* dishonest thing he'd ever done. When he was eleven, he and his sister, broke and anxious to earn money, had knocked on doors looking for work. At last, they were hired by a lady to mow a huge lawn and completely manicure the edges. They worked six hours. The lady gave them a check for $4. Joe looked at it—protested that it wasn't fair. The lady refused to pay them another penny. Joe added "teen" to the written four and placed a one before the numeral four.

"You should fight dishonor with honor," he said.

"There are going to be bids from people who know nothing at all about garbage. They won't know how to bid on the rate schedule. They just think they can get something for nothing. If I bid, it will give the council something with which to compare Wayne's bid.

"He thinks if I bid just a little higher than he, it will make his bid seem reasonable to the city council. Don't forget, Joan, the mayor's son is going to try to steal it." Joe stepped from the tub and dried himself. "Do you think I shouldn't do it?"

"I think you should make up your own mind. If and when Wayne decides to sell, he may give you first chance. That is something to think about. Also, I don't know why you want my advice. You always ask for it, argue with me, don't seem to really listen to what I have to say, then do exactly as you please."

"I know, but I like to hear what you think of things."

"I really don't think much of this. If you have to be so secretive about it . . . it must be dishonest. I know what it is . . . collusion!"

"I know that isn't what it is."

Joe's patience was sorely tried at any kind of a meeting. The business of getting large numbers of people to agree was boring, tiresome, frustrating, and vexing. He was usually tired from a hard day's work, and any city council meeting he ever attended lasted until way after his bedtime.

Wayne Sharp sat across the room. He made no gesture to indicate he was aware of Joe's presence, though they'd parted only a half hour before after agreeing to meet at Wayne's after the meeting.

The day had been hot, and the heat now caused the crowded room to emanate steam. Joe smiled to himself and thought that if it weren't for the fly, they'd all be asleep as the council droned on with its business.

Housewives in rollers and scruffy sandals, farmers in bib overalls with red blistered faces, businessmen in white shirts, and several lounging longhairs sat waiting for their special interest to come before the council.

Joe hoped they would call for a recitation of the ordinance and discuss Wayne's franchise soon. He couldn't understand why every small town in the valley made the citizens wait, while the councils went through old business, new business, inside jokes, and—always—his business last.

Tonight was no exception. As expected, the dreary business of the city had to be thoroughly explored. The lone woman on the council, a rather attractive matron, obviously enjoyed being the lone woman on the council. She seized every opportunity to let the men know how really dumb she was. She really wasn't dumb. She just wanted the men to think she was. Time after time, the meeting was held up by someone giving her obvious answers to inane questions.

They waited. One man's head began to nod. Joe fought sleep. The room began to clear as each person finished his business with the council and gratefully escaped the hot, boring room, and the babble pierced often by the shrill laugh of the lady councilman. The mayor began to speak.

"The last order of business is the discussion pertaining to the garbage franchise. While it is not the wish of the council to create undue hardships, we feel it is our duty to settle this matter in the fairest possible way for the benefit of all the citizens of the community." His eyes danced with glee as they met Wayne's. "Therefore, we've decided, after prior discussion, to call for bids due one month from tonight."

There had been no surprises. Joe hadn't expected any, but just to make sure, he'd endured the meeting. As he walked to his car, he assessed the situation. Wayne Sharp was in serious danger of losing his route. There were three people at the council meeting who were certainly going to bid against him. There could be more who hadn't come forward yet. Joe wished Wayne hadn't asked for the raise when he had. If he'd waited until after the franchise was in his hands, he could have gotten the raise. This way, all he'd done was draw attention to the fact that his franchise was up for renewal. The papers had gotten the story, and that would certainly attract other bidders.

Joe ruefully started his car. He wished he'd told Wayne he would meet him tomorrow night instead of tonight. Sudden weariness engulfed him. He knew he'd have to start at four in the morning, and as he pointed the car toward Wayne's house, he cursed softly under his breath.

The porch light was on when Joe drove down the lane. Wayne waited for him in the shadows of the porch. "Can I offer you something to drink?"

"I'd sure like a beer if you have one."

"Coming right up."

Wayne led Joe into the living room and indicated the sofa. Joe relaxed the minute he hit the soft pillows. Wayne soon returned from the kitchen and sat facing him.

"What do you think my chances are of getting the route back?"

"I don't honestly know."

"A week ago, I wanted a raise of twenty-five cents a can. Now I'd be happy if I could just keep my business."

"I know. That's the bad part of this franchise system. We've always got to face the possibility someone else is going to outbid us when the franchise runs out."

"And they can operate cheaper than we can because they don't have to buy the business like you did yours."

"I bought my business, Wayne, but you started your own, and if you can save it, you'll have something to sell."

Wayne leaned forward. Quietly, he told Joe, "Here's what I wanted you to do. I made a schedule of the number of cans and the number of stops per week. See, here, one can a week, two cans a week, and so forth. This column is the charge. I wanted you to add five cents to every figure in the column. That would show that I'm the low bidder. I figured no one else who isn't in the business would have any idea how to bid. So we'd have the advantage there.

Joe studied the chart. It was well laid out. He asked a few questions, then was satisfied. Wayne had done an excellent job in devising the form and the schedule. Joe knew he was right. No one who wasn't in the business would be able to figure out anything as concise and easy to understand as this.

Wayne shrugged his shoulders. "I thought it was the right thing to do. Maybe it is, but I've decided to forget it. If I can't get my route back without sacrificing my honor and your honor, I don't want it. As far as I'm concerned, it's in the hands of the gods—and to hell with it."

Joe looked as surprised as he felt. Stunned, he looked into Wayne's eyes and saw pride and determination. Joe grabbed Wayne's hand and shook it. He smiled and thought what a pleasure it was to know such a man existed—a man who survived without breaking faith with himself.

They visited for a while. Joe didn't want to stay longer because it was late and because he knew Joan would be waiting to hear everything that had happened. She never was satisfied until she knew every small detail. He really didn't mind telling her. As a matter of fact, telling Joan something made it better than when it actually happened. Except she had a memory like a sponge. If someone said *five* six months ago and today said *six*, she instinctively knew the right number. A red flag went off in her mind, and Joe never knew when she might insist instead of his *twenty*, it was truly only *ten*. He did have the problem of embellishing. That's what Joan called it—embellishing. If anyone else said something that wasn't true, they were a *damned liar*; but when Joe did it, he was *embellishing*. After all, he *was* her husband.

She waited for him as he expected. She was excited, anxious, and exhilarated, and wouldn't stop interrupting as he detailed the events of the evening.

"How many will bid against him?"

"I don't know. At least three . . . maybe more."

"What's his wife like?"

"She was in bed."

"What was their house like?"

"Nice and neat."

"I suppose she's one of those super housekeepers?"

"It was late."

"Oh. OK. What happens next?"

"What happens next is that Wayne submits his bid and then *we* wait until the next council meeting to see who is successful. The one who is successful will own the route. I hope it is Wayne."

"Did it ever occur to you that Wayne asked you to bid with him so that you wouldn't bid against him?"

"You're a shrew."

"I'm a realist. You're the logical one to bid against him. You're already in business. You know the business, and you've built up a certain amount of respect for yourself since you started."

"You're a shrew and a bitch."

"I know. But I'm smart. Good night."

## Chapter 12

The council postponed the hearing on the garbage franchise. Several of the bids were so poorly presented, they could not be compared. The council asked that the bids be presented in the form of Wayne's bid. Wayne was beside himself. They had used his originally created schedule structure to bid against him. He'd had a certain advantage in presenting the schedule as he had. Now that advantage was gone.

Joe had driven by the city attorney's office on the way to the meeting. The mayor's son and several other men were talking intently. Joe could see through the window. There was no doubt now there was collusion. No doubt in Joe's mind. None.

When they met after the meeting, Wayne shrugged his shoulders.

"I appreciate what you're doing, Joe. There's nothing more we can do until the next council meeting. I sure don't like the way things are going. You go home now, Joe, and get some rest. We'll keep in touch."

"I guess I will go home. Joan's waiting to hear all about the meeting."

"Bring her with you next time, Joe. It might not hurt if we have our wives with us."

They agreed that at least it wouldn't harm anything. Nothing would harm anything now.

"I've never been to a council meeting. What do they do?"

"They sit around and argue and act important."

"Is there a place for people to sit . . . I mean is it like a courtroom?"

"It's not so formal, and each town's council room is different. One town meets in the fire hall and just have chairs around in a semicircle. Where you're going, the mayor and the councilmen sit around a big table, and the people sit at the back of the room."

"What do the women wear?"

"I don't know, Joan. Wear whatever you want."

"Let's see, shall I wear my blue maternity smock or my red maternity smock?"

"Very funny."

She hadn't felt very funny. She'd felt lousy, nauseous, tired, icky, rotten, And mean. She hadn't had to tell him she was pregnant this time. He knew. He remembered. Boy, did he remember. Still he couldn't resist teasing her.

"I'm pretty good, aren't I?"

"Damn you."

"And who said 'forget the rhythm system'?"

"The rhythm system's no *goddamned* good."

"Must you swear?"

"Yes, I *must!*"

"After you have this baby, I'll never touch you again."

"Can I count on that?"

Mutual antagonism was with them the rest of the month—she, because she was pregnant; he, because he was worried. Neither knew why they snarled and bared their fangs. Sometimes it seemed they were enemies and didn't understand what war they were fighting. They had lost the closeness, sharing, and concern they'd had for each other in the beginning. Now they were competitors, each afraid the other would get the "upper hand" and each too blind to see what was happening to them and to their marriage. Edginess, snapped answers, and short tempers increased as the time for the meeting drew near. For Joan, apprehension gave way to excitement the night the bids were opened.

Everyone sat in the sweltering room in various stages of boredom. Only Joan was too curious and interested in the proceedings to be bored. Helen and Wayne Sharp sat across the room from them. Joan assessed Helen as well as she could without staring at the older woman. She was as Joan had imagined she would be—prettier, small and neat, and very nervous. She couldn't keep her hands still.

Joan, a little nervous herself, sat ramrod straight in her chair. Joe sprawled in his place. He wondered when the council would come to the franchise bid opening. He glanced at the mayor's son. The smug look on his face caused Joe to sit upright. *Something is very wrong*, he thought.

Finally, the moment came. The mayor announced that the franchise awarding had been postponed.

Everyone was stunned. No one expected *that* to happen. Later, at Helen and Wayne's, the two couples discussed the situation over coffee.

"Joe, why did they decide not to open the bids in public?"

"They had some reason. You can be sure of that."

Helen's eyes showed the strain of the ordeal. Wayne was nearing retirement. Everything they had in the world was tied up in the route. There was nothing of value to sell, except the truck. No business—unless by some miracle they'd get the franchise back. Then they'd be pretty comfortable with Wayne's social security and the income they'd get. She'd had a lifetime of council meetings—capricious, arbitrary, and emotional. God, would she be glad to have the freedom to thumb her nose at the whims and wiles of council members who become self-styled critics and judges and who, usually with a great degree of ignorance, had shaped her life all these years. No, you can't have a raise. Yes, you can have a raise. As part of your franchise, you have to pick up all the city's cans—free of charge. Free service to churches. Now Helen tightened her lips.

"Is it legal for them to do something like this?"

Wayne slapped his knee. "They seem able to do anything they want. One of my customers told me the mayor's son is going to bid one dollar for the first can with 7 percent to go to the city for the franchise fee."

Joan's eyes widened. "You mean for ninety-three cents, they'll pick up a can of garbage four times a month . . . and sometimes five?"

Wayne nodded. "The worst of it is, there's no way to stop them . . . and there's no way they can make anything but money. They don't have to pay for a route . . . and in a few months, when everything has gone back to normal, all they have to do is petition the council for a raise. They'll say they can't make money, and the council will be so sick of the whole thing, they'll grant them the raise. In the meantime, I've lost my business." He shook his head, fighting his emotions.

Helen sighed. "We've done so much work to wind up with nothing. I could cry."

Joan squirmed in her chair. "Will you men answer one question? Helen asked it earlier. Is it legal for them to do something like this?"

Wayne shrugged. "Whether it is legal doesn't matter. The expense of taking action against the city could be enormous. They probably have the right to any kind of procedure they choose. I don't know. Another thing we have to consider is that if there is too much publicity, the city may decide to run the business themselves."

"Could they?"

"All they have to do is buy a truck and go to work."

"I wonder why they haven't already?" Wayne shifted in his chair and reached for the cream pitcher. The black hair on his arms reminded Joan of a gorilla. He shrugged as he answered her.

"Lots of reasons. The main one is they've had no problem with the way things were. I've done the job well. I seldom have a complaint. When was the last one, Helen?"

"I don't remember."

"Neither do I. Anyway, Joan, another reason, and the biggest, is that historically, whatever the government does, it does with a maximum of inefficiency and red tape bureaucracy. Except for big projects costing millions of dollars that business simply can't afford, like dams—there is little government can do as well as private enterprise."

Joe accepted another cup of coffee. "I suppose it's easy to spend someone else's money, and if you get the same pay for working hard or hardly working, maybe some people don't care."

"I think we should talk to the city attorney."

They stared at Joan. She stared back. She folded her arms in front of her breasts, clenched her teeth, and closed her lips.

"Why?" Joe was the first to ask.

"If the route is lost, what difference would it make?"

Wayne scratched his forehead. "I guess it wouldn't make any difference, but what would you say to him?"

"I don't know . . . exactly. But if we don't say something or do something by the end of next week, when the franchise is going to be awarded, we might as well forget the whole thing!"

Wayne nodded in agreement. "Maybe I should go talk to him."

Joan shook her head. "I think Joe should go first—just to find out what is going on. Then you'd be in a stronger position if you should want to carry it further. The city attorney doesn't know Joe very well."

"I think Joan is right. What have we got to lose?" Helen said as she rose from the table to get more coffee.

Joe groaned. "What would I say to him, Joan?"

"Let me go with you. We'll think up some good questions to ask him. If we don't, we'll stumble through. Maybe nothing will come of it, but it does seem worth a try."

Joe shook his head. Joan knew he was tired, and the sudden rush of red to his cheeks made her decide it was time to back off and to leave. They drove home in silence. She knew he didn't like her idea. She was too smart to press the issue when he was obviously in no mood to discuss it. She'd wait until he was comfortable. Then she'd persuade him. It might take time, but she knew how to do it, and it always worked. Never give up. It was one of the things about her that was increasingly irritating to Joe. Joan was running things much too much.

The city attorney's office was lined with law books. Original watercolors of Revolutionary War English officers dotted empty spaces along shelves of beautifully bound books—part of an extensive law library. A large table piled high with papers dominated the room. On the west wall a very old map of the Pacific Northwest in delicate pastels hung on a background of the ubiquitous international building material and symbol of strength and succor—brick. It was a pink rust red and blended beautifully in monochromatic mellowness with the carpeting and grass cloth.

Mr. Johnson, the city attorney, faced them from across the table, which also functioned as his desk. He looked angry. He was. He was furious. Just who in the hell did these ignorant bastards think they were coming in to his office and wasting his valuable time? He smiled. "I don't understand what it is you people want." He shifted in his seat. Garbage. If all he had to think of all day was garbage, his life would be a hell of a lot easier than it was. *I hope this doesn't take much time*, he thought.

Joe shifted his weight in the high-backed chair and looked uncomfortable. "We're not sure what it is we want either, Mr. Johnson. I think we'd like to discuss the franchising procedure with you and find some answers to our questions."

"If you're questioning the procedure in awarding the franchise for hauling garbage in the city, and I assume you are . . ."—they nodded—"then I'll say, in my opinion, the city had every right to take as much time as necessary to make sure no errors were made. We were looking for a better understanding of the problem and the terms of the franchise by the council."

"We understand the mayor's son is bidding one dollar a month and giving 7 percent interest to the city for one can a month," Joan said.

He was too slow. Joan caught the hesitation. Then he was too fast. Bad actor.

An unseen lightning storm caught Joan. Anger flickered in her eyes. Redness rushed. "Do you mean to tell us the franchise has already been decided? Do *you* know who is going to get it?"

"Of course."

"And just who?"

"I'm not at liberty to say."

"Oh, you're not, huh?" Joan was surprised to hear her voice. It sounded as though it was coming from the bottom of a barrel. She couldn't stop. Angry words tumbled out. "Do you have any idea how this is going to look? If that bid of one dollar is accepted, it shouldn't be too difficult to prove collusion. There are a lot of good people in this community who simply will not stand for Wayne Sharp being cheated out of his route. And believe me, they'll hear about it." She gasped for breath. "Your man will be back before the city council within months asking for a raise. He'll have to because he's going to have to buy equipment and he'll have other expenses. When he does, if he does, there is going to be the biggest stink you've ever seen—or smelled. If that man gets the franchise, there's going to be more trouble than you knew existed."

They were silent most of the way home. Joan started to laugh.

"What's so funny?"

"I don't know. I was laughing at the way Mr. Johnson looked . . ."

"When you made a fool of yourself?"

"Did I?"

"Yes. When will you learn not to talk so much?"

"I didn't mean to. It sort of happened. I couldn't stop."

"You've got to learn to control yourself."

"I'm sorry. I didn't know it was that bad. I'll be better in the future."

"It probably doesn't matter. The franchise has already been awarded." He drove into the lane. "It won't be long before we know for sure who gets the franchise. Then this will all be a thing of the past."

"You're right. Once something happens, it is over. It's too bad more people don't fight for things while it still does some good."

They tried not to think about the next meeting as they waded through their chores, yet they couldn't keep their minds off the puzzle problem. Joe knew that if Wayne lost his route, it would be a matter of time before the mayor's son or someone else's son would be bidding on his route. That made him think and worry and think even harder.

At last, the night of the meeting came. The chambers filled early. The same tired faces filed into the room—right on time. The mayor stood. He looked in different directions. He waited. Silence.

"We have a lot of unfinished business to take care of tonight, and it might be quite late when we finish the meeting. Therefore, it is the decision of the council to award the garbage franchise the first thing this evening." His high-pitched voice continued. "After due deliberation and taking into account the fact that the lowest bidder is not always the one who will do the best job and also the fact that Wayne Sharp has given this city excellent garbage service at a reasonable cost for the last fifteen years, it is my pleasant duty to inform those of you here—the city is awarding Wayne Sharp the franchise."

They gasped, then babbled. Wayne Sharp's eyes found Joe's, and before the next order of business was under way, the two couples were outside on the street, congratulating each other and shaking their heads in disbelief. Someone suggested they celebrate. Soon, they sat around a cozy table in a lounge. It had been an old flour mill. Wonderful old brick, big stones, huge beams, and small, high windows had been preserved, polished, and then intimately and softly lit. Glenn Miller sent shivers down Joan's spinal column. She hoped they'd play "String of Pearls." It had been one of her favorites in high school.

They were a happy group. They laughed and talked and laughed until nearly eleven. Then Joe raised his glass toward Wayne and Helen. "To many prosperous years in *your* garbage business . . . Wayne and Helen!"

They drank. Wayne raised his glass to Joe. "To many more prosperous years in our garbage business . . . Joe and Joan."

"What?"

"Just what I said, Joe. I decided *if* I should be lucky enough to get the route back that I'd sell it. I've been in the business long enough, and while I still have my health, I'd like to let someone else worry about picking up garbage cans. Also, Helen and I have never had time to do a lot of interesting things. We'd like to travel, visit Helen's relatives in England, and, in general, take it easy. So we're selling. If you two want to buy the route, it is yours. My price is thirty thousand dollars. I want five thousand down, and you can pay payments on the balance. I own the truck, which will go with the sale and the county dump lease."

Joe and Joan looked like beached trout. Joan caught her breath first. "Oh, Joe, isn't this exciting? We have an opportunity to buy their business."

"Joan, we're going to have to think it over."

She laughed. "I see. We have to 'play business.' We never buy anything without thinking about it for a while first, right?"

"That's right."

"Look, good people, while Joe goes through the motions of whether he'll buy the business, and for whatever price you're asking, let me say that we'll take it unless we let you know differently within two days."

"Joan!"

She looked at Joe. She hadn't realized how much she'd had to drink, but there was no mistaking the angry look on his face. She giggled. She knew she'd get hell later, but now she didn't care. "Let's not discuss it anymore. Shall we have another drink?"

Helen graciously raised her glass toward the hovering waiter, "Yes, and you fellows should know enough not to mix business with pleasure."

Joan giggled. "Business is pleasure."

Joe waved off the waiter. He wearily rose. "We'll have to say good night now before I have to carry her home."

"No, Joe, let's not leave yet. I haven't had so much fun in years."

He frowned. Then he raised his arms in surrender. "OK, we can stay a little while longer on the condition that you only have one more drink."

She started to say something, but the expression on his face caused her to stop. She excused herself and went to the powder room. She took her time coming back. She hated to be criticized and found herself responding to it with a deep inner anger. What right did he have to think he was better than she? Was he the judge? The jury? Was it right that one person had the power to make another person shut up or to censor what was said? No. Damnit. It wasn't right. She might make mistakes, but no one was ever going to silence her. They might get her to quiet down for a while. But not for long. How dare anyone?

She saw Helen and Wayne dancing as she quietly took her seat. "Can we dance, Joe?"

"No."

"I love to dance. I've always loved to dance. When I was a little girl, everyone in camp went to the dances at Vine Maple—every Saturday night. It was a grange. At intermission, the ladies served pie and coffee and sometimes a nice lunch. I didn't get to go very often, but when I did, I loved it. Old ladies and small children sat on long benches around the hall. At one end, in dark slacks and white shirts with string ties, the band played twangy down-home "Tennessee Waltz"-type music. Everyone dressed up. The ladies wore frilly, slinky, velvety dresses in rich colors that blurred on the floor. The men slicked down their hair and tucked in their shirts . . ." She broke off, remembering how it had been.

"Dancing is immoral."

"I don't see how you can say that!"

"It's easy—dancing is immoral."

"What's wrong with it?"

"It's nothing but belly rubbing."

"It is not."

"It is, it's *belly rubbing*."

"If I hadn't belly rubbed with you before we were married, I'd be out there on the floor belly rubbing with someone else right now, I'll tell you." She flopped in her chair, away from him.

He clouded up. His mouth formed what was becoming his characteristic pout. He was silent. She declined to dance with Wayne when he asked her. She knew it would obligate Joe to dance with Helen, and she knew he lacked the manners to return the gesture. They left shortly.

Nearly home, Joan spoke, "When do you want to discuss the route?"

"Never."

"What do you mean never?"

"I'm not going to buy another route."

"I thought you wanted it."

"I don't want it."

"I thought you did."

"No. You did. Isn't that right? You did?"

"Well, I guess I did."

"That's right. I'm not going to get suckered into any more debts."

"What debts?"

"The route, the car . . ."

"Oh. Oh. OK, let's hear it about the car. My fault, right? It was my fault we bought the car."

"That's right. I told you we'd go look. I didn't expect to buy a car."

"Fine, I'll take full responsibility for plunging us into debt for the car." *Which we needed.*

"Yes, you will . . ."

"Great. Good night, Joe."

"Grrrrr."

# Chapter 13

She tried never to go to bed with unresolved anger between them, but sometimes he was impossible. As she felt for, found, and then replaced her rosary, her thoughts turned to the problem. She finally went to sleep still thinking about how they could raise the five thousand dollars.

It turned out there wasn't any rush raising the money. Wayne decided to let the city council catch its breath before he asked for the franchise to be transferred. It would be about six months before he wanted to sell out.

Joan convinced Joe his future lay in expanding the route. She knew fate puts some great opportunities in one's path, and it is one's duty to seize as many of them as one is able. Or as Shakespeare said, "There is a tide in the affairs of men which, taken at the flood, leads on to fortune. Omitted, all the voyages of their life is bound in shallows and in miseries."

She wasn't too concerned about Joe's reluctance to buy another route. She wished the price were more reasonable. They'd pay a premium if they bought it, but this truly was an opportunity. It was the second-largest route in the area and might not be for sale again for years. Someone would buy it. It might as well be them. Besides, the business would pay for itself in a few years, and after all, what did they have to begin with? If they lost it all, they'd be right where they started, which was nowhere.

With this in mind, Joan made an appointment for them with the local banker. A few weeks earlier, Joan had mentioned they might need a five-thousand-dollar loan. Mr. Collings, the banker, had said, "No problem . . . no problem. Come and see me when you're ready." They were ready.

Mr. Collings, small and rather delicate, was *delighted* to see them. There were few businesses in the small community, so most of the loans were to farmers. "Come right in." He motioned them from the doorway of his office down the hall and to the rear of the bank. His voice had changed from nice and friendly to pompous and arrogant. An uneasy feeling crossed over Joan, but she brushed it away. Hadn't he said, "No problem . . . no problem"? Wasn't he her friend?

Mr. Collings strutted to his chair. He indicated seats directly in front of him. They sat. He sat. He looked at them as Napoleon might have surveyed his troops—imperious.

"Now, what can I do for you?"

Joan smiled. "Mr. Collings, do you remember when I told you that Wayne Sharp might consider selling his route to us . . . ?"

He nodded.

"Now he has his route for sale, and Joe and I have decided we're going to buy it."

Mr. Collings looked puzzled. "And?"

"And we need to borrow five thousand dollars for the down payment. You said to come and see you when we needed the money." She shot a confident look at Joe. He had only agreed to talk to Mr. Collings because she had assured him he was anxious to loan them the money.

Mr. Collings smiled—and smiled. "Well, I certainly am happy you came to me before you went ahead with this business arrangement."

"Why?" Joan looked toward Joe. She began to wish Mr. Collings wouldn't say another word. He didn't sound like he was going to say anything that would strengthen her case.

He droned on. "This would be a terrible mistake for you. You would be biting off more than you can chew. I just came from a meeting of the branch managers. The only money we have to loan is for necessary farm loans to our regular customers. This recession is very serious. This is a bad time to be expanding any business, especially a garbage route. The only thing you are buying is a truck and goodwill. No. This is a bad time for any business."

He kept them two hours. He gave them a minicourse in banking, tight money, federal reserve, secondary money markets, and futures market. At last, he stopped posturing and parading. Citing their relative inexperience in business, he said *no,* again, emphatically. He seemed pleased with himself as he walked them to the door.

He and Joe would have made good bookends. Joe was smiling just like him.

"Well, that's that." Joe started the car. He was trying hard not to smile. Joan admired his control. If the situation were reversed and she were Joe, she knew she'd rub it in. But he didn't say anything to her ... He just smiled.

"For Christ's sake, do you think I'm going to let that jerk stop me?"

"Huh?"

"You heard me. We're going to buy that route. There are other banks, other people, other relatives. Someone will loan us the money. We need that route."

"I don't want any more work. You know that. I'm so lazy, I hate to do what I do now."

"I know, but you won't have any more work to do. We'll organize the route so you won't have as much work as you are doing. If you're smart, you'll be doing a lot less. Do you ever see these farmers around here working with their bodies? No. They hire people to do the work. They use their heads. It's time you started using yours."

"Why do we need to buy the route?"

"Because it's for sale. Someone else will eventually own everything that is owned now. We may never have another opportunity to buy that route. All we have to do is raise the down payment, and it will pay for itself."

He liked the idea of the route paying for itself. All they'd have to do was to make payments on the loan. If necessary, they could do it out of their present income.

"Jesus, Joe, all I ever hear from you is how you want to be rich. How do you expect to get rich if you are afraid to take a chance and do something that's a sure thing?"

"*Gamble* you mean."

"How do you think you'll get rich? Do you think a gold mine will open up under the garden?"

"I want to farm someday."

"I know. In the meantime, let's consider this. I don't see how we can do any better."

Every winter, Joan hated the old house; it was so miserably cold. When spring came each year, she forgot how miserable the old house had been—how hard to heat, and how inconvenient the bathroom and laundry facilities were. In the spring and summer, she could hang wash on the lines in the backyard under the black walnut tree. The children spent most of their waking hours outdoors playing, and on hot summer days, the old house stayed remarkably cool. The yard improved each year. Beds of flowers were added. Roses lined the south side of the yard and bordered the wheat field where the strawberries had been. Tuberous begonias bloomed in the shade of the old garage, which still looked as though it would fall any minute. The lawn was mown by an enterprising neighbor boy called in after innumerable quarrels with Joe that started when Joan said, "Please mow that goddamned lawn." Their own mower was either broken or Joe had no time. Joan computed the cost of a new mower and maintenance, and decided it was cheaper to have the work done.

If winters weren't counted, the old place wasn't too bad. The yard was pretty, the fields fertile, and the buildings looked wonderful. They'd been painted, trimmed, and even given cursory maintenance. Joan found herself dreaming more and more of a new home. They'd talked about it when they were going together. They wanted a two-story colonial—white, with green shutters and large pillars. Joan pored over *Better Homes and Gardens* and the *American Home*. She knew exactly how the house would look.

Everything was going well with the franchise transfer. They'd raised the money. Good old Grandpa. They just finished paying the last payment when Joan went to ask him for another loan. He was delighted. He was impressed that they'd paid him back so promptly, that they worked so hard, and that they were so successful. America. Where but in America could a young couple prosper so? Joan loved him. He was neat. He looked like an immigrant. He'd never lost his thick Italian accent, and when he waved good-bye to her, he flashed his perfect teeth. He had never been to a dentist or had a cavity all his life, and he was old. Wow.

The agreement was all set between the Sharps and them. There were only two problems. They were locked into $1.25 per can per month for three years because the council had written a clause in the franchise that so stipulated. The clause originally was to prevent a low bid and a subsequent raising of prices. They could live with that. Time would pass quickly.

The other problem presented a different kind of difficulty. They would have to move into the area. The city council added that requirement as a condition of the transfer of the franchise.

"It's only ten miles."

"I know, but I've lived here all my life."

"Joe, we can come and visit. I don't especially want to move either, but that is *the* condition. Right or wrong, if we want the route, we have to move."

"My family is here..."

"And how often do you go visit them? You hardly ever stop to say hello. As a matter of fact, the next time your stupid aunt comes here and acts as if I'm keeping you from visiting, I'm going to tell her the truth."

"What truth . . . and my aunt isn't stupid!"

"The hell she isn't . . . even Christina says so. And the truth is you don't want to go see them, or you would. They bore hell out of you. You don't care to hear their stories, and their cheapness embarrasses you. Fine. That's fine. But you can just stop blaming me for keeping you from visiting."

"I never told them you wouldn't let me go see them."

"Of course, you didn't. You're too clever for that. You just *imply* I won't let you go. If the truth were known, you do *exactly* as you please and *nothing* more."

"Oh, do I?"

"You're damned right you do. One of these days, I'll tell your precious guardians how I practically beg you to go see them and you won't do it."

"Forget my family. That's not the point. I don't want to leave this community. I want our children to go to the Catholic school here as I did."

"I don't see that we have a choice. You might as well start looking for a house for us in Maplewood. We can sell this place, and we should make money on it."

"Joan, I'm not moving!"

Three days later, when he came home, his eyes shone with excitement. He'd found a small acreage a short distance from Maplewood.

"We'll go see it after dinner."

"How did you ever find it?"

"I've been watching it for some time. The owner is one of my best customers. He finally put the house up for sale this week. There are seventeen acres—it's on a paved road. I think you'll like it, Joan."

She loved it. The house wasn't as large as the old one, but there were four bedrooms, a laundry room with a cement floor, and a place for her canned fruit. Venetian blinds on the windows and a beautiful Axminster rug over the wood floor made the living room warm and inviting. The house seemed in excellent condition and looked like it would be warm in winter. The yard looked good. The outbuildings and house needed painting. The owners were asking twelve thousand dollars for the property.

"Can you believe it, Joe?"

"Joan, everything is always a big bargain to you."

"Isn't it? Isn't seventeen acres and a four-bedroom house a bargain? For twelve thousand dollars?"

"Well, yes . . . it is."

"Well, yes . . . but you don't have to act like it."

"When someone tells you what they want for something, no matter what it is, you should always act like the price is too high," Joe said.

"Will that cause them to change it?"

"Sometimes. Not always, but sometimes."

"OK—I'm sorry, Joe."

"The owners will give us a month to come up with the down payment. We've got to sell our place by then."

"That shouldn't be hard to do," she said enthusiastically. "Everything is in bloom, and the grass is nice and green, and it looks good. I think we should sell it in pieces. The farmer in the rear might buy the back field . . . He's asked before, you know. He could pay cash. Then we'd still have the front acreage, and I think we could get what we paid for the whole place from that part of it."

Joe's ears perked up. He was always interested when they discussed money. The prospect of making a profit on the farm pleased him immensely. Joan didn't mention the fact that even if they could make a profit on the old place, the new one would still cost more than they would get from the sales.

"Joan, we really get along well in business, don't we?"

"That's the only place we get along, and that is because I'm smarter than you and also because you're a greedy bastard."

Joe promised he'd build a fence for the children. Joan wasn't used to living so near a road. Neither were the children. Joan worried that they'd wander onto the pavement where cars roared by. They were equidistant between two taverns. And on the only bad curve on the road. The taverns were two miles apart. In traveling between them, late and drunk drivers found the curve difficult to negotiate. They crashed. A fence seemed necessary. Joan was glad it was a paved road. She was tired of winter's muddy and summer's dusty dirt and gravel roads.

Selling the farm in St. Eames turned out to be simple. So simple they were sorry they hadn't asked a higher price. Even so, they were satisfied, and the new owner was delighted. He'd come from California, and to have an acreage and a house (even though it wasn't much) for what he would have to pay for a lot in California delighted him and his family. The neighbor bought the back field, and everything was in order in time for them to buy the new place before the thirty days were up.

They stopped in at Joe's family on the way home from talking to the owners of the new place. Joe wanted to talk to his uncle, and it seemed a good time to stop, since they had the luxury of a babysitter.

The yard light illuminated a sagging barn, garage, and grape arbor, a rotting fence, and broken back steps. The interior of the house matched the exterior. Awful. It was just awful. Chipped metal cabinets in the kitchen, limp faded curtains on dirty windows with dusty plants on sills, and old linoleum tile on the floor made the small room seem even drearier than Joan remembered it had been the first time she'd seen the room and gone into shock. Antlers decorated the living room. Joe's uncle had two interests in the world—killing and killing.

Joe's family lived through the Depression on the farm. Things had been so tough, they'd never come out of what became their private depression. Mr. Schultz thought he had to kill all the meat for the family. They seldom slaughtered their own beef, like other farm families. They hunted deer and elk and anything that moved and was edible.

The uncomfortable, hard, tattered furniture in the harshly lit living room with the austere walls invariably sent a shudder through Joan. The house reflected the people who lived in it. Every house does.

Joe's family seemed mean and spiteful to Joan. They loved to whisper and laugh about this one or that one in the community. They were always careful not to say too much in front of Joan. They still didn't fully trust her, and she hoped they never would. She knew she'd have to hit certain lows to make these people like her. Joe's aunt was a particularly bland person, completely overshadowed by his domineering uncle. Before she ever expressed an opinion, she looked at the old man to see if she had his permission to speak. Years of conditioning made her sensitive to him, and if he gave his signal, she immediately started talking . . . or stopped.

According to the Schultzes, the world was going to hell. They hated drunks and Protestants, most of their neighbors, and a lot of their relatives. The fact that they didn't like her didn't stop Joan from stating her views. Whenever she disagreed with them, the old man glared and spattered. Joe gulped and stammered. His aunt looked like she wanted her to disappear. The older woman's hands did a dance on her cheeks. They didn't visit very often, but it was always too often for Joan.

The old man was right about one thing. He predicted the economy of the country was going to hell long before it started going to hell. He knew where to get the best buys on everything—which was good—and he never bought anything that wasn't marked down in some manner.

They were provincial and Catholic, and there wasn't a Christian in the immediate family. Except John. To Joan, John could do no wrong.

This evening, Joan refused to get into an argument with the autocratic old bastard. He looked at her quizzically when it finally dawned on him an hour after they were in the house that she was particularly quiet. She was tired, and the orgy of hunting tales bored her to tears and made her feel bad as she heard about the kills and then found her eyes locked with the eyes of the stuffed elk over the living room rocker.

Joe liked to kill animals too. Once in a while, Joan was afraid he might like to kill her. Not often, though. They had a dog when they'd lived in her parents' house. It was a darling little cocker. They'd had it for about a month when suddenly, for no reason, it stopped eating. She put out food for it for three days before Joe told her the dog had had an accident.

"What happened to it?"

"It ran into a board."

Now sitting in this drab house listening to the detailed plotting of the next big kill and looking deeply into the glass eyes of the elk on the wall, Joan felt a sweep of revulsion.

"What's the matter with you?" Joe asked.

"It seems a shame for you men to enjoy killing so much."

"Who said we enjoyed killing?"

"Don't you?"

"No. We just like to hunt."

"And not kill anything?"

"We don't go hunting to kill animals. We go hunting for the sport and for the meat. The fact that we kill something is incidental."

"Not to the animal, Joe. I was reared on illegal venison. Everyone in camp lived on it. There was always an illegal buck cooling in some woodshed . . . We lived a long way from the store, and that was the way it was. And we needed the meat."

"But it's wrong for us to kill deer?"

"It's wrong for you to *enjoy* killing deer."

"We don't."

It was futile arguing with them. She'd found that out many times before. She rose to leave. Then she stood for half an hour while she waited for Joe to finish talking with his uncle. The two men kept remembering things they wanted to tell the other. She suppressed a yawn. She knew if she sat down again, they wouldn't leave for hours.

The minute they were on their way home, he impatiently asked, "Did you have to argue with Uncle?"

"Did he have to argue with me?"

"Honestly, Joan, I don't know why you insist on making them dislike you."

"Joe, I don't insist. They just do."

"Very funny."

"Why don't you go visit them by yourself? You know it always ends up this way."

"But does it have to?"

"Apparently. Accept the fact that I just don't get along with them."

"Why don't you like them?"

"I think part of the reason is the way they treated you when you were a child."

"What do you mean?"

"You told me how hard they made you work when you were a little boy. How they dropped you off in the fields in the early morning and didn't come for you until late in the day. And how they never let you spend the money you earned and how they used it for tuition . . . you know, all the things you told me."

"Well . . ."

"Look, I wouldn't have known how lousy they were if you hadn't told me. But the reason we don't get along is they don't understand me. I may as well have come from Mars. You don't either. Let's drop the whole thing."

Joe pulled to the side of the road. The headlights picked up big trees almost out of the light's path. Shrubs and bushes moved in rhythm with the wind.

"Joan, don't you love me at all?"

"Not really."

"Did you ever?"

"Probably not."

He pulled onto the road. Neither spoke the rest of the way home. When they were in bed, Joan thought over the conversation. *Probably not. Probably not.*

She hadn't really loved him, and she knew he knew it. She probably never would. She tried. She was pleasant to him most of the time. Until he made her so angry, she exploded—when he wouldn't fix something important or said he'd do something and then never did it. Most of the time, they treated each other with a certain courtesy. Sometimes she thought she should have the word *sorry* printed on a T-shirt and wear it all the time. She apologized to him often, and he made her feel so *wrong* all the time. Sorry. Sorry. Sorry. Jesus, she was sorry. She was especially sorry she had married him.

One of the rules of the Church at that time was that while separation and divorce were allowed, there could never be a remarriage that would have the blessings of the church. Marriage was forever. Whenever Joan thought of it, she shuddered. The idea of spending the rest of her life with Joe, with a man she could never please and who seldom pleased her, was dismal.

One day she found a poem that summed up the way she felt. It was called the "Three Worst Things."

To try to sleep and sleep not.

To want for one who comes not.

To try to please and please not.

## Chapter 14

They'd lived in St. Eames for six years. During that time, they'd collected a variety of belongings—a cow, a horse, some chickens, three new babies, and a fourth one on the way. Joan had no time to think, much less worry, about how things were between her and Joe. The move demanded preparation. Billing and income tax reports waited on the desk. Four of the children came down with hard measles. The baby had them the month before. Joan was eight months pregnant when the children got sick. She struggled to take care of them. They had high fevers and runny noses, and the measles welts merged and formed one large welt. The children were so sick, they couldn't blow their own noses. They were all upstairs, and Joan had to carry the two younger ones to the bathroom. The older children could walk with assistance. They were terribly sick. Joe worked late every night. Joan's sense of loneliness and isolation grew stronger.

By the time the first pangs of labor began, Joan was near exhaustion. She went to the hospital and gave birth to a skinny little girl whom they named Kit. Kit fit right in with the rest of the litter. Carol was three when she was born; Emily, two; Jackie, one. Sarah, seven, loved her sisters. Stan disliked them. He wanted a brother.

Two weeks later, they moved. They couldn't believe what they had accumulated. It didn't take long for everything to be put away and the curtains hung, and, in general, for order to reign. The house soon seemed like home. Joan had no regrets about leaving the old cold house. She often thought maybe she should have lit a match to it when they moved. That way she'd save another family from the miserable monster. But it was a roof over the new family's head, and maybe they would be more concerned about their comfort that Joe had been about theirs.

Joan vowed she would never be cold again . . . if she could help it. When winter approached and the electric sideboards proved inadequate, she made arrangements for an electric furnace to be installed. Joe protested. More and more Joan went ahead and did what needed to be done. She found if she waited for Joe to agree—it took forever. His first answer was *no*. The next thing was—how much? Too much. And never the right time.

She went ahead and did things without discussing them with him. It was better that way. She didn't have to hassle, and he didn't have to worry. And they needed so many things. She took care of the checkbook for the family and the business. She paid all bills and managed the money. Joe hated that chore, so it suited him fine. He never liked figures, and when he came home at night after a hard day's work, all he wanted to do was eat, read the paper, and go to sleep.

It didn't take them long to get acquainted around Maplewood. They attended the parish dinner (which Joan loved) and met some very nice people there. Joe wasn't too social, but Joan enjoyed meeting the women, though she was rather antisocial too. One day shortly after they moved into the house, two ladies came to visit. They represented the church and wanted to welcome the new family into the community. One of the ladies was tall and had the longest neck Joan had ever seen. The other was short and dumpy. They craned their long and short necks to see the house. Joan would have taken them on a tour, but they were so obviously snoopers, she decided against it. They left.

They lived in the house at West Maplewood and were happy there. Except for the toilet. It overflowed with regularity. Roses were planted near the drive, and the lawn was fertilized and mowed and mowed and mowed. Stan usually did it—or Joan. Joe did it twice in all the time they lived there. Somehow, he thought he had done it all the time. He was busy with the business, which prospered. He spent most of his time hauling scrap iron from the dump. Joan spent most of her time being pregnant. The rooms seemed smaller as the children grew and multiplied. Matt was born the first year there; Barbara, the second; Jean, the third.

Two months after they purchased the new route, and when they were just getting acquainted with the area, an announcement was made in the largest newspaper in the state—a new retirement development would be built in the city limits of Maplewood. They didn't know it then, but eventually, the development would swell to over two thousand units. Older people came from all over the United States to live in little houses with little rooms, little lawns, and little maintenance.

An age limitation resulted in an almost no-child development. Few dogs were fortunate enough to find eager owners. With few dogs and few children (if any), the development became a sort of paradise for older people. Living was easy, and for the first time in most of their busy lives, they could do as they pleased.

It also pleased Joe and Joan. They realized immediately what the community would do for them in terms of making their route valuable. When they first bought the route from Wayne, they had to hire one man to run the whole thing. With the beginning of construction and continuing to the present, they had had to add men regularly.

Construction began almost immediately on the project. The roads curved and wandered through the old white land that had previously grown oats. Pavement and curbing, fire hydrants, and electric poles stood amid mounds of dirt that turned to tons of mud when it rained. The first little houses sprang up like asparagus. Everyone was surprised by their apparent quality. Though modest in size and similar in design, each residence sported an individualized color scheme and landscape. Joe was amazed at the beauty of the flowers from spring to fall.

Membership in the clubhouse automatically came with the purchase of a lot. The structure resembled a colonial mansion and had game rooms, a golf shop, a coffee shop, and a large area for meetings and card parties. It was situated so that a sliding glass door led from the coffee shop onto the golf course. In spite of broken windows, these lots were favored.

Competition soon set in and found its expression by neighbor rivaling neighbor with the greenest lawn and the brightest blooms. Small flowering trees lined the streets. Residents of the development loved it, unless they hated it; then they left—quickly. Socializing became a big thing. They played cards, late, at different houses, most of which had been completely furnished with new beautiful furniture or fine old antiques. Joe and Joan liked to drive through the community at night. New furniture, new lighting fixtures, and newly cleaned glass windows made the houses seem like miniature magic doll houses.

The people came to be some of Joe's best customers. They were considerate. They hardly ever complained, though Joe gave them little to complain about. He was serious about his business and gave the very best service in the country. He went to great lengths to keep the people on all his routes happy. Occasionally, he stuck a carrying can in the back of their nine-passenger station wagon (which now held eleven) late at night to pick up a customer he had missed.

The best part about the new people was the way they paid their bills. Unlike a lot of young people, paying bills was the first thing they did at the beginning of each month. They waited for Joe to come. If they missed him one week, they'd be waiting the next. If they hadn't paid by the third week, they usually thought they had. This led to problems. They were sure they paid. Months seem to come around with surprising rapidity. They always paid the first of the month, didn't they? Joe didn't lose much, but he always knew when one of his customers wasn't out to pay on the usual day—there would be sticky problems.

Along with the housing project came national business interests. Motels, shopping centers, nursing homes, banks, service stations, restaurants, and other small businesses opened. The area became the fastest growing in the state.

A lot of the people in the project were retired and living on modest incomes of pensions and/or social security. It was even said that some of the widows and widowers lived together without being married because if they married, they might lose their pensions. A few of the residents were wealthy, but they were in the minority. Most of the people were modest people of modest means.

Maplewood soon felt the brunt of their voting power. Coupled with the apathy of the community as a whole, and the large turnout of voters from the project, school elections began to be defeated. The project voters formed a bloc of power that simply controlled not only the school elections but the city elections as well. Anything that called for an expenditure of funds was quickly voted down.

The enthusiasm with which the people welcomed the newcomers to the area turned to bitterness. The unwillingness of the older people to support the schools and the city budget became an embarrassment to the community. The older people were among the first in the nation to be concerned with inflation. The townspeople resented their attitude. A coolness soon developed between them. They destroyed the community with their votes, and every professional office in the area was filled with silver-haired men and women. When they weren't maintaining themselves, they were out in the streets learning to ride bicycles. Many a marcelled matron, attired in pants for the first time in her life, found a new challenge in riding a bicycle.

Trailers and boats were other kinds of toys these people purchased. At one end of the golf course acreage was set aside for recreation vehicles. It was soon filled with every imaginable make and model. They went boating and camping, and went to the city for symphonies and opera. They went crabbing and fishing and clamming at the coast. They took chartered bus trips. They looked happy. Shouldn't they have been?

Joan met Dora Denton at her mother's house. She liked her immediately. Dora and her husband, Art, were relative newcomers to the area. They'd moved from California. Art had been promised a job as manager of a tire store. Six months after they moved, the store went into bankruptcy. Since then, Art had searched for work and did find temporary employment in a service station. It didn't last long. Dora worked in a local bakery in order to make ends meet. They had five girls who were being taken care of by their father.

Joan felt a bond with the nice-looking woman. The situation reminded her of when they were living over the tavern. If she closed her eyes, she still could hear the song that made the whole building reverberate as it played all night . . . after night . . . after night—"Cross over the Bridge."

They *crossed over the bridge*. It had taken time, energy, and untold patience. Joan wanted things to be better for Dora and Art. She took one look at Art and insisted Joe hire him. He was tall, neat, lean, and hard, and had a winning way about him. He also enjoyed working. He proved to be one of the best men they employed.

Somehow, they'd inherited the county dump lease along with the sale from Wayne. The dump was a mile down a dirty, dusty lane. The closest house was a safe distance away. (The odor didn't usually drift that far.) The county leased the dump and all its problems to Joe. They paid him a small subsidy. In return, he had to maintain the dump, hire a man, and suffer. He suffered because he was a perfectionist. He couldn't stand to have anything out of order . . . even garbage.

In earlier years, garbage was burned each evening. Joe would have liked that solution. It was neat . . . and clean. Now because of environmental factors, a big Caterpillar (Cat) tractor covered the garbage with dirt at the end of each day. That was fine when it didn't rain, or if the Cat didn't break down. It didn't break down too often, but when it did, it was expensive to fix. Joe held his breath whenever he went to the dump until he saw the metal monster working.

Their state was famous for its rain. The water table was so high at the dump grounds that sometimes several days would pass before the Cat could get unmired enough to cover the garbage with mud. Then things were a mess . . . and Joe would be very depressed. The county commissioners were depressed too. Every person in the county old enough to dial a phone . . . did so . . . or so it seemed. They called the commissioners to complain. The commissioners called Joe. Joe couldn't call anyone. *He* was *it*. It was his garbage. His alone . . . and half Joan's.

There were days when Joe wanted to tell the county commissioners to take the dump and shove it—uncovered or covered. Prudence kept him from it. That and the fact that he got to dump free.

"What do you mean free? Last year it cost you over five thousand dollars just to maintain the dump." Joan hated the dump.

"Look, Joan, our expenses were high because of the unusual breakdowns. We had to have the pits dug. We'll be using them soon. Next year, we should come out a lot better. I don't want to turn it back to the county. The way the routes are growing, someday it will pay to have kept it."

"I suppose you're right, but if the day ever comes when a profit is shown, the county will probably decide to run it themselves."

He knew she might be right. Still it was a chance he'd have to take. In the meantime, he hoped no fires broke out under the packed garbage. When the burning of garbage had been officially stopped in the county, there had been flagrant violations of the burning code. One fellow had five fires burning brightly at his dump. Lightning. Another said *someone* had lit his dump. The accident coincided with the dumping of an unusual amount of lumber trimmings from a trailer manufacturing plant.

Joe was honest. Honest Joe. He would not have considered anything devious. However, there had been three unexplained fires. Maybe hot ashes. Maybe a carelessly thrown cigarette. The real danger . . . and constant threat . . . was spontaneous combustion. A fire could start deep underground and burn for months before breaking out on the surface sometimes thousands of yards from the source.

Joe had good friends in the fire department. None of the firemen enjoyed putting out a dump fire, but they understood his problem, and they always cooperated. Joe usually bought a few cases of beer for them because he appreciated their help so much.

There were other problems at the dump. People. Unless someone was right there, they'd dump their garbage in the middle of the road, under a tree, or wherever it was convenient for them. Joe left strict orders with the caretaker to keep all children in the car. If he didn't watch carefully, children and parents clambered through the garbage, broken glass, nails, wire, and all, like people possessed, in their search for treasure.

Next Wednesday was dump inspection. Joe's dump had been chosen. A group of state, county, and local officials were to arrive at eight thirty in the morning. It was a mess. The caretaker had been on one of his famous drunks. He always had a group of "friends" lounging around drinking and visiting at the dump. Joe didn't like it, but there wasn't much he could do about it. He could fire the man, but he liked Oscar, and it was harder than hell to find someone who would work at the dump.

Oscar's friends were a snaggletoothed, baggy suited, unshaven, soddenly happy group. They loved Joe. And they were loyal to him and each other. Whenever one of them had an extra dollar, he would buy a jug of wine and happily share it with his friends.

They always wanted Joe to have a drink with them. They all drank from a common bottle. It turned Joe's stomach. He simply couldn't bring himself to drink with them. He didn't like to hurt their feelings, but he just—couldn't.

One day early in the morning after his first load, he approached the happy group. They offered him a drink. Oscar had just opened a full bottle of wine. Joe was relieved . . . At last he didn't have to say *no*. He took a big drink.

"Say, that's good wine."

The motley group looked pleased. Smiles broke out on their craggy worn faces. They were proud.

"Know where we got that?" Oscar laughed.

"No, where?"

"We found a little wine in all those bottles over there. We put all the snipes together and got a full bottle."

"That's wonderful," Joe said. He left quickly and didn't get sick until he was out of sight around the corner.

Joe didn't have much time to get the dump in order. He'd built a fence to keep the motors and scrap metals hidden. The fence was painted a dark green to match the caretaker's shack. In the front of the fence, shrubs that had been thrown away were planted. Oscar didn't like to put things behind the fence. He had arranged a display of dump treasures, broken bicycles, lawnmowers, baby buggies, shovels, tools, and many other items. The display was right in front of the shrubs. Joe told him nearly every day to get rid of the stuff, but Oscar couldn't bear to throw anything away that was *any* good. Also, he kept the money from the sale of his treasures, so they had to be displayed to advantage.

Joe finished cleaning the dump at eleven o'clock, Tuesday night. Even in the dark it looked neat. He hated to think of anyone dumping any more garbage at the dump . . . and messing it up. He locked the gate, went home, took a much-needed shower, and crawled into his wonderful soft bed. Before he went blissfully to sleep, he set the alarm for five thirty. He had a drop box to pick up in the morning before he could play host to the visiting dignitaries at the dump at eight.

When he arrived home after dumping the box, Joan told him Mr. Crawford, who was in charge of the tour, called and postponed the inspection until the next Wednesday. By then, Joe knew, the dump would have to be cleaned all over again.

# Chapter 15

Monday morning blues affected Joe too. Usually a truck wouldn't start. Plan A was then set into motion. Joan sat in the truck to be started. Joe fastened a long chain to the special hooks he had installed on all his trucks. He towed her after giving specific instructions.

"Turn on the key and leave the truck in gear." Simple.

Then he'd get in his truck and start pulling. Joan hated to help him start a truck. She always did something wrong.

The two trucks started rolling . . . Joe's straining in front and Joan's rattling behind. The chain's tension between the two trucks relaxed, then tightened, each time sending Joan's truck lurching and her teeth rattling. Pull. Lurch. Bump. Jerk. Shit. Stop!

"What's the matter?" Joe's hysterical voice called. He tended to get hysterical—so easily.

"How long am I supposed to keep my foot on the brake?"

"Why did you have your foot on the brake?"

"So I wouldn't hit you."

"Let's try again. Please. Just take it easy and do as I tell you."

"But you don't tell me everything I should do."

"You are supposed to know *something*."

"You know I don't know anything about starting a bastardly truck! And I never want to learn! I'm going to call Daddy. He'll help you."

"No. Joan . . . we can start it."

"All right, I'll try. But don't you dare yell at me again."

On the fifth try, the truck would usually start. Joan aged five years each time a truck wouldn't start, and Joe's hair grayed—just a little.

If the trucks all started and there were no dead batteries, there was usually at least one flat tire. When that happened, the tire truck would be late, the men on the truck behind schedule, and Joan got a lot of anxious telephone calls. People on the routes were so used to having excellent punctual service that if one truck was late, they started calling.

Ring. Ring. Ring.

"Ace Garbage Service."

"This is Mrs. Spooner. My garbage was missed."

"When were you supposed to be picked up?"

"They pick up at ten today, Tuesday."

Joan noted that it was ten minutes until eleven. "One of the trucks had a flat tire and is running late. They'll be there shortly."

"Oh. All right. Thank you."

"You're welcome. Good-bye."

Ring. Ring. Ring. Ring.

There were two phones in the kitchen. The one near the sink was for business calls only; the one on the desk for family use. One rang, then the other . . . all the time. Sometimes they seemed to be trying to call each other. Joan soon developed a hatred for *any* phone. Customers called to complain, to sign up for service, to explain, to say they were going away, to announce their return, to quit, to question, or to tell Joe they had lost something in the garbage. Diamond rings were missing, or money, clothing, important papers, and other items of value. Joe spent many nights working until dawn to retrieve some of these valuables. He or the driver could usually figure out about where in the truck the missing treasure/s might be. Then it was a matter of carefully sifting through all the spoiled, smelly material until *success!*

It was nearly impossible for her to leave the kitchen. *My god,* she thought, *I'm a slave to the telephone.* And she was. The family phone rang for the children, for Joe, and for her. These calls were personal. She was the only one who received business calls on the family phone. Church business. She was thirty-three before she learned how to say *no*. They wanted her to bake four dozen cookies for the millionth parish baked goods sale. *No.* She said *no.* She'd never considered saying *no* before. The day she did, she felt good. She couldn't bake cookies for the church when she didn't bake cookies for her own family. No way.

Every garbageman in the world knows the worst possible thing that can happen is . . . snow. Joe wasn't a particularly religious man, but whenever it looked as though it might snow, he got down on his knees and prayed against it. He had to pray hard because little boys, with sleds and mittens waiting, were doing their best to intercept and cancel out his prayers.

When it did snow, roads were hidden and holes in backyards were filled. Also covered were bicycles, rakes, and other equally dangerous hazards. Walking was difficult. Carrying a full garbage can while walking was nearly impossible. Some of Joe's customers were very angry if *their* garbage wasn't picked up on time. They couldn't make it to work, but they certainly expected Joe and his men to be on the job. Work schedules geared to long summer days had to be readjusted to compensate for winter's short days and, finally, the snow. Work was lighter during the winter, but there were so many problems that everyone agreed they preferred the hot summer days with all the canning peels to the ice and snow of winter. At least they did until it was.

When the weather cleared, one of the drivers called in sick. Joe would have to run his route. Joe's back hurt. He'd lifted something wrong and could hardly bend over. It would be tortuous to climb in and out of the truck.

"If I had someone to drive, I could pick up the cans."

"Joe, I can drive."

"No, Joan. I'll find somebody else."

"There isn't anybody else. I'll call Mrs. Jamison and ask her to babysit."

"I can't let you drive a garbage truck."

"Why not? It's a hell of a lot easier than doing housework, and not half as boring."

Joan stopped the truck and helped Joe out.

"Are you sure you can work?"

"I'll go slow. I'll be all right if I don't have to get in and out of the truck."

Joan winced as she saw him approach the first can. Carefully and slowly and painfully, he raised the can to his shoulder. He made it. OK. Good. Now walk with it to the truck. Oh.

A car came around the corner. The man driving it nearly crashed into her when he saw a woman at the wheel. *For god's sake*, thought Joan, *why do men think women are only for cleaning and cooking and bearing children? Women can do lots of other things.*

The day went by slowly. Joan's legs were getting tired. The pedals on the truck were made for longer and stronger legs. Joe walked better. He straightened up about noon. *The work must be good for sore muscles*, thought Joan.

Every customer who saw Joan made the same original comment: "Who's your new helper? Ha-ha-ha! *I think I'll give the next son of a bitch who says that the finger*, thought Joan. But she didn't. She was a lady.

Efficiency was very important on the routes. Too large, they could kill men. Too small, the salary paid might be wasted in terms of work produced. It was like having three people in a single bed or one in a king-size one. Balance. That was what was necessary, and so seldom found. Joe hated to hire new help for that reason. He had convinced himself for so long the only way to make the business pay was for him to do all the work himself. With the rapid growth of the area, it became impossible for him to do that, so men had to be hired. Still, he hated to hire one and resisted until absolutely necessary, and/or he got sick of Joan's nagging him. He missed the old days when he'd collect and cut and haul huge loads of iron into the scrap yard and return home with several hundred dollars in his hand. Gratifying. He now spent his time on the route.

Art Denton was soon placed in charge of the large Maplewood route, while Joe continued to manage his original area. One man was needed to work with Art. This job paid less because this man didn't have to be as responsible as Art, who did the driving and had to keep track of the on-scene business transactions of the route. This included keeping track of who was on vacation, who was stopping service, who had extra trash or specials, and where and how to find the cans. This information was kept on the route cards, which were three-by-five recipe cards and showed the relationship of one customer to the other—for instance, white house on corner next to blue house with white fence facing Third and Alder. It was a system many businesses with established routes used to ensure—that if the regular driver was indisposed, another driver could find the house and the can (in the case of the garbage business). It made work slow and tedious for the newcomer, but the job could be done. Joe had not had such a system for years and had spent many days on the route when he was terribly ill—flu, whatever. Joan nagged, but it did no good. He never had time to change his system.

When they took over the larger route, it was impossible for him to push others as he pushed himself, and so the new system was developed. And it did work.

The trucks were parked at the house, and whenever Joan saw Art's truck, she was pleased with the way he kept it. It was always freshly washed and clean and neat inside. It reflected Art. Joe's truck looked like a garbage truck inside the cab. Joan sighed. Often their car looked like a garbage truck too. They had had to buy the station wagon for space. Papers were thrown on the floor. Mud, dirt, fir needles, and lots of litter made the car a mess. Joan hated *anything* messy, but she was a lazy perfectionist. She loved neatness and cleanliness but didn't have the energy to keep the car clean. Some days she was simply happy that she'd managed to do everything she was supposed to do: cooking, cleaning, washing, ironing, billing, banking, answering calls, and all of the other necessary things she did.

Men came to the house looking for work from time to time. Joan sized them up and, when the need arose, remembered the most impressive candidate. She knew the litany:

"Joe, you can't go on working so hard. You aren't getting any rest. You've been late for dinner for ten years. There is no sense to it."

"I can do the work myself. We can't afford to hire anyone else."

"There is plenty of money coming in. We can't afford not to hire someone. You go around all the time walking sideways. Your back hurts you so much that you can't get up or down at times. You are working too hard."

"We can't afford to hire anyone."

Stalemate.

Anger. "How in the hell do you know what we can afford? You never look at the checkbook. You haven't the slightest idea where we are financially. You know nothing about whom we owe to or what we owe or what we owe it for."

"You write down everything at the beginning of the month, and you cross out items as they are paid. I know."

"You know my method, but how many times a year do you look at the books?"

"You tell me."

"Yes, I tell you. I tell you we need X dollars to clear the end of the month. You know absolutely nothing about this business."

"I know all I want to know. All I want to do is the work. You take care of the money."

"Jesus, when I think how hard I worked to get you to let me even open a statement when we first started in the business, maybe it's time you took over the management. You have no comprehension of our profits or losses."

"I know we can't afford to hire a man."

"That's my point. We *can* afford to hire a man. You're killing yourself off is just plain stupid. You enjoy getting sympathy from people. You love it when they say *poor Joe*. Shame on you!"

"How come when we need a new truck, all I hear is we can't afford it."

"We can't afford a new truck *and* a new man. Your back is hurting, and I think we have to have certain priorities. We'll be able to afford a new truck in a few months."

"If we hadn't bought that new station wagon, we could afford a truck now."

"Joe, you know we needed that station wagon because we'd outgrown our old car that was ready for complete collapse. I'm tired of arguing with you, you silly son of a bitch. If you want to break your back, go ahead."

"No, I'll hire someone, if you think we can afford it."

"We can."

"Who do you think we should hire?"

"There was a fellow here last week. His name is Bill Adams. He lives on a farm near here. I think you know his father, Ed. He said there were five boys in the family and that he was in the middle. He doesn't go to school, and he needs a job. He's tall and not too strong looking, but he seems nice and friendly. Shall I call him?"

"Oh, I don't know."

"I'm going to call him and ask him to come over. You can't go on like this much longer."

The young man came. He entered the kitchen a bit self-consciously and seemed ill at ease. Joe smiled at him and went into his manners act. He was pretty good at it. It made Joan sick. Sometimes he was just too phony.

The children peeked at the stranger and whispered and stayed to hear every word. They were beginning to act like a little flock of lambs. They giggled.

"You children be quiet while your father talks to Bill. Bill Adams, this is Stan and Sarah and Carol and Emily and Jackie and Kit and Matt and Barbara and Jean. Children, this is Bill Adams." They giggled. Stan hit Sarah, Sarah stepped on Carol, Carol tripped over Ann, Ann fell on Jackie, and Jackie pulled Kit down with her. Matt rushed at Barbara, and little Jean grabbed Stan. What fun!

Joan worked at not smiling. "You children must be quiet while your father talks to Bill."

They nodded their heads and tried to be quiet. The men talked for a time. Then Joe rose to his feet.

"When can you start?" he asked.

"Whenever you say."

"How about Monday? I'll show you what you need to know early in the morning before I go on my route. It's not too hard—what you need to know, I mean. The work is plenty hard. If it doesn't work out, we'll know soon enough."

"Mr. Schultz, I need the job, and I'm willing to work. I want to thank you for hiring me, and I'm going to try to do you a good job."

"Fine. I'll see you on Monday."

When Bill left, Joan clapped her hands. "I'm so pleased you liked him."

"Who said I liked him?"

"I don't know, you seemed to."

"He looked a little weak . . . and I don't know if I like his looks."

"Joe, must you?" She nodded toward the listening children.

He didn't get her message. He never got her message. He didn't see what he didn't want to see or hear what he didn't want to hear. He was selective. He often became so engrossed in what he was doing that he neither saw nor heard what was happening around him. Often she asked him questions directly, and he directly didn't answer. He lived in a world of his own, and there was no room in it for her or what she felt or thought.

"He might even be dishonest."

"Joe!"

# Chapter 16

A rash of shoplifting hit Maplewood about the same time it hit the rest of the nation if an adjustment was made for east-west movement. It caused a panic among the people in the parish, the community, and the school. A public meeting called to examine the issue and (hopefully) find solutions to the problem brought an unexpected crowd of hundreds to the gymnasium of the parish school.

Father Connelly brought the large, undisciplined group to order after waves of loud conversations broke through the assembly. Bib overalls mingled with business suits, high heels with tennis shoes, rollers with chignons... everyone was there. And they all wanted to be heard at once. Interruptions caused angry exchanges.

"Silence."

Catcalls, boos, chairs scraping, tempers hissing, and radiators banging echoed off the hard surfaces of the brightly lit gym. "Silence." Father Connelly, dressed in his long flowing black robe and standing on the raised platform in front of the horde, was as ineffective as a trout pole against a whale. "Silence. Silence. Please," he begged.

Mr. Hoard stepped forward. "Quiet!"

Silence.

Before the meeting, Father Connelly had provided all of the families in the parish with a questionnaire. He wanted to find out about the attitudes of the people. Joan clutched her paper as she waited for a chance to speak. The meeting was nearly over when it became apparent that Father Connelly wasn't going to ask for the questionnaires. Joan raised her hand.

"Yes, Joan."

"I have brought the questionnaire with me that you asked us to fill out, Father." *Is that me talking? My voice sounds like it's in the bottom of a barrel. My face must be red. It feels hot. God. I am shaking. This is ridiculous. Am I making sense?*

"Oh." He seemed surprised.

"Do you want me to read what I have written?" *Hands, stop shaking!*

"Are there any other questionnaires?"

No answer. Everyone waited expectantly as Joan, the only one who had returned the questionnaire, started to hand it to the priest.

"Go ahead and read your answers, Joan. I am very interested in them."

She began to read: "The answer to the first question is *no*. I don't believe a parent is responsible for seeing that a child does his homework. It is the child's responsibility, and it is a matter between the teacher and the child (unless the child is having unusual learning problems). Two, more homework will not solve the problem of keeping children busy so that they have no time to get into trouble. As it is now, each teacher feels he or she is the child's *only* teacher. The end result is that each gives a reasonable amount of homework, but the aggregate amount causes a terrible burden. Children have no time to play or think or do anything except schoolwork—or worry about doing it. The children simply are overloaded with homework. No homework is preferable to too much." An angry murmur surprised Joan.

She continued. "Three, the practice of grounding children is an unfair punishment. Not only does the child suffer in that he is unable to see and do new things and therefore has missed valuable opportunities, but he also may become resentful and unhappy. Four . . ." As Joan read on, her voice again sounded strange. *Echo. Shrill. Me?* She finished her list. An unfriendly silence enveloped her. She sat down, stunned at the reception.

When the meeting was over, Marlene Riggs rushed over to her. Joan stood. Others circled the two women. Marlene preened. "Joan, you're absolutely right about the homework. I wished you'd a said something about lying. My god, Calvin couldn't stop. Finally, Earl cured him."

Joan wished she'd shut up. She never liked to discuss anything in public. Firstborn ideas should be nurtured and not let die. Time. She liked to wait. Marlene was waiting. "Don't you want to know how?"

"I'll listen."

"It was simple. Earl caught him one day. He took him out and beat his butt."

"That's unfair. Children lie to protect themselves or because they have a hard time separating dreams from reality." Joan sounded offended.

"Beat their butts—that's the thing to do . . ."

Marlene stood too close to Joan. The smell of her perfume, too sweet, and her breath, too sour, almost gagged Joan. She edged toward the door.

Outside it was pouring rain. Rivers ran through the parking lot; little lakes with little waves glistened in the light from reflections of the house lights in the background. Joan made a run for her car. Once inside, she shook the rain from her coat and shivered, then started home. When she turned off the main road, her eyes sought familiar landmarks. Rain came even heavier now, making it difficult to see. As she passed the mailboxes, she began to think what a fool she'd made of herself that evening. She was embarrassed to think she'd said all that stuff. When would she learn to keep her mouth shut?

Joe would be furious. She wouldn't tell him . . . but he'd find out. Someone would tell him the whole story. Someone always would tell him the whole story—how she'd spoken her piece. She'd be in trouble. Again. Whenever they went to a meeting, he made sure she kept her mouth shut. When he wasn't with her, she said what she pleased. Tonight she felt the satisfaction of having said what she thought. It felt good.

The stale smell of their early spaghetti dinner hit her as she entered the house. "Whew," she said. Joe was asleep. It seemed lately he was either asleep or gone or mad. As she inched into bed, he stirred, reached for her, and smiled. She held her breath. The sleeping tiger turned.

"How was the meeting?" he whispered with eyes closed.

"Fine," she lied.

"Anything interesting happen?"

"No. Not really."

"Hummmmmmm."

"Joe, I've decided to take a class in public speaking."

"What are you talking about?" he growled.

"When I was in high school, I was so uninhibited. Do you remember the Sophomore Follies that I wrote, directed, and starred in? I wasn't a bit inhibited then. But now I am. I need to learn how to speak in public without feeling dumb and shaking and hearing my voice sound as though it belongs to someone else."

"Forget it."

"Why?"

"I don't want you flouncing off to a class."

"Oh, you're jealous . . . is that it?"

"Yes . . . that's it. I see how you look at other men and how they look at you. You think I don't see you . . . but I do. You're a flirt. You flirt with every man you see."

"That's not true."

"It is."

"What has that got to do with my taking a class?"

"You'd probably screw the teacher."

"Joe, that's a rotten thing to say. You know I've been faithful to you. I've never even looked at another man . . . let alone fucked one."

"Joan!"

"What is the difference between *fuck* and *screw*?"

"What you said is a filthy four-letter word."

"It's OK . . . we're alone. Nobody heard me."

"I just can't bear it," his voice sounded. *Think*.

"What can't you bear?"

"To have a wife who uses that kind of obscene language. I'll tell you something else... You who flip your ass around in front of other men... you're not going to a class or anywhere else."

She enrolled in an evening class at a college forty miles away. She thought it would be easy to take the class because most of the students were young, and she related to younger people. Sadly she found she was also inhibited in front of them. The instructor, a stocky man with a friendly face, dreamy dark-brown eyes, and a pleasant manner, asked each person to introduce himself. Joan felt her throat tighten when it was her turn. She hoped her nervousness was not apparent. She felt like a fool.

As soon as they finished with the introductions, the instructor put the class at ease. He told some interesting little stories about public speakers, gave them their book lists, and discussed the books individually. Finally, near the end of the time, he gave them their assignments for the next class.

Joan had fun in the class. She looked forward to the Wednesday nighttime. Her old self-confidence began to come back, and she was learning how to give a speech. She wore skirts to class. She was unaccustomed to wearing them, and they made her uncomfortable. When she gave a speech one night, the instructor called her attention to the way she stood... with legs wide apart. She usually wore pants and had for years, so she hardly knew how to stand like a lady with her knees together. The instructor pointed out that any strange stance, clothing, or mannerism called attention to the person and caused the audience to lose interest in what the person said. The class twittered.

The next week, Joan was ready.

"Are you ready with your speech, Mrs. Schultz?"

"Yes, I am." She took three deep breaths, then began. Everything shook—her legs, arms, hands, and back. Damn. Damn. Damn. How could something that so many people did with such ease be so painful to her? She tried to slow down. Then, sensing that she might be boring her audience, she speeded up. She was pleased with her speech and congratulated herself on it.

Speech: It falls on the shoulders of a small percentage of the population to create the miracle of making solid waste disappear. The time and space is right to make the population aware of a basic problem in our society, which requires the attention of everyone. The responsibility for the problem and the solution to it lies with all the people. Health, beauty, safety, energy, and monetary savings are all problems to be solved.

Garbage begins with a natural material that is refined, processed, manufactured, sold (or not), used (or not), and then thrown away. Only there is no *away*. Away does not exist.

In the United States of America—waste is king!

We are busy burying, burning, shredding, and mutilating millions of tons of material that should never have been produced in the first place. Americans spend $4 billion a year to collect and dispose of wastes. We throw away enough organic wastes to produce the energy equivalent of 80 million barrels of oil a year. That is $2.2 billion worth. We spend 9 percent of our grocery money on packages we throw out. We import 91 percent of our aluminum needs, then throw out more than one million tons annually, worth more than $400 million.

We, ancestors of immigrants, have learned the very worst from each other. We have learned to value the valueless, to waste our time, energy, and spirit so that we can *dispose* of approximately one-eighth of our gross national product each year. Used correctly, that vast pool of energy, spirit, time, and resources could better be spent to produce a richer life for all.

Government, private industry, and the public must recognize that with these problems . . . as with other related problems . . . *time is of the essence.*

Waste is death. The Chinese know this. The Russians know this. We do not.

Joan sighed. She had gotten through it. She looked at the teacher. He was looking at her with his mouth open.

"Is anything wrong?" she asked.

"No. I'm just very impressed with what you've said."

"About waste?"

"Yes. I didn't realize what a problem it is."

"That is the problem. No one *realizes* anything. They have to be buried in garbage before they *know* anything. In New York, kids play knee-deep in it. No one cares." She made a helpless gesture and cringed.

One night after class was over and the members had left, the instructor congratulated Joan on her progress. She told him how upset she had been at the beginning of the class. He seemed surprised. He told her no one else would have known it. That pleased her. She continued to improve and found that during her effort to become better at speaking in public, she also learned a lot doing research for the speeches.

"I'm buying two scooters," Joe announced.

"Are those the little things like golf carts?"

"Yeah, Murray. The route is growing so fast, I can't keep up with it. I've got enough trucks, but I need more help. I had a demonstration the other day. One of those scooters and a truck did one of the rural routes in three hours. With just a truck, it takes at least eight hours of hard work."

"Why do you need two scooters?"

"I'll use them with two different trucks."

"Oh."

The scooters arrived the next day. Joan invited Donna and Murray to dinner when she found out how interested Murray was in the scooters. After dinner, they went to inspect the new little three-wheeled vehicles.

"Hey, Joe, let's see if they work."

"I don't know, Murray."

"Come on, Joe. You and Joan take that one, and Donna and I will take this one."

"Oh, Joe, that sounds like fun. Let's do it!" Joan cried.

"OK. They're easy to drive."

"Let's go."

Honk. Honk.

"Joe, could we be arrested for driving these things downtown like this?"

Honk. Honk.

"No. It's OK. They're licensed."

Honk. Honk.

"This is fun. They ride pretty good, don't they?"

"Yeah. They're a little bumpy, but not bad."

Honk. Honk.

"Joe, is there some way you can get Murray to quit honking his horn? People are staring at us."

Honk. Honk.

"He's not hurting anything, Joan."

"I guess not."

Honk. Honk.

"Are you ready to go home?"

"Yes. That was fun."

"They do drive slow, don't they, Joan?"

"Yes. But we're almost home now."

"Are Murray and Donna still behind us?"

"I don't see them."

"We'd better go see what happened."

"What happened? Going too fast, weren't you?"

"I got over on the shoulder too far. Gee, Joe, I'm sorry."

"No sweat, Murray. Let's get it out of the ditch."
"Yeah, we can lift it."
"You ladies stand back."
"We can help."
"No, Murray and I can make it."
"Heave!"
"Gee, that came out of the ditch easy, didn't it?"
"Much damage?"
"Just the windshield."
"Oh!"

That little scooter started its life of service with a shattered windshield.

Honk. Honk.

Bill Adams collapsed into a chair in the kitchen. He looked all in. His face, hands, clothes, and shoes were dirty. Sweat dripped from his forehead. He smelled like a garbage truck.

"Sorry, Mrs. Schultz, I didn't know I was so dirty."

"That's OK. I can wash the chair and the floor. Just don't move around in the room, please, and next time you come into my house so dirty and with mud on your shoes . . . I'll kill you."

He looked at her in surprise, then smiled. "You sound like my mother."

She shook her head and gave him a quarter smile. "I'm not your mother. And it is obvious you were reared on a farm."

"I've got an uncle who washes his boots before he goes into the house." He shook his head in disgust.

"What's wrong with that?"

"Nothing, but he doesn't accomplish anything. He's always puttering around. It takes him hours just to feed a few chickens and an old sow."

"Seriously, Bill, how did your first day on the route go?"

"Not too bad. It is really a hard job, but I didn't mind the work. When I get used to it, I think I'll like it. Right now my shoulder hurts."

He pulled his shirt aside and looked at his shoulder. A big red welt had formed where the carrying can rested on his shoulder. "Ouch." He winced with pain as he gingerly touched the area.

"Maybe you could wear some kind of pad on your shoulder tomorrow. It won't be long until it won't hurt at all. You'll learn how to lift the can and how to walk with it in such a way that it will be easier to carry."

He looked at her with disbelief. Then he looked down at himself. "Boy, I really got dirty, didn't I?"

"I don't think you will after you learn how to do things." She noted the look of distaste on the usually neat and clean young man. "Joe always gets dirty, but my cousin Greg, the fellow we bought the original route from, always looked perfect. It amazed me."

Bill took his box in his lap and started going through the stubs.

"What do you want me to do with these?"

"Didn't Joe tell you?"

"No."

"Well, the bill that is sent out looks like this." She showed him the bill, a postcard with perforations on one side. "The customer tears off the stub and sends it back with the money. The stub has his name and address on it. If you get paid any money and they don't have a stub, you have to write down on a separate sheet of paper, which you'll have in your box, exactly how much you were paid and when and by whom. Don't forget to write down everything. That is the only record we have. Did Joe tell you about extra charges?"

"No."

"He should have." She shook her head and made a sound with her teeth. Joe was getting so careless. "Whenever you pick up anything that won't fit into your carrying can, you are to charge for it—that isn't quite right . . . What I mean is if you have to make a special trip to the truck, then you charge for it."

"How much?"

"It depends on how much extra there is and what it is. I think you'd better have Joe show you what he charges extra for. Anyway, you have to mark down what it is you pick up, where, and for whom."

"How do I know all that?"

"All of the information is on the route cards. They are in consecutive order. He showed you that, didn't he?"

"Yeah."

"He'd have had to or you wouldn't be finished with your route yet. Would you like a beer?"

"Boy, I sure would."

"I'll get it." She went to the refrigerator and brought back a cold bottle of beer. She tried to keep cold beer for the men during the hot summer days. They didn't drink on the job, but they enjoyed a cold beer when they were finished with the day's work. She looked at the tired man across the room from her. *He'll do,* she thought. *He has a nice manner and winning ways.* She noticed a twinkle in his eyes; though he'd probably worked harder this day than he'd ever worked before. She handed him the bottle and a glass. He shook his head at the glass, grasped the bottle, threw his head back, and glugged over half of it.

"Careful . . ."

"Ohhhh. Good." He wiped his mouth with his upper sleeve.

"Let's get back to the extra charges. Here on the route card, there is room for you to write the date and the amount of the extra. If the charge is unusual, mark down on a separate sheet of paper just what the extra is . . . like a mattress or a box of dishes or whatever. If the person isn't a customer and doesn't pay you on the spot, write down the name, address, amount, and what it is. OK?"

"All that?"

"We have to have a record of the charges or we can't send a bill."

She went on explaining things he was to do until she was sure he understood. If any mistakes were made at the beginning, they were magnified with time. She wanted him to start off thoroughly understanding what he was to do and why. Suddenly, the aroma of the roast in the oven pervaded the kitchen.

"Oh, dear, I hope I haven't burned the roast." She ran to the oven, checked the seared roast, and added water. Then she put some flour on the rack to cook. She added onions, carrots, and potatoes to the roast. Joe liked simple foods.

Bill rose. "I guess I'd better go home while I can still move. See you." He hobbled out the door.

"Good-bye."

When he left the house, he intended to go home, clean up, and collapse into bed. He'd gone home and showered, and when the telephone rang shortly after dinner and a friend's voice asked him to go for a ride, he said, "Sure." He got home at three o'clock.

His mother's shrill soprano stabbed into his sleep. *Damn that woman,* he thought. *Why does she have to scream?* But he knew any awakening this morning would be dreadful. His head throbbed, his muscles ached, and he cursed himself as he dressed in the cold dingy room. A bare lightbulb cast shadows on the faded cabbage rose wallpaper and the dark woodwork. He sat on the lumpy mattress and tied his shoes while he stared at the worn linoleum floor. Then he dressed as quickly as he could. He didn't want to lose his job. If things went well and he had a steady paycheck, he'd move out of the house. Some friends in town wanted him to move into an apartment with them. They had parties, and girls slept over. They had lots of fun. Not that he didn't have a good time . . . He just needed a place to operate.

His gray-haired mother in her bib apron and sturdy shoes clucked over him as he tried to eat a bowl of oatmeal. He hated oatmeal. He'd always hated it. He'd hated it for years, and for years she'd served it to him. Every time he'd eaten it, he'd told her he hated it. This day with aching arms, head, bones, and fingernails, he said nothing. Futilely, he hoped that if he ate the food, his stomach would stop churning. He'd been dumb to get drunk last night. Dumb.

"How did the job go, Billy?"

"Fine, Ma."

"Is Mr. Schultz easy to work for?"

"I don't know yet, Ma. I only saw him for a few minutes in the morning."

"You don't have to snap at me."

"Sorry, Ma."

"I just wanted to know how things went."

"They went just fine. Mrs. Schultz is a nice lady."

"Is she?"

"Yes, Ma, and she's got nice tits."

"Billy!"

"Sorry, Ma. I gotta go. See you."

"Oh, Billy, good-bye."

As soon as he left the house, he was ashamed of himself. *The old bag,* he thought. *She never could take a joke . . . Everything is always so serious.* Still he was sorry he'd been so mean to her, and he determined he'd be nicer.

Arriving at his truck at six thirty, he found the route box on the seat as promised. He was a little chilled, his head still hurt, and he wished to God the birds that chirped loudly in the trees overhead would shut up.

A paper clipped to the clipboard held messages for the day. There were three new customers on his route and some other changes to be made in the cards. He read the messages while the truck warmed up. Exhaust rose in a column in the cool air. Dew covered the window and the foliage around the parking area.

At last, the truck was ready, and so was he. He hoped. He backed the truck out of its place and eased it into first. He'd learned to drive when he was six, and when he was seven, he'd driven his father's tractor in the wheat. He loved to drive. He got to his first stop, let the motor idle, and set the hand brake. It seemed to him that the ground was a lot farther down today than it had been yesterday. He hit the ground and groaned. His hip sockets sent a stab of pain through him. Surprised, he moved with caution from then on. By the time he picked up his twentieth stop, his muscles and joints were warmed up, and he felt confident that if his head cleared, he might live through the day.

Getting used to mirrors on both sides of the cab proved difficult for him. He had very little visibility, and when he backed up, it was almost impossible to see. At one of his stops that afternoon, three little boys ran around his truck, laughing as they ran.

"Hey, you kids . . . get out of the way. I'm going to back up."

Two of the boys reluctantly did as they were told. The third was not in sight. Bill uneasily idled the truck for a few seconds, then decided to back. Just as he was ready to roll, he thought better of it, put the motor in neutral, set the brake, climbed down, and went around the back of the truck. There hiding behind the right wheel was the child. Bill was furious. "Where do you live?" he demanded.

The child, suddenly afraid and not understanding that the game was over, didn't answer.

Bill grabbed him by the shirt. He shook him. "Tell me where you live."

The child pointed to a house on the other side of the street.

"Come with me," Bill commanded.

He walked swiftly, half dragging the boy behind. The other two boys followed, eager to see what would happen next and ready to run if necessary.

The child's mother paled when Bill told her what had happened. "Oh god, he could have been run over."

The child began to cry. Bill walked away, assured that the woman would be watching for him and would keep the child away from his truck in the future.

He walked around the truck to make sure there were no other children playing near it. Then he climbed into the cab. He started shaking as he put the truck into reverse. What could have happened, and very nearly did, would be hard for him to forget. He'd been lucky, and he knew it. The child's mother knew it too. *Somehow*, Bill thought, *the kid must know it too.*

By the time he picked up the last can, he was ready to collapse. It was late, and he still had to unload. He hurried to the dump. The big truck groaned under the heavy load. He swung the vehicle into position, then opened the back doors. He climbed back into the cab and worked the levers while backing slowly and intermittently jabbing on the brakes to dislodge any garbage that had hung up. He pulled forward and saw that a mass was caught. He ran the huge cylinder forward, then reversed it as he backed and again jabbed at his brakes. Several times. He heard the mass give way. Lowering the bed, he pulled the truck forward, jumped down, and closed the back doors. He was finished. It was getting dark.

He drove down the lane and into the parking area, parking near the gas tank. Joan came out to the house as he started to fill the truck. "Hello, Mrs. Schultz."

"Hi. We'll be seeing a lot of each other. Call me Joan . . . if you like. Can I take the box in for you?"

"Thanks, but I'd like to go over a couple of things to make sure I wrote everything down. I'll bring it in, in a minute."

"OK." She turned and started toward the house.

"It's none of my business, but isn't this gas tank awfully close to the house?"

"You and I are the only ones who think so. I've been nagging Joe for a long time to have it moved. It holds four hundred gallons of gas and could explode . . . I think . . . could it? Anyway, I wish he would move it."

"It does seem dangerous . . . and I can't believe you'd nag your husband," he laughed a happy laugh.

"I'm the world's greatest nagger . . . and, believe me, I have lots to nag about." She didn't laugh. The serious tone of her voice surprised him. He knew lots of women who nagged their husbands. Few admitted it.

He finished gassing the truck, then followed Joan to the house. He noticed her good strong stride as she moved in front of him. She walked quickly and, once inside the kitchen, grabbed some newspapers and spread them on a chair for him.

"Would you like some dinner? You must be starved." She watched him, and his weak protestations were made insignificant by the anticipatory look in his eyes. He hadn't eaten lunch, and he was very hungry.

"Don't be bashful. You're welcome. Joe hasn't come in yet, and dinner is still in the oven. There's plenty. I always cook too much. You can wash up in the blue bathroom down the hall if you'd like."

"I really would like that."

"Good."

Joan loved to cook, but more than she loved to cook, she loved to watch a hungry man enjoy her food. She and Joe had never come to terms about food. She loved Italian cooking with lots of garlic, tomatoes in sauce, and spices. He liked meat and potatoes. Plain and simple.

She'd just dished up Bill's dinner when she heard Joe's truck come in. In a few minutes, he joined them in the kitchen. Bill wondered what Joe thought of him eating dinner at his table, but Joe seemed to expect it. *Are we brothers under the skin? Are all garbagemen brothers? It's a terrible job. Maybe there's sympathy and empathy for each other because it's a kind of shared misery*, thought Bill.

"Are you ready to eat?"

Joe hurried to the desk. "Let me write down a message first."

"Fine."

While she waited for him to finish his business, she thought about all the times he refused to come to dinner until his work was finished. She remembered the time in St. Eames when he'd been painting the house. She'd cooked a big dinner of fried chicken, buttermilk rolls, vegetables, mashed potatoes, gravy, and a green salad. She'd called him when it was ready. He'd refused to come until he was finished with his work and the dinner was cold.

"You and your goddamned dinners," he'd said in a fit of rage. She'd heard the words often in the last few years.

Bill finished eating and turned his attention to his box. He went through the stubs for a few minutes and then wearily rose, thanked Joan (again) for dinner, said good night, and left.

Joe finished his bookwork. "Let me get my shower before I eat."

"Fine."

She turned off the oven and sat down at the desk. Whenever she had extra time, she busied herself with the bills. Every minute she wasn't working at some chore, she made out bills. She was nearly finished with them this month, and she looked forward to having them in the mail. There was a period after the bills were first sent out when she was busy answering the phone. After that initial period, there was about a full week when there was little banking or business to do. She looked forward to that brief time.

"I'm ready to eat," Joe said as she sat down at the table.

"Fine."

She watched in fascination as he bolted his food. On those rare occasions when he did manage to sit down and eat with the family, he always finished eating before Joan had dished up for the children, poured milk, and cut their meat.

He seemed to suck in the food, hardly tasting it, and his capacity was tremendous. He could eat three heaping platefuls, though he seldom did. He worked hard, and it was easy for him to burn it up.

"Garup, Sjultx, Interahful . . ."

"Wait until you're through eating, Joe."

"I said, did Bill have any problems today that he didn't tell me about?"

"Not that I know. He seemed exhausted, but no more than anyone is the first few days."

"How well I remember."

"I've got a problem, though."

"What?"

"I have to get someone to take care of the books."

"What!"

"I mean to take care of the quarterly reports for the IRS. I was up until four thirty last night. I went through each man's wages, all of the reports, and did everything I could think of to find a twenty-dollar mistake. My figures didn't compute. By the time I did everything I could, my head felt like it was going to blow off."

"Oh."

"Really, Joe, the pressure started in my toes and went up through my body like a rocket, and when it came to the top of my head, I swore it was going to blow right off. It was hot too. I suppose it might have been a hot flash, except it's about ten years too soon."

"We can't afford to hire a bookkeeper."

"Joe, I've got enough to do just making out the bills, and this report business makes me sick—literally."

"We're not hiring any more help. That's final. We'll just have to get along without it."

"That's easy for you to say. You even start to shake at seven in the evening if you have to write something. You can't do it. How do you expect me to?"

"No more hired help, Joan. That's the end of it. Now where's my paper?"

The man Joan found to do the books was very nice—and reasonable.

# Chapter 17

The envelope Joan opened marked *Fall Festival* held two tickets with $12.50 marked on each one. She set them aside until Joe came home, thinking that maybe he knew about them.

"Oh, yeah, the mayor, Willie Lutz, sent them. Valleytown is having a festival to celebrate the harvest. They're trying to raise money for expenses, so they're having a sponsor's party. I told him to count us in."

"Oh, a party. What fun!"

"Joan, promise you won't drink too much."

"You know I seldom drink."

"But when you do . . ."

"I'll be careful. What will I wear to the party? I think I have to get a new dress—and shoes. Oh, dear."

"Do you have to get into such a snit?"

"Am I in a snit?"

"Yes."

"Yes."

"Yes, what?"

"Yes, I have to get into such a snit."

"Maybe we should just forget the whole thing."

"We probably should, but I won't. I want to go . . . but, Jesus, I wish just once I could go to a party without you."

They fought about it . . . and fought . . . until it was the night of the party. Joan wore a lime-green crepe lame dress she'd ordered from the Montgomery Ward Catalog. (Thank you—Mobil Oil.) She'd also ordered aurora borealis jewelry to wear with the dress, which fit beautifully. Joe was surprised how nice she looked. So was she.

They arrived at the golf club where the party was already swinging. Excited party voices could be heard from their car in the crowded parking lot. They found their way to the upper area and entered a festively decorated room. Champagne bottles were everywhere—and laughing men and women. A small pretty woman caught Joe's sleeve as they made their way to a table. He introduced her to Joan.

"Joan, this is Marie Lutz. Her husband is Willie. Marie—Joan."

Joan leaned forward. She smiled. She wondered if her mouth looked like it felt. Like a basketball with teeth. Her jaws ached from smiling. She couldn't stop. It hurt to smile so much. "How do you do, Marie?"

"Why, I'm just fine, honey. It's been a long time since this town's seen such a pretty girl as you. Come on, come on. Let's get us a little drink." She grabbed Joan and pulled her through the crowd. Joe struggled to follow. "Give these people a drink," she commanded the bartender.

The host of the restaurant was behind the bar. He smiled at Joan. Marie shouted above the hubbub, "This is Joan Schultz, Arthur. Isn't she charming?"

Everyone standing near turned to look at Joan. She blushed.

"Honey, this is Arthur Case."

"How do you do?" Joan acknowledged the introduction, then sipped from the champagne glass Arthur handed her. She and Marie stayed in the bar area for the next two hours. People jostled them, and it was noisy. Joe found friends, and they separated themselves from the crowd. The farther away Joe went, the more Joan relaxed; the more she relaxed, the more champagne she drank, and the happier, wittier, and freer she became.

Marie introduced her to several other women her age. She liked them. They laughed uproariously at everything that was said. She watched them as they contorted themselves in glee. One scrunched down in an I-have-to-go-potty stance whenever she laughed. One put her arms behind her head. It was fun. When the dirty jokes started, Joan left.

After her fifth glass of champagne, Joan began to think she might be drunk. Then she started stopping strangers, introducing herself, and saying, "Aren't *I* charming?" She didn't care! Wheeeee. Suddenly, she was ill. Very ill. She staggered to the powder room, shocked that she could have been the sole instrument to inflict such terrible punishment on herself. God. The *powder room* was the women's locker room and had a few toilet stalls and a row of showers. She prayed she'd make it to the bottom of the stairs before she threw up. She didn't. She threw up all over the front of her beautiful lime-green crepe lame dress. Two of the women she'd met earlier came by and coaxed her into the room with the showers. One got a bucket and a mop and headed toward the door. The other tsk-tsked and sponged and tried to soothe Joan. "There, there. No harm done. We'll have you all cleaned up in a minute."

"This is so nice of you." She couldn't remember being so humiliated or so angry with herself. They were making no progress with the dress. "I'm going to get into the shower and wash it off."

"No. *No. No!* You can't do that."

"Yes, I *can*," she cried and darted to the shower. She turned on the water and let it run on her dress. Several women were in the room by now, watching her. And laughing. And laughing. One of the women who had helped her pulled her out of the shower. A voice from the group asked what could you expect from the wife of the *garbageman?* Joan heard her and started to respond, but she was too drunk and too sick, and it was too true.

Someone tied a long apron around her to cover the lime-green crepe lame that had shrunk a foot and was drip drying on her body. Joan went back upstairs, found a quiet corner, and hoped no one would speak to her. She knew she'd better not let Joe know how sick and drunk she'd been ... was. She didn't see him. After a while, she decided to go to the car. Nearly everyone had left, and the college student workers were cleaning up. She saw Joe on the backseat when she opened the car door. She carefully fished the car keys from his pocket.

When she parked in their garage, he stirred. "What happened?"

"You passed out. Honestly, Joe, if you can't hold your liquor, you really shouldn't drink."

Joe glanced up from his paper. "There's a garbage route for sale down south."

"So what?" Joan shrugged.

"I'd like to find out more about it . . . where it is and how much they want . . ."

"I guess that couldn't hurt, but the idea of buying another route leaves me cold."

Joe wrote the letter that night. Two days later, an answer came. The route was near Springdale. The price was $35,000. The owner had one truck, and the route encompassed a very large area—about one hundred square miles. Joe insisted they drive down on Sunday to look at it. By one o'clock, they were on their way. They drove south on the freeway through the beautiful verdant Williams Valley.

"I still don't know why you want to waste people's time if you're not planning to buy a route down here."

"Joan, I've told you many times . . . I'm just curious."

"You mean you're actually going to pretend you want to buy the route to get the owner to tell you about his business?"

"Yes."

"Why?"

"Because I want to."

He turned off the freeway and went into a series of turns. He seemed so confident that he knew where they were going that Joan suddenly knew they were lost.

"Are we lost?" she asked suspiciously. She thought of other times they'd been lost. Many other times. He refused to ask directions and would travel miles in the wrong direction and spend hours on a wrong road. He didn't like to ask directions. He loathed admitting he was lost.

"Just relax. We'll be there soon."

"Goddamn it, Joe! See that house up ahead. You stop there, and I'll go in and find out where we are and how to find the Larson place. Give me the address."

He made a surly face and handed her the slip of paper. She slammed the door and made her way to the farmhouse. A big slobbering dog watched her. She was afraid of dogs, but she was too angry and too disgusted with Joe to pay attention to the animal. When she had the directions and was safely back inside the car, her eyes met the eyes of the beast. She cringed. Right thigh for lunch. Left thigh for dinner. The animal looked cheated.

Soon they were on their way again and headed back toward the freeway. After a short time, they saw the house under an old oak and turned into the lane. The house was about three years old and sat bravely in an island of reddish clay dirt. No flowers or shrubs had been planted. It seemed dismal.

It was the same old story. Jim Larson's back was acting up, and he had other health problems. He wasn't very old, but his brother, two years younger than he, had just died—of symptoms similar to his, and it made him edgy. He explained that he'd found easier work and assured them the route was growing rapidly. He showed Joan and Joe a pile of letters from prospective purchasers.

"I'd like to see the books," Joan said. Betty Larson, the owner's wife, led her into the office, which was a small room off the living room, which Betty told her had been planned for a den—someday. Until then, they didn't need too much room, and it was convenient. The reddish clay dirt had been tracked over the carpet.

"When we're finished, I'd like to show you our horses." Betty Larson graciously indicated a chair for Joan. She seemed nervous about the condition of her house, which paradoxically was as untidy as she was neat. She waited expectantly as Joan looked through the papers on the desk. In three minutes, Joan could see there wasn't any point in looking at books. The books and bills were in a state of chaos. There was no order to anything. And no way to tell what was what from the incredibly messy entries. "Could I look at your bank statements?"

"Sure. I'll get them for you. Now, let's see, where did I put them?" She started pulling things out of drawers. She handed a bunch of letters with bank statements to Joan. Joan did a few computations. It soon became evident that she would have to take Betty's word for everything. It would take years and a genius to master the figures in the Larson's bank account.

"I'm going to take your word for the income." Joan was beginning to see possibilities . . . *if their figures are right, and could they lie about such a thing? Then the route could be profitable even if we had to hire someone to run it.* Yippee. "You gross about $2,500, right?"

"Yes, do you think your husband will buy it?"

"I don't know, but I'm beginning to see possibilities." She didn't care if Betty saw how interested she was. The price and terms were pretty well established. Joan knew if they didn't buy it, someone else would. There was no room for haggling.

On the freeway, Joan finally broke a thoughtful silence. "What did you think of the route?"

"Looks like a good one. He's got a good truck."

"Really?"

"Yeah."

"Joe, how bad a deal would it be if we bought the route?"

"Joan, I'm not seriously interested in buying the route. I just wanted to look at it."

"So you looked. What did you see?"

"It's a pretty good route. The guy's got a good truck, and he's anxious to sell. That's all."

"That's not all I saw. Listen. We could put a man down there to run the route and put him on a percentage. All we'd have to do is borrow the down payment and make monthly payments. The route would pay for itself."

"Oh. No. No. *No. No,* Joan. You're not going to suck me into any more deals."

"What do you mean *any more deals?*"

"You know perfectly well. No!"

"Fine, let's just forget the whole thing. But I thought *you* wanted to be rich."

"*No,* Joan."

"Joe, ordinarily I wouldn't say another word about that route. I'd just let you have your way like I do about everything else, but I think you should consider how many garbage routes are for sale."

"There aren't any routes for sale."

"And did you see the pile of letters? I read some of them. There are a lot of people interested in that route. It seems to me if you are already in the business, it would pay to buy it."

"Do you really think so?"

"Yes. We don't need any money from that route to live on. We already earn a living on what we have. It wouldn't be any trouble to own it because someone else would do all the work. It would pay for itself. Then someday we could sell it for a profit or just save the net income." She was careful not to say what she thought . . . or *spend* the money. He reacted to the word *spend* as though it were obscene.

Joe looked at her smugly. "It's too late. Jim Larson said a man was coming on Wednesday. He is going to ride over the route with him and check the books. He thinks he'll buy it. He was very interested.

"Did he put down any money?"

"No."

"Then here's what we'll do. We'll go down there after you're finished tomorrow night. I think we'll have to move fast if we want the route."

Suddenly, there was no question *if* they wanted it. They did.

"Joe, I'll call them first thing in the morning. You start early and finish as soon as you can. Then we'll go down and talk business . . . before the other guy gets there on Wednesday." They looked at each other, nodded, then began to laugh.

Everything clicked for Joe during the day. They were able to leave early that evening. Joan phoned the Larson's, so they were expecting them. At ninety miles an hour, the car took flight. Joe woke up. He was driving. He didn't realize how tense he was until he realized his hands were numb from gripping the steering wheel so hard.

"Shall we eat on the way?"

Joe hated eating in restaurants—restless and nervous; waiting to be served nearly drove him out of his mind. Joan, on the other hand, thoroughly enjoyed eating out and often wished she could without Joe to upset her. It wasn't pleasant when he was with her. He fussed and fumed and moved constantly until the best dinner in the world tasted like paper to her. They chose a drive-in along the freeway where the service was fast, the food hot, and the price right . . . for Joe.

The porch light flickered in the dusk. The Larsons waved as they pulled into the drive. Betty came from the direction of the horse barn, and Jim had just parked his truck.

"Howdy, folks," he called. His pleasant gravelly voice sounded tired as it traveled on the evening air. "I thought I'd be through with my route early today, but I had a special load of mildewed grass seed to haul. You folks visit with Betty. I'll rush in and shower. I got something on me today that smells real bad."

Joe gave the man a look of sympathy and understanding. "Go right ahead. Take your time."

"Please!" said Betty. They laughed. She turned to them and smiled. "I was surprised to hear from you this morning, Joan."

"We talked about the route after we left, and the more we talked, the more interested we became. Let's wait until Jim is through with his shower and then we won't have to repeat everything to him."

"Fine." She led them to the patio at the back of the house. They settled into large comfortable rattan chairs with heavy duck coverings. For a time, they visited, then fell silent as they watched the last rays of daylight filter through the dust-borne air. The light softened into bands of purple, red, pink, orange, and gray.

They sat in the gathering darkness. Then night descended in a blanket of black. Joan relaxed for the first time that day. It was getting late. Finally, Jim joined them; he looked shiny clean. He offered them a drink. They moved indoors into the light. Joe began to look edgy, like he'd like to forget the whole thing. He'd been hot and cold ever since Joan had convinced him it was the thing to do. She couldn't see how they could lose. Besides, she wanted the route.

"We've decided to buy your route," she said when everyone was seated. The Larsons looked surprised.

"When did you decide that?" Jim asked Joe.

"After we left you yesterday, we decided we'd look into it further."

"Well, I'm surprised. You didn't seem that interested," Jim said.

"I'll admit I wasn't until we talked it over later."

"This kind of puts me on the spot. I told you I had an appointment to show a buyer, a prospective buyer, I should say, over the route on Wednesday."

Joan moved toward the window. "If we can come to terms this evening and present you with earnest money tomorrow, I would think you'd be under no obligation to the other man."

"What makes you think that? I told him I'd show him the route."

"If he had put down earnest money or done anything to hold the route, it would be different. What happened was he wants to be shown that you have a good route—that everything is as you say it is and that he'd be making a safe investment. We are in the business. We can see by your franchises, our own experience, and a general knowledge of the business just about what you have here."

Joe nodded. "That's right, we don't have to be shown."

Joan sat down and leaned forward. "In any kind of business, money or something of value is needed to make a binding agreement. It wouldn't be wise to pass up a sure sale for a possible one. If you'll sell it to us, we can come down Thursday evening with the earnest money. We'll write up an agreement that is acceptable to you and to us. We have never been involved in a business deal where everyone hasn't been completely satisfied. If you aren't, we won't continue. If this fellow who is coming on Wednesday is more acceptable to you than we are, let us know. If he isn't, we'll have our attorney draw up the contract.

Jim twisted in his chair. He stroked his chin. "There's just one problem. We have to have cash. A contract won't do. I thought I made that clear."

Joan didn't blink. If she'd looked at Joe, she'd have seen the stunned look on his face. He had assumed from the casual way Jim had said *cash* that he'd be amenable to a contract. Now it was obvious that he would not. Everything they'd ever bought had been on contract, and he wasn't prepared for this new development. Neither was Joan.

"Then you will have cash. We'll bring $5,000 earnest money tomorrow and the balance when all of the franchises are transferred and everything is in order. We'll go over the exact terms tomorrow evening."

Joe hunched over the steering wheel all the way home. Small towns and rows of light flashed by as they passed. The car hit ninety again. It made Joan nervous. She started to say something, realized it would do no good, saw that Joe seemed to be paying no attention to his driving, said a silent prayer, then scrunched down in the seat. He was deep in thought and probably wouldn't remember having driven at all. There was no point in starting a battle. Finally, Joe looked across at her. "Well, now, smart-ass . . . where in the hell are you going to raise $35,000 cash?"

"What happened to the partnership? If we manage to get the money . . . *we did it!* If we don't . . . it's all *my* fault . . . right? Let me tell you something. I am going to get that money one way or another."

"Where?"

"Mr. Worthington." She said the words with a calm confident air she did not feel. She'd do anything to keep Joe from finding out how worried she was. She had one day to raise $35,000. They'd borrowed their limit from her relatives and his uncle. The only place left was the bank. When they'd moved to Maplewood, they started banking with the independent bank. Mr. Worthington, the manager and major stockholder, was known to be one of the most progressive and fair men in the country. They borrowed money to buy their last truck from him. He'd been friendly and gracious. Now he was their only chance. The other two banks in the community were branch banks. Joan knew it might take several weeks for a loan to be processed, and then it would stand a good chance of rejection.

Before she left for the bank, she made a list of their liabilities and assets. She also took along the last three years' income tax statements. Mr. Worthington could check over their bank statement at the bank if he wished.

He seemed pleased to see her. He stood behind a teller's window.

"Could I see you in your office?"

"Certainly." He led her into a nicely furnished office with gold carpet, good paintings, and homespun draperies. "Sit here. Would you care for a cigarette?"

"Yes, thank you." She nervously lit the cigarette, then leaned forward in her chair. Her mouth was dry. "Mr. Worthington, we need to borrow $35,000."

He didn't seem surprised. "I'll tell you what you do. You fill out a loan application, and we'll see what we can do."

"How long will that take?"

"Two or three days."

"What do you do with the application?"

"Several of the people in the bank study it, and if it is in order, the loan may be approved or not, as the case may be." He started to stiffen imperceptibly.

"Please don't misunderstand me. I wasn't questioning the procedure. I just wanted to know what was done with the application."

"That's quite all right."

"I've made a list of our assets . . . Will you look at it and see if you think I should bother to make out an application?" She told him about the route—and how if they didn't have the money by tonight, someone else might buy it later. Good garbage routes were hard to find. He listened with interest, then looked over her list.

"It looks as though you are doing very well."

"We are, Mr. Worthington. We feel it is time to expand our business. You have a reputation for treating people fairly. Just between you and me, it is said there is no committee to approve loans . . . that you do it yourself. Is that true?"

Joan watched him as he changed position, got a little tinged with red, and gave himself away with a funny little face.

"Mr. Worthington, we want to expand our business . . . you want to make loans. There just isn't time to wait," Joan said.

"I don't know what to say." He carefully weighed the situation. Joan sat silently as he struggled with the decision.

"Loan us the money, Mr. Worthington. If you don't lend it to us, you'll have to find someone else to lend it to. And you know we're good credit risks. Say yes."

He lowered the papers in his hand and looked her straight in the eye. "Is that how you get your way?"

Joan laughed and nodded. "Sometimes I'm worse. I usually go for what the traffic will bear and how important the situation is."

Disarmed by her candor, he shook his head, chuckled, and dropped his shoulders. He lit a cigarette and, between drags, said, "I'll loan you the money. At 7 percent interest."

"Six and a half."

Smoke expelled from his nose, and his eyes narrowed. He spoke through clenched teeth. "Seven."

"Seven . . . thank you very much, Mr. Worthington."

It had gone smoother than she imagined. When she told Joe about it, she was careful not to let him think she'd been concerned about getting the loan. She mentally wiped her brow and fainted whenever she thought of how she'd behaved with Mr. Worthington. Jeeesus.

They'd gone back down the valley that night, ironed out the details, made the final agreement, and shook hands all around. Then they'd found a man to take over the route. When the Larsons called and told them they were selling to them and not the other party, Jim taught him the route, and his wife took over the bookwork from Betty. They worked on a percentage and a flat wage. They were happy, reliable, and loyal. Joan was happy too. Joe hardly noticed. It was 1965. He was busy with his own route.

## Chapter 18

"Let's go visit Uncle." Joe had tired of lying on the rug after reading the Sunday paper. He suddenly felt like visiting his family . . . something he rarely wanted to do.

"You take the children and go by yourself."

"Joan, you know I don't enjoy going by myself."

"You don't enjoy going with me either."

"I'll go some other time. Let's just go for a drive."

"Why?"

"I feel like going someplace."

"Go."

"No, I want you to go with me."

"Why?"

"So I'll have someone to talk to."

"That's ridiculous. We have driven five hundred miles at a time on trips, and you know you haven't said a word."

"That's different."

"Really, Joe, I'd enjoy being in the house by myself for a change. Why don't you take the children for a ride and leave me here?"

"No."

"OK. Why don't you go down to the tavern? All your old buddies are there every Sunday. Go visit them."

"You know I hate to go any place without you, Joan."

"You hate to go any place without me or with me. Let's just stay home."

"What do you think about leasing the drop boxes?" He hadn't said anything for several minutes. She was nearly asleep as the sound of his voice cut into her spine. She jerked.

"Joe, it's Sunday. I don't want to think about business."

"Why not?"

"Because every other day that's all I do think about. I just want to stay here in this nice comfortable chair until it's time to cook dinner. I don't want to think about business or anything else. I am tired."

"Joan, are you interested in that new fellow—Bill?"

"Oh, no. Now you're going to do your jealous act."

"Are you?"

"Yes. He's got the greatest build I've ever seen, his muscles ripple, he's tan, and I'll bet he's got a great big cock." She stuck out her tongue and licked her lips.

"Joan!"

"What? Isn't that what you want to hear? Or do you want to know where he's fucking me?"

"Joan!"

"Joe, I told you I am tired. Too tired for this bullshit. Leave me alone."

The reason she was so tired was that she'd had a very bad week. It started on Monday when she noticed a taxi coming in the lane. The car stopped; the man got out and ran into the house.

"Mrs. Schultz, something is the matter with your daughter!"

"Where is she?"

"In the cab."

"If something is the matter with my daughter, why didn't you take her to the hospital?"

"The sisters said to bring her here."

Joan ran to the car. Sarah lay on the backseat. Her twelve-year-old white distressed face peered at Joan from the seat. Her body lay in a rigid line, arms and legs at right angles to her trunk. Joan had never seen anything like this. She wondered if Sarah had had a stroke. Joan made arrangements with the driver to bring Mrs. Warren from the end of the lane, then asked him to help her move Sarah from the cab to her car. As soon as he left, she called their pediatrician, Dr. Cooper, in Capitol City. He assured her he'd be waiting for them.

Joan reached over and felt the child as they drove the fifteen miles to town. She was feverish and couldn't move. *Dear God*, prayed Joan, *please don't let it be anything critical.* She drove much too fast and didn't even notice. The doctor stood waiting by his office at the clinic. He reached for Sarah's hand.

"I'll ask you to leave, Mrs. Schultz."

"Why?"

"Don't ask any questions, just go."

Dr. Cooper, Capitol City's leading pediatrician, was brusque and rude. Joan couldn't get used to being treated that way. Still he was said to be the best children's doctor in the area. Joan waved good-bye to Sarah. She nervously paced the hall during the examination. She mentally made plans to arrange things so that she could stay with Sarah in the hospital. She wondered how many months it might be before she'd recover. The next few minutes until the door opened seemed like eternity to her.

Finally, Dr. Cooper came into the hall. Joan rushed to him. Wordlessly, he propelled her into his inner office, flopped into his chair, and gestured for Joan to sit down. "Now what do you think is wrong with your daughter?"

"I haven't any idea. I thought it might be a stroke."

He looked down his nose at her. "Children don't have strokes."

"I didn't know that."

He stretched in his chair and languidly raised an arm. "Oh, maybe they do, rarely . . . but it is highly unusual."

"I didn't know what else it might be. The way she was paralyzed, I thought it might be polio . . . I just didn't know. Why are you making me guess? Why don't you tell me what is the matter? Is it permanent?"

His standard smug, self-satisfied look covered his face. "Why didn't you ask her what was wrong?"

She heard air hiss from her lips and felt her face redden. She looked through squinty eyes and said, "Because she couldn't speak."

"Come here, Mrs. Schultz." He led her to a wall with a one-way mirror. He adjusted it, and Joan looked with surprise to see Sarah lying on the examining table, swinging her leg and scratching her thigh.

"I don't understand. She couldn't move." Joan stared in disbelief.

"Of course not." He smiled his maddening smile. He'd once told her pediatricians had the highest suicide rate among doctors. She wished he'd do it now.

"Dr. Cooper, I'm tired of your games. What is wrong . . . or was wrong with Sarah?"

He folded his arms, contemplated the question, and then, in a dramatic little theater voice, whispered, "Hysteria."

"Hysteria? What is hysteria? I thought hysterical people screamed and raged and did crazy things?"

He steepled his hands and became *the expert*. "Not at all, though sometimes that is a manifestation. Usually hysterical people act very much like your daughter."

"She's all right now?"

"I wouldn't say that. Physically she's all right. But whatever caused this to happen still exists."

"You mean she was emotionally upset?"

"Exactly."

"Did she tell you what was the matter?"

"No."

"And how did you know she had hysteria and not something really wrong?"

"Hysteria is something *really wrong*."

"Can I take her home?"

"Of course."

"Is there anything I should do for her?"

"Find out what is the matter."

"Will she know?"

"Of course."

"Good."

"She may not tell you, though."

"I'll try. One more thing, Dr. Cooper, she seemed to get worse on the way into town. Why was that?"

"You were upset, and the more upset you became, the more upset she became. You frightened each other."

"Oh."

She didn't question Sarah on the way home. She had a feeling that the trouble with Sarah had something to do with the new teacher, Mr. Haas. Every day since school started, either Stan or Sarah had come home with a story about Mr. Haas. At first, Joan had listened politely and then brushed off the tales. As time went on and the daily litany became intensified and the children grew more angry and frustrated, she began to pay attention.

Mr. Haas taught at St. Patrick's school because of the shortage of nuns available as teachers. At about this time, the whole structure of the Catholic Church was changing. Fewer and fewer boys and girls entered the religious life, and the parochial schools had to hire people who either didn't want to teach full time or were not qualified to teach in the public schools. Promotions in the parochial schools were at a premium. The top jobs were taken by older nuns, and the future for lay teachers was a dead-end street.

At first, the parish hired a few dedicated teachers along with the nuns. As the years went by and the dedicated teachers were not paid what they needed and deserved, they went to work for the public school system. Fewer and fewer good teachers were available, and finally the Catholic school system could not attract them.

Mr. Haas came from a high school in Watertown. This high school was known for its violence long before *little stabbings* became fashionable.

Mr. Haas was lucky to survive, especially since he was such a perfect target—sadistic, cruel, and surly. His eyes were narrow slits, his dirty hair was dirty blond, his nails were caked, and he looked as though he seldom bathed. A four-inch scar caught him at his left cheekbone and ended at the corner of his mouth. He looked like what he was—scary.

Joan first saw him in church and thought he was the meanest-looking man she'd ever seen. She watched him and cringed when he clapped his big hand over his cooing toddler's mouth. When the child started to cry, he slapped her. Then he rushed her up the aisle. *It sounds like he's spanking her. Could he actually spank that child? That son of a bitch!* She looked over at his wife, who sat with three other scroungy children and an infant. Mrs. Haas was *young-old*. She looked twenty-five to sixty. The twenty-five was a girlish face, a slender body, and an innocent air. The sixty was the worn tension wrinkles, the look of painful despair, and the deep hurt that showed through her luminous brown eyes. The day was cool, yet the baby wore no undershirt and no shoes. His too small, too thin blanket bunched around his too large tummy.

Praise to the Lord, the Host, and Redeemer!

Stan broke his wrist. He and several of his friends, neighbors, and relatives were swinging on a ring attached to a big oak tree. The tree was at the top of a slope, and the boys took turns swinging over the slope, then letting go. It was about a fifteen-foot drop. Stan slipped.

When he came to her, Joan was amazed that an arm could look like that. It was about two inches lower than the hand, and it seemed the skin held it and kept it from falling out of its place. He was writhing in pain. His mouth was open, and he breathed in short, fast gasps. The trip to the doctor's office, the ride to the hospital, and the setting of the bone by a specialist all blurred in Joan's mind. Stan didn't remember much about the trip into the hospital either. The local doctor had given him a shot of morphine to kill the pain. He floated.

A week later, he came home from school; his jacket sleeve flapped over the unwieldy cast. He came into the kitchen, put his books on the desk, and moved out of Joan's vision to smash the wall with his good fist. He lost. Tears came to his eyes.

"What in the hell is the matter with you?"

"Oh, Mother, it's Mr. Haas. I don't think I can take any more of him."

Her shoulders dropped; her face tensed. She'd hoped the situation had improved. If she didn't stop this trouble, she could see Stan's ulcer coming back. This kind of terrible frustration could do it.

"Have you had any stomachaches?"

"He sat down on the long bench in the kitchen. For a while, he wouldn't look at her. Then he turned his red watery eyes in her direction. Tears like icebreakers cut through the sea of dirt on his fourteen-year-old face. *God, I love him,* she thought. *And that cruel, heartless son of a bitch of a bastard is causing him this pain. I'll stop him!* Stan put his head in his arms. Then he raised it and looked at her. "Yeah, I've been having stomachaches. They started about the time Mr. Haas came to school."

"I'll go talk to him."

Joan prided herself on being objective about her children. She was not one of those gooney mothers who, no matter what happened or what kind of incriminating evidence was presented, refused to acknowledge that their children could *ever* misbehave. She got a taste of that kind of thinking when she went to the sister superior to inform her that some of the big boys were chasing some of the little boys with pocketknives and telling them they were going to cut off their penises. The little fellows were terrorized.

"Not *my* boys!" Sister cried. She reared back in her chair and raised her arm.

"I beg your pardon," Joan said. She stared at her in fascination. This was not the reception she expected. She thought the sister would be happy to know what was happening so she could correct the situation.

"Not *my* boys," she repeated through clenched teeth.

"Sister, I'm telling you the truth. It did happen. I don't want anyone to get in trouble or be punished—I just want it to stop."

"*My* boys would never do a thing like that, and I do not want another word spoken. This could give our school a black eye in the community."

"Your school and the students already have a *black eye in the community*. Whenever there is any trouble in town, it is usually the Catholic kids who cause most of it. They are rowdy and obnoxious at the swimming pool, on the school buses, and wherever they gather. They instigate trouble, and everyone in the community knows it, except, apparently, *you*."

The old nun sputtered.

Joan sputtered too.

"*No*," Joe shouted.

"No, what?" Joan asked coolly.

"No, you are not going to school and cause trouble."

"Wonderful. Then you'll do it? You'll go to the school and find out what happened and why. You'll stick up for the boy?"

"Nobody's going."

Nobody's going. Nobody's going to find out the truth and stop the man who has such incredible power over the lives of those so young and eager and vulnerable. Forget it. Say nothing. Do nothing. What does it matter that one fourteen-year-old boy is wronged? Joan felt her throat tighten. Her chest felt belted. "Stan has never caused us one problem in school, except for the time when he was in the fifth grade." She smiled at the memory. The sister had insisted that Stan could not have lunch until he completed a handwritten assignment to her satisfaction. He was a terrible writer, and he couldn't. He tried. Three times. Still *no*. He was furious. He shouted that he didn't like her or the school and ran home. Three miles. The school had called and alerted Joan. When he came in, her mother, who was visiting, said to him (before Joan had a chance to say a word), "What did that old bag do to you?"

Now, Joan glared at Joe. "Don't you think you should listen to him?"

"Teachers run the schools, and they have a right to make the rules."

"I intend to cooperate with them. I just think if the man is being unreasonable, we should talk with him."

"You're not going to school."

"Do you want me to go and talk to the man, Stan?"

Resignation and defeat filled his eyes. How could he hope to find help in a home situation like this? He was damned either way.

Joan looked at him, and there was no question what she would do. "I'm going."

Mr. Haas agreed to see her after the last class of the day. Evil emanated from his Buddha body; revulsion from hers. His surly mouth with pinched thin lips sneered at her. She saw a dirty T-shirt hanging on his chest, yellowed and stained and matching his teeth.

She got nowhere. He'd rehearsed his lines. Super smooth. He had an answer for everything. He sounded *so reasonable*. *No wonder he's fooling all the people,* she thought as he droned on. His sanctimonious tones met with disbelief. He launched into a mini dissertation on the *problems of puberty*, hinted darkly at possible problems Stan *might* be having, and leered at Joan. She couldn't wait to leave. Anger girdled her, which caused her cheeks to puff and the tendons in her neck to stand out. She'd wasted her time—the only really valuable thing she had on an asshole like that. *Boy,* she thought, *all I did was supply the audience.*

The next afternoon, when Stan came home from school, he seemed to favor his arm.

"Is something the matter with your arm?" Joan asked.

"It hurts."

"Why?"

"Mr. Haas made me run three laps around the athletic field."

"He made you run with a heavy cast on your arm?" She couldn't believe her ears. Joe raised his eyes from the newspaper and shot Stan a disgusted look.

"What did you do?" he asked.

"For heaven's sake, Joe, what difference does it make what he did? He might have a permanent injury if the bone doesn't heal right."

"What's the matter with you? Don't make a *railroad crossing* out of this. Don't think about causing trouble." He turned back to his paper and made a sucking sound with his tongue. Joan shook her head and grew thoughtful. Every time she thought of the railroad crossing, she wanted to smile. It was about two miles from them. There had been several fatal accidents at the crossing mostly because there was only one or two trains a day, and everyone who used the crossing tended to be complacent about the danger. After a particularly tragic accident, Joan and a few others waged a three-year war against the state and the railroad—petitions, meetings, work, struggle, then, at last, success! Crossing gates were installed. A measure of safety. Persistence paid off.

Meanwhile, in the center of Maplewood, the main line cut directly through the core of the city. There were seven crossings of the main line that ran through the center of Maplewood. Three years after Joan's group's victory, there was still not a crossing gate in the city of Maplewood.

Now Joe said, "Kids are always getting into trouble at school and then coming home with a big story."

"Stan, I'm going to talk to Father Connelly. I want you to go with me. I think that Mr. Haas should be fired," Joan spoke without even listening to Joe. She had turned him off like a knob on a radio.

Stan gritted his teeth. He wanted no trouble. He was sorry Joan had noticed his discomfort. He was happy at school. Except for Mr. Haas. He wanted to be student body president since he was in the fifth grade. Now he was. They'd elected him by a big majority. He felt important at school. Little kids came up and said, "Hi, Stan." He liked that. "Mother, can't we just let it drop?"

"Listen to the boy, Joan." Joe's mouth had an ugly set to it. "I'm going to put my foot down. I forbid you to go to Father Connelly."

"Go to hell, Joe! Stan, Mr. Haas is not fit to teach. He possesses too many negative traits. If he is treating you like this, think how he must be treating others who may be even more vulnerable than you. He must be stopped. I believe it is our responsibility to do it. Don't you understand?" She could see he didn't. She also knew he couldn't go to that school much longer unless Mr. Haas was dealt with.

Stan (the victim) shrugged his shoulders. He'd been caught in the crossfire again. He hated getting between his mother and father. Whomever he sided with, he felt like a betrayer to the other. He didn't like the idea of talking to Father Connelly.

Father Connelly coolly received them. Joan could tell by his manner that he had not forgotten the public meeting. She was pleased that he had the courtesy to hear them out under the circumstances. At her prodding, Stan recited some of the things Mr. Haas had done since he'd arrived. Joan told the priest about Mr. Haas making Stan run around the field with his cast on.

"Well, what did you do?" He looked at Stan. His patience was wearing thin, and it was all he could do to keep from asking Mrs. Schultz and her precious son to leave. It had been a long day, and he was very tired.

Joan interrupted, "What difference does it make what he did? Any fool would know better than to make a boy run with a big cast on his arm."

"I want to know." Father Connelly relaxed a little; he felt the color in his face recede. He'd been bullied around by women like this long enough.

"I didn't do anything. Mr. Haas uses the *buddy system*. The fellow in front of me in line threw something at a girl, so the person in front of him and in back of him were punished too."

Joan shook her head. "There obviously is something wrong with the man."

Father Connelly smiled an insinuating smile. "Did it ever occur to you that there might be something wrong with the mother?"

"I suppose we always have to keep that possibility in mind," she said as she snapped to her feet.

They discussed their alternatives on the way home.

"I want you to know I appreciate what you've done, Mother."

"I didn't accomplish anything, Stan."

"You tried. I guess we'll just have to forget it."

"We can't do that. You can't go to school a whole year with a teacher like that."

"Father Connelly will never fire him."

"No, but you can go to the public school."

"Aw, gee, I've waited all my life to be in the eighth grade to be a big shot. Now I'm president of the student body. I had to work to get elected too. Another thing, I'd miss all my friends."

"A lot of your friends will go to the public school when they graduate. You can make new friends, and you know most of the public school kids anyway."

"What about Dad?"

"Oh, dear, you had to remind me."

They laughed then for the first time that evening.

"Your health and happiness are more important to me than his dogmatic views," she said.

"It'll be some fight."

"I know, Stan, but I'll win. You don't win unless you fight."

For the next few days, the house might have been a battle zone. They fought morning, night, and late at night. Each tried to convince the other that his point of view was the right one. Joe couldn't bear the thought of Stan leaving the school. The scandal and insult to the church were his main concerns. Joan fought with every weapon she had. Then she stopped fighting. Quiet resolve took over. She knew what had to be done, and that was what would be done. She thought, *Never argue with a fool—bystanders won't know the difference.*

"For the last hundred years, there has been a Schultz in a Catholic school in this area."

"We still have four daughters in school." She knew he hadn't considered the girls. In the eyes of the old Germans in the community, girls were practically worthless. It was the males who meant something.

They quarreled again, but in the morning, Joan drove into school, picked up Stan's belongings, and enrolled him in the public school. Later, she wished Joe would still be the kind of man who would get angry and then forget it. He wouldn't. He went over and over the incident for months. Much too long for Joan's comfort.

Driving Sarah home from the doctor's office, Joan realized that now her oldest daughter was having the same kinds of problems with Mr. Haas. She decided not to discuss the problem with Joe or Father Connelly. She registered Sarah in the public school the next morning. When she told Joe, she was surprised how well he took it. He had other things on his mind, and the fact of Sarah's defection didn't affect him much at all. He merely shrugged his shoulders. Joan told herself not to get any false sense of security. He might explode next month when he realized what she'd done.

# Chapter 19

Joan traveled the thirty miles to Watertown so often, she knew every landmark by heart. There were always many places to go for parts for the trucks or for office supplies or printing. The three little girls played in the back of the station wagon. They always enjoyed the trip. Except for the fear of having a flat tire on the freeway with them in the car, Joan enjoyed the drive and the girls. They often stopped at a drive-in for lunch. This gave the girls and Joan a pleasant change from the peanut butter and jelly sandwiches, which had become the only food they would eat for lunch at home.

Joe still sold metals to the scrap yards. He'd stopped hauling tin and iron, but copper, brass, aluminum, and lead brought good prices. This day, Joan was to stop and inquire about current prices at Gene Greenman's scrap yard on the way home.

The firm had recently moved to a new location. They'd outgrown the old place in the middle of town where barrels of copper and brass, boxes of batteries, and assorted containers littered and enveloped the only decent sidewalk in the area. Urban renewal had come along and paid them a sizable fee to relocate, and they were now getting used to their new facilities. They were much larger. They had room for storing metals they'd never had before. Now they could stockpile if the price went down or hold until it went up again.

Gene, the owner of the firm, waved to Joan as she and the little girls drove in. "I'll be with you in a minute, Joan."

"Don't hurry," she called. She watched the beehive of activity as trucks backed into and pulled out of the six loading stalls on the dock. Men with scales weighing metals hurried around. Gene finished his work and came over to her.

"What can I do for you, Joan?"

"Joe needs to know the current price of copper. He's got quite a bit, but if the price is down, he'll keep it."

"Tell him he'd better sell before the thieves get it." He gave her a knowing look, then laughed. Joan shuddered.

"If anyone steals any more of his precious copper, they may lose their life. He sat in ambush all one night waiting to shoot whoever stole it last time. He thought he had it all figured out. They usually steal it the Thursday before a holiday. He waited all night."

"You're kidding."

"I'm not. He hates thieves."

Gene shrugged his shoulders. He laughed a little. "Have you got time to look around?"

"I'd love to. Joe said you had a really nice place here. He said you'd built a sauna in the office."

"That's right. Come and see it."

He led Joan and the little girls through offices beautifully furnished and decorated in tones of copper and gold. The sauna was off the main office. Inch-square white ceramic tile sparkled in the sauna.

"A lot of my clients like to take a sauna. It makes them feel relaxed."

"It's beautiful, Gene."

He showed her the rest of the building. It was a far cry from the old place. Gene looked happy. Joan wondered if there was still friction between him and his father. The old man wanted to retire and still run the business. Gene wanted new and better things, including new methods and machinery. He'd gone to school, and when his education was finished, the old man let him come into the business on his terms.

Gene took to the road. He conned his father into trips around the world for business reasons. It started as a lark, but when Gene started buying and selling in foreign markets, the business prospered beyond imagination. Still the friction existed between father and son, with each complaining to Joe and Joan about the other.

Gene led them to the area where the trucks were parked.

"Here's the main attraction." He pointed toward the sixty-foot smoke stack. Beneath it, a small oven for burning insulation off copper wire and other metals was open and glowed red hot. Restrictions were getting tight, and the men who salvaged metal had very few places where they could burn because of the polluting acrid smoke.

Gene looked very pleased. "Copper wire is being burned right now."

Joan squinted as her eyes searched the atmosphere at the top of the stack. "There's no smoke—just heat rays."

Gene acted like a farmer showing off a prime litter of piglets. He threw out his chest. "That's right. It cost $50,000 to build, but it's the answer to the smoke problem. People come in here to burn their wire . . . it's just a service to them."

Joan smiled at him. "And you've enjoyed setting it up."

His face was immobile, but his eyes danced. "A little."

"A lot. You've done a good job!"

They visited a short time longer amid the hustling and bustling of the giant ant farm.

Joan remembered with nostalgia the first time she'd met Gene Greenman. Joe had taken a big load of copper and brass to Watertown to be sold. He'd saved for two or three years to have enough for a big sale. After weighing and bartering and finally agreeing on price, he and Gene had had a few drinks together in the back of the old shop.

When he got home that evening, he told Joan about the invitation. "Would you like to go?"

"Yippee. Of course."

"I haven't told you all about it."

"It doesn't matter, I'll go."

"Let me tell you about it. Gene and a friend have rented a room at the Watertown Hotel. They can watch the parade from a balcony."

"What parade?"

"The Merry-Spring Parade."

"That sounds like fun."

Because of the pressure of their work and family, Joan and Joe's social life consisted of weddings, potluck dinners, quiet dinners for four or six at home, family dinners, and dinner and a movie followed by the inevitable stop at the only lounge in town to *see who is there—do we have to, Joe?* On most social occasions, they were with people they knew. Joan hated "chitchat" and wasn't very comfortable with strangers. Joe usually fought any kind of social situation. If it hadn't been for the drinks, he'd probably never have accepted Gene's invitation. Now the drinks had worn off. He'd driven home, bathed, and changed into his best clothes. Now that he was sober, the idea of a party had lost its appeal. He wished he'd kept his mouth shut.

Joan liked Gene immediately. He was cool, nice, and easy to talk with, said witty things, and rather shamelessly ran his hand up and down his girl's (Sylvia) leg. He had big brown eyes, straight white teeth, an indolent air, and the manner of a pampered, petted Jewish Caesar. Joan watched as he tried to make Sylvia. At first, she was uncomfortable, but soon she realized that he had been drinking, so she turned her attention to Sam, his friend. Sam also looked spoiled. He had a pouty underlip, blue ambivalent eyes, small hands, and a wonderful sense of humor. Sam's date was one of the most beautiful women Joan had ever seen. Her white skin, black hair, perfect mouth, lush lashes, black eyes, long legs, dainty feet, and her elegant black satin dress with spaghetti straps combined to make her look beautifully exotic. Her dress fit like only the designer could imagine. Joan noticed there was not an extra quarter inch of fat on her entire body. Her name was Melanie, and it didn't matter that she had nothing to say. She smiled now and then. No one expected more.

After they were comfortable in the suite, a waiter brought orange and pink drinks in foot-high glasses and a silver chafing dish filled with hot hors d'oeuvres. Joan had never seen such beautiful looking food. When she realized she must be staring at the offering, she turned to watch the others. No one paid the slightest attention to the food, though Joan had never seen such a scrumptious sight in her life. They had. Often. They were blasé about a way of life Joan could only imagine.

Gene's fat friend, Sam, had only one problem in life. He couldn't find anyone who would go to Europe with him for two months. He bemoaned that fact all during the parade. Drinks kept coming, and soon the room was very festive. No one ate *any* of the hors d'oeuvres. Except Joan. Joe didn't think he'd like them.

When the parade wound out of sight, Gene insisted they have dinner in the English Room on the first floor of the hotel. Like a general, he marched into the dining room with his entourage. Soldier waiters snapped to attention. The maitre d' escorted them to their table with aplomb. They were seated. They ordered. A waiter came forward with the ingredients for a Caesar salad. He started to arrange condiments on a huge tray. Suddenly, Gene raised his left hand.

"Stop. Where is Jake? I want him to toss the salad."

"Of course, sir." The long-legged waiter rushed off to find Jake.

Jake came and started his Caesar salad ritual. He was as graceful as a ballet dancer. Every movement was flowing and efficient, and seemed choreographed. Joan thought how wonderful he looked. Joe thought how ludicrous. He would have laughed, except it wouldn't have been nice.

Gene ordered shish kebab, and when it came flaming into the room, the lights went out, and the sound of a big brass gong reverberated through the darkened room. A flaming wand lit the waiter's expressionless face. Drama and excitement like this were not Joan and Joe's daily fare. When dinner was over, the waiter brought a small dish of chocolates to the table. Joan was glad she was too full to eat any when Sam asked Joe, "Do you know what you're eating?"

"No."

"Chocolate-covered grasshoppers."

Everyone laughed, except Joe and Joan. She made a face, and he looked strange.

"What did they taste like?"

"Crunchy chocolate."

Sam and his beautiful Melanie left them at the entrance to the hotel. Joan wondered who'd stay in the room that night. She was always curious about who slept with whom.

Gene and Sylvia took Joan and Joe to a special nightclub filled with red velvet booths, red velvet chairs, red velvet walls, beautiful women in silks and satins, handsome men in dinner jackets, and sparkling mirrors. They had a few drinks and talked and listened to good music from the '20s and told a few jokes (some that Gene told weren't very nice). They laughed a lot, and finally the place closed and they had to leave. Joan meant it when she thanked them for a wonderful evening.

All the way home, they'd talked about Gene and Sylvia, and Sam and his girl, and how they'd been so much fun and so gracious and so nice.

"Oh, wasn't it fun, Joe?"

"Yeah."

"And weren't the women beautiful in the nightclub?"

"Yeah."

"And wasn't the food delicious?"

"Yeah."

"Gee, the evening was a lot of fun, wasn't it?"

"Yeah."

"We'll have to have them to dinner or take them someplace special."

"Yeah."

"I guess we shouldn't talk about it anymore, but wasn't it fun?"

"Yeah."

They were home by four. Joan wondered how she'd ever get up to go to church. But she would. She'd never missed mass since she became a Catholic. Nothing could keep her out of church. Not even a hangover.

On Monday afternoon, Joan was on her way to Watertown. A U-bolt on one of the trucks needed replacing. Joe couldn't use the truck until she brought back the part.

Cotton-candy white clouds floated in the blue sky. It was a glorious day. Joan thought it was a good thing she liked to drive because she spent more and more time on the road running errands. Their whole operation was getting very disorganized. Joe again insisted he didn't need additional help, though he was doing much more work.

"Joe, if you just managed the routes and didn't take your time and energy to work on the truck, we could be a lot more efficient."

"I do not intend to sit in an office and run the business."

"That's just the point, Joe—no one is running the business now. We both do some of it, but no one is getting a picture of the whole business. If you can stand back and be objective, you can . . ."

"What? Pick up the cans by remote control? Be an executive? A manager? No thanks. I want to see what is happening." He scoffed.

"When you get too close, you can't see!"

The part wasn't there. They hadn't received it. It was on order . . . should have been there by now. Would she care to wait?

"I have to wait. My husband can't work without his truck."

After twenty minutes, she decided to have some coffee. She'd waited long enough. Time to ask some questions. In an hour, she was back on the freeway. There was no point in hurrying now. The men would have left the garage. She stopped and picked up a barrel of chicken, then drove home. The kitchen looked as though something had exploded. Books, coats, shoes, papers, and wrappers from tomorrow's lunch treats littered the kitchen. Joe walked into the room.

"What took you so long? Now I won't be able to start until after they fix the truck, and they don't open until eight."

"I had to wait over an hour."

"They said the part was there."

"It wasn't."

"I needed that part."

"Of course, you did. That's why I drove all the way to Watertown. Maybe you'd better run your own errands."

"Calm down. I didn't have time to go to Watertown—and you know it."

That night, after dinner, Joan started on that month's billing. Joe read his newspaper on the yellow vinyl couch.

"Joe, I think we'd better turn some of the deadbeats over to a collection agency."

"We've been over that before. I'm not going to cause trouble and have a bunch of people complaining because I turned them over to a collection agency."

"Some of these people haven't paid their bill for two or three years. How long could we go on getting our lights or anything else if we didn't pay our bill?"

"I don't want them turned over to a collection agency."

"Then stop picking up their garbage."

"No!"

"Why not?"

"Because I won't, that's why."

"I hope you realize that the money they aren't paying is pure profit."

"What do you mean?"

"We pay our expenses, so any money that we don't get is profit. All of the expenses have been paid. That's where your profit goes, also for any gas and labor and other expenses to pick up the cans of those who won't pay. I think we should remember that we are running a business and run it as a business. That includes turning past due accounts over to the collection agency."

"No. No. No."

The woman from the collection agency had red hair, much lighter than Joan's, and wore a huge diamond ring on her right hand and a green scarf around her ringed neck. She arrived at one o'clock. Joe was due at one thirty.

"I'll let you tell my husband just what your service includes."

"You say he doesn't want to engage our firm?"

"No. I'm hoping you can convince him. He won't listen to me. Sometimes when someone else tells him something, he's more receptive than if I tell him."

"He sounds just like a husband." She lowered her head to laugh, and Joan noticed the rings on her neck looked like accordion pleats.

"He is," she said.

"It doesn't sound like you get along very well."

"We don't." Joan hadn't intended to discuss their personal life with this strange lady, but it seemed the lady intuitively knew that all was not *wonderful* with the marriage. Joan looked at the pretty woman. "We don't understand much of anything about each other."

Joe came in, met the woman, listened to what she had to say, and reluctantly agreed to turn over his oldest nonpaying customers to her. Her agency charged 50 percent of any money collected. The woman was happy. Joan was happy. Joe was happy—and so congenial.

* * *

The south route ran smoothly, except for a vexing problem. There were no franchises in that county, and one of the garbagemen from Pittstown spent every Saturday touring through the countryside stealing their customers. There was not a thing they could do to stop him.

It was the old story—steal the customers, then raise the monthly price. The man promised the same service for less money. People liked the idea.

"I think we should go talk to him, Joe."

"No. He'll just get irritated, and maybe he'll steal more."

"We haven't lost many customers yet, but we can't afford to lose any more. If we talk to him and tell him where our route is, maybe he'll respect our area."

"He won't. They don't have areas in Pittstown. There, it is dog-eat-dog. One time they were even offering to line the garbage cans for six months if the homeowner would sign up with a company that had already cut its prices."

"Just because it's happened before, doesn't mean it will happen again. I think we should try to talk with the man. I think we have to. It isn't fair to Tom to lose customers that he now gets a commission on."

"I'm just not going to talk to him, and that is final."

The south route had worked out better than they had dreamed—or roughly, as Joan had said it would, which was unusual. She usually was only 75 percent right. She tended to be very optimistic. But the truth was they were right on schedule. The route was paying for itself. It was making a modest growth. Tom and Debra Davidson handled it beautifully. There was little pressure on Joe and Joan from it. About once every six months, and at tax time, Joan checked over all business bills, bank statements, and miscellaneous items.

The Davidsons were doing a first-rate job. They liked the community, and Tom even taught a 4-H group in gardening. They also fit in well in the social scene of the community. Their daughter, Marcia, loved the small school and riding on the school bus. They'd found a house about two miles from town, and they planted a garden almost before they were settled.

Joan sat working at the kitchen table in their dreary kitchen. (Debra was a lousy housekeeper.) Tom poured himself a cup of coffee.

"Want one?" He indicated a mug.

"No thanks." *I really would like some coffee, but I don't think it's sanitary. I think the cups may be dirty. Or the spoons. Or the coffeepot. Yech!*

Tom sat down. "Joan, has anything been done with this guy who is stealing customers? The owner of a forty-seven-unit motel, my biggest stop, told me he was soliciting his business. He also told me the man's name. It is Jessie Lopez. His address is on this card."

"Is his phone number there?"

"Here it is. Are you going to call him?"

"Yes. It is time."

"Won't Joe be mad?"

"Probably. It seems to be his permanent state. He loves to be mad."

As she drove home through the valley, about to shut down for another day of eternity, she was pleased to see a rare display of early evening yellow sunshine mixed with one-half deep dark-gray shadowy clouds that alternated in layers over lush green low trees and emerald fields. Beauty.

She carefully waited until Joe had eaten. It was always safer that way.

"I've made an appointment to talk with Jessie Lopez."

"Who is Jessie Lopez?"

"He's the one who is stealing our customers near Pittstown."

"I thought I told you I didn't want to talk to him."

"I know you did, but when Tom went on his route this morning, he found Jessie Lopez had solicited his largest motel. If we lose our country route, what's left won't be enough to pay our expenses."

"So you called the man and made an appointment to talk to him."

"Joe, I wish you wouldn't snarl at me. Don't you see . . . we don't have any choice. We have to save what we have. If that route never gets another customer, we are all right . . . but if we lose any more . . . well, we just can't stand it."

Joe sat on the yellow couch. He leaned forward with his hands cupped between his knee. His cheeks puffed out. He blew air through tight lips. Wearily he said, "When are you going to learn to do as I say . . . ?"

"What do you mean?"

"You know what I mean—to mind your own business."

"This is my business."

Joe sat sputtering with frustration.

"I set up the meeting for tomorrow night. It was the only night this week they were free."

"You mean they're going to drive over a hundred miles just to talk to us?"

"No. We're going there."

"You know Tuesday is one of my biggest days."

"I told them we'd be there around eight."

"What am I going to do with you?"

"Why don't you kiss me?"

"I don't feel like it."

He was still mad the next night when they arrived in Pittstown. He did his usual lost routine. He refused to ask directions, and they were surprised when they accidentally came upon a neat Spanish-type house with the numbers 5674.

"This must be the place. I see a garbage truck in the back."

"Now, Joe, try to be a gentleman." Joan knew she didn't dare say much. He was at the point of spontaneous combustion. He *exploded* twice a year, and even after all these years, Joan still was in awe of his performance—and careful to put distance between them when he blew. She sneaked a sideways glance . . . he was dangerously close.

The Lopezes were from Texas; had two sons in college, a twelve-year-old daughter and a ten-year-old fat little son; collected bright-colored vases and pictures painted on black velvet; liked roses; and were very hospitable.

Andrea Lopez and Joe's aunt were much alike. Andrea didn't offer one opinion all evening. Even when a question was directed to her, she looked to her husband. He immediately answered for his wife. He said it all.

He was smiling. "I'm glad that we have this chance to talk. I've been wondering who had the route next to mine."

Joe sat forward in his chair. He was not smiling. "Now that we've met, I think we should have a little understanding."

*Damnit, Joe, can't you be a little diplomatic? Why make Jessie into an enemy?* she thought. She said, "I think what my husband means is that we need to know just where our routes lie in relation to yours. We don't want to be in the position of taking any of your customers."

Jessie took a deep breath. "I'll show you where I'm going." He took a sheet of paper and began to draw a map.

Joe looked at the map. "Some of our routes intertwine." He drew a map of how his route lay.

Jessie shook his head. "I've been trying to build my route up. We have to move to Texas in three months, and I want to make sure I have something to sell."

Joan looked at him with growing interest. "You mean you're going to sell your route?"

"As soon as we can find a buyer. It's very hard to sell a route here in Pittstown where there is so much fighting over areas."

Joan studied the map. "How many customers do you have in our area?"

"Not too many. I think I'm getting a big motel near Leaburg."

Joe choked. "That's our stop."

"Oh." Jessie seemed surprised. "The owner called me."

"He must have been shopping."

"I won't bother with them." Jessie shrugged and lit a long cigar.

Joan coughed. "Jessie, have you ever considered splitting your route?"

"Splitting the route?"

"Yes. Sell your country route to us. Your city route will be easier to sell if you don't have to sell the rural part with it, and those customers will fit in well with our country route."

Jessie puffed. He blew smoke at the ceiling. He squinted his eyes. "I hadn't thought of that."

"Think about it."

Joe shifted in his chair. At times like this, he felt like an outsider. He wished Joan would consult him before she offered her *suggestions*. Now he shrugged as he looked at Jessie and Joan in their excitement of making a deal. He said, "Go through your books and find out what you want to sell. We will pay the going rate. We'll be in touch in a few days."

Joan moved forward on her chair. "We could come down next Sunday. You should have time to get the figures by then."

"We could. That will be fine. You come on Sunday."

They said good-bye to the family after enjoying Andrea's delicious cookies with thick Mexican coffee. It was late by the time they hit the freeway. Joe quickly accelerated to *his* ninety miles an hour. As they rode through the black night, their tired, strained faces were bathed by the illumination of the soft dash lights. Joe waited until he thought it was the right time to speak. He spoke softly, and Joan thought a little condescendingly.

"Joan, would it be possible for you to keep your mouth shut when we go on trips like this? Must you go on and on? When you talk all the time, you don't listen. Most of the time, if you'd shut up, they might say something you didn't know."

He heard her hiss. "That's fine, Joe, but if I didn't say something... no one would say anything. You sit and look at everyone with a sick grin or a black scowl. Who in the hell are you to tell me when I can talk and when I can't? I have the same right to speak as any other person. Some people don't want to talk—others do. That's fine. I happen to feel that if a person has something to say and a compulsion to speak, that person has the same right as anyone else in any group. Why didn't you have more to say? You could have spoken a dozen times. You didn't say anything. I did most of the talking. If I hadn't, it would have been *silence.*"

She jerked toward the window and pulled her sweater around her to ward off a sudden chill. She wondered why she wasted her breath on him. Even now as she looked at him, she could see him forming the words for rebuttal. *Damned men. Damn them. Why did they always have to have the last word? And be right? Ego? Do women have such an ego? Yes. No. God, I don't know. I wonder.* She began to think about the men she knew. Most of them, she thought, were enchanted with the sound of their voices—and what *they* thought. They never bothered to ask another person's opinion, except on rare occasions. When they did seek another opinion, they usually asked a question; then before the other person had a chance to finish replying, they were either speaking or planning what to say next. Then they went on and on again. Joe didn't do that exactly. Mostly he just thought he was right—all the time. What must it be like to be so right so often? To never have to consider another viewpoint? To never learn anything new? What had Nietzsche said? "To have to fight the instincts—that is the formula for decadence: as long as life is ascending, happiness equals instinct."

He reached an arm toward her. She made herself small. He was up to something. He never touched her anymore, except when he wanted a concession. He glanced in her direction. "It's late . . . we're both tired. We have so many decisions and problems to work out in the next month. Couldn't we get through one night without fighting?" He pursed his lips to say more, then thought better of it and pulled his arm from her. He concentrated on his showy driving the rest of the way home.

"Would you like me to drive?" she asked.

"No."

"Why won't you let me drive?"

"Because you scare the hell out of me."

"You scare me more." Joan was silent. She thought about the close call they'd had the previous Saturday night. She'd done her usual beauty shop visit, shopping; they'd gone to dinner, sat through it without speaking, then were on their way to Joe's favorite night spot. Suddenly, from a side street, a car shot forward. Joe, daydreaming at the wheel, barely avoided an accident.

Afterward in the honky-tonk nightclub filled with smoke, red lights, candles, drunk men and women, and the smell of stale beer, bourbon, scotch, rye, gin, and brandy, Joan shuddered when she thought how close they'd come to a smashup.

They were home. Stiffly they got out of the car. Joe turned off the lights before Joan could turn on the lights in the house. She stumbled to the switch.

"Joan?"

"Yes."

"Please don't get up for me in the morning."

"I won't get up for you in the morning. I thought I was doing you a favor. I hate to get up so early. Fine with me. I'll stay in bed and sleep and sleep and sleep." *And I'll never again go with you to the joint on Saturday night. I hate the people who go there. They laugh loud. They shout. They fall down. They are disgusting. Besides, it's too expensive to go there. Those drinks cost too much.*

She was still angry when she got into bed. Joe hadn't moved when she inched her way into the sheets. *If I'm lucky, he won't move.* She held her breath, and when there was no movement, she thanked God and settled in to sleep. Just as she was dozing off, a hand reached toward her. *Damn,* she thought. *Maybe if I lie still, he'll fall asleep.* His hand moved again, this time with an urgency she knew she couldn't ignore.

"Joe, I'm awfully tired. It's nearly three." More protestations. Then she knew there was no point fighting. She hoped he'd hurry so she could get some sleep.

He did.

# Chapter 20

Twenty-four hours later, Joan again stared at the ceiling of her bedroom. She turned over and lay thinking. *Someday I'm going to have a lover. He'll be gentle and kind. He'll love me as much as I love him... which will be a tremendous amount. That's all I really want. He won't look at other women, and when I speak, he'll hear me. He'll smile a lot, and he'll be happy because I love him. He'll like my cooking, and he'll never throw biscuits on the floor because I make them with cheese and onion. Gee, what if I never find a man who'll love me like I want to be loved? I will. I know.* She smiled then and rolled over to go to sleep. Moonlight lit the bedroom, flooding in from the large windows and the sliding glass doors. They'd been in the new house for nearly a year. She smiled. She never dreamed they'd have such a beautiful home.

Construction started on the new house on September 1. The contractor, Bob Blazer, had a brother named Ray who worked with him. Bob had built some of the finest homes in the valley. Ray came directly from Phoenix where he'd been working with architects for years. Ray was put in charge of the Schultz house.

There've been foul-ups from the start. It was the year it froze so hard. A half-mile lane had been engineered through the fields, down the swale, and through the trees. Rock crushed in the hills far from town and hauled in huge gravel trucks paved the undersurface of the roadbed. Then it froze. The frost uplifted the soil under the rock. It thawed. The man from the lumberyard who drove the huge truck laden with heavy brick didn't realize what had happened until he was too far down the lane to back up. He tried everything. Back up. Go forward. Back up. Nothing worked. In order to turn around, he had to fight the soft mud inches at a time all the way to the house, around the circle, and out again. He left deep troughs of mud in a gravelly slough one-half mile long. Several thousand dollars and load after load of large aggregate and fine gravel made the road like new.

Joe hadn't even *wanted* to build. He'd fought it all the way. Faced with the reality of a growing family, of lack of space, and that a new house would also be an investment, he finally conceded. Joan had to have a house like the one she'd seen at the beach. It made her forget her colonial dream. This house was functional, efficient, practical, livable, and, most important, comfortable. It was very beautiful. Lots of wood and glass and space. The architect had studied with Frank Lloyd Wright, and after Joan had seen the house he designed, she knew she'd never be happy living in any other kind of house.

She'd found his address in Lakeside. She pulled herself up the long flight of stairs to his office. She felt strange. He opened his door with a smile, and Joan noted how handsome he was. He wore blue in different shades that matched and complemented his smoky blue eyes. He stood tall and erect, and Joan thought he might have appeared in the pages of *Esquire*—urbane, cosmopolitan, and nice. His soft voice with a definite New York accent sounded distressed. She realized she had her hand to her head. He grabbed a high stool, and she sagged on to it.

"Say, are you all right?"

She nodded her head. "I'm sorry. I'm pregnant and dizzy. I'll be all right in a few minutes. I hope."

"Now, you stay right there until you feel well." He didn't know what to do, and he nervously kept his eyes on her.

He brought her water, and in a short time, she felt much better.

"I saw the house you designed at Ocean City. I loved it. It is simply beautiful. We have to have a larger house, and I would like you to design one for us. We're about five years ahead of time financially, but I won't be happy living in any other house." She told him about the family. When she told him she had eight children, he seemed surprised and pleased.

"That is wonderful," he said.

"It is and it isn't," she answered. "It is absolutely hell to try to live in a small four-bedroom house with eight children . . . and another one on the way."

"Yes, well, I suppose you're right."

He came to their house and talked to them. Joan had several special projects she wanted incorporated into the design of the house. They seemed impossible, but when the architect found out what they were, he skillfully and quickly penciled them onto clean white paper.

He did a perfect job and graciously allowed them to make payments on his reduced fee. Joan was so pleased to have met him. He was a perfect talented gentleman.

The week before work was to begin, Bob Blazer came to them and told them he was unsure of the figures he had quoted. The contract was already signed. When he left, Joan and Joe were stunned.

"It's just not fair." Joan sat in their small kitchen, shaking her head. "He shouldn't be penalized because he didn't understand the architect's plan or how to bid on it correctly. He's honest and he's a good worker. We should build it on a cost-plus basis and not hold him to the contract."

Joe's eyes squinted. He leaned forward in his chair. "He signed a contract with us to build the house for $35,000. If he can't build it for that, that's his problem." His mouth squinched, and he seemed about to say more.

"I don't think Bob Blazer should have to take a loss on building a house—for us!"

"What if it costs more than $35,000? We can only get a loan for that amount."

"I think we could get more if we ask Mr. Worthington."

Joe reared back in his chair. He kicked his right foot high in the air. "No. I'm not going to go into any more debt just so you can have a new house."

He acquiesced. He had no choice. They hoped the costs wouldn't run too far over the $35,000. That hope evaporated when in the first week of building, the manager of the lumberyard called and said he'd made a $3,000 mistake on their estimate.

The night they sat on the floor of the half-completed structure and tried to imagine which room went with which group of studs, they had no idea the final cost would be almost exactly $20,000 more than the original bid. Joe would not have enjoyed being there at all. As it was, they heard the creek splashing and gurgling in the moonlight. Shadows from the birch trees lining the water near the pond looked like black ink. Sounds of evening captivated them and held them prisoner into the night.

The house grew and changed and came to be. Studs, which made the rooms seem small, were slowly covered with boards. Rooms suddenly formed—seemed larger. Work inched on through winter. It started to rain early that year. The workmen fought wind and rain every step of the way. Everything took longer than they imagined it would. The carpenters were perfectionists. Each mitered corner of wood fit so well, it seemed to be of one piece. They matched wood, hammered, and sawed always with an eye to perfect detail.

Double-paned glass for the windows, plumbers, electricians, and appliances were late in coming. When everything else in the house was completed, the move-in date had to be postponed two months, while the kitchen cabinets were built by Bob Blazer's favorite nephew.

Joe continued to work from early morning to late at night. Subcontracting of the work was left to Joan. She'd had to make all decisions (with the architect's gracious help) concerning materials, colors, and all the myriad choices involved in building a house. She'd had to juggle a new baby, the family, the business, and the house, with trips to Watertown for parts and items for the house.

Before the baby came, they'd slid twice into Capital City in the year's worst snowstorms. The first time was a false alarm. The second was not. Coming across a drunk driver, Joan insisted Joe call the police to get the menace off the road. Joe called from a pay phone near the hospital, while she sat hunched over her huge stomach—afraid she'd give birth any minute. They'd made it to the hospital, and a pretty little baby girl they named Jean was born on the last day of the year.

Jean was seven months old when they moved into the new house. It was everything the architect had envisioned. It suited the contours of the land—elegant, spacious, grand, efficient, and built like a fortress. Little Jean was like a princess moving into a castle. A grubby, poor little princess, but a princess nevertheless. She would never remember the old, cramped, inefficient house.

The boards and battens of the new house reminded Joan of her own childhood home. Her father, the superintendent of the logging camp, had built their house with boards and battens deep in the woods in the logging camp. The house was a cheery two-bedroom cabin with no bathroom. At first, everyone in the camp shared a common outhouse in a central location. Cold. Cold water had been piped into the kitchen. Hot water was heated in the reservoir of the woodstove. Joan's memory of the house was that it was clean, warm, and cozy with starched white curtains on the windows. She also remembered the cold linoleum floor kept highly waxed, washing machine with the gas engine her mother started every Monday, clothes drying near the heating stove on clothes racks, steaming windows, sitting by the radio with her ear to the speaker, cold beds, delicious food, and a lingering memory of pleasant days.

She remembered how they'd spent their summer in the river near the camp. All the camp kids knew how to swim. Joan learned when she was five. She couldn't imagine letting her own children be unsupervised all day, but when she was growing up, the camp kids spent every day at the river. No adult ever came to check on them, and the only time they went home was when they were forced by sheer hunger. They caught crawfish and cooked them on the big rock in the middle of the rapids. They swam and played, hiked, had wild cucumber fights and bark fights, and picked wild iris high on the big mountain behind the camp. They rode the school bus six miles over a road that made log truck drivers cringe.

Joan's reverie brought the memory of the big fir burn to mind. She was six years old, and she knew if she lived to be a hundred, she would never forget it. Smoke layered thick in the air. Red-hot cinders and blackened warm ones drifted in the air among the trees by the houses. The fire had come up suddenly; it jumped from at least a mile away. Dishes and valuables were quickly buried as flames rose above the mountain. Men with taut faces ran through the camp with fire hoses. Others manned pumps at the river. A sudden wind shift brought the raging flames too close. Another wind shift, and somehow they'd escaped the inferno. Black snags and black earth surrounded the camp when the fire died.

Looking at the new house, Joan thanked God her children would never have to live anywhere else. The acreage was a fine place to rear them. Here they could run and play. They had privacy. No close neighbors. Country silent. Country sounds. Beauty. Trees. Wild flowers. She hadn't seen the possibilities the day Joe first brought her to see the place. A lane, rutted and muddy, angled in for a half mile. Joe had been hunting when he came upon the small acreage. The owners were friends of the man who ran the dump. The place consisted of an old barn, an old house, and an old cabin . . . all about to fall down.

"Jesus, Joe, I don't think we'll want to build our house here. I don't like it at all."

They stood amid stumps left from a long-ago logging operation. When they walked, berry vines, half hidden, clawed at their legs in the tall grass.

Joe stopped. "This is where we're going to build. I want to be away from people."

"Why can't the house be closer to the road?"

"I don't want anyone to see us in a new house."

"Why not, Joe? We don't have to hide from the world."

"If our customers saw us in a new house, we'd never get another raise. If you want to build a house, this is where it will be."

That's where it was.

Jean was a good baby, and Joan thanked God for it and a lot of other things in the next few months. They'd been so poor for so long. Now it was a pleasure to have money ahead. Most of the clothes she'd bought during the years were maternity clothes—cheap maternity clothes. She always thought maternity clothes were a waste of money. She cringed when she thought about being pregnant. *Ohhhhh.* Knifelike pains in her lower abdomen had started in the third month of her last pregnancy. By the time she was nine months along, she could hardly move. Her bladder caused problems too. She leaked. She wore a Kotex most of the time to catch the drips. Her gynecologist shook his head and said she should have a hysterectomy. Joe didn't agree.

"Absolutely not."

"Joe, I need an operation."

"It's a sin."

"How?"

"It just is. Your duty is to have as many babies as God sends."

"I think I've been getting some of the ones intended for other people."

"Very funny. It doesn't change the fact that what you are doing now is committing a sin."

"I'm committing a sin? Because I need an operation? I have had nine children, my body is falling apart from the inside cut—literally. I leak urine constantly, and when I menstruate, I flow like a garden hose turned on strong. That's a sin? Don't I have a right to some kind of a life based on my needs? Don't I have a right to a healthy body? I know, as far as you are concerned, I have no right to think what you don't want me to think or say what you don't want me to say! Go to hell! I'm having the operation. I need it."

He kicked over the footstool. Then he left. His rage followed him like the tail of a bull. His face distorted and was tinged with a wonderful shade of pink that made him seem more alive than Joan had ever seen him.

The Schultz side of the family thought it was a good thing to suffer. It brought a higher place in heaven. They were good at mundane suffering, but they weren't too good at big suffering. Whenever something happened that called for real suffering, they started carrying on something terrible. They wanted others to suffer—never themselves. Joe spent a lot of time telling Joan about sin and suffering. He never seemed able to suffer on his own. Joan could do it all for the whole family. She remembered how he'd behaved in the past . . . like an authority on canon law. He'd set down rules for her to follow. Then he'd go about his business as usual.

There were days when she wished she were a man. It seemed they had the best of the marriage deal. They did nothing to help their wives with the children. She thought, *I'm the one who takes care of everything around here—the children, the house, the car, the billing, the banking. Everything. Joe comes home, eats, falls asleep on the sofa, goes to bed, yells for a towel in the morning, and acts like he's neglected if I don't want to make love all night. Boy. They have it made. Husbands. Phooey.*

When she said anything, he'd say, "Don't you think *I* get tired?"

"Joe, I don't want you to work as hard as you do. I never did. You know that, but there is a lot of work to having a family that you aren't even aware of. The clothes are clean, your meals are cooked, and the house is in order. There is no magic. I never ask you to do one thing for us, and you put forth no effort as far as your family is concerned."

"I work, don't I?"

"Ugh."

Dr. McCready examined her. Modestly she avoided his eyes. He looked at her and pursed his lips. "Have you had a period lately?"

"I'm not sure when it was. Why?"

"I think you may be pregnant."

"You're kidding."

"No, I'm not." He pulled his rubber gloves off and shook his head. We'd better make sure you aren't pregnant before we operate. Come back in a month. And, Joan . . ."

"Yes?"

"If you aren't pregnant, please don't get pregnant." He was still shaking his head while she dressed. As she left the room, he said, "I won't be responsible for this one."

She looked at him and smiled. "You weren't responsible for the others either." With that, she left him, hopped into her car, and drove straight to her favorite drive-in and had fish and chips (made of halibut), a sesame bun toasted with butter, tasty coleslaw, and a chocolate malted milkshake. As she drank the last of her malted, she thought of Joe having to wait a whole month to make love to her. Once, when they'd lived in the old house of her parents, she'd had a hydatid mole, which was a very unusual kind of pregnancy. The fetus (as far as Joan understood) turned to grapelike growths. She was three months along and was as large as if she were six.

She started hemorrhaging in the bathroom. She baptized some tissue, got weak, then called for help. Her doctor told her that the growth might come back or a deadly tumor or cancer might result. She had to have a rabbit test every month for six months to make sure there was no recurrence. The doctor told her they'd have to use birth control during that period. She told him she couldn't. He'd even called the parish priest for her in a vain attempt to get permission for her.

She thought he never did believe they had practiced abstinence for six long months. But they did. Joan was sure they could do it again. She didn't know how she was going to carry another child. She prayed she wasn't pregnant.

She was.

Chicanos lived in and around Maplewood. Unlike the Russian colony who helped and supported each other, each Chicano family was virtually on its own. They had no common link, except a desire to find a place to live in peace and some small comfort. Some of the families had a brother or an uncle or some other family member in the area, but most had no one.

In the early '50s, many families came from Texas, leaving their modest houses for shacks near the fields. If each member of the family worked very hard during the season, they could live in Texas the rest of the year in relative comfort. There were many row crops and other crops that demanded constant backbreaking labor in the area. People who could or would do the kind of work necessary were nonexistent.

So they came—mostly from Texas. Families in cars with nothing but the clothes they wore, cramped and tired and infinitely patient. Gentle people. Hopeful men, young and old, came in open cattle trucks with only a tarp for protection from the rain. Often they were exploited by greedy crew bosses.

Farmers in the area over the years changed their method of farming and the kinds of crops they grew. Each year more and more of the Chicanos stayed over the winter. The state's system of welfare made it possible for them to exist until the next harvest season. Their children were absorbed into the local school systems and, for the first time, were given a continuous education.

The farmers ranted and raved about the system. The welfare system. They failed to appreciate that, in actuality, the people of the state subsidized them by taking care of their fieldworkers through the winter. Then the farmers could exploit the workers during the summer so they (the farmers) could live in beautiful warm houses in the winter. Most held the Chicanos in contempt. They shouted obscenities at them and behaved a lot like slave owners of the old South.

At one time, the population of Chicanos grew to such proportions, these same men became alarmed and afraid for their safety. Irisher's and the Steer Inn, where everyone ate lunch and which were the social centers of town, began to be filled with Chicanos.

Tensions mounted. One night someone said something. Knives flashed. One fat townsman who was in the middle of the fracas said, "I thought I was really doing good when I saw blood on my hand. I looked down. It was *my* blood. I was cut from one side of my stomach to the other. A linoleum knife. After I realized I was the one bleeding, it hurt like hell. I'll have a scar for life. I'm just happy it wasn't my throat. We were lucky no one died—especially me."

Joan had ridden with Joe, once, to a migrant camp near St. Eames.

Water lay in pools among the muddy lane. Joan had read about the plight of the fieldworkers, but her eyes were unprepared for what she saw. The dust of summer had changed into the mud of fall. Children played in it, like pigs wallowing. Cars sat mired to the axles. One-room shacks, ten by twelve, dotted the area. Heads poked from the one door and one window of the shacks.

"My god, Joe, don't tell me people live in *these*."

"Not people, Joan, families."

"You're kidding, Joe. They look like little chicken coops. How many people live in each one?"

"However many there are in a family ... six ... eight ... twelve ... I don't know ..."

"Oh, Joe, that's terrible. How can they get away with making people live like this?"

"No one *makes* them live here."

"But they haven't anyplace else to go? ... What would happen if they had a fire and couldn't get out the door? Is there another way out?" she asked.

"No, there isn't."

Joe emptied the garbage container. He kept a close watch on the children who were attracted to the excitement, like flies to the garbage can. Finished, he started the truck, and they went bumping out the muddy, rutted lane. Joan said a silent prayer of thanks for their four-bedroom palace, which, until she had seen this squalor, had seemed woefully inadequate and much too small.

"Do you know how lucky we are, Joe?"

He was lost in thought. He had been aware of the worker's plight, but seeing it through Joan's eyes made him newly awake to the grim reality of the way these people lived. They were *society's forgotten ones*. Joe hoped he could forget them too.

Joan remembered one family who rented a small chicken house from their neighbor in rural Maplewood. There were eight children in the family. The mother, Maria Gonzales, and Joan had much in common. Joan chatted with her from time to time. The family lived there one whole summer. They papered the inside of the small structure with cardboard boxes and kept the place very clean. Mrs. Gonzales bathed the children by pouring pans of water over them. The beautiful brown babies were shaking like birds in a fountain.

Joan happened to look in the chicken house one day and was shocked to see few utensils and dishes. She especially thanked God that night that he had been so kind to her and her family, and she prayed he'd do better by the Gonzalezes.

The difference between the Russians in the community and the Chicanos was marked. The Russians helped each other and were very industrious. In a short time after coming to the United States, the young Russians had jobs in Watertown, upholstering furniture and doing other semiskilled labor. The older immigrants found these jobs for the young ones. As a group, the people were thrifty, frugal, saving, and supportive.

The Chicano, on the other hand, spent most of his money on expensive food, clothes, and new cars. The housing situation was often the last concern of the Chicano. After the first check from the harvest, the Chicano and his family turned up newly bedecked with Easter-like finery.

The Russians remained aloof from the community. The Chicanos, gregarious and warm, entered into the life of the town with enthusiasm.

Joan saw one Chicano boy who was so handsome, he took her breath away. His brown skin, big soft brown eyes, white straight teeth, soft mouth with sensuous full lips, combined with a certain challenging charm, fascinated her. In about three months, it was apparent one of the local girls had also been fascinated. She was pregnant.

The parish priest refused to marry them at first. After about a month, with exhortations from all sides (except the girl's parents, who were permanently bent out of shape because of the scandal), he relented and allowed the marriage to take place . . . at six o'clock in the morning. Joan couldn't imagine what all the fuss was about; after all, they were both Catholic.

Joan first met Father Mandell in 1950. She'd called for an appointment for instructions in the Catholic faith that summer. He'd been too busy to talk to her. One evening she and Joe had driven into the bottom and found a partying group in a cherry orchard near the road. Everyone was drunk. Joan could tell from Joe's acute embarrassment and lack of surprise that the priest's drinking was a problem. He'd get famously drunk.

Weddings brought him to the forefront of revelers, and one wedding rehearsal found him founderingly intoxicated. Members of the wedding party, out-of-town-relatives, and others at the rehearsal shot knowing looks at each other. Then a veil of conspiratorial silence descended. They knew what he had become. They loved him—and looked the other way.

A master politician, he walked both sides of the street with equanimity. Parishioners vied for his attention and his affection. He was furnished a housekeeper, a gardener, board and room, spending money, a new Buick, and God's place on earth.

At weddings, Joan watched with embarrassment as women rubbed their breasts and legs and arms and hands and anything else they could rub against him. A safe target and an elegant and attractive man, he had to practically beat the middle-aged frustrated females away.

She remembered how he'd said, "Well, you certainly have a fine family," when he'd baptized their sixth child.

"Father, you said that last year when you baptized the old baby." Joan laughed.

He looked silly.

One night there'd been a study club meeting, and Joan had asked if it was a sin for a man to be a martyr if he really wanted to die—was unable to commit suicide and being a martyr was the only way he could escape torture (Catholic martyrs go directly to heaven . . . at least they did during the '50s). When he couldn't answer her question, he'd become angry.

The Schultzes' country calcification met with contemptuousness by Father Mandell. He'd been reared in fine Eastern traditions. Life among the uncivilized filled him with disdain. Carefully hiding his true feelings, he flourished in the town for many years. Most of that time, he spent tyrannizing the populace with proclamations concerning the latest *sin*. Everything was—and everyone agreed. Heads nodded. Eyes closed and stayed shut. The devil was everywhere.

Keeping *sin* out of St. Eames was no easy task. The man who took the job was a master, even though he had to contend with such downfalls as the yearly rodeo, summer swimming, beer parties, trail rides, bus trips, hay rides, backseats of cars, wedding receptions, and the woods and trails around the lively little town.

Joan thought Father Mandell did a particularly good job on eulogies. He had a gift for making the worst sinner into a veritable saint. The magic of death instantly transformed the offender. It did make the family feel better. Except for the fact that he was getting to be an old man. Joan wished he would be around for her funeral. He said the nicest things. She doubted anyone else would.

She wished she'd stop thinking of him. She could see him trim and tall, his black cassock flapping as he moved with precision, grace, and speed. His white hair contrasted with his steel-blue eyes with crinkles at the corners.

She missed him. He'd been sent away. Moved to another parish, his health faded and his spirit crushed. He'd been overlooked for a move for years until a new archbishop went over the list of parish priests and discovered the error. Everyone in the chancery office knew how dangerous it was to leave a priest in a parish for such a long time. Everyone in St. Eames was sorry to see him leave. Except those who weren't.

Joe detested the Chicanos and the State Immigrant League, which had become a force in the community. They assisted the Chicanos in day care, job finding, and myriad problems bred by ignorance and poverty.

Murray was having a beer when Joe picked him up at the little tavern on Third Street. He stuck his head out the door and called to Joe. "Come have a beer with me."

"Sure." Joe was happy to stop for a short time. He'd worked hard all morning, and it was getting warm.

"How come you're picking up garbage?"

"It's my job." Joe shook his head.

"I didn't mean that. I thought you were off the routes."

"I am and I'm not. Whenever someone doesn't show up, I work on the truck. Otherwise, I'm spending most of my time on the drop box truck."

"So you need a man."

"I sure do."

"Why not hire a Chicano? They need work, and you need someone to help."

"You sound like Joan. I wouldn't have one of those lazy bastards working for me for anything."

"They're not that lazy. They pick more berries than any white person I've ever known."

Country Western music, which Joe detested, suddenly reached his consciousness. He hadn't noticed it until now. He hadn't noticed the stale beer smell either. The music, smell, and dark lighting were all wrapped up in a big net of unpleasantness with him in the center. He had to get out of there. He thought of the Chicanos in the fields where he worked as a boy. With resignation, he answered Murray, "They leave half the berries on the vine. They scoop through the rows. It's a shame the way they ruin the plants. I wouldn't have one of them work for me for anything."

"Well, hey, who am I to tell you how to run your business? Seems a shame, though, that you can't take advantage of the latest government subsidy. The government pays part of their wage for several months of training. It sounds like a good program for the Chicano and the employer."

## Chapter 21

The man Joe hired through the program, Jesse Gomez, had just arrived from Texas in a car crowded with his wife, Lupe, his six children, and everything he owned. Jesse was so happy to get the job; Joe felt a little ashamed.

The first week on the job, Jesse looked like a ghost walking. He wasn't used to the climate or the hard physical labor. Most of the men of his height and stature found jobs where their flying hands were put to work, not their backs. They seldom did such hard work as carrying garbage.

Joe peeked his head into the kitchen early the next Monday morning. Joan looked at him through sleepy eyes. Her muscles ached. She hated to get up early in the morning. But she did. Some mornings when she awoke, her body wouldn't move. For a time, she would think she died during the night. That's how she felt this morning. Tired. Exhausted. Dead.

"Jesse's baby is sick. He wanted to take the day off work to go to the doctor. I told him you'd take the baby." Joe shook his head in disgust. "Can you imagine taking a day off work to take a baby to the doctor?"

"It's hard to believe anyone could be so stupid," Joan whispered, shaking her head.

Joan did what was necessary, found a sitter for her own children, then hurried to the address Jesse had given Joe. Jesse had rented a grotesque, old, dilapidated, two-story dump in a shabby part of town. No grass grew. Hard-packed dirt under the trees would turn to mud when the first rain came. There was no walkway, just a packed dirt path leading to the soiled front door. Joan knocked. She waited. She knocked again. Jesse's wife, Lupe, answered the door. She seemed distraught. She motioned Joan inside. The house stank. Joan tried to imagine what combination of ingredients could produce such a smell. Whew. Lupe brought the baby to the living room. A neighbor would stay with the other children. Joan nudged Lupe toward the door. Her sympathies were aroused by one look at the very sick baby breathing laboriously. Her skin looked feverish, and she was completely still. Not even a tear.

When they arrived at the doctor's office, Joan was relieved to see only a few cars ahead of them. The doctors in the only clinic in town had long since stopped making appointments. They saw patients as they arrived on a first-come-first-served basis. The critical or seriously ill patients were sometimes given priorities, but the others often had to wait as long as three hours.

The baby still had made no sound. Experience told Joan that when a child is too sick to cry, there is every cause for alarm.

The office nurse came into the reception area. "What can I do for you, Mrs. Schultz?"

"I've brought Mrs. Gomez in with her baby. The baby is very ill."

"Fine. Here's a form . . . We'll need to have it filled out."

"Mrs. Gomez speaks no English, and I don't know Spanish."

"Oh, dear." The nurse looked perplexed. Her brows knit together, and she pursed her lips. "Does her husband speak English?"

"Yes. He speaks very good English."

"Then he can probably read it too. Have him come in as soon as possible. In the meantime, the charge for the doctor's call will have to be paid in cash."

"What?"

"The doctor will not see the baby unless the bill is paid in advance."

Sudden anger caught Joan. "The baby's father just started working last week. The family has no extra money."

"I'm sorry. If they can't pay for the office call, they can't see the doctor."

"I can't believe this."

"It is true."

"Let's do this . . . If the bill isn't paid within a reasonable time, charge it to our account."

The nurse grudgingly agreed.

Joan had an insight into a totally different world that day. She and Joe had been poor, but they always had someone they could turn to in an emergency. In the world she'd glimpsed . . . the world where a sick child could be denied medical care because the parents had no money . . . there was no hope at all.

The respect Joan had always felt for the medical profession turned to righteous anger. The baby with its strep infection would be all right in a few days. The greed of doctors who pushed people through the examining rooms like cattle and could refuse to treat a sick baby for lack of cash would ooze through society and cause a disease so devastating in itself that all society would be diminished.

She wondered as she passed the doctor's house on the way home what kind of man he was. She saw children swimming in the new pool. What was the justice that let one man live like a king and another in poverty? Did doctors deserve such luxury? Or anyone?

As darkness caused evening's heat to change into night's chill, Joe's truck came banging down the lane. The lane was different now. Dustier. Dirtier. Deeper ruts. Joan waited for him under the trees near the gas pump. She decided to wait to talk to him until after he had eaten. He might be in a better mood then—maybe.

The smell of gas as it ran into the truck filled the night. Finishing, Joe took Joan's hand, and they walked toward the well-lit kitchen. Joan busied herself at the stove, while Joe collapsed on the couch.

"You'd better go wash. Your dinner is almost ready."

"Mmmmmmm."

"What?" She turned to listen, then looked and saw he was engrossed in the evening paper. He wasn't paying the slightest attention to her.

"Joe, please get washed for dinner."

He glared at her, turned back to his paper, and continued reading. Finally, he rose and made his way to the bathroom, muttering to himself as he went. Joan turned back to the food. *He probably won't like what I fixed him tonight either.* She seldom fixed anything he liked. Except steak.

She watched with fascination as he bolted his food. His eating habits always amazed her. He could clean a plate faster than anyone she knew. He gulped his milk, patted his stomach, then flopped onto the couch with lightning speed. She waited awhile. Then when she could see he was in a better mood, she thought she had picked the right moment.

"Joe, I went to the bank to see Mr. Worthington today."

"Mmmmmm."

"I asked him if he'd lend us $3,600 to pave the lane."

"Don't be ridiculous. We are not spending money to have the lane paved."

"I think you should think about it, Joe. We have three estimates on the paving job, though the one from the man in town is two years old. We might want to talk to him again. I think we should have the man who lives near the grade school do the job. He's a local contractor and has a reputation to maintain and also a lot of competition to buck. I think he'll do the best job at the lowest cost . . ."

"No. No. *No!*"

"And we've got to consider the damage those deep ruts do to the trucks and the cars. It is getting very hard to drive down the lane. There's so much dust in the summer that it's impossible to breathe. It is very dirty in the house too, with all that dirt coming in. In the winter, mud is tracked in."

"No. No. *No!*"

"There's one other thing we have to consider. It wastes a lot of time to have to drive so slow on the lane."

"I told you—*no*. I mean—*no*. And I don't want to hear another word from you."

"Look, Joe, I'm tired of nagging you. Just who in the hell do you think you are to tell me *no*? I have some rights in this marriage and the business, you know."

"Oh. Oh. Here comes the part about your being the brains behind the business. Right?"

"I wouldn't say that. Except, of course, you know I'm smarter than you."

Their voices rose. She'd made him angry at last. Now she would taunt him. There was something about the way he became lividly furious that brought out the perversity in her. Once, she'd made him so angry when he was driving that he'd taken his hands off the wheel and roared like a lion. She couldn't stop laughing, but it scared the hell out of her.

He had his stubborn-child look on his face. "The lane is not going to be paved. I'll find something to patch the holes."

"You said that before. You've done nothing about it. It's easy to make promises. A promise made is a debt unpaid. And, brother, you have lots of unpaid debts. You never keep your word."

"I'll promise you this—we are not having the lane paved."

The paving man was happy when Joan called early the next day. He said he'd call and tell her exactly when he'd be able to schedule the job.

"Joe, I'm going to take the children to the beach for a week. I'm all caught up on the billing, and the paving man wants to pave the lane day after tomorrow. If we're around, they'll track black asphalt into the house. You can come out on the weekend and bring Stan and Sarah with you."

"I don't think you should go."

"Why not?" she asked, though she knew *why not*. Joe hated to have her out of his sight. He also hated to have to wait on himself. If she were gone, he'd have to get his own meals (which he was completely incapable of doing) or eat out. If he ate out, he'd have to come home, however, change clothes, then drive into town and find a place to eat. It was easier if she stayed home—for him.

"I don't want you to go."

"I know. I'm going." She looked forward to taking the children to the ocean. They seldom were able to go. Usually on a winter Sunday, every year or so, they managed a trip. "The children love to play in the sand."

"Go! Go! Go."

"I'm *going!*"

By the time she finished washing, packing, and loading the car with enough clothes, shoes, and sundry to keep her and the children covered for a week, her enthusiasm had waned. The coast trip didn't seem nearly as exciting as it had when she'd first thought of it.

They stopped for groceries halfway to the coast. By some coincidence, all the children had to go to the bathroom at the same time. The store manager refused to let them use the facilities, which were for *employees only*.

"You'd better let them in . . . or I won't be responsible for what might happen."

He shrugged in surrender and opened the door.

After an hour and a half of fighting, crying, singing, shouting, getting stepped on by the old baby, and one emergency stop for carsickness, they arrived at the beach. Joan found a large tumbledown cabin on the beach for $50 a week. She couldn't believe her good fortune . . . until she got into bed that night with two children. It listed to the right, was lumpy and damp, and had a musty odor. When she finished her prayers that night, she added, *Please, God, don't let anyone wet on me.*

The next morning, everyone woke early because of the strange beds and different sounds of the ocean. The older of the seven children spent that day and the rest of the days at the beach, playing in the sand in their bathing suits, running in and out of the cabin, and making friends with other children from the nearby cabins.

By some miracle, the weather stayed beautiful all week. It was neither too warm nor too cold. The sun came up early in a soft violet light that reflected on the ocean in front of the cabin, stayed out in a cloudless sky, then sank in a glorious fiery red blaze.

While the children ran, played, made sand castles, and looked for seashells, Joan, the ubiquitous mother, read, visited with other mothers, fixed simple meals, and completely relaxed. The garbage route and Joe seemed faraway. She was surprised how little she missed him—and a little ashamed.

One day, she walked back from the small grocery store to find the owner of the court working on the garage at the rear of his house. She stopped to chat.

"How are you doing there, Mrs. Schultz?"

"Just fine, Mr. Hardin. The children have never been happier. Even our toddler, Barbara, goes on the beach to play. I'm afraid to leave her alone very long, though—she likes to eat sand. She produces bricks." Mr. Hardin caught the twinkle in Joan's eyes. They laughed.

"One of our boys used to do that."

"What are you going to do—paint the garage?"

"Yes, I'm trying to make the place look good. We're going to have to sell. My wife has cancer of the bone, and we have to get closer to Watertown to her doctor."

"I'm sorry to hear that. I hope she'll get better. Have you set a price on the property?"

"Yes. I'm asking $16,000. That includes the lot, which is 200 x 200." He indicated the boundaries. "Those three cabins on the front will have to be torn down eventually, but that cabin near the fence and our house are in real good condition."

"What would you need for a down payment?"

"I'd take a thousand down and carry the contract. I need the interest to supplement my social security."

"That sounds like a really good buy for someone. Are you sure you're asking enough?"

"We've had the place twenty years. We bought it for next to nothing. If we had time and wanted to stay here, maybe we could get more for it . . . I know we could . . . but we have to sell soon, and I'm not interested in making a big profit."

They chatted for a while. Joan noticed how inefficient Mr. Hardin had been with his repairs. Everything he had done looked a little messy—a little off center and askew. Joan thought about the property as she worked. Mr. Hardin was actually making a gift of the place to whomever had the foresight to meet his very easy terms. The cabins could be rented for enough to make the monthly payments. Maybe two or three families might pool their money and buy it. *I'll tell Joe about it when he comes.*

She looked across the blue Pacific. She felt the same as she had when she was six years old and had seen it for the first time. They'd lived in the logging camp, which was thirty miles from the ocean. The narrow, unpaved road made driving difficult most of the year. So it must have been summer. She remembered the view from the highway near the top of Mount Takawana. She would never forget it. It was a clear sunny day. Looking out over the glimmering green-blue ocean from that height made her feel suspended. To the right looking down the coastline, blue sky, dark-green trees, beige sand, and white lacy saucer-shaped waves etched a picture in her mind she would always remember—like a dream. But it was real.

She and Joe had looked for a beach house on other trips to the coast. Everything they'd found was overpriced, hard to maintain, in a poor location, or just too awful. Joan wanted a house on the beach. For once, Joe agreed.

The day before Joe came, she noticed a FOR SALE sign on a charming Cape Cod right on the beach. As soon as she could, she knocked on the door.

"Hello." The woman who answered spoke in a soft pleasant voice. Joan noticed how small she was. Her curly gray hair peeked around the edges of a bright blue silk scarf. She wore a neat apron and a pretty smile.

"I saw your sign . . ." Joan looked beyond into the comfortable living room . . . "and I'd like to see the house."

"Of course, Mrs. . . . ?"

"Schultz."

"Mrs. Schultz—I'm Mrs. Goodwin."

"How do you do? I'm planning to buy a house at the beach, but I don't know that my husband is. If it's any bother for you to show the house to me, well, I may not be a prospective customer at all."

"It's no trouble. We just put the sign up last night. So far, three other couples have already looked at it. Come right on in."

The house was compact, warm, nicely decorated, and in excellent condition. Joan pictured herself sitting in the living room, looking at the ocean from the huge window.

"My husband spends every weekend working on the house. It's his relaxation."

"He certainly takes good care of it. Why are you selling?"

"My husband does nothing but work on the house every weekend. We have hordes of relatives and friends who come in on us. We've awakened many Sunday mornings to find the house full of people I have to cook for and wait on. And they like *steak*, thank you. There is no way to stop it, and we're just tired of that kind of life. We've decided to spend the rest of our lives doing what we want to do without being pressured by other people. Of course, Mr. Goodwin will miss this place—his hobby is carpentry, but we can find something else for him to do."

"How much do you want for the house?"

"We're asking eighteen thousand dollars. We're selling it furnished."

Joan was thinking how the house would suit them. They would have a lot of things to buy—sheets, linens, silver, dishes, and all the other necessities.

As if reading her mind, she heard Mrs. Goodwin say, "We're going to leave the dishes, silverware, blankets, and everything but our personal possessions. We have everything we need in our home in town."

"That would be wonderful for whomever buys it. It's quite expensive to buy everything at once."

"Well, these things aren't new . . . but they're serviceable."

Joan noticed the dishes were an old pattern she loved. Marjorie Bunker had a set of them in camp years before. *Fiesta*. Rainbow colors. Heavy ware.

The house had four bedrooms (one overlooking the ocean), two down and two up. There wasn't a lot of storage, but for a vacation house, it was quite adequate. The lot was landscaped and had a small easy-care lawn in front. The house looked solid on the ridge; the garage was hidden under the first floor from the beach side. Steps led from the driveway near the street up to the front door. A deck was attached to the fence on the south and to the entry on the north. A flagpole with a weathervane and an attractive gate leading to the beach were in the northwest corner of the fifty-by-eighty-five-foot lot.

Mrs. Goodwin showed her everything. She was very gracious especially considering that she pretty well knew Joan was not a completely serious buyer. They parted company at the gate, and Joan walked back to the cabin on the beach. She didn't know why, but she was very happy.

When Joe came the next day, she was beside herself. After he'd had a chance to catch his breath and tell her how wonderful the new lane was (like it had been his idea) and unload his clothes, Joan told him about the properties that were for sale.

"This probably would be the best buy from an investment standpoint, but you and I have no extra time to manage any income property. It sounds like a gift, and probably is, but I think the house would suit us best. Will you go look at it with me?"

"Before we go home. I want to enjoy the weekend. I don't want to think about buying anything. I'm afraid I'll have to say *no* right now anyway. We just built our house three years ago, and we're going to have to buy a new truck..."

"I know we will, but I just want you to look at the house."

"Not now. No."

"All right. Forget the whole thing. You seem to want to have a big family so you can say you have a big family. It makes you look like a good Catholic. You don't fool me. What do you do to make their lives any better? Every time they need something, you fight with me about it. If I take them to the doctor, you complain. You never want to spend any money for their pleasure or enjoyment. I know you are a masochist and you thoroughly enjoy being miserable."

He snarled. He'd been in the small smelly shamble of a shake shack for all of five minutes, and already he was sorry he had come. He watched her through narrow slanted eyes. She killed him. He decided to play his trump card, the one that always made her furious. "You really should go to Hollywood. You'd make a wonderful actress!"

It worked. Her eyes flashed. She parted her legs and dug in for heavy battle.

"Another thing," he said, "I don't enjoy suffering."

"Bullshit. You glory in it. If someone says *poor Joe*, you love it. You wallow in it. Well, I don't think you are fair or honest or just with your family."

"Don't you mean *you*?"

"Yes, I mean me. I also mean the children. You treat them the same way you treat me."

"All this because I say *no* to a beach house?"

"All this because you say *no* to everything. I think if you have a family, you should try to make life better for them—not worse. I know you think we never can afford anything, but it's just not true. There is plenty of money left over after we pay our bills. We could afford it nicely. I think you'll just have to admit you are a tightwad. Just remember all those years when we had *no money*—when we couldn't buy *anything*. Now we can."

Joe hated to be called a tightwad. His uncle had been called that for years. Joe hated the word. He went to great lengths to avoid the label. He made a big show in restaurants of picking up the check for people. He wouldn't allow anyone to pay for dinner or drinks. Most of the people they knew were quite content to let him pay their way. Joan found it distasteful to be pleasant to the freeloaders Joe cultivated.

He stretched. Arguing bored him. Joan seemed to enjoy it, but he thought it was stupid. He'd do as he damned well pleased, and no woman nagging, shouting, cajoling, or begging would change him. Not him. He sat thinking for a short time, then said, "There's one thing about having a beach house. We could let the men use it and deduct it from our income tax."

"I don't think I'd want to have other people use my house."

"See how selfish you are."

"Maybe I am, but I would hate to have other people sleep in my bed, wash my dishes, or be responsible for my things."

"Oh, well, we all know what high standards you have."

"I'm glad you *all* do."

His inadvertent compliment made him choke. He coughed and reached for his trunks.

"Are you taking the children into the ocean?"

"I don't know if I want to."

"They'd love it if you would. The only time I let them go wading is when they are with an adult. The ocean is too dangerous."

Joan thought about the eighteen-year-old girl who had drowned near the rocks on her birthday. The coast guard came to retrieve the body, which floated on top of the waves. Rip tides moved her body a quarter of a mile in a remarkably short time. A coastguardsman in a bucket from a helicopter futilely reached for her time after time. The beach was lined with people watching the heartbreaking scene. Joan would never forget the light-green water with the lighter-green lace that formed after the white caps crashed. The girl's body in the black maillot appeared, then sank from sight. Horror. Poor girl.

Joan remembered when she was fourteen and had gone swimming in the ocean at Oceanview with some boys from Seattle. It was during spring vacation. The beach was crowded with blankets, bottles, and basking students. The ocean was ice cold. Two of the boys were lifeguards, or she was sure she'd have been floating in the surf too. They'd swum out . . . far out . . . beyond the breakers. She was a good swimmer, but she expended all her energy going out. She was unable to swim back. She panicked. The undertow carried her out to sea. She had no strength to resist. One of the lifeguards swam over to her and told her to float on her back. He laughed at her and calmly told her the undertow was a few inches under the surface and floating above it would take her safely to shore. Weary and very grateful, she did as he said and was soon on the beach.

Since that day, she'd had a deep respect for the ocean. She insisted her children take certain precautions. After a time, they didn't mind the restrictions—after the ocean surprised them too a time or two.

She looked at the beach and saw Joe racing with the children. They seemed to be having a grand time. She took her book and collapsed on the blanket spread waiting for her in the warm summer sun. A gentle breeze blew from the ocean. She closed her eyes and imagined she was in some far-off country. When the sun is warm, one can be anywhere one chooses.

The next day when the last grain of sand had been dutifully swept from the cabin, the last piece of cheese packed away in the car, and the last child sent to the bathroom, they were ready to leave.

"I hoped before we left you'd go see the house with me."

Joe had been in a pretty good mood that day. He surprised her by smiling two or three times. She'd been thinking what a wonderful difference it made. His beautiful almost-black eyes looked happy and carefree. *Maybe it's too hard on him to be the father of a large family, and to have a wife like me, one who won't do what he wants her to do—or be what he wants her to be. He should have been a bachelor. Actually, he is a bachelor,* she thought. She wondered where she'd gone wrong. He did absolutely nothing for himself. He expected her to wait on him. Sometimes she didn't mind and even enjoyed doing things for him. But it rankled her that he *expected* her to fetch for him. Big chief chauvinist. She wondered if it was because he was German. She remembered reading that the way the men of a society treat the women is the measure of that society's degree of social and cultural progress. America's society rated low.

"I guess it wouldn't hurt to look at it. You big kids watch the little kids. Your mother and I are going to look at a house."

As they approached the house, he slowed his pace. "Joan, I think you should know that if we buy this house, we will have to use it as an income tax shelter. If the men can use it, it will pay for itself."

"Joe, you don't know anything about our finances. You still don't know what we owe or what we have coming in or anything. Don't you think it a bit unfair to put that condition on?"

"Do you want me to look at the house or not?"

"Yes."

He liked it. Joan still had to convince him the house was the buy of a lifetime. He was convinced . . . pretty much . . . and surprisingly signed an earnest money receipt that night.

The Goodwins had last-minute regrets. They turned their thirty-foot boat around halfway to town. The next morning, they woke up in the house, again considered carefully, and realized they really did want to sell. Joan and Joe would have cancelled the sale if the Goodwins had wanted to. They didn't like to do business unless everyone was satisfied.

It wasn't long before the papers were signed, the contract recorded, and the property changed ownership. The house would be easy to maintain. Joan looked forward to many happy weekends.

# Chapter 22

They went to the coast a few times that fall for the happy weekends. Joan spent Friday packing, Saturday relaxing (between meals), and Sunday cleaning (between meals). It didn't take her long to figure out that the beach house should be used when there was at least a week's time to make it worth cleaning.

The men were getting a lot of good out of it. The young unmarrieds went out for big beer busts. Whenever one of them had the house, the word got out, and the entire over-twenty, under-thirty population of Maplewood turned up there. Beds were broken, windows were smashed, curtains were torn, carpet was burned by hot coals from the fireplace, and cigarette burns dotted the soft cushions. The last straw was when one of the young workers brought dirty sheets from all the beds home for Joan to wash.

"It's not working out, Joe—the men are ruining the house."

"Who's doing the damage?"

"I don't know. The ones who are married leave it in pretty good condition, even though some of the new sheets are disappearing."

"Joan, I think you just like to complain."

"Joe, I have *always* hated to think of anyone sleeping in my bed and using my things. I went along with your scheme so you'd buy the house. Now it just isn't working out. No one gives a damn about the house because they don't have to pay for it. It doesn't belong to them. No one is responsible for anything about it. If the oven is dirty, they ignore it. Each one who uses it expects the next person to clean up after them. Haven't you ever heard the old saying: A horse with many owners is poorly saddled?"

"Where's the paper?"

"Will you please listen to me?"

"No."

"I want to stop people from using the house."

"Look, it's gotten to be kind of a fringe benefit."

"Unfringe it."

"No."

"Pay them a decent wage, and they'll be able to rent their own motel. And a maid can clean up after them instead of me."

"Jesus, you do get dramatic. You really should be in Hollywood."

"Joe, I'm stating a fact. Those people are ruining our nice comfortable beach house, and you're letting them do it because you haven't the guts to tell them they can't use it."

"They enjoy the beach."

"So do I . . . but not after they've torn up the house."

He sauntered out of the room, leaving her in angry frustration. She thought of hitting the wall with her fist as Stan did when he was angry. *She* didn't want to hurt her hand. She'd been hurt enough by her temper. In earlier years, she'd given vent to her anger by throwing things at Joe or at the walls. She'd stopped that too when she threw a bowl of cornflakes, with milk and sugar, against the wall only to have it disintegrate into thousands of slivers of glass mixed with cornflakes, sugar, and milk. That cured her. From then on, she'd been careful what she threw, but she still had a temper. She surprised herself now as she rushed after him. She tore the paper from his hands.

"You son of a bitch . . . listen to me."

"I've had enough. I don't want to listen to you." He pushed her into a chair. She looked at him in surprise and jumped to her feet. She grabbed him by the shirt and spun him around in a circle. Buttons popped.

"Are you crazy?" He looked at her in disbelief.

"Yes. I'm crazy." She bared her teeth and did the vampire thing with her arms.

"You tore the buttons off this shirt my aunt gave me. I might as well throw it away." The petulance of his manner and the whiny sound of his voice and the truth he spoke (she rarely sewed on a button) made her laugh. She couldn't help it. It started in her throat and went down to her stomach. He stood looking pathetic. Him and his new shirt, now a hopeless rag, made her laugh and laugh.

"Don't you laugh at me!" He clenched his fists, his lower lip protruded, and he menacingly glared at her.

The madder he got, the harder she laughed. He was a ridiculous sight with his shirt hanging loose, his T-shirt bunched over his belt, his pants cuffs around his heels, and the fantastically funny expression on his face. He sputtered at her, then turned and left the room.

"Come back and fight like a man," she called, still laughing. Her stomach hurt, but she couldn't stop.

When she'd gotten herself together, she went into the bedroom and apologized to him. She was ashamed of herself—for having lost her temper and for having laughed at him. (But he was so funny.)

"What's happening to us, Joan?"

"I don't know, Joe. I think we never should have been married."

"Don't you love me, Joan?"

"I love you in a lot of ways, Joe. There are many kinds of love or parts to love. I want to take care of you and keep your clothes clean and cook good food for you. I love the brave way you do a terrible job so well, and I admire your endurance. I don't want to hurt you. I don't want you to be unhappy. I want to fight your battles for you and with you. I love you like one of my children—or a brother. Can you understand that?"

"I do. What went wrong between us, Joan?"

"I don't know, Joe. We were too young to get married in the first place. When I told you I loved you, I wasn't being dishonest because I do love you, but I wasn't *in love* with you, and I didn't tell you that. I think the truth is that I should have told you, 'You have a nice cock, and I like to make love with you, but we're not matched.'"

"I think our interest in each other has been more biological than logical. There is a relatively new field of study called sociobiology that indicates the genes are responsible for the kind of mates we choose. Maybe my genes were in love with your strong legs and your beautiful body. It's an interesting theory."

"We've never understood each other. Over the years, we've grown far apart in our interests and tastes. You like to kill animals. You have never read a book. You think symphonies are for creeps and that real men don't go to them. You like it when other people have trouble, and you think it's funny when things happen to them that are bad. You have no compassion for me or for anyone else," Joan said.

"Am I so bad?"

"Maybe it isn't bad . . . but it's not right for me."

"Joan?"

"Yes?"

"What's going to happen when you really fall in love with someone?"

"I wonder if I ever will."

He'd rolled over and gone to sleep quickly. She lay wide awake. There were so many things she wanted to tell him—so he would know. If she could find words to describe how she felt, she knew it was futile to say them. He wouldn't hear her. If he heard, he would not understand.

She thought of the sweet smile on his lips every morning as he awoke. He was never grumpy or grouchy in the first five minutes. She blinked through tears as she thought how it had been for them. She saw them as they walked to the rodeo grounds the year Stan was a baby. She wore white pants and a peasant blouse. Joan's aunt had cut his hair with her clippers. They went out of control, and she ruined him—knicks, all over.

He looked like he had been attacked. He was mortified. As they walked, they were laughing and holding hands.

She flopped over on her stomach. *I must get to sleep. I have so much to do tomorrow.* She was sleepy, but she didn't want to forget her prayers.

*Dear God, why can't life be as I imagine it should be? Why can't Joe understand me, and why can't I understand him . . . just a little? I want to tell him I must have the right to think what I please. He'd never understand he tries to think for me. I've told him we each have a life, and if he is allowed to think for me, then he has two and I haven't any. I'm going to have to tell him again, but how can I make him hear me? The truth is, he doesn't want to hear me. As long as he gets his own way, he's happy. Who isn't? I want my way. But my way is right. I wish he were as good as I thought he was when we were married. I mistook weakness for goodness. His heart grew smaller and smaller as the years went by. I wonder why? God, what makes some people want to think the worst of others, and what makes them want to hurt their own family and be so nice to everyone else?*

*I'm only thirty-one. I don't see how I can live with him the rest of my life. God, it sounds like a death sentence to say it—all my life. If I live with him the rest of my life . . . I won't have lived at all. What a shame. I really like to live. I think life is neat. But if I have to live with Joe the rest of my life, it won't be worth living. He takes the joy out of life.*

*God, I remember how smart I thought I was when I was sixteen and we were married. I thought I knew everything there was to know. It didn't take me long to find how wrong I was. It is kind of amazing how much I did know. Joe was even dumber than me. In a way, I guess, we reared each other. Only somewhere along the way, he went off the track, and life got to be too much for him. Or maybe it was just that he thought life was supposed to be unpleasant. Suffer. Suffer. I wonder why he likes to suffer? He really seems to enjoy it. I don't. There's so much to learn in life, isn't there, God? Well, I'm sleepy, so I'll say good night and thank you, God, for giving us enough food to feed our family, for the shelter we have, and for the warmth of our house. God, we're so lucky to have what we do. Thank you. Good night.*

She woke feeling wonderful. She rolled and stretched and wished she could spend the rest of her life right there in her bed. She couldn't. She had to pee. She heard Joe in the bathroom. He always took so long—shaving. "Joe, will you be finished soon?" She hated to be in the bathroom with him. It was small, and she liked her privacy.

"I'm almost finished."

"Good." Thank God.

"Do you remember that tonight is the Knights of Columbus Sing-Along?"

"Yes, I remember."

"It starts at eight, and I'm supposed to pick up my hat and vest from Murray."

"So?"

"So will you get them for me? We should be there a little early, and I won't have time to run over to his house after I finish my route."

"Sure, I'll get them. I'd like to visit with Donna anyway." She made a mental note not to take the children. Donna's were spoiled, and they loved to fight and run and yell—just like hers. She'd leave hers home. Otherwise, she'd never get a word in with Donna. She didn't anyway. Murray's mother was staying with them. She stayed within earshot all the time. Joan was frustrated when she returned home.

Joe was late. When he saw she wasn't dressed for the sing-along, he said, "Joan, I want you to go with me."

"Sorry, Joe, I've decided that I've gone to my last social function. I may never leave the house again . . . for the rest of my life. I'll never again go to any kind of a party. I don't enjoy such things, and then you make me feel terrible afterward."

"What will people say if you don't go with me?"

"I don't care what people say."

"I do. And I don't want any scandal."

"How can there be a scandal if I don't go?"

"Well, then gossip."

"Call it what you will. Tell them I've got to get the bills out. That's true. I'll be billing this evening as I do every other evening."

"All right, I'll tell them that, but I don't see why you can't come with me and behave yourself like the other wives."

"Because I am that unique individual *me*, and I don't do what others do."

He left in a flash. She was glad when he was gone. She felt free. Lighter. Always. It had been years since she wanted him near her. She thought of the early times and realized then she'd been hoping for a bright and happy future. Well, it was here. And it wasn't. Why did the "happy ending" elude her now? Hadn't she done everything she was supposed to? She'd cooked and cleaned and smiled and been gracious when her heart was breaking because something sad had happened. She wasn't one to ask for sympathy. And she didn't get any. Now it seemed she was beginning to seek it. From herself. Self-pity. Ugly. Necessary.

After he left, she bathed the children, put them to bed, then later checked to see if they were covered. She sat billing in the basement while she watched TV, and by ten, she noted that she was over halfway finished. She heard a car drive into the front circle. Brakes shrieked. The sliding glass door slid open noisily.

"Who is it?"

It was Donna and her friend Shirley. They called to her. They'd been drinking. They were loud—and happy. Joan shook her head. One of the most offensive things in the world to her when she wasn't drinking was someone who was. She knew she'd better answer or they'd wake the children.

"I'm down here," she called as they clambered down the steps. "What are you doing?"

Donna focused on her. Her top button had unbuttoned, her makeup was smeared, and her hair looked straggly. She faintly resembled her usual neat, fastidious self. She smiled. "We've come to take you to the party."

"How nice of you. I'm afraid I can't go. I'm not into singing along anyway. The children all cringe and say, 'Please don't sing, Mother,' when we're in church."

Shirley cackled a silly little cackle. "We're going to take you back with us, if we have to drag you."

They pulled her out of her chair. The bills she'd been working on fell to the floor. They weren't fooling. They did intend to drag her.

"Let me go. I'll get dressed and go with you, but I want you to know if there is any trouble, it's your fault."

"Posh, there's not going to be any trouble." Shirley grinned stupidly. "We're going to have a good time. We just couldn't let you be all alone while we had all the fun."

She knew there was no point arguing with them. They thought they were doing her a big favor, and if she didn't let them and get them out of the house, the children would wake up. It was easier to go. They wouldn't understand her reasons anyway. She wondered what Joe had told them about her staying home. *Anything but the truth,* she thought.

"Make yourself at home while I dress . . . and I want you to know I'm driving."

Donna's eyes widened. "How come you're driving?"

"Because you two are too drunk."

They giggled. What Joan had said was the funniest thing they'd ever heard. Ever.

"Will you please be quiet down here? The children are asleep."

She tiptoed to Sarah's room, told her she was leaving, then checked the children before she went to dress. Donna and Shirley made strange sounds in the kitchen, while she forced first one leg and then the other into a pair of panty hose, which had been engineered to transform women into instant cripples. She twisted and stomped. Then she was in. She heard glass break while she dabbed on mascara. Something slammed. Joan hurried.

When Joan entered the kitchen, they looked at her in admiration. They were sitting with their heads one foot apart, being very quiet and listening to each other in glassy-eyed determination. They rocked gently in unison like two birds on a wire.

"I'm ready."

"Gosh, kid, you look great."

"Thank you."

Donna and Shirley laughed and talked as she drove carefully into town. The strange car felt cumbersome to her. It was stiff and unresponsive. She was glad she'd insisted on driving. She hadn't realized how drunk they were. About a mile from the parish hall, they'd lapsed into silence and were almost asleep by the time they parked near the entrance.

Music sounded from the hall. Lights. People singing. Men whizzed around the tables, serving sausage and beer. Some saw them arrive and shouted to them. Shirley and Donna, subdued and a little diminished, led her to their table in the middle of the hall. Crepe paper streamers and colored paper camouflaged the bright basketball lights on the ceiling. Burlap wrapped around the grillwork of the windows ensured privacy, absorbed sound, and improved acoustics. Still it was a gym.

Joan sat next to a man they told her was Donna and Murray's guest, Harold. His paunch hid his legs. He had white hair and a pleasant face. His wife, Harriet, across the table resembled a fragile, starving bird. Joan tried not to look at her, but she was fascinated. Harriet looked as though she might break. The raised contours of veins on her tiny hands forced the skin into unusual patterns as Joan watched in fascination. The veins moved back and forth as Harriet moved her fingers.

"How about some popcorn?" Harold said as he dumped popcorn into Joan's glass of beer, laughing uproariously as he did so.

Almost as a reflex, she said, "I don't want any," and dumped the glass on the table in front of him. He tried to move out of the way, but in an instant, his huge pants were saturated. Joan couldn't believe she'd done such a thing, but she was angry enough to feel he deserved it.

"Jesus." He moved to soak up the beer. He laughed a nervous, silly laugh and called for a white-hatted knight to bring a towel. "We've had a little accident here."

She leveled her gaze and looked at him coolly. "It was no accident. Won't you excuse me?"

She pushed her chair back and headed for the kitchen. No one wanted her to stay at the table, and she wished to God she hadn't come. Being sober in a group of drunks did not appeal to her. Joe looked around and did not smile when he saw her come into the kitchen. He was filling pitcher after pitcher with cold amber beer. She didn't smile at him either—just glanced in his direction, then moved to the far side of the kitchen and leaned against the big stove with two monster ovens that once produced delicious lunches for the parish school. Now the only time the stove was used was for parish dinners. The pilot light was off, and the odor of gas emanated from the stove and permeated the kitchen. She chugged the beer, then got another glass and returned to her safe space by the stove. Everyone laughed and joked in tight circles near her. She tried to make herself disappear. Suddenly, she was utterly bored. She knew she never should have let anyone talk her into anything she didn't want to do. It never worked out. She had to learn to listen to herself. It was hard to say *no*. She'd made another mistake. *When I make a mistake, I pay for it—and pay.*

Someone moved near her. She turned to see who it was. Bud Stone smiled. He managed one of the branch banks in town. Joan had seen him on occasion about loans when they lived in St. Eames. He was nice—and good looking.

Joan drank four glasses of beer in a very short time. She felt better and better. Except her feet hurt. She considered going back to the table but thought better of it. She didn't want to be bored to death. And Bud Stone was not boring. He put his arm around her waist, smiled insinuatingly, and tentatively touched her thigh. She reached for his hand and held it tight so he couldn't move it. She didn't want to cause a scene . . . and it wasn't all that unpleasant.

Bud looked at her. His big brown eyes with incredibly long lashes melted her. "Meet me outside."

"What?"

"Meet me outside."

"You're crazy!" she said with her mouth open and her eyes wide.

He strode for the door, leaving it open for her to follow. She giggled. Then she walked to the door and shut it. She hurried through the ancient kitchen to the door marked GIRLS. Tipsily she struggled with her girdle. She simply could not budge it. It rolled around her hips and cut deeply into her legs. She moaned. Her bladder had been signaling her brain for some time. Now she felt pain. Finally, with one long pull, the girdle moved. She pulled and tugged and staggered around in the cubicle. She managed to pull it down enough so she could go. Tears came to her eyes in grateful relief. *Boy, God sure knew what he was doing when he fixed people so they could pee. Thank you, God.* She stood up, pulled and tugged at the girdle to get it up, felt like she'd fought a ten-round battle, then went to check her makeup and wash her hands. She moved in slow motion; she was in no hurry to join the others.

By the time she finally came out of GIRLS, the party was breaking up. Joe waited for her, his face distorted with anger. He glared at her. When she saw him, she pretended she didn't.

"Joan!"

"Yessss, sirrr." She stood at attention and saluted him.

"Get to the car."

"Yesss, sirrr."

He followed, then passed her and had the motor running when she got in her side.

They rode in silence until she heard him sob.

"Joe, are you crying!?" Her voice was astonished, baffled, and anxious.

"What if I am?"

"Why are you crying?" She had felt like sleeping, but the obvious distress Joe displayed sobered her. She'd never heard him afraid and desperate before. "What's the matter?"

"You . . . you know what's the matter."

"I do?"

"Yes . . . you whore . . . you sinner."

"Me?"

"Yes. You!"

"What did I do?"

"I saw what happened . . . I saw it all."

"Are you drunk, Joe?"

"No, I'm not drunk. I didn't even have one beer. I saw the way you and Bud carried on all evening. I was ready to throw a pitcher of beer at the two of you. I saw you start out the door, and then when you saw me watching you, you turned back and went into the restroom. I saw Bud come in and wait for you outside the door until his wife came and got him. I saw it all. I could have done something then, but I didn't want to make a scene. So I waited."

"Waited?"

"Yes. I'm taking you home, then I'm going to find Bud Stone."

"What are you going to do after you find him?"

His voice grew soft. He whispered. "I'm going to find him and kill him."

Suddenly sober, Joan couldn't believe her ears. "Joe, that's ridiculous. Nothing happened between me and Bud Stone. I didn't see you watching me. I can't see that far without my glasses. I had no intention of going outside with him."

"Then why did you go to the door and not go out when you saw me watching you?"

"I . . ." She knew there was no sense trying to tell him. His mind was made up. There was no one quite as unreasonable as Joe.

"Where do you think you'll find Bud?"

"Everyone was going to the Chinese restaurant after the sing-along. I'll find him!"

The car skidded to a stop in front of the house. Joan looked at Joe in the light from the dash. She shuddered. He looked exactly like the devil.

"Get out."

"Joe, please don't do this!"

"Out!" He leaned over and pushed her from the car. His strong hands dug into her arms as he leaned toward her. She made one last effort to stay in the car, but when he stopped the motor and started to get out his side, she scrambled for her door.

"*You're crazy!*" she called as he zipped behind the wheel. The car headed toward town through the soft summer night. The moon hung bright, and millions of stars twinkled in the Milky Way. Joan watched the sky and the car from their bedroom until the car disappeared at the end of the lane. She noted the time. It was one thirty. At four, she fell asleep. Joe was not home.

She woke the next morning to find Joe's bed empty. She hurried into the kitchen. He'd already left the house. She was sure he had not killed Bud Stone, but she spent the day in apprehension waiting for some word about what had happened.

When he came home that evening, he acted as though nothing had happened. She should have known he'd behave like that. Whenever they had a fight, he'd go off to work and come home having forgotten all about it. In contrast, she'd spend the day brooding, and by the time he came home, she'd be madder than ever.

He didn't say a word, and she didn't question him. She was glad Bud Stone hadn't been murdered. She liked him. He was a handsome son of a bitch.

# Chapter 23

Joan hadn't expected Joe to be early, so she hurried to fix dinner, while he impatiently and abstractedly thumbed through the desk. "Hey! What's this?"

"I can't see. What does it say?"

"It says seven fifty for an office call for Jesse's baby."

"They wouldn't accept Jesse's credit, so I told them to put it on our bill if he didn't pay."

"You what?"

"I told you . . . I told them we'd pay it."

He sputtered and slavered, and shock waves seemed to catch his heels. "I won't have it. I won't have it."

"Will you please not get so upset! Dinner will be ready in a few minutes. We'll talk about it after we eat. You'll feel better then." *I hope. Music to soothe the savage beast. Hell. Food does it a whole lot better.*

"I won't feel better then. Joan, you're always doing something for those crummy people. You waste gas collecting food and blankets for them. Now I'm paying their doctor bills. I didn't want to hire him in the first place."

"Not until you found out you'd get a subsidy on his salary. You'll have to admit he's a good worker."

"He's still a Chicano."

"No Chicano would be in this part of the country if it weren't for the necessity of their labor. They are the backbone of a very lucrative farming industry. If it weren't for them, this would be a depressed area. Those people are human beings, who, in reality, sustain the *farmers.*

"My uncle never used them . . ."

"Because he didn't raise crops that needed labor."

"He doesn't want them in the country."

"I know. He inherited his farm from his parents. He thinks he owns the whole country and that the Chicanos should be run out."

"What's wrong with that?"

"Look, Joe, I can see your uncle wanting to preserve the land and the way he lives. He likes it. But these people weren't lucky enough to have parents who owned land. They come from big poor families. They have nothing. It's up to those who have something to see that other people exist in some sort of dignity."

"It's their own damned fault they're poor. Look how hard my uncle worked for a living."

"He inherited the land."

"And had to work it for the last fifty years to earn enough to pay taxes and live. And look how hard I work."

"You've been lucky, Joe."

"*Lucky!*"

"Yes, lucky. You were able to earn enough money to support our family, build this house, and buy the trucks we had to have. *Lucky.* What if things had turned out different and you'd have had to work in the lumberyard for the last fifteen years and you had to support us on what you made? You'd be driving around in an old car with a pee-stained mattress on top . . . for sure."

"Don't hand me that. If I hadn't worked so hard, we'd have nothing now."

"I'm not saying you didn't work hard! You've worked so hard at times, I prayed you'd stop."

"Stop? I couldn't stop. We needed the money. We always needed the money."

"There are other things in life besides money."

"What?"

"Music . . . art . . . books . . . lots of things."

"And how do you get them? With money."

"There's no point in arguing with you, but I do think you should thank God you are able to live the way you do."

"This isn't the way *I* want to live."

"I know how you'd like to live. In a tent, you'd like to live in a tent, with no running water, no lights, no inside plumbing. You'd like to be primitive."

"No more. No more!"

"God has been good to you."

He sat silent for a fraction of a second and then continued talking. "And those stupid people have baby after baby."

"Look who's talking!"

"Yeah, well, I pay my bills."

"They probably use the rhythm system. What do you think they should do, Joe? They're Catholics—what can they do? The pope refuses to allow other kinds of birth control. They're just doing what they think is right . . . just like everyone else."

"Putting their doctor bill on my statement?"

"My statement."

"Yours?"

"As much as yours."

"Oh, is it?"

"Yes. I work as hard on the business as you do. I also take very good care of the house and the family. You do nothing for the family—and you know it. I consider the business as much mine as yours."

"Oh, you do, don't you?"

"When I come back in my next life, I want to be a man. All they have to do is have a penis and balls, and the world is theirs—and the business. Let me tell you something. I have as much an interest in the business as you."

"You stupid woman! Don't say I do nothing for the family. The family wouldn't survive without my working."

"A father is supposed to give more to his family than money."

Everything was ready, so she busied herself dishing up, muttering as she did so. Joe helped himself as fast as the food was placed on the table. By the time the children had been served and their meat cut, he had finished his meal, as usual. Joan sat down at her place and ate in silence. She thought of a million things she could say, but she didn't want to upset the children. They hated quarreling, especially at dinnertime.

Joe stood and went to the yellow couch. "Are you going to take care of Jesse's bill?"

"Next time I see him, I'll tell him about it. I'm sure he didn't have anything to do with it. I think they didn't bother to bill him."

"Humph." Joe rattled his newspaper in irritation. "Humph." Rattle. Rattle. Rattle.

Joan finished her dinner. She was tired. She was also grateful that she had organized a system for the girls, which left her free after dinner. They took weekly turns. The chores were divided into four areas. One girl cleared the table and stacked the dishes. Another loaded the dishwasher, and swept and cleaned the kitchen (worst job). Another bathed the babies and put them to bed. Another straightened the living room and playroom (best job.)

Joan's evenings were free, but she usually made out bills, often working into the early hours of the morning. She found it nearly impossible to do her work during the day because of the constant interruption of the telephone, workers, and children.

Dr. McCready would make arrangements for her to have the hysterectomy as soon as possible after the current baby was born.

Joe didn't like the news. "I'm going to see Father Connelly. I still don't think you should have the operation."

"It's my body. You have nothing to say about it."

"Joan, I just don't want you to commit a sin."

"There is no sin to it. The only sin that I can see is yours. You are going around discussing this with your family, my parents, and anyone who will listen to you. It is a private matter."

"I haven't talked about it to many people."

"I'm surprised you'd have to discuss it with anyone. You are so secretive about everything. You don't want anyone to know anything about your business. You didn't want to build your house where anyone could see it because someone might think you were doing well. When we buy a new car, you hate to drive it because someone may think you have a new car. You've never told anyone I was going to have a baby. You've kept very quiet about everything. Now, all of a sudden, you seem to have to have other people's opinions on something that is no one's business but mine—and yours . . . maybe."

"What do you mean *maybe?*"

"I'm the one who feels like I'm coming apart when I'm pregnant. Not you. I simply cannot be pregnant again. You should be able to understand that. I am not a machine, or maybe I am? I am literally falling apart. When I'm pregnant, it feels like a butcher knife is pushing on me from the inside out. It is very painful. I can't turn in bed. I get locked into a position between sitting and standing, and I can't stand up for a half hour. I am immobilized. That's when the children do all sorts of terrible things. Because they know I can't get them. They dance around me and say, 'Yah. Yah. Yah—Yah. Yah. Yah.' I have to have the operation whether you like it or not."

"I *don't* like it."

"What have you liked in the last fifteen years?"

"What does that mean?"

"Just that I'm tired of your scowling face. You never smile . . . unless someone dies. And the only time you laugh is when someone is having trouble . . . like a car accident or a divorce. You never smile."

"There's nothing to smile about."

"Bullshit."

"I don't see what you have to be so happy about all the time."

"Neither do I."

Amy came. Joan marveled at the beauty of the child. Physically, she embodied the finest features and qualities of both her mother and her father. Her flame-red hair and almost-black eyes were set off by creamy skin that blended with her hair. She was a fine baby. The children adored her. So did Joe and Joan. She never cried unless it was necessary—that sort of thing. She was considerate from the first.

Apprehension overtook Joan the night before the operation. Dr. McCready came to see her and explained the procedure. His pragmatic manner did little to alleviate her anxiety. She felt the same way she had when she was six and she and her sister, Grace, and Dan Bunker went to Boroughs to have their tonsils taken out. All the way in the car, past Newabram, Ocean City, and through the Chinatown section of Boroughs, Joan insisted on being *first*. They'd gotten to the hospital, and she'd been frightened by the smell, the sterility of the shiny white walls, and the waxed brightness of the halls that echoed strange noises. She'd started crying.

She was last. When she awakened, Marjorie Bunker stood over her with a glass train engine filled with brightly colored candies. She tried to cry, but no sound came from her sore throat. They'd told her it wouldn't hurt. She never trusted the medical profession again.

Now, Dr. McCready's assurances met with silent contemplation. She found silence the best way to hide distrust. She listened while he explained that the uterus would be taken out through the vagina. She couldn't imagine how he would do it, and she didn't care. She wished it were over. The thought that she'd never have to be pregnant or go through nine months of misery or give birth to another child made her almost deliriously happy . . . except she had to endure this final torture. Delivery rooms, operating rooms, surgical procedures, needles, hospitals, and everything connected with them brought her heavy chest-filling dread.

"It won't hurt a bit." Dr. McCready said. Then he smiled and left the room.

"What if it does?" she called after him. He'd been her doctor for all the children, except three. She respected him. He was coolly professional and efficient—and kind.

The next morning, a nurse woke Joan for her first shot of the day. She immediately went back to sleep; was wheeled from her room, up the elevator, into the operating room; was operated on; was taken back to her room; and finally woke a little nauseous about six o'clock that evening. She couldn't believe she'd slept through the whole thing. She decided that the things one worried about the most seldom happen. She was thankful it was over, and before the night shift came on, she was begging for food.

Except for a pressure on her bladder and pains in her legs from the tight surgical stockings, she felt wonderful. She stayed in the hospital three days, read, wrote letters, slept, and ate. She found the food exceptionally good and gained five unneeded pounds while she recovered.

Joe was supposed to come for her at noon on Sunday. He was late. She dressed and sat in the hard vinyl chair in the hospital-pink room to wait for him. By two o'clock, she heard the nurses whispering in speculation. She began to feel weak and wished she'd asked them to wait until she left to make up her bed. It was made, and she couldn't crawl back in. She wished she could.

She called the house. No answer. *Joe must be on his way.* Sweat broke out on her forehead. She felt cold and clammy, though the day was warm going on hot. She'd thought she was fine, but now a trembling started, and she knew she must be weaker than she'd thought. She longed to be home in her own bed. Four o'clock came.

"Your husband is here, Mrs. Schultz." The smiling nurse ushered him into the room.

Joan felt like crying. Joe walked in as though nothing had happened. He didn't say a word about being late. She didn't trust herself to look at him. She was afraid she'd start to cry and never stop. And she hated to give him the satisfaction of her tears.

When they got to the station wagon, she found it packed with seven of their children and a strange couple with a little baby.

"We're taking them to Lerner," Joe said as he settled himself behind the wheel. "Sarah stayed home with the *new* baby."

The old baby, Jean, started to howl when she saw her mother and crawled over the seat and elbowed her way onto Joan's lap.

"Joe, I can't hold her."

He pretended not to hear. He was intent on driving and playing to the couple in the rear. She was too weak to protest, and if she held the child a certain way, it didn't hurt too much. She felt like screaming. Everyone was delighted with the drive, the company, and the fact that she was coming home. They took the strangers to Lerner, then headed North.

"Tell me how you happened to have those people with you, Joe?"

"Now I suppose you're going to make something of that too, huh?"

"I just wondered what they were doing with you."

"If you must know, they were hitchhiking on the freeway, and when I saw the baby without a hat in this heat . . . I just had to stop."

"Oh."

"Isn't that right, kids?"

"Yes." "Yes, Daddy." "Yes." "Uh-huh." "Yeah." "Yes."

"You're always the one who complains because I don't have a heart. Well, make something of that."

"It was nice of you to pick them up . . . but I wish you would have taken them home before you picked me up."

"Can't *I* ever do anything right?"

"Joe, I don't want to complain—it's just that I don't feel well."

"There is no pleasing you. If you hadn't had that operation, you'd be feeling just fine."

They rode on through the hot sticky afternoon. Traffic was light on the freeway. Occasionally, a semitruck whooshed by and sucked them into its wake. Joan wished she were home. The baby's shoes dug into her legs. She knew enough not to try to restrain her. Nothing makes a toddler so active as restraint.

"I'm hungry, Momma" came a voice from the rear.

"My name is *Mother* . . . Haven't you eaten?"

A chorus of *nos* rose from the rear.

"Joe, didn't you feed them?"

"I've only got two hands. I didn't have help this morning. The babysitter left last night. I had to get their breakfast, dress the baby, see that the house was clean . . . so you wouldn't complain . . . and then we drove all the way in to get you?"

"Where was Sarah?"

"She stayed with a friend and got home just in time to take care of the new baby. I still don't like her name. Amy. Amy," he sputtered.

"So you had to do everything *one* day. I've been doing everything for years, pregnant or not, and no one's ever gone hungry before. Is there anything in the house for sandwiches?"

"No. I thought we'd pick up groceries on the way home."

"We'd better stop and feed the children. They can't wait until we get home and shop and prepare dinner . . . Besides, I don't feel well enough to prepare anything."

"So you're going to complain again. I thought you were feeling so well. You said you felt just fine last night. Now you're sick."

"How many days have I been sick since we were married?"

"I don't know."

"You've cooked dinner *once* in all the time we've been together. Remember when you fried potatoes and put too much pepper in them? When we lived in West Maplewood. And the neighbor boy came while you were cooking, watched you for a while, then said, 'That's *woman's work.*'"

"I remember. I almost threw the little bastard out."

Joan waited in the car while they ate. While she waited, she wondered what Joe would do if she were seriously ill. *Probably shoot me, like he would a horse, and take pleasure in pulling the trigger. Dear God, thank you for making me so healthy.*

Joan recovered in a remarkably short time. With each passing day, she became happier and happier. She'd never have to have another period in her whole life . . . and she was only thirty-one. She tried to explain to Joe that since the doctor had not removed her ovaries, there was virtually no difference in her body chemistry. He distrusted everything she said, doctors in general, and concluded that since she had had the operation, she was a *neuter.* His stupidity and insensitivity caused her to close the door on him more than before. She simply gave up on him and enjoyed the new freedom she was experiencing.

By the time a few months had passed, periods, pregnancies, and everything connected with them were just a memory. Throughout the years, when she'd been pregnant or knew she would be, she dreamed of the time when she'd no longer have to worry or cope with such things . . . and miraculously here it was.

The baby was good. The older children adored her. They lived in a beautiful home; the business prospered beyond belief. Everything that had been a problem no longer was.

Just when Joan relaxed, Ohio Lowden came into their lives. They'd met him for the first time at the first meeting of the Garbagemen's Association. He was brash, loud, argumentative, and constantly irritating someone. Few of the men liked him. He had a proclivity for doing and saying the wrong things.

Soon after they met him, Joe came home and told Joan that Ohio was the one who'd been nosing around city hall, trying to find out if he could bid on the development when it was in the planning stage.

"Didn't he know you had the route?"

He had known. He'd also known when they dealt with other owners for their routes, and he kept himself informed about their franchises, since some of their routes bordered his, and he would have liked to scoop them up. Joe said he was a first-class jackass, and Joan wanted nothing to do with him. One day the phone rang. It was Ohio.

"Can I speak to Joe?"

"I'm sorry, Ohio, he isn't home."

"It's really important that I speak to him."

"I'll give him the message."

"OK. My number is 433-0980. Have him call me, will you?" She heard arrogance, petulance, and a tinge of anger in his voice.

"As soon as he comes in." *You bastard.*

As soon as he came in, she gave him the message. He shrugged and pulled his brows together.

"I'm not going to call him," he said.

"Why not?"

"He's fighting with the people who sold me the truck bed on that last truck. He wants me to back him up. He ordered a truck from them, then found another one. Now he says he's not responsible for the one he ordered because it took a month longer to deliver than it was supposed to."

"Where do you fit in?"

"He wants me to say I heard the owner of the company promise him that if it wasn't delivered on time, he didn't have to take it."

"So for once, Ohio is in the right?"

"Yes, but I'm not going to get involved. I have to do business with those men, and I'm not going to stick my neck out for him."

"I don't blame you for not wanting to get involved in something that doesn't concern you . . . but if the man gave his word, it shouldn't hurt you to say so."

"That's the point . . . He was drinking and doesn't remember . . . at least he says he doesn't."

"How did you find out about it? Did Ohio tell you?"

"No. They told me about it when I went in yesterday for an adjustment."

"Oh, all you have to do is call Ohio and tell him you don't want to get involved."

"Joan, I'll handle this my own way . . . I'll call him later."

He didn't call him later. Joan reminded him several times, then knowing anything she would do would be futile, simply wrote it on his work pad filled with other old *things to do* and went on about her business.

Ohio called several times. Joe refused to answer.

Joan considered Joe a first-class procrastinator. His habit of putting things off until they simply couldn't be ignored drove her up the wall. Poor maintenance caused the trucks to break down; low tires went flat because of negligence. Joe's lackadaisical attitude about the equipment was reflected in every other way he ran the business.

The fall meeting of the Garbagemen's Association was the next weekend. The first person she saw when she entered the spacious hotel where the meeting was being held was Ohio. He was talking to Joe. He wasn't smiling. Joan came up in time to hear parts of the following conversation:

"Hey, old buddy . . . how come you didn't call me back? You could have called me collect."

"What?" Joe sounded as though he'd never heard of any message from Ohio. Joan couldn't believe her ears. She strained closer so that she could hear every word and yet not let them see her.

"I called your place, and your wife said she'd have you call me. I really needed you to back me up."

"Gee, Ohio . . ." His voice sounded *so* sincere and *so* friendly. Joan nearly gagged. "Joan never gave me the message. I guess she's just got too much to do with the kids and all . . . I don't know what we're going to do.

I guess we'll have to get the office out of the house. Sorry, pal, maybe I can make it up to you in some way."

*Joe, you dirty son of a bitch, you just cannot tell the truth.* Joan edged into the rest room, seething with anger and filled with an intense desire to go tell Ohio the truth. After a few minutes, her anger subsided, and she realized she shouldn't make a scene and let everyone know what a spineless bastard she was married to. She wondered how many other times he'd used her as an excuse when it suited him. She pulled herself together and walked out into the lobby.

"How nice to see you, Ohio." She looked directly into his eyes. He shuffled his feet, looked at the floor, then excused himself, murmuring something about having to talk to someone across the room; he fled.

Joan looked at Joe with innocence. "I wonder what's the matter with Ohio? Is anything wrong? Was he mad at you for not calling him back? Or did you?"

Joe's face had turned red the minute he saw her. It got redder and redder as she looked at him. He wondered how much of the conversation she had heard. She gave no indication that she'd heard anything, and Joe slowly relaxed. She was no longer angry. She felt sorry for him, and a little contemptuous.

## Chapter 24

Summer turned to autumn. Then winter's cold came to match the coldness that developed between Joan and Joe. Increasingly as the months wore on, their relationship took on an entirely new dimension. It was imperceptible at first. Then each person began to go his separate way. Joe's interest continued to be working, bowling, hunting, and Saturday night nightclubbing. Joan busied herself with the children, business, classes, and avoiding Joe whenever possible. She was completely turned off by him. They were like strangers living in the same house.

Joe knew there was something wrong, but he didn't know exactly what it was. He had a strange need to be near her, perhaps sensing that he was at last truly losing her. Whenever he came into a room, she had to leave. He suffocated her with phony, almost frantic affection. She couldn't bear to have him close to her. She couldn't explain to him, and he wouldn't have understood if she had. She didn't understand it herself. They hardly spoke. They were polite to each other (though Joe tended to be surly), and his temper became sharper.

"I want to know what's the matter with you." Joe's voice suddenly sounded reasonable.

"I don't know."

"I know. It's the operation. You're mentally unbalanced because of the operation."

"Jesus, Joe, do you have to start that again?"

"Yes . . . I think that's what's the matter."

"Dr. McCready said there is no difference in my hormonal balance. I still have my ovaries . . . which you well know."

"What's making you act like this?"

"Like what?"

"Like not wanting to screw? Not wanting me to touch you?"

"You mean *make love*. Joe, did it ever occur to you that I've had it? I've knocked myself out trying to be a good wife to you, and I simply cannot please you. No matter what I do . . . it's wrong or it doesn't suit you. You are never happy with my efforts. You're ashamed to be my husband. You are embarrassed by my behavior, the things I say, and the way I say them."

"That isn't quite fair."

"It is. And every time you've made love to me (except at three o'clock in the morning, which incidentally is a terrible invasion of my privacy and very distasteful), it's because I reached for you. I wanted your affection, and the only way I could get it was to pursue you and to beg for it. You are the coldest man in the world. Now, frankly, it is not worth the effort. When you do *fuck* me, it's for two minutes. Then you roll over and go to sleep. It's hardly worth getting undressed. You make sure you're satisfied, and you have absolutely no consideration for me." She sighed. She felt like kicking something, then sat down on the bed and looked around at the room. It was beautiful. The light wood of the hemlock, one-by-fours; the floor-to-floor-ceiling windows; the sliding glass doors that led to the deck where she liked to sunbathe; the special carpet made of mill ends in lovely tones of copper that gave the room a soft, warm, and comfortable aura; and the carefully placed lighting fixtures all combined to create an atmosphere of peace and tranquility. Now she knew it was all unimportant. She'd worked so hard to make a home. A good home—where her family could be happy. *What was it Mrs. Soames had said in Thornton Wilder's* Our Town? *She said, "I always say the most important thing is to be happy—just be happy, that's the important thing."*

Now looking around their bedroom and seeing it through tear-filled eyes, she thought, *I've never really been happy here. I've made no one else happy either. There's no point to the whole thing anymore.*" She heard Joe talking. Talking. Talking. When she could listen, she heard him say,

"But, Joan, I love you."

She turned to him and looked at him with hatred poorly concealed on her expressive face. "Don't you dare say that to me again. That's all you ever say. 'Joan, I love you. Joan, I love you.' It's so easy for you to say *I love you*. What I want is a man who shows me he loves me. Talk is cheap."

"Please, Joan, I want you to love me."

"Did you love me yesterday when you had that fit and threw an orange juice against the wall . . . in the glass that broke and cut my hand? How much did you love me then?"

"Oh, Joan . . ."

"When you throw food on the floor because you don't like my cooking . . . how much do you love me then?"

"Forget it. I don't want to make love to you."

"How can you make love when you don't even know what it is? I simply cannot be treated like a subhuman and then fucked."

"I wouldn't touch you with a ten-foot pole."

"And sometimes I think I'm not lucky."

"You bitch."

"Good night, asshole."

She couldn't stand being near him, and as the weeks wore on, she began to plan a trip to the coast for the summer. She'd take the children, and they could spend time on the beach, while she and Joe sorted out their lives. She could get someone to come in and take care of the business and Joe for a few weeks. She could come home and take care of paying the bills, a chore she knew she'd have to do. She made plans in silence.

It was during one of these days when Joan was making silent plans that Bill walked toward the house with his shoulders set in such dejection that Joan watched in fascination. She'd seen the same set of the shoulders in her grandfather when he came in from a particularly hard day in the fields, in her own father on hot summer evenings when he climbed down from the mulligan that brought him in from the woods, and in Joe when he'd had a specially bad day. But she'd never seen it in Bill. Bill always walked with a bounce, and he seldom was without a smile.

"Whatever is the matter, Bill?"

"Wha . . . oh, Joan, I was thinking about something else. You startled me."

"Sorry. What's the matter?"

He collapsed into the desk chair. "I'm tired of the mess the routes are in."

"What do you mean?"

"You know a lot of the customers are new on my route. It would be so much easier if I could reroute the whole thing. The way it is now, I have to backtrack, and you wouldn't believe how inefficient and aggravating it is to have to cross the same intersection several times a day."

"Bill, you know I don't have anything to do with the routes. I just take care of the office, make out bills, pay payments, fix reports, answer the phone, get parts, take gas out to out-of-gas trucks . . ." They both laughed at her recitation. She said "damn" when steam from the potatoes she was draining burned her. She set the pan on the burner, then came around and stood across from him.

"I . . . seriously, I know little about the trucks—as a matter of fact, I hate them. I hate any kind of machine. I'd rather do anything than have to deal with machines. I've had to drive the trucks from time to time . . ."

"That doesn't surprise me."

"I've had to. I don't mind. Sometimes I've liked it even though my legs were tired at the end of the day. Joe takes care of the trucks. He doesn't know much more than me, and I'm afraid he doesn't do a good job of properly maintaining them. Since I don't know anything about them, I have to assume he does what he's supposed to do. I know he doesn't. He doesn't fix anything until it breaks. He is negligent about maintenance, but frankly *I* haven't the energy to handle that end of the business."

"I know how busy you are, Joan. I can't believe you do as much as you do."

"There's always time to do what a person wants to do—and has to do."

"Maybe."

"Bill, I'd really like to know more about the way the routes are set up. If they're inefficient, they should be changed. The problem is Joe hasn't worked on all the routes. The only ones he knows are the ones he worked on or has set up. We inherited the routes as they are when we took over. All the routes have exploded with growth since then."

Bill leaned forward in his chair. He spoke quickly and with great interest. "Do you really think Joe would consider rerouting my routes?"

"Let me handle Joe. He hates change—any change, but he loves money! If there's a way to save money, he'll like the idea."

"That's wonderful." He sat up straighter and started to smile.

"I do wish I knew more about the routing of the routes. When we first started in business, Joe used maps. The routes changed so fast, the maps were outdated in no time. For years, whenever he had a backache or any kind of problem, he had to work. No matter what! Wind. Rain. Hail. Snow. Sun. No one else knew the routes."

"Gee."

"Yeah. But finally I convinced him to take the time necessary to make out a card for each customer and where they were in relation to others so that anyone could go on the route, and even though they might not be as fast as the regular driver, they'd at least be able to do the job."

"Those cards work very well."

"You know, Bill, you're the first man to take an interest in the business enough to make a suggestion like that. Most men don't care about the company, except to get their paycheck."

"I don't know about that."

"OK. That really isn't fair of me, is it? I guess I should say, all in all, we've got a great bunch of men working for us who are very loyal and don't complain, but they don't make constructive suggestions. That much is a fact."

"They *complain* to me."

Her neck stretched as she looked up. "Oh? I wish I'd hear them. What are they suggesting?"

Bill started to speak, thought better of it, then left the air heavy with his silence. "It's nothing to do with you," he said finally.

"It's my business. Anything that affects my business has to do with me."

"It's not something a man discusses with a woman."

She felt her face turn red. Her eyes narrowed. Her jaw hardened. Bill looked surprised. He was sorry he'd said anything. Very sorry. Her brows arched. She knew instinctively that somehow this concerned Joe, and she knew she had to hear it. "As long as I sign a man's check, that man discusses business with me." The words shot out. Her anger surprised her.

He knew she was right and didn't waste time talking. He shrugged his shoulders in defeat and glared at her. "Just remember, you asked for it."

The tension eased in her upper body. Then she felt her legs relax. Smugly she thought how she'd deliberately challenged him and how easily she'd won. She stopped a little victory smile from dancing to her lips. No point in rubbing it in. She leaned back in her chair and waited for the litany. Then "Mother . . . Mother . . . Mother." The children surged up the stairs for dinner. Their favorite cartoons were over; that meant dinner. She didn't want them to interrupt *this* conversation, and she didn't want them to spoil their dinner with a piece of fruit so close to mealtime. She signaled for Bill to wait and hurried to the refrigerator for celery sticks. She hoped they'd go for the deal. Celery sticks now and chocolate sundaes for dessert. She seldom baked. Time was too precious, and sugar too destructive. They usually had fruit. Sometimes ice cream. The children accepted the trade with a minimum of fuss. If they'd known she didn't want them in the kitchen, they never in the world would have left. But she fooled them—acted like she didn't care.

She settled in the chair. Bill seemed relaxed. He'd had time to gather himself together. He realized he'd been on the verge of telling her to shove her job and stick her "business" up her ass. He thought maybe he should have done that, but he knew she was right. And he did like her. They'd gotten on very well from the first day he'd come to work. He never really liked Joe. But he needed the job. He wished he'd never opened his mouth. He sucked in his breath and began again. "Just remember you asked for it."

She nodded.

"There are a lot of things wrong with this operation. Frankly, I'd rather discuss them with Joe than with you. I feel this is like talking behind his back . . . It's kind of like showing a child his father's no good."

"Like telling a woman her husband's a jerk?"

"Maybe."

She nodded and sighed. "Let's set some ground rules so you'll be comfortable. Whatever you have to say that is about Joe, I will try to remember it's about *your employer* and not *my husband*. You have a perfect right, and I hope you will discuss these things with him. I feel the same distaste you do for someone who is unwilling to face the person he accuses. I feel I should know what is going on and what the men are unhappy about. If I don't know, I can't do anything to change the situation. If Joe doesn't want me to know, he'll never tell me. It is very important to me to run it well and to do a good job with it. I neither want to be unfair with any employee. They'll tell you that. I need to know the problems, and I appreciate your telling me. I certainly won't hold it against you. You might keep in mind, as you go, that no woman wants to admit she married a jerk."

He chuckled. She laughed lightly, not because it was funny, but because it was true.

"OK, I'll just lay it all out, and you can think what you will."

"Fine."

"In the first place, we are underpaid. The men who work under the union get a lot more every month than we do. Whenever we break down, we have to wait for the truck to be fixed. then we have to finish our route, no matter how late it gets. Joe tells us he'll help us, but we've found out he often comes home and takes a nap. Other times he doesn't show up until the job's finished. Frankly, he just doesn't keep his word."

Joan started to defend Joe from long habit, though Bill's complaints were the same as hers. He motioned her to silence and continued. "You asked for this, now you listen."

She saw he was getting angry. She put both hands palms up in a mollifying gesture. He continued. "The other men and I are tired of wondering if the brakes on our trucks are going to give out. Mine did last week . . . and don't tell me I should tell Joe. I told him. The brakes weren't fixed. The next day I almost ran into a truck. I was going downhill so fast, I thought I was flying. I almost hit a truck and then a little boy on a bicycle. Do you know what would have happened if I had killed that little boy?" His breath came in short spurts; his eyes snapped.

"I'm on your side" was all Joan had time to say before Bill rushed on.

"So the brakes aren't fixed, the clutch goes out . . . a tire is flat when we come to work . . . the gas tank is empty whenever someone leaves the spare . . . the pay isn't good. We get nothing but promises. If you want to be in business, I suggest you run this business like a business. There's so much negligence and poor management that I'm surprised you make a living."

"Are you finished?"

He searched his mind for other things he might have forgotten. His hand gripped his head, then slid down his cheek. "I think so . . . no . . . wait a minute. That lazy son of a bitch out at the dump should be fired. He lets people dump right in the roadway because he's too lazy to come out of his shack. When we come in with our trucks, we're blocked off from dumping."

"Now are you finished?"

"No. I also want . . . the men to be able to sit down with Joe and discuss solutions to some of these problems." For the first time since he started talking, he scanned her face to see how she'd taken the deluge of information. Her expression hadn't changed.

She said, "I appreciate your telling me all this. Some of it I already knew, some I guessed. I'll do what I can to see that something is done about the things you've told me. I will tell you what to do about the most important one—your safety. Whenever you feel something is wrong with one of the trucks, you drive it to the garage. That's the best way to handle that."

"What about, Joe?"

"The best way to handle him is not to bother him about it. He doesn't object to having the trucks fixed so much as he doesn't want to be bothered with having to have them fixed. Do you understand what I'm saying?"

"Yeah, he wants to have a business and take the profits, but he doesn't want the headaches."

"Just do this. Whenever your truck needs to be fixed, or any of the other trucks need repairing, just take them in, and I'll come and get you."

"I don't know if I like taking that responsibility."

"You take the responsibility. I'll not only come and get you but also back you up. It's your neck—literally."

"And what about you, if Joe objects?"

"I'll handle that when I come to it. Of course, I'll expect the men to use discretion. If the trucks are taken care of properly, it'll save us money in the long run."

"Yeah." Bill seemed satisfied.

"Yeah, I know." Joan understood.

Bill stood to leave. His long legs pulled earthward at the thighs. Extreme fatigue. His body begged to be taken home to shower and bed. "I'll talk to Joe about the other things. It would really help if I could reroute my route. I think most of the other men would like to do theirs too." He had to leave; he couldn't talk anymore. "Thanks for listening," he said as he walked out the sliding glass door onto the patio.

"You did me the favor." She smiled at him. He was quite a man, and she admired him more than ever. "Good night, Bill."

She hurried to the stove and quickly dished up dinner. "Children . . . children, come and eat your dinner."

They clambered up the stairway like monkeys let out of cages. She didn't have to ask them twice to eat their dinner. "Do you know what Grandma used to say?" They moaned as they always did when they knew she was going to inflict one of her *sayings* on them. She ignored the moans. "She said, 'Hunger is the best sauce.'" Moan. Moan. Then they laughed. Through the din, she heard one of the girls say, as she directed her gaze at Joan, "There but for the grace of God, go I." This time *she* groaned. It was practically her favorite saying.

Wind blew across her face. It was cold. Goose bumps rose on her body. Sand stung her arms. Overhead wispy clouds played near, around, and under the sun. When Joan came to the beach and found her favorite place in the dunes, it was warm. The blue sky was so blue, it looked unreal. She'd burrowed into the sand—warm and comfortable. Now it was cold. Maybe if she stayed for a while, it would warm up. She hoped so. Her younger sister, Ann, was on the way. She hadn't been miserable very long when she heard her sister calling.

"Where are you?"

"Here."

Ann came over the crest of the dunes like the Pied Piper. Instead of being followed by rats, she was followed by adoring children.

"What are you doing in that bikini?"

"Hiding here in the dunes, trying not to sexually excite, entice, and/or otherwise unduly enflame the adult male population."

"You look awful," she said, then stood, staring at her sister.

"I know. Relax. Tell me, little sister, how are you, and how long can you stay?"

"I'll be here three days, if you'll have me. Then I'm going to State University to look over the housing situation."

As the sisters visited, the children drifted off. They went to play in the shallow creek that flowed across the sand into the ocean and to finish the fort they were working on by the water's edge.

"What have you been doing here all week, Joan?"

"I've been reading and eating and sweeping sand and making out bills in the evening while I watch television."

"It looks like you've been eating a lot." Ann, still staring, let her eyes sweep Joan's girth.

"I have, Ann. I just can't seem to get enough cookies, candy, buttered popcorn, ice cream, chocolate, and potato chips into my mouth. I eat when I'm not hungry and when I am—too much."

"Sounds like you're a compulsive eater."

"Maybe I am."

"Is something bothering you?"

"Whatever is bothering me isn't important. Next week I start the modeling course."

"So Mother finally talked you into it, huh?"

"Not really, though she's been wanting me to do it for years . . . and wear falsies."

"She wanted me to wear them too."

"I kept telling her, 'Look, what if I were beautiful? I'd have more trouble than I have, and I have enough as it is.'"

"What made you change your mind?"

"I'm sick of myself. I'm sick of looking like I do. I'm sick of not knowing how to do things . . . I think it did you a lot of good to take the course. You always seem so poised, and you look so good . . . but you did before you went to the school."

It was true. Ann had been a pretty girl from the start, and the classes not only seemed to make her look even better but also gave her a certain confidence she hadn't had before. Sometimes, though Joan was almost thirteen years older than Ann, it seemed to her that they were contemporaries. It also seemed to her that Ann was much more sure of herself than she.

"Have you ever been thin?"

"Not really thin, but when Kit was a baby, I weighed 139. I had a twenty-six-inch waist, and I really looked good. The reason I lost so much weight was because Kit had colic, and I slept only two or three hours a night. I thought I'd die. Sometimes I think back and wonder why I didn't. You probably remember when I was thin—in the little house at West Maplewood? You babysat every Saturday?"

"I don't remember that you were ever thin. Were you thin long?"

"I got pregnant with Matt. After that, I thought, to hell with it . . . Now I'm through having babies, and I'd like to look nice and feel good the rest of my life."

"That's good!"

"Or do you think I'm being foolish to take the course? I certainly have no ambition to be a model."

"No. I don't think it's foolish."

"Neither do I, I suppose. I don't wear any makeup, except lipstick and mascara, and I don't even know how to put it on or what to buy to make myself look better. I suppose I'll learn all about makeup?"

"You'll learn about makeup and a lot more. You'll learn about nutrition, exercise, clothes, posture, and how to walk, stand, and sit. You'll learn about a lot of things, and you'll enjoy it. You'll meet other women who have the same interests you do, and you'll have fun doing it."

"I hope you're right. But what other women would be stupid enough to have the interests I have? Rinsing diapers and running a garbage business?"

"This is a great way to run a business. Are you sure you've got everything under control?" The warm sun peeked through the cloud checkered sky. She raised her face to worship like a Druid. "Do not worry, little sister. All is well. Aren't I lucky to be here? Aren't we?"

Ann nodded. She hadn't realized how good the sun could feel. She drowsed in its warmth. "I'm surprised he let you come," she murmured as she lazily soaked up the afternoon sun.

"It's funny how Joe fools everyone, but he's never been able to fool you, Ann."

"No. And he never will." She cringed when she thought of him. She'd liked him well enough through the years. He'd never done anything to hurt her. But she hated the way he treated Joan. Maybe he couldn't help it. Joan seemed to defend him enough, but Ann hated to think her sister would marry a man like that.

"I told him I was coming, and I came. We haven't used the house much at all. Joe's always got some reason for not wanting to come out, and he hates to have us leave him alone. Although he likes to have the house to himself. Sometimes he hates to have the children in the house with him . . . but he doesn't like to take care of himself. He's a puzzle."

Ann reached for the suntan lotion. Her slender fingers massaged it into her fair skin. When she finished, she lay back on the green wool army blanket that Joan favored for sunning. She yawned, looked at the sky and the bright sun, gave a contented purr, and turned on her stomach. "I remember how he used to lie on the floor and act like he was having a heart attack because the kids bothered him so much."

"He wasn't acting. I'd have to take them out of the house so he could be alone, to save his life."

"Yeah, I remember. Why did he have all those kids if he can't stand to have them near him?"

"Catholic." They both said the word at once. Then they laughed.

Joan shook her head. "The church says you're to accept all the children you're sent."

"Even when you can't stand to be in the same room with them?"

"I don't know. All in all, the children really haven't put him out all that much. I'll bet if someone asked him their middle names, how old they are, or what grade they are in, he wouldn't know."

"I'll bet he wouldn't. He seems to love them, though."

"Nothing ever stays the same. Sometimes he loves them. Sometimes he doesn't seem to. It depends on what has happened to him and to them. And how he responds to them. He is so taken up with his business that he seldom has time for the children—or for me. As long as they don't bother him and stay out of his way, he loves them. Strangely, he always seems to adore the baby. Whoever is the baby!"

Ann turned on her side and looked at Joan. "You never seemed unhappy when you were pregnant."

"I never was, though I was miserable because I hurt so bad. I accepted the fact that I was pregnant. I knew if I wasn't pregnant one month, I would be the next. I never questioned it. This may sound strange to you, but I treasured each child as they came—more than the one before. I was so impressed with how precious they were. That's one reason they're so spoiled. It's hardly in my heart to spank them."

"I've seen some dandy spankings."

"*On the other hand*, I refused to be disobeyed. If I say I'm going to get my wooden spoon *if* they do such and such, and they do such and such, I have to give it to them. I've chased children all over the orchard, especially Matt and Emily. And I do not give up."

Ann laughed. Joan was *so* defensive. "You're a good mother."

"And you're a good auntie. All the children adore you. You've done so many nice things for them—and me."

"If I have anything to do with your taking the modeling classes, the whole family should love me."

"They do! Don't make me nervous. I might need some cookies."

"Are you really upset about starting the classes?"

"Yes. I'm too old to have to be taught how to do things."

"I don't believe that?"

"I guess I don't, or I wouldn't!"

# Chapter 25

Joan smiled and thought how it had been. It was one of those rare days in late fall when the sun shone all morning. She had finished doing her daily floor washing, and the kitchen was beginning to dry. She noticed her mother's car coming down the lane. She rarely visited at the house. They saw each other at an occasional Sunday dinner or a short visit now and then. In an emergency, Joan's mother would babysit.

Rose Powers got out of the car and was smiling as Joan opened the sliding glass door onto the patio.

"How nice to see you, Mother. What brings you here on such a beautiful day?"

"It is beautiful, isn't it?" She looked around at the trees. There were several species in the grove at the back of the lawn. Each had a particular kind of beauty and was a different shape and shade of green. Two huge old maples stood near the fence denuded of all their leaves. Beyond the fence, the valley spread far below but was not visible from their vantage point.

"Come in. Do you want a cup of coffee?"

"I'd like some tea." She knew Joan and Joe seldom drank coffee, and she didn't like to drink it when Joan made it. She made it so seldom, she never found out what she did wrong. Rose listened for the children. "Where are the girls?"

"They've gone to play with the new neighbor girl. She lives in the house at the end of the lane. Her mother called and invited them. They were so thrilled to be able to go all by themselves. The babies are down for their morning nap. This is the first time I've been alone in months. It feels funny. I think I could get to like it."

"Do you listen to the radio?"

"There's one someplace in the bedroom. I seldom have it on. When it's quiet, I enjoy it. It's so noisy around here that whenever it is quiet, I love it. I enjoy listening to the wind, and I love the sound of rain on the roof. We can hear it good because of the way the roof is constructed."

"I'm glad it isn't raining today."

"Me too. Do you want to go into the living room? I haven't been in that room for months . . . except to vacuum and dust. I think I'd like to relax in there."

Joan's mother led the way. Joan balanced teacups, sugar, cream, and tea on a large plastic tray she'd found on sale for $2.99. It was one of her better finds, and every time she used it, she felt smug.

They sat in comfortable chairs close to each other, and while the tea steeped, they chatted. At first, they spoke in generalities. Then her mother leaned forward and said, "Joan, are you feeling well?"

"I'm fine, Mother."

"Maybe you should wear a little makeup—you look pale."

"I wouldn't know how to put on makeup or what to buy. I should do something, though. All I wear is mascara and lipstick."

"You should go to the modeling school Ann went to."

"I don't want to be a model."

"I know, but you could look a lot better than you do. You're a pretty woman. If you knew how to wear makeup and fix your hair . . ."

"And lose forty pounds."

"And lose forty pounds."

"Mother, I'd feel silly taking a modeling class. A woman my age should know how to do things. All the girls in the classes are in their teens and twenties. You just want me to be a lady. I think you're a little late."

"All the girls aren't in their twenties. When Ann took the class, several older women were in it. And believe me, they looked good when they graduated."

"OK, Mother, you're right, I should take the class. I don't know how to walk or sit like a lady . . . or anything. But what kind of trouble would I have if I should be beautiful? You don't know how jealous Joe is . . . and I'm not going to bore you with details, but I have enough trouble as it is without being beautiful."

"Joe would be happy if you were more attractive."

"Don't kid yourself!"

"You just don't want to do it."

After her mother left, Joan stood looking at herself in front of the mirror. She calmly and objectively surveyed her physical self. The image reflecting from the mirror did little to inspire her. She was pretty in a healthy sort of way. She looked clean and neat, even though she was overweight and felt like a big fat clod. She looked at her flat chest and wondered why her mother had forgotten to mention that she should wear falsies, as she did whenever a discussion of this kind started. She laughed at the thought of it. With each successive pregnancy, her breasts had grown smaller. So much so that after number seven was born, Joe had started to laugh one night when the baby was a few weeks old. "They look like apricots," he'd squealed as he convulsed with laughter. He couldn't stop. He was weak when he finally caught his breath five minutes later. Joan wouldn't have felt so bad, except it was the first time she'd heard him laugh in months.

Now, as she thought of the time it would take to put on makeup each morning and the hassle Joe would raise if she spent the necessary $500 on such a course, she decided to forget the whole thing.

She did try. It came to her at odd moments. She forced it out of her mind only to have it tap-dance on her brain. Classes. Worry. Should I? Yes. No. Why? Why not?

"Joe, what would you say if I told you I'm considering taking a modeling course?"

"I'd say forget it?"

"What if I really wanted to?"

"I said—no."

"Joe, I'm sick of the way I look. My hair's a mess, my figure is gross, my skin looks like hell. I think I should go."

"*No!*"

"Let's not talk about it anymore."

"Fine."

"Wouldn't you like me to look nice for you, Joe?"

"If I say I would, you'll go sign up for the class, then tell me it was my idea because I wanted you to look good."

"Oh, Joe, I wouldn't do that."

"You've done it before."

"Bullshit."

"See how you are."

Anger swept over her. Every other year they'd spent the $500 and more on hospital and doctor bills to have a baby. Surely she should be able to spend that money on herself now that she could no longer have a child. She was sick of the old maternity tops and the pants with the elastic inserts for her big, big stomach. It wasn't fair. She hardly spoke as she undressed for bed.

Silence unnerved Joe. She was usually so verbal.

"Get some sleep and forget all about going to any modeling school. I never heard anything so ridiculous in my life." He started chuckling. "Don't make any plans to go, you hear?" Chuckle. Chuckle.

"Yes, Joe." She shut her eyes and began to visualize how she'd look when she was beautiful. Then she thought, *Joan, maybe you shouldn't embarrass yourself by going to a modeling school. The sound of it seems silly.*

*But then, you don't have to be like you are forever. You want to look better. You just don't like yourself. What if people laugh at you for going to a school for young girls? When have you ever cared who laughed at you? And what if they did laugh at you? Are they living your life. And who are they? You can't name them. You don't even know who they are. You are afraid of what the unknown they will say, when what they say matters not at all. You should be afraid of what you will say . . . not they. They don't give a damn what you do. They could care less. And if you are going to be embarrassed, you should be embarrassed because you're fat and because you don't look good. You go to the school, and maybe you'll be able to like yourself. Maybe you'll even be pretty. It won't make any difference to Joe. He'll be jealous of you anyway. You wonder if he's looked at you in the last five years. You wonder if he's ever seen you? You have to live with yourself. You might as well enjoy it.*

She tossed, tugged at her sheets, plumped her pillow, then stared at the ceiling of the darkened room. She shut her eyes, and immediately she saw a flurry. The years. The years had gone by in a flurry. Bills. Babies. Bedlam. A kaleidoscope of memories: clothes hanging on the line, dried, and gently blowing in the warm summer air; green, green grass; and the Cecil Bruner Climber. She could smell the flowers as she inhaled the day. It could have been any day. Through the mist of memories, she heard and saw the children swinging, playing in the sandbox, sliding and shouting in the snow. She saw them in their bath, hungry at the table, running and screaming through the house. Each time she pictured them, they were a little older and in a different place. Now it was hard to believe the children had once been roly-poly balls of gurgles and coos. She laughed when she thought how carefully she'd prepared for each baby, like an absolute mother hen. She'd found soft flannel receiving blankets and diapers, pretty little knitted gowns, and all the rest of the paraphernalia the current baby would need. She saw little scrawny cowboy legs in big booties, flailing arms, and baby fists so long ago.

Joan called the school the next morning . . . to find out if a class started soon. Yes.

"There is? It starts in two weeks? I have to come in and sign up?" She told the woman she'd be in the next day. She found a babysitter, went through the usual dos and don'ts, and was on her way by eleven thirty. Her soaring spirits turned to apprehension as she came closer and closer to the city. Streets still soaked from a sudden downpour that had missed the freeway, glistened in the early afternoon light.

As she parked the car in a lot near the uptown address, doubts came rushing back. With sweaty palms, she clutched her purse and a big, brown umbrella. Resolutely, she climbed from the car, turned to the attendant, and showed him the address. He stretched his arm and pointed to an elegant building about a block away. Joan smiled, thanked him, and was on her way. Her chemise blew about her unsteady knees, which were connected to her shaking high heels. Her eyes widened as she saw the lobby of the building. Fine old marble walls with gilt mirrors in clusters showed to advantage in the early afternoon glow. The elevator's pecan doors opened, and Joan stepped into a mirrored interior with a thick purple carpet.

The elevator opened directly into the lobby of the school. A beautiful girl, black haired, violet eyed, and creamy skinned, sat at the desk directly in front of Joan. Her long, red lacquered nails held a pen primed to write. She was speaking into the telephone. When she saw Joan, she smiled and motioned to her to be seated.

Joan looked around. The lobby office looked like a set from a movie. Something with Doris Day. It was beautiful. Purple. The carpet, walls, and accessories were purple. Different shades of the color were everywhere. Joan noticed a sign that said in script "powder room." Her bladder signaled that she'd better take advantage of the opportunity, so she slipped into the room. It was fantastic. Mirrors, gild, purple paper, purple accents. It seemed almost a desecration to use it.

When she returned to the sofa in the lobby, the girl was finished with the telephone.

"Miss Yvonne will see you now." She smiled at Joan and led her through a hallway covered with pictures of former beauty queens and other faces Joan recognized from the society pages of local newspapers. She watched the girl walk in front of her. She was tall and slim with a good straight back. Her hair seemed more blue than black. She paraded just a bit as she walked, and Joan smiled in spite of her nervousness. "Here you are," she said to Joan and indicated a door for her to enter. Then the girl nodded, did a fast turn, and walked smartly away, leaving Joan feeling fat, frumpy, cloddish, dumb, and gross, and wondering why she hadn't been satisfied to stay home and stay that way.

The woman at the desk could have been forty or eighty. An ageless face looked at her through eyes that could have seen many, many summers. She was elegantly dressed in a beautifully cut purple wool suit. Her golden blond hair swept up from her neck and swirled around her crown in a classic coiffure. Her skin stretched across high cheek bones and had a luminous quality. She smiled and, in a deep throaty voice, asked Joan to sit down.

"Joan Schultz." She read from a card while surveying Joan across the desk.

"Yes . . ." Joan answered, "Miss Yvonne."

"Please call me Yvonne," she said crisply as she began to write. "When did you want to attend classes?"

"As soon as possible. I have a long way to go."

"Joan, I was hoping you'd come in to sign up. I have just one opening in the class that starts in two weeks on a Tuesday. There won't be another class for you until spring."

"Then I'll sign up now."

Miss Yvonne smiled. "Why don't you do it as a surprise for your husband?"

Joan laughed inside. What a surprise it would be for Joe. Miss Yvonne had no idea!

"Joan, we give figure counseling. We'll teach you makeup, wardrobe, nutrition, and so many other things. Have you read our brochure?"

"Yes, I have. I must say I need to learn all you teach."

Miss Yvonne leaned forward and said in a conspiratorial tone, "We can help you—that I know. Miss Eloise will take care of you from now on."

Miss Eloise magically appeared. Joan waved good-bye to Miss Yvonne and said hello to Miss Eloise, a vision, perfectly groomed, coifed, gowned, shiny and bright, with a soft purring voice, who held out her hand to Joan and ushered her into another mirrored purple-carpeted purple paradise distinctive with a wreath of white feathers on the west wall.

Ten minutes later, Joan presented her stub to the parking attendant. She caught a glimpse of herself in a window and silently said "good-bye" to what she saw. She smiled when she thought how slim she'd be . . . and she would. She promised herself. The attendant brought the car, and it whisked her through town, onto the freeway, and halfway home before she was aware she was driving. The realization that her actions had been automatic brought her up short, and she tried not to think about the school or Joe's reaction to it. Before she turned her full attention to driving, she decided she'd better wait until he was very receptive before she told him what she'd done.

She didn't get a chance to tell him all that week. Each night she thought she'd tell him, but he was working late, and by the time he came home, showered, and ate, he was too tired, and it was too late for her to spring the *good news* on him. By Sunday, the tension was acute for her. Joe seemed to be in a very good mood all that day. The children spent most of the day playing in the far corner of the basement. It was relatively quiet and peaceful in the living room where he'd spent the afternoon in front of the portable television watching a football game. Joan decided she was too tired to start the war she knew was inevitable, so she'd wait until the following night. No matter how late it was or tired she was, she'd have to tell him then.

\* \* \*

He was furious. It took an hour to calm him. "Why do you insist on going behind my back?" he shouted.

"I don't have any other choice."

"Couldn't you discuss things with me before you go ahead and do them?"

"Joe, I had no choice. If I wanted to get into the class, I had to sign up that day."

"And you just *had* to get into that class."

"I wanted to."

"You wanted to spend my hard-earned money on a stupid modeling class?"

"It's my money too."

"Oh . . . now it's your money. I don't see you out earning any money. How is it yours?"

"You son of a bitch! I work just as hard as you."

"OK. OK. Let's not start that. What if I spent that kind of money on myself?"

"You do."

"How?"

"It costs a lot of money to go hunting. Guns are expensive. That scope you bought was over $120. You bowl every week. That costs money."

"And you smoke cigarettes, so we're even."

"I hate you. And I don't like your stupid aunt either."

"What does my aunt have to do with this?"

"I don't think she taught you any manners."

"She taught me not to spend $500 behind my husband's back."

"Every other year I've had a baby . . . that cost at least five hundred dollars. This year I'm going to improve myself instead."

"If you were going to improve yourself, I wouldn't mind."

"Do you mean that, Joe?"

"Yeah. If they teach you to keep your mouth shut and not talk like a logger, I wouldn't mind a bit."

"And polish your shoes and kiss your ass."

"You just do as you please, don't you, Joan?"

"Yes, and I'm going to continue."

"We'll see about that. I'll find a way to stop you. You'll go to that school over my dead body."

She was early and sat waiting in the classroom for the others to come. She made a point of being early. She hated to have everyone look at her. She had found it pleasant to be alone and not have anyone to talk with or listen to. She was tired of being bored by people. She decided just this week that if anyone bored her again, it would be herself.

She'd arranged everything at home so she could leave by five. Dinner was in the oven, and Sarah could dish it up. She leaned back into the soft sofa at the rear of the classroom. Her eyes closed, and she wished she had time to take a nap. When Stan and Sarah were little, she'd napped every afternoon when they did. She hadn't napped now for years. She wondered why she was so tired. She had read that people who are unhappy often try to escape by sleeping. Maybe that was what she was trying to do—escape from Joe, and the fight they'd have when she got home. He'd told her not to come. Here she was. Wicked little snickers escaped. She felt smug. One giant step for her womanhood. Yeah!

Miss Eloise came through the stairway entrance. She walked with a controlled bounce, carried her shoulders high, and rolled her hips in a slightly suggestive manner.

"Good evening, Joan."

"Good evening . . . I was beginning to wonder if anyone was coming."

"We're still a little early. Would you like to come into the exercise room?"

Miss Eloise led the way into a large room about forty feet by fifty feet. At one end was a portable stage with a runway, a mirrored wall, and a few props placed casually on the stairs leading to the stage. A stereo occupied the southeast corner of the room and was set up in front of another mirrored wall, which was in line with the first. A row of doors opened into the hallway, and on the opposite wall, windows faced the street two floors below.

One by one the girls came into the room. They were little and pretty and young. There were twenty in the class. Two other older women came just before Miss Eloise called the group to order. Joan looked at them and wished one of them was as heavy as she. Neither was. They were just a little overweight—and dumpy.

"Now, girls, the first thing we're going to do is take your height and weight and measurements," Miss Eloise said as she pulled out a doctor's scale. "Please take off your shoes and form a line to the left."

Joan chose a place near the end of the line. As the girls inched forward, each person in turn was weighed and measured. She wished she could disappear. She didn't mind telling what she weighed, but she hated to have to be weighed in front of others. By the time it was her turn, some of the girls had gathered in small groups and were chatting, so the audience she anticipated had dispersed.

Miss Eloise measured her around the bustline, waist, hips, thighs, calves, ankles, and wrists. Beneath the present measurement, she wrote down the desired measurement. And beneath the present weight, the desired weight. Joan cringed when she saw how many inches she'd have to lose—and pounds. She rolled her eyes and wondered if she'd have the strength of character and will to shape up.

"Now, girls, we're going to learn some exercises. We'll spend time doing them every evening before class begins. We will also weigh in at the beginning of each class." With that, Miss Eloise began bending, stretching, leaping, pulling, pushing, and contorting with surprising dexterity, though Joan guessed her in the early-sixty range. She looked great. Her skin and hair were youthful, but there were signs of aging around her elbows and upper arms. The most exciting thing about her was the look of panache in her eyes. Joan liked her and admired her style. Each week of the classes, as Joan would come to know, Miss Eloise wore a different color, always coordinating her accessories and her costume to that one color. Her champagne-colored hair and her flawless complexion were complemented by any color she chose.

They exercised for a long, long time. Miss Eloise called out from time to time, "If you're tired, stop now . . . If not, go on with me." Joan thought she'd probably die and have to be removed by a tow truck with a winch. She was exhausted after the first few minutes. The admiration she'd felt for Miss Eloise turned to amazement. Here was a woman probably twice as old as she doing things with her body that Joan couldn't believe—or do.

Diet sheets were handed to them as they left. The overweights had to reduce, and the underweights had to gain. Joan glanced at one thin girl's diet. Milk shakes were circled. She envied the girl. Her diet featured skim milk, cottage cheese, vegetables, fish, and fowl. It sounded dreary and drab—and icky.

The weeks passed quickly. Each Tuesday a different subject was taught. The exercises and the weighing and measuring continued. Joan couldn't believe the transformation in the girls, and they couldn't believe the transformation in her. One girl with big eyes and drab blond hair, whom Joan felt was rather ugly, looked so glamorous with her makeup on that all the class stared. Then they busily put on their own. They started with moisturizing lotion, then foundation, blusher, eye shadow, eyeliner, false lashes, lipstick, lip gloss, and finally eyedrops. They smiled at each other in wonder. *Wow. How lovely they were. All of them.*

She tried to keep the fact she was going to the class a secret, but it was impossible. The children told their friends; they told the men; and Joe, still angry, spouted off about it whenever anyone would listen.

She felt the same though her appearance had changed. One after another told her that she was not the same person. As she became slimmer and slimmer, she wondered if she was. They cut her hair and frosted it in the beauty shop next door to the school. Miss Eloise helped each one in the class find just the right colors and kinds of makeup to complement her complexion and coloring. Joan was pleased with the way she looked, and she couldn't help wondering what others thought. One day, when Bill finished writing messages after work, she decided to ask him.

"Do you think I've changed, Bill?" As soon as she asked, she felt foolish, like she was fishing for a compliment. She wished she'd said nothing. She was pleased, however, with his answer.

"You look different, but *you* haven't changed. You're as nice as you always were."

"No one else thinks that. They think because I look different, I am different. It's not true. I think the same things I always thought. I feel I'm the same person, and I always will be no matter what makeup I do or don't wear."

"You're just as pretty without makeup as you are with it."

"What a nice thing to say."

"I mean it . . . you're a pretty woman."

"Oh, dear."

"Don't be embarrassed. Hasn't anyone ever told you how pretty you are?"

## Chapter 26

Joan managed another week at the beach in late August that year. It was cold. A chill wind blew as she ran from the icy water. The children hurried home, while she ran to retrieve her jacket. As she picked it up, she glimpsed a very fat man lumbering toward her. He breathed hard from (it seemed to her) the small exertion. As she moved toward the house, he called to her.

"Mrs. Schultz." Puff. Puff.

"Yes?"

"I'm Ace Peters." Puff.

"The twins' father?"

"Yes." Puff. Puff.

"I'm happy to meet you. My girls have enjoyed playing with the twins. They like them so much."

Joan and Ace chatted for over an hour in the cold until a sudden rain joined the biting wind. Joan ran for the beach house. Ace puffed home. She was fascinated with him and hadn't met anyone in years she liked as well. He was the fattest man she'd ever seen. Several times that evening, she wondered about him and why he was so huge. They'd talked about food a little, and it was obvious Ace liked to eat. He'd told her about a place nearby where they made peppered bacon and how to deep fry unpeeled quartered potatoes. He'd been rather silent about his wife, and since Joan hadn't seen her on the beach with the children, she wondered about her. Later in the day, she was jarred when her girls came running in.

"Mother! Mother!"

"Yes, girls?"

"Mr. Peters likes you."

The girls had been with the twins on the beach, and as they removed their wet sandy shoes in the back entry, they seemed unduly excited.

"I like him too."

"He told the twins you were a nice lady and that you're going to visit again tomorrow."

"Yes, that's right."

"Mother, is that what you call a date?"

Joan thought quickly. Joe would have fits and probably accuse her of a romantic interest in the man if he ever heard the word *date*. She brushed the thought aside. Even Joe wouldn't be jealous of a man who weighed at least four hundred pounds.

"It's kind of a date. It's more like an appointment. Mr. Peters and I are meeting after lunch tomorrow. We're going to visit, while you children play in the ocean."

"Mr. Peters writes children's books . . . The twins have three of them."

"How nice. He said he was an engineer."

"He does that too, I guess."

Joan hurried through her work the next morning. She couldn't wait to finish lunch. Ace Peters had captured her imagination. He was the most intellectually stimulating man she'd talked with in years, and they had shared an instant rapport. He was waiting for her.

"I was hoping you'd be here," she said as she fell to the sand.

"I've been here fifteen minutes."

"I wish I'd known . . ."

"Why?"

"I'd have come early too. I enjoyed visiting with you more yesterday than I've enjoyed visiting with anyone in years. You made me *think*. I haven't done that for so long." They laughed. "Could I go and invite Mrs. Peters to join us?"

"She won't come."

"Is she ill?"

"Joan, I don't usually discuss it, but the truth is my wife is a schizophrenic."

"I don't know exactly what a schizophrenic is . . ."

He took a breath and began to recite like a small boy in grammar school: "A major mental disorder of unknown cause typically characterized by separation between the thought processes and the emotions, a distortion of reality accompanied by delusions and hallucinations, a fragmentation of the personality, motor disturbances, bizarre behavior, and so forth, often with no loss of basic intellectual functions."

"How terrible for you. I am sorry."

"Don't be. There's nothing you can do about it." He turned his head and didn't say another word for the longest time. Joan didn't know what to do—whether to say something or not. If she did speak, she wouldn't know what to say, so she said nothing. After a time, Ace turned to her.

"Is it hard for you to take care of her?" Joan asked.

"It is. She's been in and out of mental hospitals ever since the twins were born." She fell silent and seemed deep in thought. Joan asked if she was ever dangerous.

"She's never tried to harm me or the girls. Sometimes she is suicidal. Schizophrenia is a form of mental deterioration. One never knows."

"Should she be alone?"

"She's on medication. Right now she's sleeping."

"How sad for you."

"I never think of it that way."

"How do you think of it?"

"You want to know, huh? All right, let me see if I can tell you. I was in the Veteran's hospital being treated for obesity. I weighed 415 pounds. I lost a hundred." He laughed at the memory. "Of course, it took me seven months on a strict diet, but I was losing. Sharon got sick, and I had to leave the hospital and care for the twins. I gained the weight back in three months. I was under a strain. I had to find a sitter for the girls and do all the housework and cooking, and I spent many nights at the hospital. I organized a group of people to visit the patients and act as a support system for them. We had a group of patients that met once a week. Since Sharon became sick, the hospital is my second life. I managed to write three children's books, which have sold well, so I've taken a leave of absence from work for the next six months to spend as much time as possible with my family."

"How good of you," Joan said. They settled back and watched the children in the surf. A long time passed. Finally, Joan spoke.

"I wonder what Joe would do if I ever became seriously ill?" She hadn't even meant to say it aloud. After she did, she was sorry she had because Ace's answer haunted her for months.

He'd said, "You must know the answer if you have to ask?"

She'd never thought of being seriously ill or having a chronic disease. Now she thought of it . . . how it would be between her and Joe. She knew he'd never take care of her. The few times she'd been sick . . . really sick . . . he'd ignored her. She remembered lying in bed hearing children fight, run, scream, and cry. Terrible sounds. She'd been too sick to get out of bed, and she'd lain for hours before her "nurse" Joe came to see if she needed anything or to feed her. She'd felt helpless and dependent, and she hadn't liked the feelings or the treatment she received. Ace Peters made her think. The thoughts made her cringe.

Joan laughed when she thought of the fights they'd had. It seemed the intensity of the fights directly coincided with their age, physical condition, and degree of tolerance. The first really good fight she remembered ended in her taking her very best yellow satin nightgown with ecru lace—the San Francisco honeymoon vision—and ripping it right down the middle. She remembered how good she'd felt when she heard the fabric tear. Later, she wasn't so happy when she realized what she'd done. She also threw things at Joe—anything—until she realized she could *kill* him (or make a terrible mess). Then she never threw anything. She learned—and learned.

When they were young, it was survival of self. As they became older, Joan found herself more and more doing anything to avoid open war. The demands on her time and life were such that she had no energy left to try (and never succeed) to get Joe to see her point. When they were young, one of her favorite tricks had been to lock him out of the house after they had one of their most ferocious fights. He invariably stalked out in anger. His unwillingness to stay and fight it out frustrated Joan. To get even, she'd secure every window and door. Somehow he'd find a window to climb in, and then the fight would continue—all night, some nights.

When they moved to St. Eames, the doors had no locks. During one fight, when he'd taken off to anywhere else, she took hammer and nails and nailed the doors shut. She settled back in her favorite chair and waited for him to come home. She smugly congratulated herself. *I've fixed the son of a bitch this time.* She knew he wouldn't be able to get in. All windows on the lower floor were covered with plastic to keep the wind out. *He can't open a window. Ha-ha-ha.*

She heard him drive in two hours later. She went into the kitchen. She heard him try the door.

"Let me in!" He sounded mad.

"No. You stay out."

"Let me in!" Madder.

"You can't come in." *Tee-hee.*

"Let me in." Menacing.

"You've been bad, and you can't come in."

At last, she had the best of him. His voice sounded as though he might strangle (himself or her) as he pounded on the door. She smiled to herself and did a little jig, sliding her logger's wool socks on the just waxed floor.

With a great crunch, he jettisoned into the kitchen. They looked at each other in surprise. Then they laughed—and laughed. They laughed so hard, their stomachs hurt. That's the way most of their fights ended.

They saw their stupidity or just got busy and forgot what they were angry about. At least Joe did. He would leave the house furious, work hard all day, and forget what they were fighting about. Joan, on the other hand, remembered every inflection in Joe's voice, his unfair treatment of her, and everything else pertinent to the cause. Five years later, she still remembered.

They'd kissed and made up for years . . . Sometimes the making up was more fun than the fight. At least he'd pay attention to her when they were fighting. Looking back on it, she had to admit she had not always been fair—like the time Joe's aunt had the mistaken idea that she, Joan, was forcing him to work long hours, like a slave driver.

"Will you please tell your aunt I am not making you work so hard?"

"You tell her."

"She won't believe me. She thinks I'm driving you to work all those hours."

"You aren't."

"I know I'm not, but she doesn't know I'm not. You act like I force you to work. The truth is, you aren't crazy about being home . . . or coming home on time for dinner . . . or doing *anything* around the house."

"Yeah. Yeah. Let's not get into that."

"OK. I'm tired, and I don't want to fight with you, but the next time that old bag . . ."

"Don't you call my aunt an old bag!"

"The next time that old bag comes here, I'm going to tell her a thing or two. She drops in with her friends on tours without letting me know they're coming, and I dearly don't like it."

"Don't you say another word against my aunt . . . Your mother isn't so hot either."

"I thought you liked *my* mother. She's been good enough to you. Every time we have a fight, she always says . . . *Poor Joe.* You just love to be *Poor Joe* . . . I wonder what she'd say if she knew you didn't like her."

"I didn't say I didn't like her." He stretched his neck in an awkward way.

"Next time we're having Sunday dinner with my parents... I think I'll just tell them how you feel about them." She shot him a smug glance. She'd won. Yippee.

Although they fought in private, they never had a quarrel in public. Everyone thought they got along well. They detested married scenes and battles. From time to time, their friends had quarrels in public. It seemed so tacky. Once, a friend of Joe's slapped his wife at a gay Christmas party for smoking a cigarette. The pall that descended on the house ruined the evening. Joan shuddered at the thought. How mortified the woman must have felt to have her face slapped in front of all those people.

She left Joe once—for two days. Later, she thought she should never have gone back. She'd been cooking smelt, which she had cleaned (a job she found detestable). Joe came in from work grumpy about something that was wrong with the truck. Usually she sympathized with him, but that day she had troubles of her own.

"Will you please just get ready for dinner? I don't feel like waiting all night for you to wash."

He'd looked at her in surprise. She hadn't meant to sound so snappish. She was tired of waiting forever for him to come to the table. They'd had quarrels about it often. She felt food should be steaming hot to be palatable... He was just as content to eat it lukewarm or stone cold.

"Look," he glared at her, "I'm tired of having you nag me about coming to the table to eat."

"That's fine, because I'm goddamned tired of calling you ten times every night. I suppose that means you'll start doing what I want you to do and you won't have to be nagged anymore."

She couldn't remember who threw the first fish. She probably did.

Joe dressed carefully in his new clothes. For the first time in his life, he had more than one suit hanging in the closet, shirts and ties that matched, and long socks that were almost knee-high just like Mr. Worthington's. He hummed to himself as he put on his shoes.

"How do you like your shoe shine?"

"Fine."

"Is that all?"

"Yeah. How do I look?"

"You look very handsome, sir." *Like a little boy on his first day of school.*

"I have to hurry to make the meeting."

"What meeting is this?"

"The county solid waste meeting."

"How is it you're going?"

"I am a member of the commission."

"How did you get to be a member? I don't recall anyone voting for you."

"I told you I started going to the meetings. Then they sent me notices, and suddenly because I always showed up—I'm on the board."

"It doesn't make sense."

"What does?"

Nothing. Nothing made sense. When you thought something was going to be good, it was bad. When you thought something was going to be bad, it was good. If you looked forward to a party and thought it would be fun—it wasn't. The imagined boring evenings turned into gay affairs. You never know where you are. All the signposts and landmarks have changed. Where you used to go right, you now go left. People are not the same either. Those you thought were happily married are divorced. Those who seem always on the verge of divorce—never do. It is a strange world—*and exciting.* You never know where you are, but you know you've never been there before, and neither has anyone else.

"I still wish I could go to the meetings with you."

"Not these, Joan, they're really boring. I just want to be in on the ground floor. When they start making important decisions that will affect us, I want to have some clout."

"I wish you'd let the county take over the dump, and you concentrate on picking up garbage. That dump has cost us a lot of money."

"Sometimes I think we were better off when we had one truck."

"Very good thinking. You say that all the time. When we had one truck, we had six children, and you had to work every minute. Now you can go to meetings, buy new clothes, go to nightclubs, and you are never without money in your pockets. I remember when, for years, you didn't have an extra dime for a cup of coffee . . . when you had one truck."

"I guess I just felt better then."

"I don't think you did. I think you think you did. You aren't working half as hard as you were then. I think you are a lucky man to be able to have the time to do what you want to do."

He stretched. Then he flopped onto the bed. "I'll tell you a secret . . . I am really a very lazy man."

"Good God, I've been married to you for five thousand years—don't you think I *know* you're lazy? Why do you think I nag you? If you weren't lazy, there would be no reason to do that. We must acknowledge, though, that you are a very hard worker. You work hard enough to earn enough money so that you can hire people to do the jobs you're too lazy to do. Besides, everyone is lazy at times. Except me. I'm perfect."

"I don't think you're all that *perfect*, but you never seem to be lazy."

"Joe, I have too many things to do. Too many details. The things you don't do can be done by someone else. What I do—no one could or would consider doing."

She knew it was true. Something else was important too. The work she did satisfied her sense of self-achievement. She felt wonderful when she completed tiresome, necessary jobs. She experienced a sense of accomplishment when the laundry, kitchen, and cleaning were finished. She loved to see the house sparkle. It rarely did.

Joe looked at the clock. "Oh, I hate to get up. I've got to get out of here. Pull me up."

She walked to the patio doors with him, and he pecked her on the cheek as he headed for the car. He checked his vest pocket to make sure he had his papers. When the car turned out of the lane, he waved to her. She took a Coke from the refrigerator and started planning her work. She busied herself with the routine she'd developed to do the housework.

Her way of doing things was efficient and left the afternoons free for bookwork or other things. She silently thanked God that she now had household help two days a week and didn't have to do the heavy cleaning. This was added to her standard daily prayer of thanks that the family had enough food and clothing and a roof over them. They had been so poor for so many years that she never forgot it or forgot to be grateful. They were so fortunate.

By late afternoon, the sun shone on a small patch of grass in the landscaped yard. The table with the glass top made a perfect place for Joan to work, so she moved outdoors to catch some sun. The glare on the table blinded her. She leaned back in her chair and, with the warmth penetrating her bones, felt what it must be like to be in Cannes or Mexico or Portugal or any of the exotic places where the sun shone. None of those places could have been any more wonderful than where she was.

Beads of moisture formed on her face, and she felt the salty liquid run down her cheek and tickle her lips. She wiped her face with the back of her hand, then moved the table into the shade. In a few minutes, her eyes adjusted to the darkness, and she began to work. Time passed, and the pile of finished bills grew as the stack of blank statements disappeared.

The children came and went and came back. The men drove in. One by one they sprawled on the ground by the table. Tired and thirsty, they laughed and joked as they drank chilled bottles of beer Joan kept for them on hot days. They reminded her of her father. Their clothes were dirty, and they were sweaty, like he'd been. He would sit on a chunk of wood by the back door, unlace his caulked shoes, glug his beer, and then breathe a great sigh of relief. He'd felt better, revived, like these men.

They teased Joan, then one another. Joe's car pulled into the drive. He walked over to the group with a certain arrogance that was new to him. He held up his hand in greeting and motioned to them to stay where they were. "No one is leaving. Get the boys another beer, Joan."

"Does anyone want another one?"

They did. She returned with the bottles, passed them around, then sat down, conscious of the contrast between the men who had worked hard all day and the man who coolly held court. The men enjoyed themselves anyway. They laughed and told stories and relaxed. Then someone mentioned Nixon.

"That son of a bitch!" Joan couldn't help herself. She detested the man. When he was first elected, she looked at the picture of (to her) an exquisitely ugly man and almost cried.

The men laughed nervously. They knew about the running quarrel between Joe and Joan concerning her language.

"Joan!"

"And he's a *bastard* . . ." She looked at Joe in defiance. How dare he? How dare he criticize her in front of the men? How dare he go off, leave her to do the scut work, then come home and *criticize* her. She shot him a warning glance. He was righteous indignation, new arrogance, old church, defender of truth and morals, and plain holy anger. He looked at her with contempt. "You talk just like a logger!" he sniffed.

"That does it!" She threw her pen onto the table with a fury that surprised her—and everyone else. Her jaw locked. Her eyes were slits. She very deliberately rose from the table and walked to the house. When she caught a glimpse of herself in the mirror in the hall, she groaned, "My god, I've created a monster."

*Sarah should have called by now*, thought Joan as she finished cooking the spaghetti. It was delicious, like her Grandma's. Joan closed her eyes and visualized her grandma standing in front of the chrome-encrusted, heat-emanating wood cookstove with the warming ovens on top. Her hair, held in place by large tortoiseshell pins, escaped in places and formed a halo around her head whenever light from the window caught it just right. A chef's style apron covered clean blue cotton clothing of a practical design. She wore a man's flat-knit cardigan, thick stockings, and sensible shoes. She'd been up since six, when she and Grandpa got up to milk the cows. The rest of the day was a slow, steady maze of feeding chickens, working in the garden, and doing other unending chores that ended with milking the cows.

Her grandma worked efficiently, carefully, and steadily. She muttered to herself. *Probably mad at Grandpa*, thought Joan. Then the little old lady turned and smiled at her. How had Joan forgotten how much she loved her? Or how kind she was? And understanding?

Grandma offered Joan a taste of her spaghetti sauce. It was delicious. Now Joan put her tongue to the corner of her lips in anticipation as she stirred her own creation. She inhaled the aroma bubbling from the sauce—and kept remembering. Just then, the phone rang. She rested the wooden spoon in the dish on the stove and answered it. She sighed with relief when she heard Sarah's voice. The game was over and could she "come pick up me and Peggy Ross?"

"Stan, will you please pick up the girls? I have to finish dinner."

He looked at her with resignation. He hated to ferry his younger brother and sisters anywhere. When he first got his driver's license, he wanted to drive everywhere. Now two years later, it was a chore. He looked down at his paper, grimaced, then nodded his head.

Turning back to the receiver, Joan assured Sarah that she and Peggy would have a ride home, then hurried to the stove. The spaghetti was nearly done, and she didn't want to ruin it.

Stan turned as he started out the door. "Where does Peggy live?" He held up his right arm in its heavy cast in a questioning gesture. He'd broken his wrist again in a wrestling match at school and was just now getting over the anger, frustration, and pain of the injury.

"East of town . . . about two miles out. The girls will direct you. Come right back . . . I'll hold dinner for you."

"Go ahead and eat. I want to pick up a book at the library."

"OK. Thank you, Stan."

"No problem." With that, he strode out the door to his green Torino. She saw him swipe the fender with his good arm. He loved his car and took excellent care of it.

"Come and eat!"

"In a minute. Just let us finish this program."

"It's over. Come right now."

"Awwwww."

"Turn off the television and come and eat!"

"Coming."

"Joe, will you please come to the table?"

He lay down on the couch on his stomach with the newspaper spread on the floor. He continued reading.

"Joe, dinner's ready."

He didn't seem to hear. The children straggled in one by one.

"Tomorrow after school, the only thing you children can have to eat is a slice of bread and butter."

"That's no good . . ." "Yuck." Oh, no," they objected.

"If you're really hungry, it's good. My mother always said, 'If you're really hungry, you'll eat bread and butter.'"

They groaned. Joan looked at them and said, "When you eat late in the day, you spoil your appetite. I think everyone had too many cookies."

"Not me." "I didn't." "I only ate three." "I saw Matt take four!"

"OK. OK. No one ate too many cookies, so everyone is hungry? Mungulata."

"What does that mean?"

"I think it's an Italian word for *eat your dinner!* Joe, will you please come to the table?"

He rolled over and stretched. He blinked his red, almost-black eyes. "Be right there." He yawned.

Joan shook her head. Sometimes she wondered why she even bothered cooking. All the effort of shopping, preparation, cooking, serving, and cleaning up was lost on her family. They'd yell like banshees if their meals weren't ready, tasty, and substantial. Yet they took them for granted in an arrogant offhand way—and her. *Maybe I'll go away for a week and let them see how necessary I am to them and how much I do for them. They wouldn't care. They wouldn't miss me. They'd buy a barrel of Twinkies. Yum. Yum.*

She dished up the little girls' dishes, then passed the food on to the others. Spaghetti was one dish all the children liked, and it was easy to make.

Joe sat down at the table and glared at her. "You know I hate spaghetti."

"I thought you'd gotten over that."

"I'll never get over that."

"When we were at Mother's last week, you took three huge helpings of *her* spaghetti and would have gone back for more, only she ran out. You liked it well enough then."

"I didn't like it. I ate it because there was nothing else to eat."

"You said you liked it. You licked your lips and said, 'This spaghetti is delicious.'"

"All right, your mother makes better spaghetti than you do!"

"I use her recipe."

"*I* don't like yours."

"May I suggest you not eat it?"

"Couldn't you fix me something else?"

"I don't have anything else. Besides, I'm going to eat my dinner before it gets cold." With that, she started eating. The children giggled self-consciously. They never knew how to behave when their parents had a quarrel. Mostly they were quiet and watchful. Joan felt her face redden. She was tired of being humiliated in front of the children by Joe, whom she now referred to herself as the *son of a bitch*. She wondered if he thought it was fun to prepare dinner and then have the father act like that in front of his children. No wonder they turned up their noses at so many foods. She decided that the next time he let the children have dessert when they hadn't finished their meal, she'd raise hell.

Joan looked at him as he petulantly sucked spaghetti from his fork. His manner made her lose her appetite. She wished she weren't sitting across the table from him. He soon forgot he didn't *like* spaghetti and began to gorge himself. Joan watched in fascination as he wolfed down the food. She had never seen anyone eat so fast. He could be through eating before she could serve the children's food and sit down to her own. Fast.

The phone rang. Joan started to answer, then turned and shouted, "Quiet!" then into the telephone, "Good evening."

"Mrs. Schultz?"

"Yes."

"This is Peggy's mother. Stan had an accident in front of the house."

"Is anyone hurt?" Joan snapped to attention. The children stopped talking.

"I don't know. I think Sarah has a concussion. The ambulance is on the way."

"We'll be right there." She hung up the phone and looked at Joe. His face had no color. He started trembling. "Joe, she didn't know how bad they've been hurt. Let's go. Children, we'll let you know how everything is as soon as possible."

Joe started for the car. Joan ran and jumped in. He fumbled with the keys.

"Do you want me to drive?"

"No, I'm fine."

"Are you sure."

"Yes."

She didn't like the look in his eye or the way he jerked the car into the lane. "Joe! Be careful."

"I'm all right."

She gripped the handhold on the door as they raced around a corner. Joe's face intently followed the road. He was going much too fast.

"If you don't get hold of yourself, *we'll* have an accident."

"I can't help it." He slowed down a little. His foot shook on the accelerator.

"Please let me drive."

"No. I'll go slower."

As usual, he assumed that if he agreed to something, that would be enough to satisfy Joan. Having agreed, he continued to speed. She'd lived through enough traumatic events to know that in an emergency, the first thing to do is control yourself so that you can think clearly and calmly and hopefully take care of the situation. Joe had a tendency to panic. As the car flew through the night, she laughed ironically—people always think that women panic.

As they came on the scene, ambulance lights flashed in the middle of the road. Police flares illuminated the face of a state patrolman who stood directing traffic, his flashlight waving in the night. Joe skidded to a halt as close to the ambulance as he could get. A big egg truck awkwardly straddled the right-hand ditch.

Joan ran from the car and found Stan dazed and bleeding in the Rosses' front yard. An ambulance attendant was trying to corral him.

"I can't leave. I can't leave," he said as he held his head and moaned.

The attendant looked at Joan and saw her distress. "He'll be fine, lady. He's just dazed. I think he should go to the hospital for a checkup."

"Of course."

Sarah was being led from the house by another attendant. She looked at her mother with unseeing eyes. Something was very wrong with her. She stumbled and weaved as the attendant and Joan helped her into the ambulance. Peggy, looking very somber, climbed into a seat near Sarah. Mrs. Ross, obviously distressed, stood wringing her hands in dismay.

One of the attendants came back to shut the door. "I'm sorry, ladies, only one of you can ride in the ambulance."

"Mrs. Ross, you go with them. We'll follow in the car."

Siren blaring, the ambulance headed for the hospital. Joan hurried to where Joe stood talking to some men. He seemed intent on getting the details of the accident.

"Let's hurry, Joe, I want to go to the hospital."

"We can't go yet."

"Why not?"

"Dean Black is on his way."

"Joe, we don't know what's the matter with Sarah and Stan. Peggy doesn't seem to be hurt. I think she's in shock... but something is wrong with Sarah."

"The policeman thinks Sarah hit her head on Stan's cast. She was in the backseat. When he thought he was going to crash, Stan put his arm back instinctively, forgetting his arm was in a cast. Stan was not at fault. As he started to turn into the Ross driveway, after signaling, the egg truck started to pass. See, there are signs saying, *No passing next 1000 ft.* See them?"

"Please, let's go."

"No. Dean will be here soon."

"Will you tell me why it is necessary to talk to our insurance man?"

"Just calm down. He'll be here soon."

"I can't calm down. I don't know how bad the children are hurt. Please take me now."

"No. We'll wait."

"I'll take the car and leave you."

"Joan, be reasonable. He'll be here any minute. I'll talk to him, and then we'll be on our way."

"But why do you have to?"

"I just want to, that's why."

"You're thinking about the money, aren't you?"

"Not at all. What a thing to say!"

"You drove like a maniac all the way over here. Now you don't seem to care if the children are all right or not."

"But they are all right. We saw that with our own eyes."

"They're alive. Sarah certainly must have a concussion. Stan may be in shock. We don't know how they are."

He stood looking at her with a contemptuous smile. "Yes, Dr. Schultz."

Dean Black drove into the yard right then. He jumped from his car and rushed to Joan. She hated him. He put a conciliatory arm around her and said, "I'm sorry," as though someone had died. Cloying. He cloyed.

She slipped from his grasp disgustedly and glared at Joe. "Five minutes, Joe, then I'm leaving."

She turned but not fast enough to miss the knowing, mocking look that passed between the agent and Joe. *You bastards*, she thought. When Joe got into the car and slammed the door, he turned on her. "Now why did you have to be like that? Dean is in Rotary and belongs to the Chamber and the Lions. You shouldn't have treated him like that."

She glared at him and didn't trust herself to speak. They rode in silence. After what seemed an eternity to her, they arrived at the hospital. Stan met them at the inner desk.

"Hi. I guess you can see I'm fine." He turned to show them his back. It was swollen and bloody. It looked as though he'd been whipped with a cat-o'-nine-tails, and little pieces of gravel showed in the wounds. His bandaged face looked old and worn. Joan grimaced.

"Is your wrist all right?" she asked.

"It doesn't seem to hurt at all . . . but I think my car's totaled."

"Don't think of that now. How and where is Sarah?"

"She's right in there." He pointed to a room filled with nurses, orderlies, and doctors. A doctor bent over Sarah's still form. He looked up as Joan approached. "Are you her mother?"

Joan nodded. The sight of the pretty girl so pale and still brought a constriction to her throat.

"She has a concussion."

"I thought she might."

"We don't know how bad it is, but we want to keep her overnight for observation."

"Fine."

"You could take her home if you prefer."

"I wouldn't prefer. I don't know what to look for, and I'd feel better if I knew she was in the hospital getting good care."

"I'll make the arrangements."

Sarah opened her eyes. "Mother."

"Yes?"

"I feel awful."

"I know, dear." Joan held her hand and looked at her intently. Except for a faraway look in her eyes and a strange slowness to her speech, Sarah seemed all right. "You'll feel better in the morning after you've slept. Go to sleep now."

"My head hurts."

"There's a big lump on your forehead. You hit Stan's cast."

Joan stayed in the room until Sarah fell asleep. Then she whispered to the emergency room doctor, "How often will you check her?"

"At least every two hours. I'm sure she'll be all right. You'll have to watch her closely for several weeks after this. Sometimes it takes that long for anything to show up."

"I know. Several of my children have had concussions."

He looked at her quizzically. "How many children do you have?"

"Ten."

"Ten?"

"Ten."

"You don't look old enough to have *ten children*." As he spoke, his face turned red. He hadn't meant to be so personal.

Joan smiled. "No one is ever old enough to have *ten children*."

"I guess you're right," he mumbled.

She stepped into the hallway. Joe had been in with Sarah for a few minutes. Then, restlessly, he'd left. The smell of ether nauseated him, and she knew he'd be as far from the odor as possible. She found him and Stan in the waiting room.

"Can she go home?"

"Tomorrow morning if she's all right, which she hopefully will be."

Stan rode to the hospital with her in the morning. The doctor wanted to check the swelling of the lacerations on his back.

"Do you think she'll be able to come home?"

"I hope so. I didn't get a chance to call the doctor, but if she can't come home, she'll need a toothbrush and comb and some of her things."

"I want to see my car on the way home. I still can't believe it's a total wreck."

"Better the car than you. I am sorry that you had the accident. We can go see the car if Sarah feels well enough."

"I wouldn't have had an accident if that jerk hadn't tried to pass me on the hill."

"I'm really glad it wasn't your fault."

"What difference does it make—my car is just as wrecked?"

"If it were your fault, we'd have insurance problems. And frankly, I'd never feel good about your driving again."

"That's dumb. Accidents do happen."

"So do carelessness, inattention, negligence, and stupidity. I want you to be a good example to the other children as they grow up."

"I am sick of being a *good example*."

"Is it that bad?"

"Yes. I never can do anything. I always have to be a *good example*."

"Can you imagine what kinds of problems I'd have if you weren't a *good example*? The hope of the world rests in a good example. Things are far from perfect, but if you *got away with things*, everyone in the family would too. In order for me to maintain any kind of control in the family, you have to behave. The others learn from you. Chaos and confusion would run rampant. If you didn't mind, no one else would," she said, then laughed.

"I didn't ask for a sermon," he replied tautly.

"You know, Stan, I think where I made my big mistake was in trying to reason with you. Maybe I should have beaten your rear end."

"I've had my share."

"The trouble with you is you just got too big for me to spank too fast."

"Do you remember when I kicked you at the dentist's office?"

"I haven't forgotten, neither has Dr. Lowry."

"I don't see how you could have let that big man pick on your little boy."

"My little boy needed his teeth fixed."

"Yeah, but I had been to too many doctors by then. Anyone in a white coat scared me to death."

"You got so red. You must have been terrorized."

"I was. I must have made you mad when I kicked you."

"No. I was used to you. Dr. Lowry was mad."

Stan laughed. He wondered, as the miles passed, if he'd ever want to drive again. The memory of the crash, the sudden tearing, screaming, grinding crash, filled his consciousness. It had been so sudden. He'd seen the big truck behind him and had started his left turn signal in plenty of time. Just as he'd started his turn, the truck driver decided to pass. Crashhhh. Screechhh.

"I think I'm lucky to be alive," he muttered.

When they saw the car parked in the old barn that the tow company leased, Joan was amazed Stan hadn't been killed. The roof of the car was two inches from the steering wheel.

"Sarah, you wait for us in the car. You look shaky."

"I will. I just wanted to see with my own eyes. This car is wrecked! I can't believe we could live through such a crash."

"Don't you remember anything at all?"

"Peggy and I were in the backseat talking, and the next thing I knew, I woke up this morning with a headache in the hospital." She shuddered, and as she did, a chill rushed through her. She hadn't realized how weak she was. She crawled into the station wagon and watched her mother and Stan as they inspected the damage.

"Stan, how did you manage to escape with a few cuts on your back?"

"All I can figure is that at the moment of impact, I fell into the passenger's seat. My legs were on the driver's side, and the rest of me was on the other side of the car. I was lying on the seat when it was over."

"Thank God you and the girls weren't hurt a lot worse."

"I don't know if I will ever drive again."

"You will, Stan. You'll just be a lot more careful and defensive. Then one day you'll suddenly be very complacent. That's when someone will crunch you again."

"Thanks a lot!"

"It happens to all of us. That's why there are so many accidents. People forget."

"Not me!"

"Not *I*."

"Not *me!*"

## Chapter 27

Joan lay on the window seat in the living room. She sighed. Looking up through double-pane crystal windows, she watched huge billowy clouds float happily by. She found faces in the clouds and animals and scenes. She was here and now. Happy. Content.

A sense of satisfaction enveloped her. Through all the poor years, through all the struggles of building the business and rearing her family, through the times of striving and straining, at last everything was right in her world. The children were miraculously well and strong. To the unprejudiced eye of the mother, they were an *absolutely adorable* group of children. Maybe the old sociobiologists were right after all; maybe the important thing about mating was the improvement of the races. The children seemed healthy and strong. Most of the time, they had a good color—not as high as the Swiss, but very pleasant. In winter, their color, at times, was so pale for so long that Joan would worry. The doctors said it was the state. And most of the other children she saw looked the same.

As a group, they were wild and rowdy. Looking back on it, Joan could see that as many times as she and Joe butted heads, it was only natural that their children should be nitty-gritty fighters. Nobody ever gave up.

She remembered with horror the many trips to the doctor, dentist, or? *Perfect* angels at home; at the office, they went off course. One hit one. Another hit one. One hit three. Cry. God had certainly deserted her then. She knew what happened. At home they could be controlled or ignored. In the small confines of an office, especially one filled with sick patients, feverish babies, etc., Joan found herself unable to control them.

When they went shopping, it was like an absolute zoo with all the animals loose.

The children had caused no real trouble. They didn't slash tires or steal gas or . . . The thing that pleased Joan so much about the children was that they were so good-natured. They had fun. They loved each other. They helped each other. They could laugh at themselves, and they shared a certain contempt for the contrived.

She wondered how they had turned out so well. For one reason, she thought, they have taken care of each other in many ways. That made them much closer than other children. Sometimes the best plan is no plan at all. Who knows? The accounts balanced. In time, the children would all go to good schools. Heaven on earth.

The old captain had been right on course. They had enough customers to earn enough money to maintain their equipment, buy needed items, and give the men a raise. Every month a healthy surplus built up in the vaults of silver far beneath the city streets. Expenses paid—and savings. Who could ask for more? Less energy expended. A dependable income for the next few years.

It had been hard—hard for Joan and hard for Joe. How he had managed to carry all that weight on his back for so many years was a mystery to her. His legs were hurting—and his back. She felt her own body soften and relax. How wonderful. Peace in our time.

She had known it would be like this, like a happy ending. There were no happy endings in the real world—only in our hearts. That's what she'd thought. It felt good. All the old anxieties born of need and reared on tension left like gold leaf—in layers. She hummed. Then she lowered her lashes and began to pray. *Dear God, thank you for helping me through another day. Without you, I wouldn't see the beauty I see, or seeing wouldn't appreciate it. So, God, so something I did was right. I know you know I've tried. I think I've done my share, don't you? I can't remember when I ever enjoyed hurting others. I always feel stupid when I try to explain myself to you. You know me. You are in the very essence of my spirit. Anyway, God, I've got to go. But before I do, know that I deeply appreciate the way you have assisted us in our lives, both personal and business. Because of you, we are finally going to move the office from the home. More and more we will be able to spend time with the children and each other. It will be so nice to rest!*

She thought of Joe. She knew she could not change him. He was himself. *Jesus, what an awful thing to happen to a man—to be locked into himself and never see another side of a question or be able to listen to another point of view. Well, hell, I've lived with him this long. What if he isn't quite the man I want him to be? He has a lot of good qualities. And I can go on living my own life excluding him as I do anyway. At last, we have security. The office will be gone. The phone will stop ringing. Yippee! And those huge trucks won't be near the house.*

She blinked and looked up at Joe, who stood towering above her. She smiled and stretched.

"Oh, Joe, I am so happy. For the first time in years, I am truly happy."

"Don't be *so truly* happy yet."

"Why not?"

"While you were gone today, I had a call from John Sharp's brother, Edgar. He's ready to sell."

"We aren't buying."

"Oh, yes, we are."

"No. No. No. You promised." The idea of taking over another garbage route with all the intensive problems that entailed left Joan cold.

"This is the way it has to be. I'm still going to be a millionaire," he said expansively.

"Why?" Joan asked. "You have everything a man could want. You have a healthy family, fine house, space to spare, green grass, orchard, good water, abundance of food—what more could you want? Why do you want to work harder—lose your sleep and your health in search of money? We've both done so much. Can't we rest? We'll be completely out of debt in a little over a year. We don't want to take on another route right now, especially *the biggest in the state.*"

"I've already talked to one of the men. He could run the route for us . . . on a percentage . . . same as usual," Joe said. Then in a voice that sounded remarkably like hers echoing through the years, she heard him say, "It would pay for itself in a few years."

Joan sighed and shook her head and shuddered. "Where would we get the down payment on a two-million-dollar route?"

"Mr. Worthington."

"You are serious, aren't you?"

"It's too good an opportunity to pass up."

She looked at him. He stood imploring her to understand, to agree with him, and to know his need. He stood on one leg with the other bent at an angle. He seemed a little shorter than Joan remembered he had been when they were young, but he stood straight and proud. Exhilaration gleamed in his eyes as he waited for her to speak.

*Dear God, she silently cried, why did you have to do this to me? Just when everything seemed so perfect. Now, God, you and I know what we are going to have to do. We are going to have to divorce this man. He has shown us in a million ways that he does not love me. There will never be enough routes, enough savings, enough stocks, or enough anything. I'll be careful not to destroy the business. He'll probably never remarry. I can't help that, though. I can't imagine him without a woman. I'll lay my plans well. As far as I am concerned, this is the end.*

She heard his pleading voice through the fog of her tortured thinking. "Joan, Joan, say something!"

"Shit."

# # #

Edwards Brothers Malloy
Thorofare, NJ USA
May 12, 2015